VELVET PURRS IN PARADISE

DYKKC BDSM Erotica Romance Series: Book 1
(A Domination and Submission Romance Novel)

LEYA WOLFGANG

Velvet Purrs In Paradise
All rights reserved.
Digital version: © 2013 Shadows and Light Press
ISBN: 978-0-9867775-2-3
Print version: © 2014 Shadows and Light Press
ISBN: 978-0-9867775-1-6
Calgary, Alberta, Canada
www.DYKKC.com
www.Facebook.com/DYKKCnovels

Warning: Adult Only Content. Not suitable for readers 17 and under. This work of erotic fiction contains strong language and graphic sexual content, and includes themes of Dominant/submissive relationships, light bondage and discipline, anal play, pet play, testing the boundaries of consent, kidnapping, betrayal of trust, and broken hearts. But it also contains the balancing forces of personal growth, respect, love and romance, and the redeeming power of forgiveness. And, of course, hot, kinky, dirty sex!

This story is a work of fiction, as are the people (except for the named artists whom I admire), businesses, locales, and events. The characters live in the author's active imagination (driving her crazy) and are used fictitiously for entertainment purposes only. This work is not to be construed as a how-to guide about the BDSM lifestyle.

DEVIL YOU KNOW KINK CLUB, DYKKC, WHERE WICKED DREAMS COME TRUE, the DEVIL YOU KNOW LOGO, and BELLADONNA GENTLEMEN'S CLUB are trademarks of Shadows and Light Press.

Cover: Leya Wolfgang

DYKKC Front Entrance Image: © hifijohn. A special thanks for the right to use this image. http://hifijohn.freeservers.com.

Additional Image from Dreamstime.com: © Syda Productions.

Velcro® is a registered trademark of Velcro Industries B.V. (Thank God for Velcro®!)

< ♂ + ♀ >

Watch the video trailer on YouTube at
http://leya69.me/17ysVMn

Devil You Know Kink Club™
Where Wicked Dreams Come True

< ♂ + ♀ >

Acknowledgements

I can't begin to say how grateful I am for my dear friends JC and BH. Whether you kept me sane while the rest of my life fell apart during this writing, or gave plot feedback at various points of progress, that the book is in readers' hands now is largely because of you pushing me onward. You reminded me that spending my time telling stories is the life I came to live and that all the sacrifice is worth it. EG, thanks for being a cheerleader when I was coming down the home stretch.

I'd also like to say a big thank you to the three editors who heard and commented on my first page at a local writers' conference. Your generous critiques gave me the confidence to believe I might have written something worth reading and to send it out into the world.

Bless you all.

Dedication

To all you romance and erotica readers who doubt a man and woman can fall in love in less than a week, this story shows you how it can happen—breath by breath, word by word, kiss by kiss, thrust by thrust.

.

Table of Contents

$< ♂ + ♀ >$

Thrill Me, Fill Me, Will Me

As you thrill me, spill into me, Beloved,
My barricades crumble, and I am exposed.
As you thrill me, spill into me, Beloved,
My wild heart splits open, and I am revealed.

As you fill me, spill into me, Beloved,
My ego fades away, and I am lost.
As you fill me, spill into me, Beloved,
My essence radiates, and I am found.

As you will me, spill into me, Beloved,
My ambition falls apart, and I am empty.
As you will me, spill into me, Beloved,
I kneel down, your humble slave, and I am fulfilled.

© 2007 Leya Wolfgang

x

"Weeping may stay for the night, but joy comes in the morning."
~ Psalm 30:5

Chapter One – Forbidden Fruit

Friday Night, September 14

"Don't you dare come, sub. When are you allowed to come?" *Damn.* My eyes water as The Saint follows his sharp command and question with a vicious slap to my already reddened inner thigh. Fresh stains of fat fingers blossom on that tender flesh. My Top has easy access because I'm on my knees, strung up, bound with my legs splayed wide open for him.

A shudder of wicked delight zings through my body. *Yum.* The image of ripe golden fruit dripping with juice makes my lips purse, and my snug back hole puckers in anticipation of being stretched and stuffed. I never imagined I could be so turned on by something so forbidden.

"No, Sir. Only when you're between my peaches and only when you give your permission, Sir." It's such a dirty thing to give voice to the even dirtier thing we will soon do. My eyes almost cross with the effort to stay this side of the abyss as his unrelenting fingers plunge in a steady rhythm into my aching pussy.

"Where, miss priss?" *He doesn't fool me.* The gentleness of his tone warns he's at his most dangerous, dangerous to my resolve to not disappoint him.

"In my tight, fuckable ass, Sir." He's the one who calls my firm globes "lush peaches." The Saint prefers I use profanity. Me, not so much. I'm a good girl, or I try to be, and he gets a real kick out of watching me squirm when I say bad things on his command.

Ever since claiming my anal virginity during our second scene, Dillon St. Laurent, known in the club as The Saint, makes sure he gets some back door action every time we're together. He doesn't just want it; I know he's almost obsessed with it because he's very vocal while sliding between my sweet cheeks. Part of the appeal for me, what makes me tremble, is how he moans in pleasure when he's in deep. My desire to please this strong, stern, sexy man, to send him to paradise, is instinctive. My heart soars whenever I succeed.

The Saint leans toward me from a thickly padded, black leather ottoman. The over-stuffed, wingback chair I'm kneeling on is the only kindness he afforded me when he tied me securely—bindings at more points than usual—and spread me wide open to give him unrestricted entry to my most intimate places. We sit at the same height, eye to eye, and I take a direct hit of his burning gaze.

"Damn, you have such a beautiful body, priss." This large and powerful man doesn't go for the petite types—Dillon says they're too breakable. I'm not small at 5'8" and carry a little extra padding. "A classic hour-glass figure," he says as he glides his calloused fingers over my glowing skin, soothing the sting where he smacked me. His complimentary appraisal warms my heart. I used to think my body was just plain, old fat. Now, with all the attention and praise I've been getting here at the club, I finally appreciate my curves.

Dillon grabs hold of my hair and snaps my head up. *Damn him.* He insists I wear my long, raven locks in a thick braid when we scene. He can't resist tugging on the hair rope to get my attention, like he's doing now, or coiling it around his hand and leading me about as if I were on a leash. At work, I always put my hair up in a bun or French braid. No one leads me around in the outside world; I'm the boss. But it's another universe here inside Devil You Know Kink Club, affectionately referred to by its members as DYKKC. That acronym always makes me blush. It's the stupidest thing, but "dick" is the one word for penis that I have trouble saying out loud.

My big, beautiful bad boy leads me up close to the peak of ecstasy for the third time tonight. Usually, he'd have some sympathy and be ordering me to come right about now. My sanity is slipping away, but, with a valiant effort, I hold on. Another severe slap to my thigh brings me back.

"Pay attention. Look at me, priss." Dillon's gravelly voice softens slightly when he adds, "Don't you want this, my little sub? Isn't this what you asked for?" A quick pang of shame jolts through me. *I asked for this.* His pacifying voice has insinuated itself into my subconscious and has made me want, made me beg, for many wanton things since we met. He is a maleficent corrupter. They call him The Saint, but I know he is a demon.

"Yes, Sir. Please, Sir. I need your fat cock in my tight ass." He loves to hear me beg, even if I hate to hear that weakness in my voice, the yearning for connection and completion. The problem is that I do need Dillon and what he is doing to me right now far too much. Every cell in my body is tingling, every synapse in my brain exploding like popcorn. The stimulation assaulting all my senses overwhelms me. I breathe deeply and slowly to try to still my body. My attempt is futile. I'm just a puppet, and, tonight, Dillon is pulling all the strings, like the Master he is. The best I can do is force myself to hang on and follow the steps he's making me dance.

My ears pick up every crazed pant of both Dillon's and my breath and every obscene squelch of his fingers pumping in and out of my slippery pussy. My nostrils inhale the heady aromas of seasoned leather and our combined sweat and musky arousal. Floating on top of that complex bouquet is his crisp cologne that reminds me of salty sea breezes. My tongue darts around my mouth, still savoring the aftertaste of Dillon's tart ejaculate.

My eyes behold the handsome face of the Dom pleasuring me; his youthful skin radiates dark passion. His skill and experience say he's older than he looks, early to mid-thirties. When he's ridden by lust like this, I can't get enough of him. Despite my moments of feeble begging, knowing that I have the power to drive him to such a fever is an intoxicating and addictive elixir.

I long to slide my hands, which are inconveniently tied behind my back, over all 6'3" of his artistically muscled body as it glistens from frenetic exertion. Not only am I hungry for what he's doing to me, I am ravenous for all of him—his charisma, his potency, his intensity, his control. I simply can't resist him. I just want to eat him up, consume him the way he consumes me. Our appetite for each other kicked in from the moment our eyes met.

< ♂ + ♀ >

The first time I saw The Saint, I'd only been a member of DYKKC for two weeks and had ventured out on a Saturday night without an escort. I couldn't sit at home after paying the price of admission. I was crazy nervous but determined to explore. After hanging out in the common playroom for a half hour, not finding anything or anyone to tickle my fancy, I ventured upstairs. I was apprehensive and excited about what lewd and lascivious scenes I might chance upon. A small crowd halfway down the hall caught my attention.

Dillon was running a disciplinary scene with a tall and skinny redhead in one of the private play areas. The door to Playroom No. 5 was wide open, so I assumed they wanted to be heard as well as seen through the observation window. He looked delicious from a distance, and I was compelled to get as close to him as possible. Ripples of restless energy coursed through me as I skirted the knot of voyeurs at the window and tiptoed to the edge of the doorway.

I was drawn in and held by eyes that glowed as blue-black as a stormy ocean. To this day, I get lost at sea every time I stare into them. The entire world drops away when I gaze at Dillon and he gazes back at me. Nothing exists except for those wild eyes of his, framed by the perfect assemblage of high forehead, straight, narrow nose, firm pink lips, and square angles of jaw and chin.

The phrase "dark and brooding" would accurately describe this intimidating Dom if it wasn't for his soft, strawberry-blond hair. With the straight locks combed away from his face and brightening his appearance, he is merely fierce. And he was fiercely focused on the redhead. I shuddered to think how intense it would be to have the force of his attention directed at me.

He was bare to the waist, wearing only tight, black bicycle shorts that hid nothing. I was entranced by the way his skillfully sculpted muscles wrap around wide shoulders, thick arms, straight spine, narrow hips, and long legs. *How tight could he wrap his muscles around me?* His stride was as graceful as the gait of a prowling panther as he circled his distressed sub. Her forehead pressed against an iron pole, and a metal collar kept her head in place. Wide bands of the unforgiving material shackled her wrists in front of her, and similar cuffs at her ankles kept her legs spread wide. It looked like she was in the contraption backward.

I could only see the sub's profile because she was turned facing the side wall, but her long hair hung down and hid her face. Her muffled cries indicated that a gag of some kind was stuffed in her mouth. As if being confined that way wasn't torture enough, a rod and clamp locked a wand massager in place over her pussy. I could hear the tool droning away on low speed.

That wasn't the extent of the sub's suffering. Every muscle in Dillon's arm strained to stay in check as he stood back and dropped whiplashes on her tender skin with the control and precision of a sharpshooter. He decorated the meaty parts of her athletic body with an intricate pattern of bright red welts. Each crack of his 3-ft. bullwhip was as sharp as a spike, nailing my feet to the floor. The harshness of his handling of her body and the degree of control he exerted on her petrified me, but I couldn't look away.

When she let out a particularly loud moan, he approached her side and pulled hard on her chestnut-red locks, drawing her head back as far as the ring around her neck would allow. She dropped a ping pong ball she'd been holding, and he reached down and turned off the vibrator. His spandex-clad buttocks clenched, tantalizing me then and each time he leaned in to whisper in her ear. *Is he taunting her or reprimanding her? Or is he praising her?*

"Had enough, have you? You've done well. What a good girl you are," he crooned in his low, raspy voice. That bluesy tone just about dropped me to my knees when I heard those first words spoken loud enough to carry. When she moaned again, so did I. Dillon startled and zeroed in on me, glaring at me for my audible intrusion.

His chest was heaving, certainly from exertion and, if the hefty protrusion in his shorts said anything, from arousal as well. Dillon's eyes widened and stared, telepathing to me his anger, severing the sensual cord keeping me spellbound. My shoulders crumpled, and his clear disapproval made me whither as limp as a delicate Morning Glory in the late afternoon sun. Already I was attuned to his authority, needed to please him, and regretted failing him.

I hung my head but kept my misting eyes locked with his. That was when I saw another emotion flaring in him. His lips puckered like he was considering something before he turned back to concentrate on the discipline he was doling out to his bottom. He had dismissed me, and the loss chilled me as thoroughly as if he had doused me with a bucket of ice water. The whole exchange had taken no more than three seconds, but it seemed to stretch forever.

I stumbled from the doorway, disconsolate but unable to leave him. Through the window, I watched the session progress, my golden eyes turned green with jealousy. Each time he made the sub come, my body weakened as if I was going to pass out. Writers use the phrase "she fell apart" to describe a woman's orgasm. My God, she really did look like she was bursting at the seams. I could almost see light pouring from the cracks. The sight left me breathless.

When he finally removed her gag–her balled up panties–she begged him to take her ass. I'd never considered anal before beyond fantasy, but my cheeks clamped together and let me know that I was right there with her, wanting what she wanted. The woman next to me put her hand on my shoulder when I whimpered. I didn't want Dillon to do it. I didn't want him inside her. I didn't know who he was, and he scared me shitless, but I wanted him in me. I knew I was losing my mind because I was so wet from how much I wanted him. It was ridiculous. We had made eye contact for mere seconds.

Dillon struck her butt again and again. I could tell he did it hard because of the sonic booms pealing out of the doorway and the high-octave screams bleating from her mouth. The redhead begged over and over, and he leaned in and said, "No." I couldn't turn off the tears streaming down my face. I'm sure his refusal had nothing to do with me, but relief flooded my body and eased every aroused and covetous cell.

My nose pressed to the window as Dillon released the woman from the pole apparatus. He cradled her in his arms and carried her to a gilded divan. He lay down with her, stroking her and pressing soft kisses wherever he could reach. She was hidden behind the bulk of his beautiful body, but I knew that if it were me curled up beside him, I would be wearing a smile as wide as the Grand Canyon. Especially when I heard her gasp and sigh, obviously from being stroked to another satisfying release. As it was, knowing that she hadn't received the gift of his massive erection was enough to cause a wicked grin to split my lips.

With the action over, the crowd wandered off in search of new scenes to spy on or perhaps to star in their own scenes. I lingered. I stared as he stretched his tall body and pushed up off the divan. I sighed when he spread a blanket over the sub and tucked her in. I moaned softly when he laid a tender kiss on the top of her head.

I was so engrossed by the sweetness of his aftercare following the bitterness of his aggression, trying to understand the cravings mewling in my belly, that my brain didn't register Dillon walking away from her. The click of the door closing triggered a gasp from both of us and sent me whirling to face him. Our eyes locked, again for only a few seconds, and then he brushed past me without a word or a backward glance.

Our encounter made a lasting impact on me and was the source of countless wild, warm and wet fantasies over the next week. I didn't realize it at the time, but Dillon had been as deeply affected as I was. The rest, as they say, is history.

$$< \male + \female >$$

Tonight, I kneel before him, roped and tied like a fatted calf, the sole focus of his talents. The heavy jute ropes binding my naked body dig into my wrists, elbows, breasts, waist and ankles, sending continual tickles of pain dancing through me. Despite the ache, which hovers close to the upper limits of my tolerance, I struggle against the rough restraints. I am helpless and at The Saint's mercy, such as it is. Instead of feeling powerless and imprisoned, I feel free. I have no decisions to make; I only have to obey Sir's commands. And I can't run from the depravity that I really shouldn't give in to.

After checking that the ropes aren't cutting off my circulation, Dillon's long, thick fingers—three of them—continue their ceaseless probing, slithering in and out of my grasping channel. His persistent thumb presses against my exposed clit. I'm primed to ignite and explode like a Roman candle.

All the excitement fizzles with Dillon's rapid withdrawal. I know that I am here for Sir's pleasure, to serve him, but the teasing is getting ludicrous. Ultimately, we're both supposed to get something out of this; that's why the Top/bottom dynamic is called a power *exchange*, isn't it? All I'm getting is a boatload of frustration. I glare at him, trying to convey my distress and discontent without using words. The Saint forbids me to speak unless asked a direct question, and I have no desire to challenge his authority; his punishment when given, as I know all too well, is swift and uncompromising. I'm willing to risk a spanking for a mind-blowing orgasm but not for merely speaking out of turn.

"You were going to come, weren't you, slut?" I cringe at the pejorative term as a swell of lassitude slumps me forward. I know the members here at DYKKC think "slut" is a term of endearment, but it hurts my pride. My heart sinks as I flash back to the crushing memory of my high school senior prom.

< ♂ + ♀ >

The night surpassed every young girl's fairy-tale fantasies. The pageantry was designed to enchant and sweep sweet young things off their feet, tumbling the last holdouts of the HEA myth head-over-heels into dreams of eternal love. I naïvely succumbed.

My boyfriend and I began the evening with a romantic dinner at my favorite steakhouse, and I was floating on a cloud by the time we left. Jed detoured en route to the dance. When he pulled his dad's Lincoln Continental into a dark parking lot, I began to deflate.

I knew what he had in mind, but I was unsure of what I wanted. We had only been a couple for three months, and I hadn't let Jed do much more than heavy petting above my waist and on top of my clothes. But I was sitting beside the boy I loved. His broad smile buoyed me back up, and I let my guard down.

Jed made the most of my weakened defenses. He leaned over the center console and, after a quick, crushing kiss, slid his sweaty hands under my skirt. My own hands had been the only ones to touch me with the intent to tease and excite. It was a new thrill to have his strong hands on my skin, one so great that I couldn't think clearly to stop it. Before I knew it was happening, Jed was pumping his little soldier inside me like he was trying to pound an enemy to a pulp. The harder he rammed, the louder I moaned and the deeper I surrendered. It seems I liked rough fucking right from the start.

The poor boy didn't last long, but neither did I, which was a bit of a disappointment. He grunted in my ear as he shot his load, and I howled as my first non-self-induced orgasm flattened me. I had never come close to a release that monumental by my own hand, and I was shocked that the pleasure could wreck me like that. Jed turned sweet again afterward, and that made me want him more. I began scheming ways to get him alone for practice time.

My dreams and fantasies crashed down later when I overheard him telling his friends how easily I had spread my legs for him, offered up my cherry, and given him what he wanted. "The slut is a real screamer. You should have heard how much she loved it, how much she wanted my big dick. She begged for more." I slapped his face and fled from the gym.

I was humiliated, mortified, absolutely crushed. Jed betrayed me and belittled the intimacy we shared together. The whole school knew my private shame in three minutes. My skin crawled like I was dirty, cheap. *Why was it wrong to be with the man I loved? Why is sex something for a guy to brag about and a woman to be ashamed of?* If I was a slut, then so was that sleazy pig. Besides, I might not have told him to stop, but he hadn't exactly asked for my permission.

He was the one who was wrong, but the guilt slashed deep. I was inconsolable for two weeks. My faith in boys was shattered. I didn't sleep with anyone or even have another date until my junior year of college. Unfortunately, that didn't work out so well either, and relationships have been difficult and short-lived ever since. I guess I could say I have trust issues. No wonder I'm still single at 32 and having kinky sex with men who aren't even my boyfriend.

< ♂ + ♀ >

"Answer me, sub!" Dillon yanks on my braid and stretches my neck. He is angry that I have drifted off again and haven't answered him within a nanosecond. He can read my body like a book, so denial is not an option. That would just make things worse for me.

"Yes, Sir. I was very close. Thank you for bringing me down in time, Sir." My smile is weak, and there is a hint of snark in my voice. The reply is a little over the top, a bit saucy. My body is nearing the ends of endurance, and I don't have the resources to behave like I should, but I don't want a spanking for coming ahead of schedule.

Dillon's strict, sharp edge keeps calling me back for more, but I haven't quite figured out why his cragginess is so alluring. Still, he usually balances out the roughness with gentle caresses, lingering kisses, and kind compliments. I never have to guess why my Top is angry, or disappointed, or pleased. Tonight, I wonder what I did to deserve the coldness that borders on cruelty. I glance at the St. Andrew's Cross on the opposite wall. *Thank God he doesn't have me strapped to that.* In the mood he's in, I shudder to think ...

The two of us have played together half a dozen times over the last five months. Each time, we negotiate what kind of scene we will indulge in and what my limits are. I'm really not into pain, and I don't like to be punished. And public humiliation? Prom night was enough for a lifetime. I'm not willing to go as far as any of the other bottoms at DYKKC, and that has earned me the name miss priss.

I've observed several of the extreme scenes Dillon has run with other bottoms, ones who are gluttons for pain like the skinny redhead. I can't compete with that kind of staying power, as much as I wish I could. Hand spanking is the only form of corporal punishment I can tolerate him dishing out.

Dillon drove me to the limit a couple of times by whacking me so hard and so long that he made me wail in agony. I almost had to safeword out of the scene both times, but I persisted for beautiful Dillon. I couldn't give in until I had won his approval. Considering that he doesn't like breakable women, I'm mystified but grateful that he deigns to play with me when my limits are so narrowly defined. Still, I suspect that it's not my body he is trying to break.

The Saint is one of only three Tops that I scene with at Devil You Know. *Hah! Only three.* I say it like it's no big deal to be juggling multiple guys when I only ever dreamed of finding "The One." But, honestly, each man is a treasure, for very different reasons, and I couldn't possibly say no to any of them.

Dillon, my ferocious panther, is my current favorite, but not my first dashing Dom. The Squire owns that privileged distinction.

Chapter Two – On the First Day

Six Months Ago

Serendipity delivered an introduction to DYKKC at my feet.

On a late Friday afternoon, I had just downloaded an erotica novel onto my e-reader for my weekend's entertainment. I should have waited for the privacy of my office. I was at work at the state School of Law Library where I'm the Access Services Manager. That's a fancy title for Chief Librarian. One of the lawyers who used our research services, a regular flirt, slinked up behind me at the Reference Desk. The graphic cover and suggestive title were on display for him in glorious color as he leaned over my shoulder.

A rather embarrassing conversation stemmed from his sneak peek, at my cleavage as well as my reading material, but ended with a summons from James Burton, Esq. to attend Devil You Know Kink Club as his guest that night. I agreed readily, though I'm sure he wouldn't have let me refuse, but I wanted to retract my acceptance as I watched him strut out the door. I sagged under the weight of what I had done; I had taken the first step of an epic quest of self-discovery for which I had been obsessively *planning* for years.

Even arriving at the planning stage of my exploration required a feat of bravery. I used to be vivacious, adventurous and outgoing, but Jed and every other guy I dated knocked that out of me. Every hurt or rejection shook my confidence. I retreated into a safe shell. Friends drifted away as I let myself become a shy, self-conscious and dull adult. I lived a drab vanilla lifestyle. Each lonely day was like the one before it—ordinary, ordered, following a routine of work, exercise, meditation, reading and sleep. Luckily, I was blessed with a few girlfriends who stuck by me and sometimes dragged me out with them. I even ventured to a dance club now and then if I could hide in a corner. I doubted I would be able to hide in a fetish club.

A friend in college turned me on to meditation. I latched on to spiritual teachings as a way to help me rebuild my sense of worth and find out who I am in the great existential context. The only problem with that was that I stuck to the straight and narrow, following the path of the righteous. I expanded in some ways and shrank in others. I turned myself into a goody two-shoes as I tried to suppress any acknowledgement of having a lusty nature. There was no way anyone would mistake me for a slut again.

My life changed drastically three years ago when my mom and dad were killed in a horrific, fiery crash with an 18-wheeler. My precious spirituality was of little use to me as my human heart grieved the devastating loss of the only people who loved me unconditionally. For the second time in my life, I was inconsolable. It was too soon for them to be gone and for me to be alone.

Pangs of unwelcome emptiness still rip through me at times and tear my life into shreds. Then it takes me a while to start piecing myself back together, until I remember the promise I made myself at my parents' funeral. Their deaths drove home the fact that we never know when our time will run out. I had to start living.

Something most definitely had been missing from my life. I suffered a crushing blow when I realized that I had been using meditation as a way to escape the world rather than to engage fully with it. Rather than trying to keep one foot in each realm, I needed both feet in the celestial *and* both feet in the material. I needed to become more human and, more particularly, a *female* human. My course was set. I began to explore my sexuality in the only way I could do it safely, through books. I freaking love books.

I tested the waters with charming and innocent romance novels. These fluff pieces were my gateway drug. I started to look at the world differently and learned a new vocabulary. That was when I developed my penchant for purple prose. I'm well-educated, well-spoken and well-read. I adore the classics and lofty tomes that inspire deep thinking. Yet my guilty pleasure is reading trashy tales with flamboyant descriptions of voluptuous bosoms heaving and steely swords plunging.

What I immersed myself in were politically incorrect bodice-rippers, the ones where the heroine fights the passion burning deep in her heart and her loins and either ends up shamelessly throwing herself at the hero because she can no longer deny his mastery, or is overpowered and devoured by the beast because he can no longer control his hunger. All ending happily ever after, of course.

I dove into the deep end of erotica as I yearned for racier titles, swamped by stories of dark desires and consuming cravings, freaky fetishes and carnal lust, demanding Doms and obedient subs, corruption of innocence and indulgence of perversion, and pleasure wrapped in pain. Basically, bodice-rippers with an edge.

There was something about the BDSM lifestyle that called to me. Not all of it by any means, but a latent aspect woke in me. My dark side was fertilized by sweet romance, nourished by unbridled passion, and ripened by wicked want. The seed had always been within me, though I didn't know it, nor could I have had a clue what kind of fruit it would bear, until I budded and blossomed.

I am a submissive.

The revelation was epic in terms of self-awareness and paralytic in consequence. After spending almost ten years trying to not be a slut, I faltered. I couldn't move beyond the label. I didn't know what to do about submission. I wasn't brave enough to taste it, let alone embrace it. The only way of indulging my disconcerting desire to fully give myself over to a masterful man was to live the decadent and debauched scenarios vicariously through the characters playing with each other in my e-reader.

That, of course, is why I agreed readily to meet Jim. He didn't have to seduce, or trick, or coerce, or force, or blackmail me into it as happens in some of the more ridiculous novels I read. I wasn't a naïve, 18-year-old virgin anxious to explore but unaware of the dangers. I wasn't desperate. *Okay, so I was desperate.*

Jim offered me the golden ticket to the kind of excitement I read about and dreamed about. I seized that free pass, clutched it protectively to my aching bosom. But the difference between getting kinky in fantasies rather than real life is as dissimilar as the visual appeal of a picture of a lake and the sensuality of cool water flowing through your hair, seeping into your eyes and ears—and every other orifice—while floating atop gently rippling waves.

From the first time I saw him, I couldn't deny that Jim's physical presence appealed to me. My fingers itched to trace along his strong, square jaw and bury themselves into his soft, sandy brown hair. He keeps it short on the sides, but a longer wave peaks and sweeps rakishly across his high forehead. He stands several inches over six feet tall, and, even in my heels, I have to tip my head up a bit to look into his rich chocolate eyes.

The problem for me was that he seemed too laidback and didn't radiate that spine-tingling charisma that I was looking for. His good looks alone weren't compelling enough for me to risk getting over my timidity. I had rebuffed all of his earlier invitations for a date; his latest invite at the beginning of that week was to his 30th birthday party to be held a couple of weeks later. In the end, what drew me in was the lure of exotic adventure that he hadn't offered before.

That first night, as Jim drove us to the club, I was freaking out and kicking myself for being too stupid, for getting myself into something that wasn't just a bit out of my comfort zone but was in a whole other solar system. Jim was considerate and understanding of my apprehension. He held me close around the waist, and my courage swelled. I stood taller as we walked through the door.

When I remembered to breathe, I was proud of my boldness and was exhilarated to be with Jim. He shape-shifted into someone I didn't recognize. I saw confidence and a powerful presence behind his roguish arrogance. I took Jim's outstretched hand and was happy to follow where he led. We were there as companions only and not to play together. Still, the feel of his hard body bumping up against mine certainly got me in the mood for what I was about to encounter. My panties were damp before I even saw a kinky thing.

The stately, old edifice built of massive sandstone blocks was at one time a diamond exchange and bank. The columns alongside and the lintel above the old, blue wooden doors are intricately carved. I expected a rich, old-world atmosphere inside. After we passed through the coat check, my eyes blinked in complete surprise at the modern décor of a nightclub called Night Moves. I was disappointed that the place is just like any other upscale bar.

We walked among a cluster of low tables and leather club chairs. Along the wall to the left is a long bar. The mirrored wall is covered with tiers of glass and chrome shelves displaying bright bottles and pyramids of colorful cans. A small dance floor spans the back wall, probably 30 feet in width and 20 feet deep. Tall tables and stools scatter around the edges. Every surface is black or chrome, the lighting neon and ultraviolet. The only difference from any dance club I had been to is the three metal cages suspended over the dance floor from the 25-ft. ceiling. They housed two naked women and one young man gyrating to the booming music.

"I need a stiff drink," I shouted to Jim. I needed help to relax and to warm the cold apprehension curling in my gut.

Jim flashed a killer, white smile. "No alcohol here. Booze and sex together may be fun at private parties," he said, "but they are a risky combination at a BDSM club. The liability is just too great where matters of informed consent are at stake." In my line of work, I am well-versed in the matter of legal liability and can see the point.

"Only *virgin* cocktails, Erin." It turns out the pretty display at the bar is an exotic selection of juices, syrups and cordials. With a sly grin, he added, "We *really* like virgins around here."

When I had left my house that night, I didn't feel virginal. I thought I was flashing too much skin in the low-cut, cream top and short, black silk skirt I put on. I did wear high heels, but they were more suited for the office than a club. Anyone else would have said I was dressed like a prude compared to the people I was meeting.

Jim guided me toward the teeming dance floor. I was definitely the most conspicuous person out there, for what I was wearing rather than what I wasn't. Even Jim fit in, and he was fully dressed in skin-tight, black leather pants and a simple, black silk T-shirt. Somehow he looked sexy, and I looked like a stereotypical librarian.

I soon forgot about my attire because I was going mad watching Jim's narrow hips pumping in time with the driving beat of the techno pop. The man can really work his *assets*. I had to hold myself back from jumping him as the music pulsed through my bones and desire pulsed through my girly bits. The vision of the cage dancers swaying seductively above me heightened my arousal exponentially.

The predatory glint in Jim's eyes set me on a slow simmer. When he looked at the junction of my thighs and licked his lips, I boiled over, stumbled and grabbed his rock-solid bicep for support. That misstep was all it took for Jim to swoop in and grind his hard body against my soft one. He wrapped his arms around me and twisted until I was crushed against his swollen groin. One hand snaked up to release my long, black hair from the bun it was wound into; the other grabbed my butt. The raw sensuality of Jim's gyrations really shook me. I hadn't believed that men as hot as him were real.

I wasn't sure what to do with my own hands, so I wrapped them around his shoulders. I was uneasy about Jim moving in that intimately and that quickly, and I was embarrassed that I couldn't find the impetus to push him away. I don't think I would have succeeded anyway; his hold on me was unbreakable. What choice did I have but to cleave to him for the ride? "Oh well," I thought with a guilty smile as I spread my legs a little wider and let him press his thick thigh in between. With our limbs woven together, I had never felt so sexual, so womanly. *Thrilling and threatening.*

I almost lost it when a barely dressed woman with fake boobs snuggled up behind me and jammed her hands in between Jim and me to fondle my natural breasts. Never mind the fact that she was a stranger, I don't do women. I'm not against it in theory if that's what turns a gal's crank. Personally, I would rather have a hot, throbbing cock filling me instead of a hunk of cold, inert plastic, even if it is strapped to a beautiful, warm body.

When Jim saw the panicked look in my eyes, he shoved hard against the woman's shoulders and dragged us off the dance floor. I was very grateful for his rescue, but I really wished I could have ordered a martini or two to knock back right then.

A mature and distinguished man wearing a huge, white diaper and a blue baby bonnet toddled up to us. He popped his thumb out of his mouth and thrust his hand forward.

"Squire. How are you tonight, Sir?" I was grossed out when Jim shook his spit-covered hand.

"I'm well, davey. You shouldn't be alone. Where's your Mommy?"

"She's out back having a quick smoke with the other grownups. She'll be right back. alyce is keeping an eye on me. Who's your lovely playmate, Squire?"

"She doesn't have a name yet. Let's just call her that. playmate." I opened my mouth to say that I did indeed have a name. The hard look from Jim made me shut up quick.

"It's her first time at DYKKC and on the scene. She's a fet virgin. I'm honored that she's letting me break her in." He turned to me with a kind smile. Then he shocked the shit right out of me when he leaned in and sucked my chin fully into his mouth ... and bit me. *What the heck was that? And why did my knees just go weak?*

"Good for you, Squire. playmate, you've got yourself a good teacher here. He'll show you the ropes ... and the whips and chains." He giggled like a precocious little boy at his silly joke.

"Mommy!" davey squealed with delight and tottered off to be cuddled up by a pretty blonde. He laid his head on the tall woman's bounteous bosom and grasped at her killer curves. I thought it was sweet and the most natural thing in the world. Not kinky at all.

"I'm sorry, Erin. I should have thought to talk to you about this. In the interest of some semblance of anonymity, no one is allowed to use real names here, even if we do know what they are.

"For tonight, why don't we stick with playmate? I think it's kind of hot, and I don't know of anyone else using that alias." Through lips twisted into a wicked grin, he faked an Australian accent and added, "I most definitely want to *play* with you, *mate*."

I couldn't think of a more appropriate name off the top of my head, not that I could think of anything at all because of the sinful message that flickered across Jim's face. Besides, I agreed with him. The name was pretty sexy. plaything would have been demeaning, but playmate appealed to the part of me that wanted to be adventurous with men and maybe a little bit bad.

"You can call me Squire, but I'd be happier if you call me Sir."

Jim placed his hand at the small of my back; his fingers burned into me like a brand. The name choice was already having a psychological effect on me. I was keyed in to Jim's, or should I say The Squire's, masculine vibe. Of course, the way he humped me on the dance floor might have had something to do with my exhilaration. A vague notion that maybe I wanted to play with him, in this place, was sprouting up toward the light like a tender shoot bursting from fetid, fertile soil.

$$< \male + \female >$$

We mingled for about an hour before Jim ushered me through sliding glass doors on the wall opposite the bar and into a large room he called Purgatory. I crash-landed onto another planet. Foreign sights, sounds and smells assailed me. Sexual energy crackled through the hot and humid air. Despite the crazy antics I saw in Night Moves, I wasn't prepared for bizarro world. I was able to hold my fears at bay as long as I clung to Jim for safety. He was my anchor to the real world.

This room is about two-thirds the size of the dance club and a lot cozier, in a twisted kind of way. It is almost womb-like rather than hellish. The ceiling is lower, only about 15 feet high. The walls are rich scarlet, and the floor is hardwood stained ebony. Utilitarian wall sconces cast subdued light around the room, and strategically placed spotlights create a sense of theater and high drama. Sensuous and dark music always thumps in the background, most of it in the same vein as my favorite band, Depeche Mode.

Four support posts in the room do double duty as bondage stations. I ogled the subs in various states of undress, attached to the posts in various manners and presented to the rank and file in various lewd positions. My stomach twisted as their Doms or Tops pestered or punished or pleased them in a multitude of ways. The four corners of the room are dimly lit and furnished with intimate groupings of couches, divans and wingback chairs. I mainly averted my eyes because the people were also in intimate groupings. I wasn't quite ready for orgies.

As distressing as the whole landscape looked to me, a tremor buzzed through me and straight to my clit. I didn't want to be turned on by any of it. Reading fiction and spying on made-up characters was okay in my mind, but being a voyeur in a human zoo didn't seem right. No matter where I turned, degeneracy was on display, just inches from my tingling fingertips. I was helpless to ignore it, getting horny and wet regardless of my righteousness.

A 10-ft. square and 4-ft. high platform dominates the center of the room. Stairs and a heavy brass handrail lead up one side. Spotlights at the four corners, with corresponding down-spots in the ceiling, illuminated the couple on the stage. That night there were red filters on the lenses casting an eerie glow over the scene playing out. I had no idea what to make of the main attraction.

In the very middle, a naked woman hung in suspension. Her wrists were bound in wide leather cuffs and shackled to a bar that spread her arms up and out in a V. The bar was attached to a chain that looped through a ring in the ceiling. A crank on the wall had been used to ratchet the chain so taut that her toes barely touched the floor. Her ankles were similarly bound and spread about three feet apart, further diminishing her stability. She was almost twisting and swaying in the wind. When I closed my eyes, I tapped into the frustration she was feeling from being nearly but not quite on solid ground.

The woman's Dom reclined in a lazy pose on a metal stacking chair in front of her. At random intervals, he dipped into a bucket and pulled out his ammunition. He pelted his sub with little, wet sponges that splatted in random places on her voluptuous body. Mixed in with her glistening pussy juices, trickles of icy water ran down her quivering legs and off her flexing toes. Since the scene was already in progress when we walked in, we didn't know whether the Dom was taunting the sub for the fun of it or was punishing her because she deserved it.

A swath of heavy lace around her head blacked out the beautiful brunette's sight, ensuring that she could never prepare for the next missile flung at her or for where it would land. She squawked and jumped every time one hit its mark; my body twitched in sympathy.

Her Dom laughed, as did some of the spectators. In a hushed voice, Jim explained, "They must have the Dom's permission. It's a club rule that a Dom has the right to punish anyone disturbing a scene or speaking to or touching a sub unless invited." So *what about the bitch who groped me on the dance floor?* The sub screamed and came unglued when one of the spectators retrieved a sponge from her Dom and bombarded her from behind in a sneak attack.

After watching a few scenes, some titillating like that one and others more dark and disturbing, Jim urged me up a narrow stairwell. He followed close behind, his greedy fingers sinking into the tender flesh of my derrière. About halfway up the stairs, Jim's grip changed, and he held my hips in place. He was a few steps below me and, leaning forward, his head was level with my rear end.

I recoiled when his nose nudged between my legs. The breezy sound of him having a good, deep sniff appalled me. *Brazen beyond belief!* My pussy, however, meowed and purred. In her Morse code language of clenches and releases, she let her approval be known.

Jim slapped each globe of my butt hard, jiggling the plentiful flesh, and pushed me onward. Once we made it to the top, me on very shaky legs, I saw four doors along each side of a cavernous and shadowy hallway. Each room, except for No. 8, had an observation window we could spy through with the other avid spectators. "The glass is just like they use in police interrogation rooms," Jim said.

I shuddered at every successive room, if not at the activity going on at the time, then at the equipment that suggested what might go on. I was also still quivering and creaming from our clandestine escapade on the darkened stairs. By no means was that daring or wild, not compared to future delights I would discover. For a first visit, the incident was enough to rattle me and entice me. I quickly succumbed to information and sensory overload, so Jim whisked me away to a trendy but vanilla lounge for that drink I needed.

"I'm curious, Erin, about your impressions of the club. Was it all too frightening for you? Or are you intrigued enough to want to explore further? How brave are you willing to be?" Jim leaned in and twirled a lock of my hair while he waited for my answer. As I considered my response, I swirled my glass of merlot and inhaled the fruity fumes before swishing a sip of the ruby nectar in my mouth. The researcher in me had started right from the get-go gathering data on what I wanted to try and what I didn't.

"You've seen the kind of books I read, but not a lot of what I saw matches up with my imagination. I was queasy most of the time. I crossed a few activities that I had wondered about off of my 'Want to Try' list. Now I know for certain I'm simply not interested in them. But, geez, I'm also flat-out terrified of certain styles of play, if you could call it play. It seemed more like torture to me.

"In all honesty, I was shocked by a lot, particularly that monster of a man, the one with salt and pepper hair wearing head-to-toe black leather. He whipped the stuffing out of that delicate-looking blonde who was shackled in heavy chains. My body jerked every time his bullwhip smacked against her skin. I don't think I care much for anything that looks painful ... but the glossy patches on her thighs made it look like she was enjoying herself."

"Trust me, she was." Jim shuddered. I wasn't sure why.

"I have to admit, the older couple in Purgatory wearing the latex suits intrigued me. I could see every bounce of lush curve and undulation of hard muscle." I licked my lips as the images lit up in my mind. Their most private parts were displayed through cut-outs in the rubber. The stunning brunette wore red, and her silver fox wore black. Exquisite bodies of all shapes and sizes decked out in outlandish fetish wear had paraded by me, and I had wanted to touch them all. The visual appeal seduced me. I appreciated each individual as a fine work of art. *Masterpieces.*

In a shaky voice, I said, "I'd like to go back, maybe try something on the tame side, as long as you'll be with me." I didn't know him very well, but I felt safe with Jim. He seemed perfectly harmless. I had paid close attention to his reactions to the club action. I figured he was either a good poker player, or he wasn't too excited either by the really extreme scenes of impact play or humiliation. Except for whatever his shiver hinted at when I mentioned blondie.

"Of course. It would be my pleasure." Jim's eyes brightened, and his smile smoldered. I just about came when he kissed my palm and sucked on my thumb. As we parted company, he invited me back to DYKKC for Saturday night the following week. It would be my initiation as a new player in the BDSM community.

"I would be honored to have you as my sub for the night," he said. I guess it was obvious that I am no Domme. I may take charge at work, but I doubt I'll ever be comfortable leading in this arena.

I accepted Jim's challenge while hoping that I would be able to go through with it. I was tired of my lackluster life and ready for adventure. I had no one to answer to but myself, and this was what I wanted, if I could just keep my courage up. I did follow through, and that decision changed my life.

$$< \male + \female >$$

A week later, Jim and I had dinner at a swanky Italian restaurant before going to DYKKC. He was sweet and attentive, paying me sincere compliments, especially on my simple, royal blue, sleeveless dress. He said he liked how it draped on my curves. The way he kept skimming his fingers along the smooth silk covering my thighs and eyeing my body throughout our meal unnerved me at the same time that it got me all hot and bothered.

We talked about what I was willing to try and what was definitely off the table. "I'd like my first scene to be pretty mild. I just want to get used to showing myself in public." For a non-slut, that was probably going to be traumatic enough for one night.

My first test came right at the coat check when we entered the club. I hopped like a scared rabbit when Jim tugged at the zipper down my back. He quickly peeled off my dress—my shield—folded it carefully, and slipped it into a cloth bag. The attendant took a sideways glance at me before she slung the bag over the hanger holding my coat. She looked like a scared rabbit herself, sporting only bunny ears and a powder-puff butt plug.

Jim pointed out on my first visit that the nubile, female staff, at least those who are subs, hop about in exactly the same kit and bare feet, except some wear a modest, red thong with the bunny tail attached to the string up their crack. The provocative Dommes on staff promenade around clad in red leather bustiers or corsets, hot pants, and, of course, red stilettos or boots.

The imposing Dominant male employees strut their stuff in black leather pants so tight they look like they are sprayed on. Bare chests peek from behind their black leather vests. Footwear seems to be an individual choice. The hot, submissive males kowtow to patrons in nothing but black leather G-strings. I said a silent "thank you" to management for the dress code.

All staff, as fits their station, wear either a black collar dangling a dog tag engraved with the DYKKC logo or an elegant silver rope chain with the logo etched into a silver medallion. I was relieved when Jim identified the Dungeon Monitors, who also wear a red armband on their left bicep. Knowing there would be DMs roving around Purgatory, the private rooms and the dungeon who made sure all members and guests played safely was a big comfort.

Jim stepped back and took his time appraising my body. His pupils dilated wide, almost eclipsing the chocolate ring around them. He drew in a few erratic breaths as he mentally mapped my almost-naked territory. He ever so slowly dragged his pointed tongue from the right corner of his mouth and along his puffed-up bottom lip. He flicked his tongue in, moistening it before tracing from the left and over his full upper lip. I neither dared nor needed to look for further signs of his arousal.

As Jim had requested, I wore the most daring outfit I owned at the time. I didn't think when I bought it that I'd be exposing myself publicly in the skimpy, black, peek-a-boo halter and thong set. Everyone could see my nipples through the fine, fishnet mesh of the bra. They were hard and erect, but the tightness of the fabric squashed those buds back flat into my ripe flesh.

"Perfect," was all Jim said on a steamy breath. I sighed at the sound of his silky, smooth bass tone. That one word was all I needed to calm my wildly beating heart, at least to a level where I was no longer on the verge of passing out. He swiped his finger through the fringe of black tassels swinging under the cups. The G-string barely covered my top-secret parts. A circle of matching fringe skimmed the tiny V of mesh covering my neatly trimmed bush and tickled along the top of my butt cheeks. I did my best not to fidget or hide myself, chanting in my head, "Be brave, be brave."

My Dom for the night, The Squire, looked as sexy as all-get-out. Staring at him was what had gotten my nipples hard in the first place. Rich mahogany leather pants accentuated his long, athletic legs and drool-worthy butt. The downside of those pants was that they kept his package tightly contained and concealed, although I did notice some curious bulges in his pockets.

A matching vest atop a skin-tight, white T-shirt highlighted the ripples of an upper body he clearly spends a lot of time shaping. A few sandy curls peeked above the V-neck. He cast a devastating grin at me and, with a twinkle in his hypnotic eyes, reeled me close and laid a warm kiss on my cheek. I closed my eyes, sinking my fingers into his bicep to regain my composure. I didn't want to let him see so early how much a simple gesture like that affected me.

Jim startled me when he fished a black leather collar from one of his pockets. Without a word, he pressed his chest against mine, reached behind me, and buckled it securely. We hadn't discussed this, but I didn't make a fuss. I was here to explore and wearing a collar for play seemed harmless enough.

"Nice look. Tonight, you belong to me, little sub." *Property ownership? Seriously? Perhaps not harmless after all.* "Don't worry. I'll protect my playmate." His crooning tone soothed my nerves but melted my muscles; I slumped against his strong body. That was when he attached a leash to the ring in the front of the heavy collar.

When I saw men and women being led around like animals the week before, I had thought the implication of ownership was totally degrading. Yet, here I was, collared and leashed like an obedient pet, and, suddenly, I had no resistance. Susan B. Anthony must have turned over in her grave as I set the feminist movement back at least a hundred and fifty years. You could have knocked me over with a feather, but I couldn't deny my acceptance. A sense of peace that I couldn't express or even comprehend washed over me.

That, in my naïveté, was how I felt that night. I have never let Jim collar me again, even though we play together about once a month. Jim's a great, fun guy, but, even with the transformation I saw come over him when we walked into Devil You Know together, he is not strong enough or serious enough for the responsibility of ownership. I'm not about to give that much control to someone I'm just playing with. If I ever let someone collar me again, and I'm not sure I will, I won't take it lightly and neither will he.

< ♂ + ♀ >

Jim tugged gently on the leash and guided me into Purgatory, straight to one of the hitching posts that was unoccupied despite the room being packed. A *coincidence?*

As he unclipped my leash, he barked out, "Stay." I looked at him, my eyes blank of response, but obeyed. Jim threaded the leash through one of the post rings and then through the leash loop. The clip snapped loudly when he fixed it back to the ring in my collar.

Once he had me chained in place, I started to tremble, wondering what would come next. A small, curious crowd gathered around us, and the tremble increased to a shake.

Jim came close and stroked my hair as he spoke softly. "Breathe, sub. You're safe, baby girl. No one is going to touch you. They only want to look at your beautiful body."

I shook my head vigorously, flinging a few tears from my eyes. The warning about not speaking unless spoken to had been delivered and understood, as had the talk about safewords. Jim asked, "You don't want them to look at you? Do you want to use your safeword?"

"No, Sir," I peeped.

"Then what is it, sub?"

"My body isn't beautiful, Sir. It's too big." There isn't a single body at DYKKC that I don't think is beautiful. Even the overweight woman being strafed with sponges the week before is gorgeous to me. So is davey's Rubenesque Mommy.

Thanks to that asshole boyfriend in college, I had trouble loving the more-than-generous curves I acquired after Jed's betrayal. Even all the jogging I have done since my parents died hasn't completely erased my love handles and muffin top. I unkindly judged myself as perennially tubby. That's another reason I never took Jim's flirting seriously. I couldn't imagine that a god like him could ever be interested in a marshmallow like me.

"I don't want to hear you talk like that again, sub, or I'll have to take you over my knee." I snapped to attention. I'd read enough naughty books and had seen enough red asses my first night at DYKKC that I didn't want Jim laying his hands, or something more sinister, on my tender behind. No one had ever spanked me, not even my parents. This "play" session was turning out to be far more humiliating than I had anticipated.

Jim spent agonizing minutes running his fingers all over my body. As he skated along, he pulled at the ribbons at my back and neck. My top sailed to the floor. When he dropped his hands lower, he plucked on the ribbons at my hips and tugged the G-string from between my thighs. I hadn't planned on getting completely naked, and the shock had me hyperventilating. I covered myself to hide my vital parts and my excess weight. My Dom took control, speaking in calming tones and gripping my wrists.

"Look around you, sub. There isn't anyone here who will judge you. This is what you asked for. Just let yourself go." *I can do this.* I finally caught my breath and gave in as Jim pulled on my wrists, drawing my hands away. I watched the emotion dancing in his eyes. He looked like he was unveiling a marble statue or work of art. A cloud of butterflies fluttered in my heart. Things were not going according to my original plan, but I was glad to have my exposure over all at once. I was also oddly relieved to not have made the choice myself. I was getting a feel for the appeal of submission.

Standing in the middle of a crowded room in only my birthday suit and heels suddenly wasn't nearly as embarrassing as I expected, thanks to Jim. He found special compliments for each part of me that he brushed his long fingers over. He *oohed* and *aahed* and sighed, as did the spectators watching closely. One rather rotund man in a black, spandex bodysuit incited my nerves by inching his flagrant erection closer. *Is that hard-on because of me?*

Jim placed a tender kiss on each of my cheeks and a single, wet smacker of a kiss on each perky nipple. He treated each butt cheek to a sharp smack with a heavy hand. A hot blush flared on my face when he ran one finger across my slit and brought it up gleaming.

"Mmm. So temptingly juicy, my little playmate. And delectable." I gawked as his thick tongue licked his finger clean. The act was dirty, and the most erotic thing a man had ever done to me. Sure, I'd had a man taste me before, but the tone of Jim's voice, his unwavering stare, the slow flickering of his tongue, and the popping sound as he removed his finger were all sexually charged. On the periphery, I could see several men and even a few women shifting their attention to Jim sampling my nectar. He was that hot. One tall, lean man with a bullwhip coiled at his side smacked the leather against his hip. Jim and I both stared hard at him in disapproval.

Tears of gratitude welled up in my eyes and threatened to spill over by the time Jim finished praising my body. No man had ever appreciated me in that way, but a skeptical voice inside said that he would say whatever he needed to say to get inside my pants—not that we had broached the possibility. I know that not all domination involves sex, but my optimistic voice hoped.

"Do you believe it now, sub?"

"I guess so, Sir."

"Do you think I'm lying to you, sub?" He sounded a little cross.

"Oh. No, Sir. It's just a new concept for me. I guess old habits and ways of thinking are hard to break."

I almost choked on what he did next. Jim turned to the crowd and asked, "Who would like to tell my pretty playmate how lovely she is? She thinks her mirror works differently than my eyes do."

Voices on every side showered me with words of admiration. Jim stepped back, and the spectators advanced. A sickening wave of claustrophobia swamped me even though they stopped short of touching me.

I wanted to bolt out of there, until one man stepped directly in front of me and stole my full attention.

He didn't put so much as a pinky finger on my skin, but his gaze roamed across each inch of me, the action every bit as tactile as if his hands were tickling and tracing all over me. He captivated me with his smoky gray eyes, and I gave him a nervous smile. *Shit!*

Just as intently, I studied the man, fixing him irrevocably in my mind. Waves of black, silken hair float against a strong jaw that angles down to a sharp chin. I'm not a fan of facial hair, but I like the way his straight, broad nose is underlined by a lush mustache. His is neatly trimmed and satiny soft, the perfect foil for plump, kissable lips. Heavy, dark stubble enhanced the sinful look of the fine specimen of hard masculinity—he was no pretty boy. He seemed vaguely familiar, even at that first look. I scrinched my eyes tight and saw a hint of the devilish face of the DYKKC logo.

He was a big man, even though he was an inch shorter than me with my heels on. While broad-shouldered and solidly built, it wasn't his hard body that made him seem huge. His aura and his presence filled the room and screamed, "Dom!" His energy bumped up against me before he even moved an inch. I pegged him at about 35 or 36, and I sensed a maturity that had nothing to do with his age. An air of authority that Jim can't match swirled around him.

When the man did move closer, he put one foot between mine. The space between us was paper-thin, but he still didn't touch me. Sparks of electricity arced across that sliver of space, and a thousand needles pricked my skin. How any woman would ever be able to resist him is beyond my comprehension. He was elemental sexuality. I almost did an old-fashioned swoon when his hot and damp breath blew across my ear as he whispered to me.

"You are a tempting little treat, aren't you, pet? Creamy white skin that looks so soft and tasty. Pretty, pink nipples blossoming like fragrant rosebuds. Dark, curly snatch, like a woman instead of bare like a child. Strong, shapely thighs to squeeze a man tight. Hmm, I wonder what else squeezes tight ... I do hope I get a chance for a lick and a nibble of you." The low rumble deep in his throat reverberated in my sopping pussy. It was a primal sound, the kind capable of giving birth to universes.

Excuse my language, but ... Ho-ly fuck! No man had ever talked to me like that, or growled at me like that. He might as well have run over me with a steamroller. I hadn't even gotten a growl out of Jim at that point. Comparing them now, Jim yips like the trickster he is, a coyote; the sound coming from the Dom was the husky yowl of an Alpha wolf, the leader of the pack. I noted a faint hint of a suave French accent in both his words and his snarl.

He filled his lungs with my light, floral scent before he turned away, and I had my own full sniff of his earthy musk. I tracked his movements as he walked off, particularly the rotation of his hips and the swagger of his sexy ass. From shoulder to coccyx, his torso forms the most perfect triangle I have ever seen.

I later found out his Dom name is Master Ronan, but the rest of the world knows him as Dr. Christophe Serle. It was only two weeks later when he got his first taste of me and became the second Top I play with at DYKKC. He's very skilled and very attentive, so he's in high demand as a Service Top among the unattached bottoms. Add in the fact that he travels frequently, and that means he's not around much. Time with him is rare for me. *Such a pity.*

Jim crushed his lips against mine an instant after Christophe left. *Dominance!* I wondered if those two had a history or if they were just posturing for each other and to warn off others. As I melted into Jim's kiss, he held my upper arms in a firm grip while his tongue ravaged my mouth. My head spun, and I thought I was on the brink of fainting. Jim grounded me with an assuring tone.

"Thank your admirers, sub, for their attention. They've been generous with their compliments." I nodded to Jim and turned in a slow circle. I made tentative eye contact as I offered them smiles and hushed words of gratitude.

Just like the week before, I was surprised that everyone around me seemed normal. Despite what they did to each other, no one looked like a deviant. They had all just been incredibly kind. I even saw a couple of people I recognized from my everyday life, and though I was still too shy to speak to them, I didn't think it would take me very long to feel comfortable and like I could fit in.

My admirers shuffled off. Jim detached my leash from the post and then clicked it back into place on my collar. "Follow me, playmate. You were magnificent, such a brave girl. I'm so proud of you. Now, I have a reward for you." I glowed happily. I felt like I'd accomplished something important, for both of us. My joy lasted only until Jim snatched up my bikini set and led me naked up the stairs and to the door of Playroom No. 1. Things were about to get serious. *This isn't a game.* Trepidation filled me as I fretted over his idea of a "reward."

I needn't have worried at all. Jim teased and pleased and played with me for almost two hours. Except for one little hiccup at the end, he had me screaming in delight over and over again.

Later that night, I wrestled with my conscience, questioned my moral character, and examined my needs. There was no point in deceiving myself. *I'm hooked.* My need for erotic adventure, for learning about myself, outweighed my fear of the unknown. This was the launch of the odyssey for which I had longed for years. I analyzed my financial records to figure out how I could pay for my own DYKKC membership. "I really want to know those devils."

Chapter Three – Cardinal Sins

Friday Night, September 14

After four close calls, I'm ready to move this show along and get my well-deserved orgasm. The Saint, the sexy bastard, is not. He unfolds his long, lean body and rises off the footstool. He cups my face in his huge, hard-skinned hands. The pressure is anything but light; it's crushing. *Dammit!* He pulls me up hard, hyper-extending my neck as he almost lifts me off the chair. Our noses kiss when he bends down, and his silky, blond hair tickles across my cheeks.

"You. Will. Not. Come. If you do, I *will* punish you. We've had this discussion too many times. Do you understand, sub?"

"Y-yes, Sir." I have no doubt that he is serious; he's done it before. He didn't think Jim was strict enough in training me to control my orgasms, so he made it his duty to give me some very intense lessons that convinced me of the wisdom of self-discipline.

"It's a good thing you remembered how to respond this time, you naughty sub. But, to remind you who the Top is here, you need to pay the price for your earlier transgression." Dillon releases my face and drops me back onto the chair.

Wait. What transgression?

"You know that when you speak, your answers are to be concise. Thanking me for stopping you from coming was a breach of protocol. I don't appreciate being sassed." I'm used to the dark Saint finding flimsy excuses for spanking me, and his face contorts into an expression that looks like anticipation. But, when he walks away, I realize he has some torment other than spanking in mind.

He reaches into a pocket in my knapsack. In the interest of health and safety, I bring my own toys with me to the club. I wince at just the sight of the nipple vices pinched between his fingers. I'm not a fan of clamps—my breasts are too sensitive—but I tolerate them for Dillon, and only for Dillon. These are steel, each one a u-shaped frame, closed off by a crossbar along the top. A second bar attached to a long screw adjusts the pressure of the nasty device. They were a gift from Dillon. *Such a romantic.*

Dillon leans in to me and takes my left nipple into his mouth. He sucks hard for a few seconds to distend the bud and clamps his teeth in a callous chomp. I jump in outrage and cry out. "Ow!" That earns me a light smack on my cheek and a stern look. *Seriously?*

I close my eyes and breathe, trying to regain my composure. The soothing smell of leather floating in the room calms me—until the shock of cold metal on my skin is followed by the bite of Dillon compressing my nipple in the vice. For such a tiny gadget, it delivers a heavy dose of pain when in the wrong hands. Tonight, those hands belong to The Saint, only he's more like the Marquis de Sade. Any other sub would think I'm exaggerating grossly, but it feels accurate to me. My Top has always encouraged me to go to the edge of my tolerance but has never hurled me at it like this. I really don't know how much more stimulation my body can take.

My other nipple gets the same barbaric treatment. I gasp a few more breaths into my lungs, and I am barely able to bear the vices. Dillon strokes around my breasts, soothing, then licks and gently suckles my aching buds. *Who the hell is this guy tonight? He is taking pain and pleasure to another level.*

"Do you want to use your safeword, sub?" I quickly shake my head. I really *should* because, as much as the clamps hurt now, they're going to sting like a mother when he gets around to unscrewing them. The only reason I don't stop is because he owes me one hell of an orgasm after all this bullshit. One thing is for sure, I don't dare say anything else at this point. I'm positive the opposite is true, but at times like this I think he's a misogynistic prick. He wants to see how far he can push me ... but he never goes too far.

"Good girl. Now, where were we?" *Good girl. Ohhh, good girl.* I want to stay mad, but every tiny sign that I've pleased him makes my heart thump wildly. This is why I let him use the clamps. The way his breath stutters, the way his eyes rage, the way his tongue points and flicks along his top front teeth, the way his chest rises, the way his groin surges, these are the signs of how turned on he gets seeing my nipples squashed and seeing me twisting in agony. I shouldn't let him do it, but his response to me slays my objections.

I can't wait for him to turn me around and bury his mighty cock in my butt so he can come and then I can come. No such luck. He soundly smacks the outer side of each already abused breast as he eases back down on the ottoman with a nonchalance that irks me. He drops a hand down his side to get something I can't see. I hear a loud, steady hum, and my eyes open wide in disbelief. *The sadist thinks I'm going to be able to tolerate the wand right now? Hell no!*

Dillon positions the head of the massager against my pussy, jiggling it back and forth until it covers my slit and works its way up between the protection of my labia and onto my naked clit. Even on the low setting, in only ten seconds I'm writhing uncontrollably from the vibrations emanating from the "nasty stick." The ropes are starting to abrade my skin and the rawness stings.

"What will I do if you come, sub?"

"You'll punish me, Sir." I can't disguise the anguish I'm suffering right now. I'm straining to hold off my orgasm, and then the bastard dials the wand up to high. I don't care who peed in his cereal this morning; I shouldn't have to suffer for it.

I let out a howl just as Dillon pulls back the wand. I'm dazed by a hard slap on my mound. "Hold it," he snaps. Then he laughs and brushes his fingers along the insides of my thighs. I throw the stink eye at him and get another slap over my pussy in payment. This isn't so much fun anymore. Except for the anticipation of what he's building me up to. I can't believe what I'm willing to put up with to get an orgasm, no matter how out-of-this-world the climax is when his finger is on the ignition button.

"You know the rules, sub. Hang in there a little bit longer while I get you ready to take my big cock in your little back door. It's going to be hard and fast. You'll swear it's too much. You'll beg me to stop, but you'll take what I give you. I'm gonna pound your peaches until I blast deep in your ass. When I come, you're going to milk for all you're worth. If you do it right, I'll let you come. And you'll thank me with a smile ... like you always do." *Seriously, who says stuff like that?* His raunchy words make me hot, but the reason for my burning blush flips between being disgusted and being delighted. The timbre of his rough and ragged voice edges me closer toward delight. And he won't just *let* me come, he'll make sure of it. *Yes.*

The Saint finally acts like he really is a saint as he reverently glides two fingers on either side of my overly sensitized little nub and slips a third inside my clenched channel. *Now, this is pleasure.* A little moan of appreciation rattles up my throat, almost like a purr. I'm kicked out of heaven when Dillon thrusts the wand back on top of my poor, mistreated clit. Once he has the vibrating head right where he wants it, his eyes glaze over. His attention is somewhere other than where it should be. He barely pulled off in time before; he better be able to do it again because I can't hold back for long.

I'm squirming like a worm in a rain puddle, and more moans leak from my mouth. The jerk has his eyes closed now. He might even be asleep. I should say something before it's too late, but, dammit, I won't let this villainous Dillon heap more abuse on me for speaking.

Oh Christ! My orgasm slams into me with the force of a World Series champ knocking one out of the park. Dillon jolts up and drops the wand, but I'm already flying over the left-field fence and nothing is going to stop me from relishing this rush. Or so I think.

I crash back to earth with a thud as Dillon slaps my face with just enough force to make my teeth click. "Bad sub! You weren't allowed to come. Now I have to punish you."

He lifts me off the chair, flips me around, and sets me back down. I almost tumble onto the floor before he steadies me. In this position, the ropes that once gave me freedom now feel like prison bars strangling me as they bite deeper into my limbs. I'm used to harsh with Dillon. It's part of our game and why I come to him instead of always playing nice with Jim, but he's gotta slow down.

"Yellow! Sir, please." I try to shout, but my voice is a bit muffled with my face smushed into the back of the armchair.

"miss priss! Bad sub. You disappoint me. You disobeyed a direct command. I gave you a chance to use your safeword, and you didn't take it. So you will take the punishment you deserve. What kind of Dom would I be if I let you trick your way out of the spanking you have earned?" *What?* Before I can plead my case, Dillon lights a fire on my ass with a wicked whack of his palm. I just know he's been waiting for this chance.

Dillon's hands are huge and strong, like bear paws. As wide as my cheek is, he covers most of it in one swat. With my butt up and the muscles stretched, that strike goes beyond spanking to what I call a whoopin'. Another and another follow hard on top of each other. He lands at least ten excruciating blows before he relents.

"Dillon, stop. Please stop." This time, my cries carry.

"You *will* address me as Sir, and you *will* speak respectfully to me. Are you a submissive or not? Yield and take your punishment."

Another four thumps land on my burning butt, but they don't hurt me nearly as much as my Top questioning whether I'm a submissive. With just a few words, he's dismissed everything I've done for him, given him, given up for him, become for him. His chastisement cuts me to the very bone. I always do my best to please him, push myself to please him. This conflict and his anger turn me into a little girl, unsure, trembling, shamed. Being on the receiving end of my big, beautiful bad boy's ire is one of the worst wounds I've ever suffered. Fear impairs my brain; sorrow maims my heart. I need to stop this.

Even with my neck twisted into the chair-back, out of one eye I see Dillon step back and pace. He's panting like he's trying to regain control. *This is new.* He's never been truly angry before when he's punished me. *How much am I supposed to take? Everyone has limits, should have limits.*

"Red, red, RED!" I scream at the top of my lungs. "Untie me, you bastard. It's not my fault. You fell asleep."

"Well, you should have said something, shouldn't you, priss?" He actually has the gall to say that to me, like he's not responsible for falling down on the job.

"Of course I couldn't. What did you expect after you literally put the screws to my nipples just for saying 'thank you'? You are way over the line here, asshole. End this now. Untie me and get these damned clamps off me." I'm quite comfortable with profanity right now. My whole body is twitching and jerking from the pain load and the anger surging through my veins. I struggle for every breath. Tears stream down my face, and snot runs from my nose. *He knows me. Why can't the bastard see I'm messed up?*

I really need an intervention. I doubt I'm going to get it, but I say a prayer for help. Unless a Dungeon Monitor happens to poke his head in on a whim, I'm on my own. It's my own damn fault. I don't like the whole being-on-public-display aspect of club play. Dillon is the only one of my three Tops who grants my request for privacy and pulls the drapes across the observation window. Because we've played together safely on several occasions, and with Dillon being a long-standing member, the DMs didn't see any reason to check on us during our last session. I was glad of that, until now.

"Sir, please." I'm begging and pleading. "My butt really hurts, and I can't take any more. Please, Sir."

Dillon takes a deep breath, sighing, and strokes my behind with gentle pats. He leans close to my ear, nuzzling me with his nose, and speaks in a low rasp that, at any other time, would have sounded tender and made me pant.

"We negotiated that I could bind you and play with you within your limits. Now we know what those are. Thank you for telling me. But *we* negotiated that you would not come without permission and that I could punish you if you did. I was lenient, sub, only 16 light swats. No more spanking, baby; you've taken your punishment well. But, in case you've forgotten, *we* negotiated that I get your ass and *then* you get to come. Be a good girl for me. Just relax while I give you everything you begged so sweetly for, priss. Is that okay, baby?"

Those words push me too far, and I finally lose it. Not in the sense of going all apeshit. I wish I could do that. Instead, I close down. I give up and give in.

Dillon, this Dom that I cared about and trusted, strips away all the personal power that I ever gained with my awakened sexuality by breaking the cardinal rule—a safeword must always be respected immediately, no matter what the other party wants.

I stop all struggle and flop limp as a rag doll. Dillon is too far gone to realize what's happening, that I've left, floated out of my body. "What a good girl. Thank you. Let yourself enjoy this, priss. You're so beautiful, baby girl, and I want your ass so bad." He glides his hands over my numb bottom before he maneuvers my knees to the edge of the seat. My head is crammed down into the corner.

I look down from the ceiling, see my ass sitting high and ready. The glob of cold lube dribbling just above my clinched anus doesn't make me shudder. Nothing hurts. A vague thought drifts through my brain that I'll be in a world of hurt when I re-enter my body.

He strokes his left hand up and down my back while his right one spreads the lube. "That's my pretty girl. What a stunning glow your ripe peaches have." The jerk chuckles like he's proud of what he's done. He whispers sweet nothings at me. *Now you want to be a nice guy? Screw you, Dillon.*

I watch him opening a condom wrapper and hear the creak of latex being rolled on. At least he doesn't break that rule. He settles a bony finger against my rosette. "Relax for me, sub. Come on, baby girl, wiggle your beautiful butt. Let me in. I know how much you love this." He coaxes and cajoles like he thinks I'm cooperating with him. I'm not ... because I'm not there to fight him anymore.

No, no, no. Please, no. No, no, no, no, no, no. My mind should be screaming, but I only hear distant whimpering.

"Baby girl, what's the matter? Tell me what happened. Are you okay? Talk to me, sub." I'm sucked into a vortex and land with a bump. My eyes flicker open. Dillon is beside me, and I realize I've been mumbling "no" out loud. He shakes my shoulders to break me from my trance before he carefully lifts and turns me. His face broadcasts sheer panic, and his pupils bloom like black buds.

"My safeword. You didn't stop. Please don't rape me." My sobs are heavily laden with soul-crushing despair.

"No. Oh, my God. No, baby. Never. I would never. I thought you changed your mind, that you wanted this. *Christ.*" He dashes across the room for a pair of EMT scissors. With shaking hands, he hacks at the loathsome ropes. As soon as I'm free, he cradles me in his arms and stumbles to the couch. Dillon looks as terrified as I am.

"Baby, I'm sorry. Shhh. You're okay. Shhh. I'm so sorry." He swaddles me up in a blanket and pulls me onto his lap. "Erin, baby. I'm sorry. This is gonna hurt, but I've got to get these clamps off you. Breathe deep, baby girl. Are you ready?"

I'm not, but I screw my eyes closed tight and inhale as much oxygen into my lungs as I can. Searing pain explodes over first one nipple and then the other as pinched nerve endings spark again and scalding hot blood rushes back into vessels constricted for too long. I'm convinced that my delicate skin is melting.

Uncontrollable tremors rock through me. As catastrophic as a nuclear blast, stress hormones detonate and blow all my circuits. I liquefy and dissolve. As the blackness takes me over, I wonder whether I'll ever be able to pull myself back together again.

$$< ♂ + ♀ >$$

The sound of two male voices calling to me draws me back to the land of the living. Another, calm, nurturing voice in my head, decidedly female, warns me not to move quickly. She's my higher self, my usually silent witness, the best version of me. She's like a spiritual wonder woman, and she calls herself Evanya. I typically only hear her wise words when I'm deep in meditation. She's got to be wondering what kind of an idiot I am to have gotten myself into this fucking disaster. *Oh, that pun is so unintentional.*

She tells me I'm alive and that I am untouched. Not true; my aching muscles and joints tell me I've been touched rather savagely. Evanya can mind her own damned business. I've got the reality of this clusterfuck to deal with, and she's not helping with her take-the-high-road attitude. *It's too soon for sweetness and light.*

I force my eyelids open, moving only my eyeballs toward Luke who is standing to Dillon's right. I say to the Dungeon Monitor, "Get him out of my sight."

"You're right, priss," Dillon interjects. "We've both had a terrifying scare. Luke should leave so I can give you aftercare, and we can talk about what happened in private. I need to make sure you're okay." He turns my face toward himself. His smooth move gives me one critical piece of feedback—my neck hurts like a sonofabitch. I look right at the DM even though I have to move my aching neck again.

"Help me, Luke. Get me up, and get this bastard out of my sight. Now." I can't find the strength yet to raise my voice, but I still manage to impress the seriousness of my request on the right party. The DM, who goes by the handle Luke Skywalker, finally figures out that I'm talking about getting rid of Dillon. He springs into action, ordering Dillon to let me go as he scoops me out of his arms. *God, I love protective men.*

"Do you need a medic, priss?" He assesses my respiration and gaze. Dillon is hopping about like a Jack Russell terrier on speed.

"Yes. And I want that asshole to have a drug test. Keep him away from me and make sure it happens. Please, Luke?"

"Drug test? What are you talking about, priss? I haven't taken any drugs." Dillon is beside himself. "Why won't you let me help you?" Luke must be using "The Force" because he shields me with his body and single-handedly keeps the lunatic off me.

"How else would you explain your behavior tonight? You torture me and then you fall asleep. You punish me for your own mistake. You ignore when I call 'yellow' and keep going. And after you ignore 'red,' you try to rape me, in my ass." I cringe as I hurl the ruinous accusation, but it's out of my mouth before I can clutch it back. I'm careening down a track I can't disengage from, fueled by physical pain, emotional torment, and stress-chemical overdose. I'm in pure survival mode, and Evanya may as well be a galaxy away.

"Are you going to tell me you did all that stone cold sober?"

"I didn't rape you. I stopped! I didn't even put a finger in you." True, but, at this point, that sounds like a technicality to me.

All the ruckus lures another DM into the room. After hearing my allegations, Luke shouts at the other DM to restrain Dillon. An epic battle ensues. The DM eventually pins Dillon to the floor and gets a pair of cuffs on him.

In the meantime, another DM rushes in, and Luke directs him to clear the growing crowd of spectators. *So much for privacy.* Even if only one member saw and heard even a little bit of what has been going on, it will be all through the membership within 24 hours. I doubt anyone missed hearing me yell that odious word. I shrink back into myself as the echo blasts in my head.

I'm still shaking in Luke's arms when the medic arrives. The DMs try to hustle Dillon out of the room so I can be examined without the bastard squawking at me. I don't want him to ever see me naked again. Dillon does not go quietly. I can't believe he doesn't realize how much he hurt me. And how much he scared me.

I have the right to say what happens to my body. Well, every human being has that right. I used our prearranged safety valve, and, Dom or not, Dillon had no right to dismiss that. He should have stopped right away, not taken his sweet time about it. He's been around the BDSM scene long enough that he should know that.

The medic employed by DYKKC calls himself Dr. Yuri. Not many get the reference to Russian literature. He takes my vitals and tells me that all my readings are out of whack, but there's no need for paramedics. That suits me fine because I feel violated and exposed enough. I'm not going to the hospital for further humiliation.

Thank goodness for autopilot, that self-preservation instinct, because there is no way I should be able to function and think about what needs to be done. I ask Dr. Yuri if he will gather the evidence I'll need *if* I decide to call the cops. He nods and snaps pictures of the visible wounds like the deep rope burns and the bruising around my nipples. Then he checks my limbs.

"You seem to be okay, priss. Pulled muscles and strained joints, but no serious damage. I suggest you get your neck checked out though. I'm concerned about that. Even if it's a chiropractor, get some x-rays taken to rule out whiplash or dislocation."

"Thanks, Dr. Yuri." All I can offer him is a half-hearted smile.

"I have to write up an incident report and attach the pictures for the club's insurance, so I'll make sure you get a copy of it." *Great, naked pictures of me out in the wild that I'll have no control over.*

Luke says he will write his own report and add to it that I was unconscious when he arrived. He was on a random check when he entered the room. That's a shock and another strike against Dillon; he should have hit the panic button to call a medic when I passed out. He has First Aid training, but that's not the point.

"priss, I'm not saying I don't believe you, or that I don't think something went wrong. I don't honestly know what did." Luke's eyes focus on the floor while he talks, and he scuffs his boots along the hardwood. "I can't say anything in my report that I didn't see for myself. All I know is that, after I opened the door, I saw The Saint rocking you in his arms. He was really worried about you.

"I've known him since I started here; he helped with my training. It's hard to believe he could do something like ..." He's avoiding the hideous word, and I understand why. I'm queasy myself because something about it sounds really wrong. Still, I bury my misgivings because I can't believe Luke's siding with Dillon. *I'm the victim.*

Luke says they will need an incident report from me as well, but he wants me to go home and take care of myself. Someone from management will contact me tomorrow to get my side of the story.

"What I really need right now is a hot bath, otherwise I won't be able to move tomorrow." Dr. Yuri tucks a bottle of muscle relaxants in my hand and kisses my cheek. This time I can give him a full grin. We make arrangements for one of my sub friends to gather my belongings and take me home. She's known around DYKKC as alyce. Some think it's a reference to *Alice in Wonderland*, but it's just a mash-up of the letters of Lacey Harris's first name. The DMs will be occupied interrogating Dillon, so no worries about running into him on my way out. I couldn't bear to hear him prattling on about how he did nothing wrong and that he wanted to talk about what is "all just a misunderstanding."

< ♂ + ♀ >

With lots of help and physical support from Lacey, we head home. Because she is driving, I left my keys with Luke when he promised to deliver my car to my place. I freak out a bit and swat at Lacey's hands as she tries to help me put on my seatbelt. The idea of being restrained right now makes my heart race, so she just lets me be. I'm grateful she doesn't try to get me to talk; the peaceful ride home allows me to calm down a bit.

This woman is a godsend. I wouldn't have made it inside without her help to hold me up as we stumble along the front walk and up the five stairs to the door of the tiny, one-storey house I grew up in. It's already past midnight, but Mr. Bilson's curtains are fluttering in his kitchen window. *Doesn't that old man ever sleep?*

My next door neighbor is quite the nosy parker. He'll be on my doorstep in the morning with some concocted story that will give him the chance to meddle. He likes to be "protective" as he calls it. I'll just have to tell the old fart I got drunk. He'll *tsk* and tell me drunkenness is shameful. I'd rather he believed that lie than have him know the truth. The thought of him knowing my perversion makes me shiver, as does the chilly wind that whips around us and makes me brace my battered body. At least this early cool weather will give me a reason to wear long sleeves and slacks. I'll be able to hide my injuries. *It's weird the way my mind is focusing on practical details like that instead of what I should really be concerned about.*

Lacey has such a big heart. She's given up her own scene to be here and take care of me. I know that she was really looking forward to her session with Master Zephyr. She is the delicate blonde and he the mean monster who was whipping her into a frenzy the first night I went to DYKKC with Jim.

She has a huge crush on Master Zephyr and hopes that one day he'll be more than a play partner. I can't see it. For one thing, the age difference has to be at least 25 years, if not more. The other reason is that Lacey is the perfect submissive, and I don't think that's what he's looking for. I've seen the way he watches the owner of DYKKC. She's a very intimidating Domme, Mistress Raidne. I can't begin to imagine the fireworks if those two powerful forces ever get together. *I wonder which one would come out on top?*

Lacey is sweet and perfect, helpful and kind, anticipating my needs without hovering. She takes charge immediately, heading to my modest kitchen to brew a steaming pot of chamomile tea. She brings a fragrant cup to me in my en suite bathroom and lets me lean on her so I can get into the hottest bath I can stand.

I have a beautiful, refurbished claw-foot tub that I love soaking in. Right now I wish I had something bigger. It's plenty deep enough but quite narrow, and my distressed limbs protest when I tuck them in tight. I sink all the way into the froth of sea algae bath foam, instantly relaxed by the tangy scent and heat. The water stings my rope burns, but that soon eases, along with some of my muscle ache, thanks to the Epsom salts I added. I let myself be transported to a tranquil place by Deva Premal's angelic voice chanting to me from the bathroom stereo. My favorite track on the *Embrace* CD is "Shante Prashante," a chant for peace and release from fear.

I soak for almost an hour, letting the water and music heal my aches and begin to soothe my soul. Evanya tries to talk to me, but I'm not listening. I stay focused on the words of the sacred chant. I block out everything else, even Lacey perched on a stool in the corner. Usually effective, chanting is a mere band-aid in my current state, but at least I'm not falling apart and bawling like a baby.

Lacey smiles and holds out a clean, fluffy towel for me. I step into her open arms as she wraps the towel around me. I slump against her, tired, weak and grateful. Lacey is not exactly short at 5'6", but she seems petite because of her trim, lithe body. Her shapely legs reach to heaven, so it's only her torso that is short. Still, in her embrace, I feel like a small child.

I'm not nervous about being naked and cuddled by this woman, which is surprising. I guess I don't feel any sexual charge between us, just sisterhood and a flowing of nurturing feminine energy. That's what I need most right now.

I may not be attracted to women, but if I ever do decide to experiment ... She's a stunner. When Lacey takes the time to put her long, straight, blond hair in spiral curls like she did today, it's a silky riot. Her narrow face ending in a sharp chin matches her slender body. Her denim-blue eyes are as soft and inviting as old jeans. And, man, when she smiles, a dimple pops up in her left cheek that just does something to my heart.

I don't get why some super-hot Dom hasn't snapped her up. I can understand why none of them, not even my three Tops, have wanted a more substantial relationship with a wuss like me. I'm not edgy enough, nor will I ever be. But Lacey's gift for giving pleasure and her appetite for pain are as sinful as her body. I would have thought that would be an irresistible combination. I don't know why, in the five years she's been at DYKKC, no one worthy of her has seen her as the angel she is. I wonder if that's the problem— maybe she's been there for so long that she's old news. She's certainly not old, only 28, but perhaps she just blends into the background now. As if that could even be possible.

Tonight, all I care about is that she's willing to be *my* angel. Lacey's hands feel like heaven as she tenderly massages smelly antiseptic cream into my worst rope burns. I move tentatively as I pull cozy yoga pants and a sweatshirt over my beaten-up body. I'm ready for the oblivion of sleep. All I want to do is to forget about the drama and trauma of the last four hours. I pop a couple of muscle relaxants and gingerly lower myself into bed.

Without discussing whether she is staying or leaving, Lacey slides in beside me, for nothing more than compassionate companionship. I'm relieved. Dillon doesn't know where I live, but it wouldn't be too hard for him to find me if he was highly motivated. Having Lacey here, I don't have to worry about him tonight. I know she won't let anything happen. With a slightly calmer mind and the drugs and tea countering the adrenaline still metabolizing in my system, I pass out almost as soon as I lay my head down.

Chapter Four – Sanctuary

Saturday Morning, September 15

Bright light on my eyelids wakens me. *It can't be morning yet. I closed my eyes only ten seconds ago.* I assess the state of my body before I try getting up. Everything, and I mean *everything*, still hurts like hell. I know from past intense workouts that the second day is always more painful. Times like this, it would be way cool if magic was real. I could wiggle my nose and teleport right into a hot tub.

I slowly lift my eyelids and, once again, can only look as far as I can see by swiveling my eyeballs. My neck is frozen stiff. A thin sliver of filtered sun shines into the room through the corner of the west-facing, long window high above my bed. It must be getting late if the sun is beginning to peek through.

The room comes alive this time of day, and I feel my mood lifting already. I wallpapered a feature wall in a modern pattern of pink roses and green leaves that is cheery without looking too girly or frilly. With the subdued, green linens on my king-size bed and the airy, green drapery framing the French doors that open out to my backyard, I feel like I'm in a spring garden year round. I spot

Lacey rocking in the wooden chair by my dresser. She's wearing her white leather bustier and micro miniskirt from last night.

"Morning." Even my throat hurts, and the word comes out in a froggy croak. The newspaper she's reading crinkles, and her head pops above the pages.

"Good morning, sunshine. How are you? Ready to get up? It's way past noon already." I look at her with a frown.

"I can't believe I slept so long. Those muscle relaxants really have a kick. They haven't done much else though because I don't think I can move yet. I'm going to need help." Lacey stands and smiles. "If I haven't said it enough already, thanks for looking after me, Lace. And for staying. Don't you have clients today?"

Lacey is kind of a celebrity in the local fashion scene. She's an A-list hairstylist and esthetician with her own salon and day spa downtown. She's done well for someone so young. Not content to just manage the business, her number-one priority is taking care of and pampering the clients she still sees. She says her work allows her a deep sense of fulfillment when she nurtures people and makes them glow. That instinct is one of the reasons she's such a good submissive. Lacey falls naturally into the role of pleasing her Top.

"I rescheduled my clients and called in a manager. I thought you might need me today." She pauses briefly and clears her throat before saying, "You know, I'm sorry for what happened to you. I've bottomed for Dillon, and I always worried that he might get a bit too rough with you. I'm glad I could be there for you when it happened." I can't fault her mistake. She wasn't in that room and doesn't know what went down.

"It was more than that, Lace. I'd like to talk about it once I'm in the tub, if you don't mind. I need to get it off my chest before I have to write my incident report. Will you listen to my side of the story?"

"Of course. I'll put on the kettle and run the bath. Then I'll come back and help you out of bed, okay?" I give her a big smile and whisper "thanks."

All settled under the slippery bubbles with a cup of Earl Grey and a plate of toast with strawberry jam, I begin my tale of woe. Lacey doesn't interrupt, but I can see by the rapid flight of expressions across her face that she will have plenty to say when I finish. I try to steer clear of any emotional embellishment and stick to the facts. I don't want to talk about my feelings because they're still bloody. I need to translate what happened into words to try to shake my disbelief that the assault, if that's what I want to call it, ever happened.

"That doesn't sound like Dillon. You're sure it wasn't a horrible misunderstanding? You're still pretty new to BDSM. Sometimes a scene can get hot and heavy. It doesn't always work out the way you expect if signals get crossed. Especially when you're playing with someone who's as naturally aggressive as Dillon. You have to step back and talk to each other during aftercare, particularly if things go sideways." Her use of Dillon's word "misunderstanding" rankles.

"I know it doesn't sound like Dillon. But that guy last night wasn't the Top I play with. He wasn't even the Top I've seen you and the other subs with. He totally lost his focus and then ignored both of my safewords."

"And you weren't playing out a rape fantasy?" I understand her question. Forced sex is not an uncommon fantasy, especially in our community. The scenarios can range from being coerced into giving in to a Hollywood-handsome and charming Alpha male, like in the old bodice-ripper novels, to something more dark and violent.

But, it's just a fantasy, lived out in a woman's imagination or carefully negotiated and roleplayed safely with someone she trusts. Even though it might get blurry at times, there's a line that can't be crossed. No woman ever wants to actually be forced and taken against her will. And no one has the right to take what isn't freely given.

"What Dillon did came too close to reality for me. I was terrified when he said he was going to finish our scene. He really lost it, broke his discipline and broke the rules. He was out of control. I've seen him on edge, but never angry before. I didn't feel safe or that it was sane or consensual."

"You said he didn't complete the deed, that he stopped and cut off the ropes in a hurry to get you free. Erin, he didn't even take the time to untie them. What did he say to explain himself?"

"I didn't give him a chance to tell any lies." I can't say any more. Lacey blows out a lungful of air and frowns. She looks like she wants to say something about that but asks instead what I'm going to do.

"Maybe you should talk to Jim. He's really worried about you. I saw his number on your phone when he called this morning. I hope you don't mind that I answered." She looks at me sheepishly.

"Thanks. I can't talk to anyone else yet. And I certainly can't see anyone. I think I'll check into a hotel for the rest of the weekend so I can have some peace and some space to figure this mess out."

"Awesome idea. I know you don't want to hear this, but Dillon sent a bunch of texts. I didn't read them, and maybe you shouldn't either just yet, but you'll have to deal with him at some point. Just give yourself a bit of time to calm down." She pauses for a moment.

"Okay. I'm going to give you my two cents, and then I won't say any more. Unless, of course, you need to talk later." She takes a deep breath, squaring her shoulders.

"You will have to do something. I don't know what, that's up to you, but Jim says he's getting phone calls. The membership is buzzing and rumors are already flying. That's not a good thing for you. Right now, all anyone is hearing is Dillon's side of things, and he's defending himself, saying you made false accusations."

"The way I see it, in the absence of clarification from you, he's going to be more popular than ever because of your claim. Instead of expecting him to answer for the safeword shit and for hurting you, every sub with a secret fantasy of being ravished is going to line up to have him make her wildest dreams come true."

"Damn. You think so?" Lacey's reply is a solemn nod. "What a freaking mess. I won't be able to keep this just between him and me, will I? I'll have to go public at DYKKC, whether I want to or not."

Lacey rests her hand on my shoulder to comfort me. It also feels like a gesture of solidarity. "I like Dillon, or, I should say, I did like him. I want you to know that I'm on your side. Until you figure out what you want, I won't bottom for him anymore." I notice that she doesn't say she won't ever bottom for him. I don't think she entirely agrees with me, but she's sticking with me. She's a good friend.

"Thanks. I can't tell you how much it means to me to know I'm not alone in this. All I ask is that you don't make a big deal about it. Promise you won't make a spectacle and do something noble like defend my honor and freak out on him in front of others."

"Well, I'd really like to string that ass up by his balls and give him a golden shower in Purgatory, but I promise not to do anything loud or showy. I don't want you getting hurt any more than you are."

"Thanks, Lace. You're the best. Now, I'm shriveling like a prune. You've got your own day to get on with, and I want to get out of here and into a hotel before anyone comes looking for me."

< ♂ + ♀ >

I didn't quite make a clean escape before arriving here at the hotel. As I predicted, Mr. Bilson was at my door two minutes after Lacey left. This time, he didn't bother with a fake excuse for butting in. His bushy brows waggled as he said he saw me staggering.

I gave the annoying man my prepared answer. I said I was fine and didn't need the help he offered. I've known him since my family moved into the neighborhood when I was seven. When my parents died and I moved back into the house, he took it upon himself to act like a father to me. I kind of feel for the old man. His kids live on the West Coast and don't come home anymore. I should be grateful that he wants to watch out for me, but there's always a creepy way his watery, gray eyes look me up and down and a disturbing undertone to the way he speaks to me. His concern today was patronizing and hostile. I felt like I had been slimed after talking to him. *Maybe his freaky vibe is why the kids never visit.*

Before anyone else could get to me, I fled as fast as my ruined muscles would take me. I brought only a small overnight bag, my laptop, two bottles of wine, and a stack of DVDs. I made a pit stop at the grocery store for Epsom salts, more antiseptic cream, chocolate —lots of chocolate—and cashews.

The cost of the junior suite I'm in will be a big hit to my credit card, but it's worth it. The jetted tub in the room is a necessity in my condition and not a treat. Dr. Yuri advised me to soak often.

I stretch out on the king-size bed with the just-right mattress and brilliant white, Egyptian cotton sheets. Satiny softness cools my bruised and scraped skin. The whole room, while modern, is done in a cozy, classic color scheme of cherry wood, creams and golds, with a cranberry-red armchair that pops against the opulent palette. The best part, of course, is the spa-style bathroom with the swimming-pool-sized tub. Too bad this isn't a holiday. I could really enjoy this luxury.

My first priority is to shut out the rest of the world. With a quick call to my Reference Head's voicemail, I book two days off work. I see Dillon's texts, but I can't handle his shit yet. I fire off a terse message. 'Haven't read your texts. Can't talk now. Don't contact me. Give me time.' I'm not sure why I even give him that much courtesy instead of telling him to piss off. Ingrained manners, I guess.

Jim is going to worry, so I send him a short text. His instant reply asks how he can help. I respond that there is nothing to do yet, but I'll let him know if and when there is. I ask him to stay away from Dillon and not take matters into his own hands. His last message is, 'XOXOX.' I know what that cheeky bastard is like. That wasn't a "yes." I just hope he doesn't make this whole debacle worse by trying to be my white knight. *I always wanted a white knight. Why does the idea make me nervous now?*

Christophe texted me, too. I sigh a heavy sigh. He's thousands of miles away in Iraq for a month with Doctors Without Borders. *How did he hear so quickly?* My text won't convey a tone of voice or show body language that he could read, but I know not to lie to him.

'Hurt but no permanent damage. Will heal quickly.' He offers to kick Dillon's ass.

'Lucky for him u r on other side of world. Thx, but I'll handle it.'

He wants me to video call him so he can see for himself that I'm okay. *Not a chance.* I tell him to give me a few days. He's not backing down, but I finally put him off until tomorrow. We arrange a time, and he sends his final text. 'Wish I was there priss. Think of my healing hands on yr beautiful body, easing yr pain. Til 2moro.'

Oh, I do think about that. I shouldn't. I should be disgusted by the thought of any man touching me. *But it's Christophe.* With my eyes closed, I imagine stepping out of the bath last night and into his strong arms instead of Lacey's.

When Jim introduced me into the BDSM scene, I thought I was just looking to explore and get comfortable with my sexuality. And maybe be a bit naughty. Joining DYKKC was only supposed to be a bit of risky fun. That's how it has been with Jim and even Dillon. Not so with Christophe.

Every time Christophe, as Master Ronan, tops me, I have a very potent and *very* satisfying experience. I feel safe with him; I feel cherished by him; I feel powerful with him. A session with Master Ronan is more like a therapy session—with erotic fringe benefits.

Each scene is more than mere hot sex, although there's plenty of that. *Oh là là!* He has a level of skill that lets me trust him to do things to my body and my mind, to push my limits beyond what I'll let Jim or Dillon do. He is often hard and unrelenting in his demands while we're playing, but he has a way of helping me bare my soul and dump emotional baggage. I always feel like I should be the one to give him aftercare in gratitude for how much he helps me.

Even so, I've found lately that I'm almost eager to hurry through the scene, even the sex, to get to the aftercare. It's hard to explain. I never thought I would be lucky enough to learn firsthand about pleasure and pain from a man like him—not that there's a lot of pain. To be in the arms of this compelling man and have him go all soft and tender after a taxing session blows me away. Our bodies twined together makes me feel like all is right with the world.

He seems like the perfect man, everything I've ever hoped for. I *should* be in love with him; I'm just not. He doesn't feel like my soul mate. Maybe it's because our relationship is lived inside a bubble, or because I know our connection is only temporary. Or perhaps it's because I only know Master Ronan and not the real man. *What would happen if I met Christophe Serle in the real world?*

I don't want whatever it is that we do have tainted by the ugliness of what's going on with Dillon. *He can't see me battered and bruised like this.* Christophe makes me feel invincible, and I don't want him to see me broken. I sure can't have him thinking he has to rescue me. Even though I feel like a victim, I couldn't bear having him think of me as one. That would be a failure too great to bear. I'm going to have to deliver a performance worthy of one of those little gold statues and hope that he doesn't see through it.

So, would I prefer him to be the one who wrapped me in that towel? No. Lacey was the one I needed. Her tenderness, free of sexual tension and expectation, was a balm last night. Confiding in her this afternoon was cathartic, to a point, but I had to leave when I did because I could feel emotions bubbling up, hints of self-doubt, rage, terror, despair and vulnerability. Even something that felt suspiciously like guilt. I wasn't ready to give in to any of that yet. I wasn't ready to appear that weak, not in front of someone as strong as Lacey. If I had let one tear fall, I wouldn't have stopped crying until there was nothing left of me.

I type a brief message to Lacey to let her know that I'm settled but don't say where I am. The only one I tell is my friend Jessica. I'm ashamed to let her see me like this, but I need her talented hands of silk and steel. I thought about booking a masseuse from the hotel to keep things impersonal, but there's no guaranteeing the quality of massage I'd get. I suck it up and make the call.

I've got two hours to kill before Jess arrives. I can't delay writing up the incident report and emailing it to Mistress Raidne. I know it will take all two hours because of all that emotional stuff I've been sweeping under the rug. It's going to get ugly. Already the pressure is building in my waterworks. The dam is sure to burst; the weepy flood will leave devastation in its wake.

$$< \male + \female >$$

I'm a basket case by the time Jessica sets up her massage table. After too much time wallowing in blame and self-blame, grief, fear and righteousness, I'm glad to see her smiling face, until she asks about my puffy, red eyes and runny nose and why I'm in a hotel.

"I had a rough night," I squeak like a timid mouse. She gasps as she peels back the sheet covering my body on her table and sees the full scope of the trauma. It's impossible for her to not ask.

"Leave it alone, Jess. No questions. All I need, all I can handle right now, is you giving me the best massage ever."

"Did you call the police? Whoever did this much damage to you needs to be behind bars, Erin."

"You don't understand the lifestyle. It's not that bad. Just a few scrapes. No broken bones. I haven't decided what to do yet."

"What's to decide? Someone did a number on you. He needs to pay. End of story. Look, hon, I suspect you're into some kinky stuff. I've seen your red ass before, remember? So you like it a bit rough. Who doesn't? But this is different. You can't tell me you enjoyed who and what hurt you this bad." I can't muster my usual appreciation of her tenacity and no-BS approach to life.

I bury my face into the hole in the table's headrest so Jess can't see my lip wobbling and my cheeks flushing. Her tone is not supportive; it's judgmental. I don't need this right now.

I try to lighten things up to distract Jess. "Sometimes feeling good hurts and leaves marks. You've never seen how badly bruised I am after your massages." Honestly, this isn't much different.

"Sorry 'bout that. You should have told me, but don't change the subject. It's not like you to take matters of right and wrong lightly. You called the cops last summer after you saw that dog left inside a car, and you always report drunk drivers."

"It's not that simple. Those were dangerous situations."

"You're shitting me, right? Look how beat up you are. That sure looks like a dangerous situation to me." *Was it? I'm not so sure.*

I peer up into Jess's heart-shaped face. "It's over with. Can we please just drop this? If you're my friend, let it go." She agrees, but she's not very happy about it. I know because her soft brunette curls falling on her cheeks can't ease the hard look she gives me.

Jess performs her usual miracles. Despite the severity of my injuries, her results are quite impressive. After the massage, she does her woo-woo reiki healing on me. Even though I'm in touch with my spiritual side, I have never let her do any energy work until now. *This is crazy. This stuff really works.*

Her hands are no longer touching me, but I'm not imagining the intense heat pouring out of her fingers. Tingles dance all over me like I'm standing under a steaming shower. The sensation is almost like the one I had when I first met Christophe. Everything hard and tight inside me just lets go. My body is less achy, and I float on a fluffy cloud. I swear that some of my bruises even look like they have faded a little. She lets me rest on the table for a few minutes before she packs up and leaves.

Relief floods over me as Jessica walks out the door. She was starting to make me feel guilty for not calling the cops, as well as guilty for thinking that maybe I should. It's easy for her to say what I should do; she's not the one struggling to deal, and she doesn't have all the facts. Everything went wrong so fast last night that I'm not really sure what to think. I can't stop seeing Dillon being led out in cuffs. I don't know if involving the police is the right thing to do.

I sink into the giant whirlpool tub after dumping a whole carton of Epsom salts into the water. I am completely and utterly drained. I chant along again with Deva Premal for a hit of happy thoughts as I drift away on the turbulent currents of the pulsing jets.

My frail body is grateful for the luxury of the plush hotel towels. My stomach, however, complains loudly about not being treated as well. I only ate a couple of pieces of toast at breakfast and a protein bar on my way out the door. A light dinner of a chicken Caesar salad and garlic toast from room service silences my growling tummy.

If only it was so easy to quiet the voices in my head. Meditation doesn't calm me tonight. Relaxing on the bed, I try to decide how to entertain myself so I don't have to listen to myself rehash last night. I did all the contemplating on that mess I can handle for one day while I wrote my report. I shuffle through my stack of DVDs and nothing appeals. Flicking aimlessly through the channels on cable brings the same lackluster result.

If I had my craft kit with me, I could easily kill a couple of hours whipping up one of my naughty creations. But I can't go get my supplies now because Dillon might be lurking about. He sent another text during dinner, which I did read. His words made me worry that he might show up at my place. No way am I strong enough to handle an encounter with him yet. My thoughts and feelings are still all over the map. I might have been a bit hasty in vilifying him; it wouldn't be the first time I've over-reacted. The thing is, I'm likely to do it again if I don't get a grip on my emotions.

Booting up my laptop, I plan out my next kinky project. I totally lose track of time and have a lot of fun choosing the materials to create something extraordinary. I place the order, excited for the arrival of the goods. I smile as I picture the finished result.

It's finally 10:00 and late enough for me to call it a night without feeling like a baby. I swallow a couple of muscle relaxants before doing my nightly routine so the pills will kick in by the time I hit the pillow. Heavily medicated, I drift off quickly, not worrying about what I'll have to face tomorrow.

$$< \male + \female >$$

Sunday Morning, September 16

Waking up this morning is a lot easier than it was yesterday, especially after almost 12 hours of sleep. That's 12 hours of recovery time, 12 hours of not thinking, and 12 hours of not feeling. I'm grateful for any minor miracle at this point.

With checkout time only an hour away, I won't be able to get my shit together in time. Since I'm off work tomorrow, I call the front desk to extend my stay one more night. I snuggle back into bed for another half hour, proud of myself for taking such good care of me.

A quick bath spruces me up well enough that I'm eager and able to venture down to the restaurant for brunch. It is Sunday after all. The meal won't be as stimulating, gastronomically or otherwise, as Sinful Sundays at DYKKC, but the chef always puts on a lavish spread. Friends sometimes come here for the buffet, so I tuck myself away in a corner. No one knows what I'm into, and I couldn't begin to explain if anyone saw my injuries.

Stuffed and sated after three trips to the buffet, I head back to my room. I have to get myself functioning before I go back to work, so I try some gentle stretching. I go slow and easy, pleased that my range of motion is better. Then I try to lift my hands above my head.

Holy Mother! Shooting pain ignites a chain reaction of twinges and seizures through all my joints and muscles. My neck is still *majorly* messed up. For the next few minutes, I look like a funky chicken as each contraction or extension sends another body part into a reflexive jerk. I sound like a funky chicken, too. Each painful movement sparks a squawking *ooo* or an *ahhh* or an *ouch*. I am not amused by my comedic antics. I've never been a fan of slapstick.

Now that my body has calmed down, I'm exhausted and covered in sweat. *Time for another bath.* It's excruciatingly clear that I'll be seeing the bone crusher tomorrow. The irony that it's going to take more torture to make me feel better is galling. Relaxing in the tub, I face up to the fact that I've stalled long enough. I have to deal with Dillon's texts at some point. I might as well do it now.

"Wow. You're pretty pissed, aren't you? What the hell, Dillon? I'm trying to ruin your reputation? Asshole, you defiled my body. Guess who's the only one with the right to be pissed? It's not you."

Each subsequent text is nastier and nastier. I had been willing to concede that we both made mistakes, take my share of the blame, but this attitude changes everything. I'm as hot under the collar as he is. I don't think I've ever been this angry in my life.

"It's a good thing we're not in the same room, otherwise I'd scratch your eyes out or damage something a bit more sensitive. Well, you idiot, at least you're giving me more ammunition if I decide to come after you."

I thought about that a lot at brunch. He didn't penetrate me after I said "stop." Saying that what happened in my mind between when I said my safeword and when he cut the ropes was a sexual assault is a bit of a stretch. Just because I feel violated doesn't mean anyone else would see it that way. It would be one of those he-said-she-said situations. *Who is going to be more believable?*

I've helped enough lawyers do research. Sexual assault charges are hard enough to prosecute in favor of the victim when there's a stronger case than I have. Then there's the added strike against me of where and when the incident happened, even though it shouldn't matter. No means no.

Setting aside my own personal concerns, which I'm no longer in a hurry to wade through, I have to think about my friends at DYKKC. If I go public, I'll put every member's privacy at risk. There are a lot of high profile people like Jim, Christophe and, especially, Master Zephyr who could get burned in the crossfire.

On the other hand, after my talk with Lacey yesterday morning, I don't want anyone else to get hurt, especially some vulnerable sub who thinks Dillon is going to play nice while she's living out her fantasy of being taken by a romance novel hunk. I know a lot of the women like it rougher than I do, but physical damage is not the only kind of pain he could inflict. There was nothing nice about what he did to me. Even if I can't exactly call it rape.

The tone of Dillon's texts makes me wonder if maybe he has a screw twisting loose in his head. I better get my own head on straight before I send any message back to him. I have to be really careful what I say. If I decide to press any charges and bring his texts into evidence, then my replies will be under equal scrutiny. I think I'll have to check with Jim on this one.

I survive the day by self-medicating with a movie marathon and wine. It is a toss-up between muscle relaxants or wine, so I pick the good stuff. I stretch out on the bed with a plate of chocolate and cashews beside me. Every one of the movies makes me cry, comedies and romances alike. With the macho hero saving the day, the action movie is, big surprise, the most painful to watch.

I've got barely 15 minutes before Christophe's call, so I set up my laptop on the glass-topped desk and sit in the ergonomic chair with an added bed pillow to cushion my butt. I chant for a bit to get centered before I try to pull one over on Master Ronan.

< ♂ + ♀ >

My acting skills are abysmal. How stupid to think I could fool a doctor. It takes Christophe all of two seconds to figure out my neck is badly hurt. We argue about me going to the emergency clinic. I'm glad he's not here to go all Dom on my butt and force me to go.

He finally drops the issue but harasses me until he drags the whole freaking story out of me. Now my stomach is tied up as tight as if Master Hitoshi used it for Kinbaku bondage practice. I give him an abbreviated version of events but enough detail that I'm feeling sick. I didn't want this coloring our relationship. *So much for that.*

Christophe shocks the heck out of me when he talks about cutting his trip short to come back to help me. *That's crazy talk. Why would he do that when we've only done four scenes together?* He's just my Service Top; I'm just another bottom to him. I sometimes wonder if maybe we have a special connection, but I do know it's foolish to hope that it could ever be the real thing. *It's a fantasy, right?*

"Give me your word, Christophe, that you'll finish your tour. You've only been there a week, and they need you in Iraq. Those people are truly suffering; I'm not. I'll be fine. Promise me. Please."

"Are you forgetting who you're talking to here, priss? I'll come home if I damn well want to." *Stubborn ass.*

"Don't call me priss. We're not at DYKKC, and I'm not forgetting, *Christophe*. I am not your sub, and I'm not your bottom right now either. If you're my friend, promise me you'll let me deal with this."

He's forgetting the last session we had, where he taught me how to deal with my bullying boss. The new Associate Dean of Library Services had been running roughshod over my staff and me. Master Ronan worked my body and mind long and hard until I learned about professional and personal boundaries. He's crossing a personal boundary or two here.

"Alright, *Erin*. I'll stay, on one condition." I should have known he wouldn't give an inch without taking something in return. It would never do for a Dom to appear to be topped by a bottom.

"Read Dillon's texts to me." *Dammit.* I don't want to obey his command, but I can't risk him coming home either. As I read, even with the fuzzy resolution of the video feed, I can see his jaw might shatter from how tight he is clenching it.

"Self-centered tool." He opens his mouth to say something else but snaps it shut. The hiss of static on the line is deafening. He's silent for almost a full minute.

"Christophe? What are you thinking?"

"Don't worry about it, priss." *Oh, oh. priss again.* He's dropped into Alpha mode. *Hello, Master Ronan.* I threaten him with a steely glower that he can't mistake. "Just trust me, priss."

"No. You leave Dillon alone. *You* have to trust *me*. Let me handle it, pleeease." No luck. That's one concession he won't commit to. I plead with him not to make things worse for me, but begging gets me nothing. *I guess he doesn't think my boundaries apply to him.*

I'd really like to trust him. I'm just scared that anything anyone does at this point is going to push Dillon too far. It's a safe guess. Another text just came in, one I'm *not* going to read to Christophe.

'Need to talk. Don't make me hunt u down priss. U won't like what happens.' Now I'm officially rattled. I've got to get Christophe off the call as quickly as possible.

"I'll call again Wednesday night at 9:00 your time, priss." That's fine with me. I'll deal with his bossiness later because, right now, I can't think any further ahead than the next five minutes.

"I'm sorry this is happening. I wish I could do more for you, Erin. Now I want a promise from you. Please be careful, sweetheart.

Don't take any chances. Dillon could be lurking anywhere." This is *aftercare* Master Ronan. His honeyed words sound soft and sugary. His affection is a genuine tasty treat. My eager tongue slides across my lips in anticipation of a bite. Except, he's not here right now, nor do I want him to be—no matter how hungry my body is for some man candy.

"I promise, Christophe. I'll be okay. I'm a smart cookie, and I can take care of myself. But thanks for your concern. You're a good man, and I'm lucky that you're my friend."

"If I was there, I'd have you wrapped up safe and sound in my arms. That prick would never come near you again. You wouldn't have to worry about anything, and you wouldn't be sleeping alone tonight in some dismal hotel. priss, when you go to bed, close your eyes and feel my body pressed up against yours. Let me hold you all night and kiss all your troubles away."

"Christophe?" *Really?* This is an interesting development to put it mildly. Those aren't words a buddy would say, and who the hell is saying all this? Christophe or Master Ronan? *Shit, I don't need this kind of complication right now.*

"I've got to go, priss. My shift starts in 15 minutes. Be well, sweetheart. I'll talk to you on Wednesday, but make sure you call if you have any more trouble. Promise me."

"I will, Christophe. Thanks. You be well, too. Keep your head down. I worry about you over there."

"I'm okay, sweetheart. Just worry about yourself. Bye for now." With that, he blows me a kiss and leaves me hanging. *What the hell was that all about?*

Before I can panic about Dillon's latest text, I need a moment to panic about all that romantic stuff at the end of the call. Christophe has never called me "sweetheart" before, and he just did it, *several times*. "What was all that about me not sleeping alone if he was here? We've never seen each other outside of the club, let alone spent a whole night together. What is he thinking?"

If things weren't royally screwed up right now, a girl might want to consider this change of Christophe's attitude for longer than a minute or two. Then again, if things weren't screwed up, there might be nothing to consider further. This is exactly why I didn't want this nonsense with Dillon between us. How do I know what's real and what is Christophe just being a protective Alpha?

"Enough! What the hell are you going to do about Dillon, Erin?" I shout to get my own attention and get back to what's imminently important. It f-ing sucks that I'm forced into this position, but I can't put off calling Jim any longer.

I grab my phone; Dillon's latest text is emblazoned across the screen, a glaring digital threat. Visions of a wild cat pouncing and ripping me apart flash before my eyes. Shivers of fright gallop through me. A crushing weight bears down on my chest, cutting off my air supply. I can't stop shaking, and a jackhammer pounds on my head. *This must be what a panic attack feels like.* Resting my forehead on the cool glass of the desktop doesn't help. I pace the room, trying to shake off this spine-chilling premonition of doom.

After chastising myself to "get a grip," and trying to ground myself by eating six squares of 90% dark chocolate, the debilitating tension begins to ease and wane. It's too soon to have a third bath. Instead, I crawl under the covers and curl in the fetal position. I hit speed dial to connect with Jim.

$$< \male + \female >$$

I pour out the whole story, this time including all the gory details. I even tell Jim about my call with Christophe, minus the perplexing other-than-friends undercurrents, but add my concerns about what he could do to Dillon all the way from Iraq.

"Geez, Erin. I'm so sorry. What can I do? I can be at your place in ten minutes."

"I needed space, so I'm at a hotel. Jim, I really didn't want to get you involved in this. But, as much as I need to handle this myself, Dillon's last text really has me spooked. I've never been afraid like this before. If you really want to help, talk to Dillon and tell him to back off until I'm ready to talk to him. Will he listen to you?"

"Just leave it to me. No more worrying. I'll take care of him."

"Please go easy on him. Not for his sake but for mine. If he feels like he's being attacked ... Well, you know what a cornered animal is like. I'm pretty certain Christophe is going to go at him hard and make a mess of things. Use your superior lawyer skills and be diplomatic, please." I don't care about Dillon's feelings, except for how they could push him to retaliate.

"Just trust me, Erin. It's getting late. Put it all out of your mind until morning. Try to get some sleep and let your body mend. I'll be in touch after I've talked to Dillon." I tell him how grateful I am for him helping me and believing my side of the story. He doesn't respond to that, just says goodnight. I do put Dillon out of my mind. Christophe is another story entirely.

For weeks after a scene with Master Ronan, my fantasies are filled with his larger-than-life presence. I've built him up in my mind to be a superhero. He's helped free me from some of my demons and slayed a few of my inner dragons. He's led me on a quest for the holy grail of my womanhood, my own superhero status as a strong, sexy female in charge of her own destiny.

"Who wouldn't idolize that kind of leadership? And crave it constantly? And the sex is *fanfreakingtastic*." I'm glad there's no one around to hear my confession.

All the scenarios I create in my mind, as sexy and loving as they are, can only be built based on what little I know of Master Ronan. All the pictures that haunt me are set either at DYKKC or at my place. I can drop him into my world, but I don't have a clue what Christophe's world is like. I can't begin to imagine what kind of life we could have together. The dream always falls short of fulfilling what I need most in my life—a real man to love and to love me back.

These new hints he dropped have really messed with my head. *What if he is my soul mate?* There's a possibility that I'm just scared to admit it. *Should I thank him or curse him for opening up new possibilities in my fantasy world?* The one question I've never tried to answer in any of my daydreams is how much control this strict disciplinarian would exert and how much of me I would have to submit. I'm too afraid that he will need something I can't give him.

Chapter Five – Judgment Day

Monday Morning, September 17

The perky tune of notes tapped out on a xylophone wakes me at 7:30. The receptionist at my chiropractor's office sets me up with an appointment at 10:00. *Hallelujah!* I have time for one long, last soak in the decadent tub. Now that I've been spoiled, I'll be saving up for one of these babies for my place.

I arrive at the pancake house beside Dr. Jefferson's office just before 9:00. I need something substantial and fortifying, so I order a platter of waffles, eggs and bacon.

"Be careful. Don't get sucked into that comfort-food downward spiral again. It got messy after senior prom. You don't want to go there again." Evanya can't seem to help offering unsolicited advice now that she's found a way in to my waking consciousness. I ease my guilt by promising her I'll eat a salad for lunch and stir-fried veggies for dinner. But right now, my waffles are drowning in maple syrup and butter, and I want them in my tummy.

I walk out of Dr. Jefferson's office feeling better physically. The x-rays took longer than expected, but they came out clear, thank goodness. I'm ticked that I had to dance around my injuries with my vanilla Doc. He was just like Jess, except he tried to pressure me into going to the police. He was livid that I haven't filed a complaint and threatened that he could do it as my doctor, even thought he had a duty to do it to save me from what he called "cowardice." My aversion to his and Jessica's advice about police intervention says something I don't want to hear yet.

The only way I could get Doc to back off was by threatening to find another chiropractor. I'm surprised he bought my bluff, but he knows now where I draw the line. After a few snaps and pops, my neck swivels freely again and hurts only half as much. Alternating heat and ice will take away the rest of the pain and stiffness in a day or two. I'm glad I'll be good for work on Wednesday.

Before I pull into my driveway, I circle the block to be sure I have no uninvited visitors waiting for me. Dillon sent a text while I was in Doc's office asking, 'Where r u? U didn't come home last night.' *He's stalking me now? And he knows where I live!*

It seems that neither Jim nor Christophe have gotten through to him. Or maybe they did, and he just didn't like what they said. There's no sign of his SUV, so I grab my things and walk quickly up my front path. I'm almost home free when Mr. Bilson pounces.

"What's the matter with you? You're hurt, aren't you?" I tell him that I'm fine. He thinks I'm lying and says he knows I wasn't drunk the other night. He wants to carry my bags, but I don't want to let him in my house. He tries to snatch the bags from me. As I pull back, I wince in pain. I look down, horrified to see that my sleeves have ridden up and that my black and purple bruises and red rope burns are in plain sight.

"Erin Piper! Did one of your *boyfriends* do this to you?" I don't answer, so he motors on, spittle spraying from between his paper-thin lips. "Your father would be appalled by some of those tarty outfits I see you leaving the house in like you did on Friday. You can't dress like a floozy and expect to stay out of trouble. I hope you were at least smart enough to report this to the police." I stare at him, my mouth gaping like a goldfish sucking pond scum.

His attack turns scathing when I say there won't be any police. I wish people would stay out of my sex life. I put my foot down, literally. My shoe stomps down, missing his foot by an inch. I storm off. *It's none of his damn business. Why does everyone think they have the right to run my life? I get to decide what's best for me!* Dillon's rebuke pops into my head. "Are you a submissive or not?" Well, I've got no Master, so I'm still the Mistress of my universe. *So there.*

In a royal huff, I unpack my bag and then head to the kitchen. I make the salad I promised Evanya, not caring that all I have left in the fridge are a few scraps of wilted veggies. I'm too annoyed to pick anything fresh from my kitchen garden. I eat with my right hand while the left holds an icepack to my neck. The ice helps cool my emotions as well as my injury. Mr. Bilson has disturbed me more than I want to allow him to, and it's feeding my other fears.

I'm worried about what Dillon might do. This tension is really killing me. I need to talk to someone who knows him and might have a clue of how to make him understand. Maybe Steffie Harris who owns DYKKC can help. The pun makes me snicker. I can see her collaring a sniveling slave named dick and leading him around on a leash. "Ha! I'd love to see her try that with Master Zephyr!"

Steffie has always been nice to me, but she can be very nasty to naked men. She certainly knows about keeping bad boys in line. Maybe she can give me some tips.

$$< \male + \female >$$

Ridicule and scorn spew from Steffie's hard mouth the moment the severe redhead glances up from her desk. "Well, you're stirring up a real shit storm, aren't you, little miss priss. I don't understand how you can make up such outrageous lies about The Saint. Saying he raped you is beyond heartless. How can you do such a harmful thing to him?" I used to think of Steffie as mysterious and exotic. Right now, with the ugly sneer on her pale face, she looks like the Wicked Witch of the West. I'm clueless as to how to respond to this full-on attack and freeze where I stand.

"You may have conned your play partners with your lies, even my sister-in-law, but I've always seen right through your innocent act." I forgot that Lacey is her ex-husband's sister. *Oh God. It'll kill Lacey if her own sister-in-law ends up with Master Zephyr.*

"Mistress Raidne. Did you read my report?" We're in the club, so protocol requires me to address her respectfully regardless of how I feel about her right now, but no way will I bow or lower my eyes.

"What a load of bullshit." She snorts; the woman actually snorts at me.

"I didn't say anything about rape. I was a bit distraught when I used that unfortunate word. So, exactly what part of my report are you having trouble with?"

"That The Saint did not have your consent. You entered that room with him voluntarily, didn't you?" I nod. I'm not saying I didn't. *So, no support from this contingent of the sisterhood then.* The contempt she hurls at me is like a physical assault. The force of her disdain dislodges my feet, and I plop down in the black leather visitor chair in front of her slick glass and chrome desk.

Like Night Moves, everything in the room is chrome or black, except the instruments of discipline hanging on the walls, the red tool chest, and the steel cage in the corner. The room won't put people at ease, at least, not anyone from the vanilla world. I imagine those who frequent the dungeon would feel right at home.

Steffie has to be either really stupid or really scared. No savvy business person would deliberately antagonize a woman who might have been sexually assaulted on their premises. Putting me on the defensive is sooo not working in her favor.

"You're twisting things a bit, Mistress Raidne. I said I withdrew my consent and used my safeword. When he continued, that could be considered assault." The words don't feel right coming out of my mouth. Evanya pipes up and agrees, but I stuff her back down.

"There is no way that someone with The Saint's experience would ignore a safeword. It's not possible. We've never had any complaints of any impropriety in all the years he's been a member here. I can only assume that you either didn't say your safeword or that you didn't say it loud enough for him to hear." *Bitch just called me a liar.* It's always the woman's fault, isn't it? Like Adam couldn't have said no when Eve offered him the apple? That attitude just makes men look like spineless wimps. I'm not the one to blame here.

My research told me to expect reactions like this when claiming sexual misconduct. After Lacey, Jim and Christophe took my side without question, I had hoped to escape the whole blaming-the-victim mentality. Steffie should be bending over backward to appease me. Well, her Domme bravado won't work on me.

"You would be wrong in that assumption. Very wrong. Not only did he ignore my warning safeword, but he ignored my failsafe. When I screamed it at him. Over and over again. Is The Saint saying I didn't use my safeword?" She sits as quiet and still as a block of granite. *He's not denying it then.*

"Something was off with him Friday night. He wasn't himself. Everything happened just as I said it did in my report. He didn't back off until I freaked out."

"I can't see it, priss. Not The Saint." There's something in her tone and the way she casts her eyes downward that gives me the impression that there's something else going on with her. A Domme would never lower her eyes to a sub. *She's hiding something.*

"Maybe not the man we know. He was rude, insulting and mean. For real. He lost his concentration and pushed me beyond limits that he knows very well. He scared me, Mistress Raidne. But the texts he's been sending me since are more disturbing." I pull out my phone and show them to her. She softens during the minute that she's reading. In the next moment, I witness her pull herself up by the bootstraps and reassemble her armor.

"Well, I don't know what you would expect after your wild accusation." I show her the photos Dr. Yuri took, even though they are in his report. The evidence is lit up brightly for her on the phone screen. She refuses to look; I can see her focus is just off to the left. *Like she refuses to believe me.*

"You've read the reports from Dr. Yuri and Luke, I presume. I was in rough shape after The Saint was finished with me. And he didn't hit the panic button when I passed out."

"We've both seen worse, priss, on a regular basis. You're here and seem just fine. He couldn't have hurt you that bad."

"My chiropractor would beg to differ with you and so would my massage therapist. Regardless of what other women let happen to them, The Saint knew this was too much for me. AND he ignored my safeword. I want to know what you're going to do about it."

I stick my chest out and fold my arms across it. I'm trying to puff myself up like a cute, tiny robin does when he gets all aggressive and territorial. I will not cave in to her. I've got to at least pretend that I'm tougher than she thinks.

"If you choose to play our game without learning the rules, you have to accept that when you play with fire, sometimes you're going to get burned. I warned him you'd be trouble when you wouldn't take any classes in submission." My shoulders jerk against the back of my chair as those verbal blows land with deadly accuracy.

"I don't intend to do anything at all for you. There is no evidence of what you're claiming other than a couple of photos of a few minor rope burns and a report that you had a sore neck. Given his dedication to developing his skill and your status as an untrained cherry, I'm not about to ruin The Saint's good name. He's a good man." If I'm honest, I don't think I want that either, but she's taking a pretty ballsy position that's increasingly fraying my nerves.

Her defense of Dillon was fierce, like a mother bear protecting her cub, but she ended on a soft, almost wistful note. *Holy Shit! Now it all comes together.* I don't know why I didn't clue in before. It was Steffie that night I saw Dillon running the scene with the redhead! I thought she was a hard-core Domme. I had no idea she is a switch. That partially explains her bizarre reaction, but I don't care.

"Well, if you won't do anything, I guess we'll let the police decide what to do. If you aren't prepared to ban him, I'll be calling the cops. Tell him to stay away from me if he knows what's good for him."

"You don't want to threaten me, priss. I've had enough posturing from Master Ronan and The Squire. The Squire seems ready to walk, which wouldn't be such a great loss. Master Ronan plans on being a bit more disruptive, but I'm not worried that he would jeopardize his status here for the likes of you. You can't scare me into doing something that isn't right." Her claws are out, and I think she would dearly love to shred me if she could get away with it.

She thinks Jim is a lightweight. While I agree he can be a little flippant at times, it would be a grave mistake for her to forget that he's a lawyer who loves taking on a good cause. I sure wouldn't want to find out what kind of creative ways he could come up with to make things rough for both her and her business.

What I find the most intriguing is the nebulous way she refers to Christophe doing something "disruptive." On one hand, it's kind of fun watching Steffie squirm; on the other, I'm pissed that whatever he's said has got her hackles up. It's certainly making this situation a lot more difficult and stressful than it needs to be.

Of course, her whole stance is totally ludicrous, as is mine. I can smell the fear wafting from Steffie's every pore, and I seem to be lapping it up like it's some sort of mood-altering drug. My emotions around Dillon and this situation keep bouncing back and forth, almost as if I have a raging case of PMS.

"We'll just see what the police have to say about what's right. Have a good day, Mistress Raidne. I think it might be a while before you have another one." I stride out of the room with steel in my spine and jelly in my gut. I have no intention of making that call, but it sure feels good to scare the crap out of her. That's exactly what I've done, if the way she's shrieking my name is any indication.

Remembering my promise to eat stir-fried veggies for dinner, I stop at Fong's on my way home to pick up some Chinese takeout. They're known here for their fresh and fabulous food but not the ambiance. I've got nothing to do but stare at white walls and replay my perplexing conversation with Steffie while waiting for my order.

"Idiot. *Idiot!* You really screwed that up." I let Steffie push my buttons and get the better of me. I didn't plan on threatening her or demanding that Dillon be banned. It was a total knee-jerk defense. I just don't understand why I'm not able to rein in my emotions. I can't find my equilibrium, but I'm going to have to.

As much fun as it was at the time to scare Steffie, I have to be smarter and avoid her from now on. Antagonizing her further would be a tactical error. She's in a very strong position to poison popular opinion against me in the community and fortify Dillon's reputation. I smack my palm on my forehead and sigh. *What am I thinking? She's probably already launched a full-scale "Hate priss" campaign.*

< ♂ + ♀ >

Tuesday Morning, September 18

I just about have a heart attack when the doorbell rings around 10:00. I peer out the kitchen window cautiously. The breath I had swallowed explodes out of me when I see the delivery man in a brown uniform. My relief turns to joy as I fling open the door. My highly anticipated package is here. The courier smiles at my smile and flirts a little with me. A week ago, I would have been flattered and flirted back with the young, good-looking guy. Not today. What Dillon did, it seems, has made me wary of strangers.

I file the thought away and skip to my workshop with the box clutched tight against my chest. This room used to be my bedroom. The only three things remaining from my youth are a twin bed shoved up against one wall and a nightstand with a lamp. The rest of the blue room is taken over by a wide but shallow work table, cabinets and stacks of boxes. A pegboard on the wall adjacent to the table is covered with a vast array of tools and implements hanging from the hooks. Even the closet is filled with supplies. No one knows what really goes on in this room.

I snatch the box cutter, slice open the tape on my box of goodies, and spill the contents all over the work surface. *Beauteous baubles.* I dive in and completely immerse myself in my secret project, measuring, snipping and hammering. My total focus clears my mind just as if I was meditating, and the rest of the world ceases to exist.

Before I realize it, six of the most peaceful hours I've had in weeks have flown by. I forgot all of my troubles while indulging in my private fetish. I hold my creation, my most elaborate to date, up to the late afternoon sun shining through the blinds and admire the artistry and allure of it.

I grab a hanger and slip my masterpiece on. It looks stunning hanging in the closet at the front of my collection. All the energy I infused into its construction was like an affirmation, the start of me rebuilding my life. I am tempted to wear it now, but I'll save this little number for a special occasion. I wonder what that will be and when it will happen.

A wave of giddy joy fuzzes my head, partly because I'm proud of the work I've just done and partly because my stomach is empty and my blood sugar is a little low. A survey of the contents of my fridge yields scant results. I finished the salad veggies yesterday and the eggs and bread this morning. There's not much I can do with milk that's on the edge of turning sour and a shriveled apple.

I usually hate shopping, but it seems like such a normal thing to do, and I need normal right now. I hop in the car for a quick trip to the grocery store and load up with a few days' worth of food, including a T-bone steak and some mushrooms for dinner and chocolate chunk ice cream for dessert.

I'm feeling pretty content as I push my shopping cart to my car. I dig for my keys to lock my purchases into my trunk, and the short hairs on the back of my neck tingle and stand on end. I scan the parking lot and, out of the corner of my eye, I see Dillon headed my way. He has hunted me down after all.

Before panic kicks in and my flight instinct takes over, my heart lurches at the sight of my beautiful bad boy, and then I scramble into my car and squeal out of the parking lot. Channeling my inner movie stunt driver, I make several quick turns. He's not in my rear view mirror when I look back. I continue to drive for a couple of miles away from my house and pull into a fast food joint.

My wild eyes dart around the parking lot. With all the adrenalin and cortisol pumping into my bloodstream, I'm shivering like a fraidy-cat. I sit for five full minutes, letting my breath normalize and my sweaty skin cool off. Convinced that Dillon hasn't caught up to me, I grab my phone. As much as I hate to do it, I call Jim again to intervene on my behalf. Someone has to get it through Dillon's head that I need time. I want to talk to him. Really, I do. I'm just not ready, especially now that he's pulling this crazy shit.

It's been half an hour, and Jim finally calls to say it's safe to go home. He really wants to come and keep me company, and I almost give in. I'm so raw and tired that strong arms and soft kisses would be nice. I'm not sure why I can't just let him give me some comfort.

When I get home, I leave my car out of the garage; I'm too drained to fumble with the groceries in the tight space. I unload the shopping bags and trudge from the driveway to the house. My feet drag like some mobster has fitted me for concrete shoes. I don't have even a spark of energy left for grilling steak after I put away the food. I don't mind because my ice cream is melted. It's a good excuse for being bad. I dump the thick liquid in the blender with some frozen berries and whip up an awesome milkshake.

I slurp the shake down for dinner while relaxing in a steamy tub of bubbles and crash into bed only an hour after the sun sets. My dreams through the long night are filled with perilous chases on tricycles, drowning in vats of melted ice cream, and Steffie laughing maniacally after tossing me naked into her steel cage.

$< ♂ + ♀ >$

Chapter Six – Hell Hath No Fury

Wednesday Morning, September 19

My muscles protest mildly as I roll out of bed. For ten minutes I stare into my closet, and I can't figure out what to wear to cover my bruises. The fear of being questioned about my absence and having my injuries discovered the way Mr. Bilson found them makes me rethink everything. *Maybe I should wait another day before returning to work.* The healing properties of a steaming shower and the need to hang on to some control sway my decision.

An eerie sense of déjà vu stops me cold when I reach my driveway. Last night, Dillon sent me a text with just one word. And there it is on the rear window of my car—huge letters spray painted in bright red. BITCH.

I stamp and snort like a wild stallion and buzz like a swarm of killer bees. "Well, you're a bastard! Where do you get off calling me that? Leave me alone!

"That does it. You're going to wish you had stayed away like I asked you to. You had to push me, didn't you, Dillon?" I spin on my heels and slam my heavy front door shut once I'm inside.

I stab the little numbers on my phone to make two calls. First, I call work and beg off another day. Second, I call the Police Department to report a stalker. The receptionist is very pleasant. She takes my name, phone number and address and says someone will phone me immediately.

Three minutes later, a woman identifies herself as Detective Jarvis from the Domestic Violence Unit. She and her partner will be at my place within 45 minutes. *Good. The sooner, the better.*

After I hang up, I make a hasty dash to the main bathroom. Cold sweat trickles down my back and glues my blouse to my shoulders. I heave violently but somehow keep down my breakfast. The warm washcloth I swipe across my face rubs off most of my makeup, revealing how paper white my skin has turned.

"What have you done, Erin? Are you sure you want this? It could get very messy for everyone. Well, whether you're ready or not, the cops are on their way. Get your act together so you don't babble like an idiot when they get here." Evanya tries to butt into my pep talk, but I silence her before she can dissuade me. I finish cleaning myself up and put on the kettle. I text Jim while the water boils.

'Dillon pushed too far. Have called cops. Will be here soon. Thought u should know.'

'Will be right there.'

'Please don't. I need to do this alone.'

'You need representation. I'm coming.'

'Thx but don't. Will call after. Luv u.'

'Luv u too.' Jim and I know we *luv* each other, not *love* each other.

Dangling my head over the toilet aggravated my neck, so I sit with my tea and an icepack while I wait nervously for all hell to break loose. Evanya yells at me that I should have let Jim come over. She says I need a calming influence. I tell her I can't let someone else fight my battles.

$$< ♂ + ♀ >$$

The chiming of my doorbell scares me out of my chair, and I slop my tea all over my kitchen table. "Well, priss. Suck it up. Here goes nothing." However bad I think it's going to be, I'm sure it's going to be ten times worse.

I'm a nervous Nellie as it is, but, when I open the door, stress hormones pump into my system double time. A short and stocky young woman stands in front. Her dirty blond hair is pulled back into a tight bun. She has a pretty face and bright green eyes, but her severe expression detracts from her beauty. She doesn't just look sour, she is sour; I can feel it. Under an open, black wool coat, she wears a black, man-tailored suit and steel blue shirt. Her vibe and her attire say she's not the type you want to mess with.

I look behind her and my lungs collapse. Because towering over her is a drop-dead gorgeous man. If Jim, Christophe and Dillon are perfect 10s, this man is several notches above that. The rising sun hits him from the side, highlighting his statuesque frame. His black leather bomber jacket outlines broad shoulders and nips in to accentuate a narrow waist. His black dress pants drape stylishly on long, strong legs.

Before I make an idiot of myself by staring too long, the woman says, in a very manly tone, "Ms. Piper, I'm Detective Jarvis, and this is Detective Vaughn. We spoke a short while ago. May we come in?"

I nod my head and snap back to attention. "Please." I usher them in, stepping away from the door and deeper into my foyer as they crowd in. The tiny space seems even smaller than it is with Detective Vaughn and his larger-than-life fabulousness filling it up. He closes the door behind him, and my eyes close while I try to reel in my hormones.

I thrust out shaky hands for their coats and quickly hang them up. My breath catches when I see the crisp, white dress shirt straining against the man's expansive chest. I know this isn't a social call, but all I want to do is play the good hostess. I need something to keep me busy and keep my mind off what's about to come, and off Detective Dreamy's rockin' body.

"Let's sit in the kitchen, shall we? I'm afraid I don't have any coffee to offer you, but I just made a pot of Chai spice tea if you'd like, or I have orange juice."

Detective Jarvis's refusal is terse. Detective Vaughn graciously accepts tea and lights up the whole room with his charming smile. *Like a shining angel. An avenging angel.*

His face is radiant and strong and square. *All male.* My lips want to kiss along the sharp planes of his jaws, and my tongue is tempted to dip into the shallow cleft in his blunt chin. In the center of all his magnificence is a perfectly straight, patrician nose that I would dearly love to rub my own up against.

Sitting below a prominent, high forehead and broad, bushy brows, ice-blue orbs sparkle at me from beneath heavy lids. Lush, black lashes relieve the coolness of his steady gaze. His soft, jet black hair is close cropped, but I can imagine it an inch or two longer with gentle waves that would surely feel luxurious if I were to run my fingers through them. It's not fair, but the wisps of silver at his temples are damn sexy. Crow's feet at the outside corners of his eyes and the laugh lines bracketing his generous mouth tell me he is likely pushing 40.

Time stretches as I continue to stare. His early-morning skin is smooth and fresh, but the hint of a black beard has me dreaming of heavy stubble rasping along my thighs come the dark of night. It seems I'm changing my views about facial hair for yet another man.

As for his body, it is perfection. He stands probably 6'4" or 6'5". His frame is strong and sturdy, the epitome of masculine beauty. He is lean and athletic, not muscle-bound—just the way I want a man to be, if I'm allowed to have my preference. His arms look to be about the right length to wrap right around me and strong enough to carry my generous curves off to bed. He makes me forget I'm supposed to be pissed at the male gender right now. I swallow hard and stifle a moan. I need to dial back my lust.

As I turn to pour his tea, I mutter to myself, "Smarten up, Erin. An avenging angel? What kind of sappy crap is talk like that? As for carrying you to bed? So what if he's freaking hot. Big flipping deal. He's here to help you, not to seduce you. You're a sick woman."

"Is everything alright, Ms. Piper?" *Good Lord, did I say that out loud? I would just die if I said that out loud.*

"Fine, Detective. And it's Miss Piper, but I'd be more comfortable if you call me Erin." I'm relieved beyond words that he doesn't seem to have any idea what I was mumbling about.

My head and heart may be telling me to forget about men, but my body seems ready to dive right into his arms. *Traitor.* My hips throw a little extra swagger in their sway as I walk over to him with a steaming mug. My nipples stand at rigid attention underneath my bra. And, yes, I detect a slight dampness in my knickers. *No, no, no. Not good. This is so wrong.*

Detective Vaughn's long, lickable fingers brush against mine as he takes the mug from me. It's a good thing he has a firm grip on it because my hands start to shake as a surge of electricity jolts up my arm and explodes throughout my whole body. The only other man I've had such an energetic reaction to is Christophe. He didn't touch my skin when we met, and the sparks only felt like tiny pin pricks. This is like being shot at rapid-fire by a nail gun.

"Thank you, Erin. Call me Jerry, and my partner is Ellen. Perhaps we should get down to business. Could you please tell us why you called?" *Sure thing, when I remember how to make my vocal chords work.* His voice is rich, low and sexy, Sam Elliot kind of sexy, and oozes over me like sticky, warm honey. My toes actually curl. It's a primitive response shared with our monkey relatives to help us hang on and not fall out of trees during orgasm. *You can shake me out of a tree any time, Detective Dreamy.*

My chest heaves as I gasp in several deep breaths. I place my palms on the heavy, maple table and slowly lower myself into the padded dining chair. No more stalling. I make a couple of false starts before I can make any words materialize.

"I'm being stalked by a former friend of mine. He's sending threatening texts, showed up while I was getting groceries last night, and you probably saw what he did to my car overnight."

"Hard to miss, unfortunately. Why do you think he's doing this to you?" asks Jerry.

"This past Friday evening, we were, um, intimate. I told him to stop, and it kind of took him a while. He did eventually, but not before scaring me, making me think he wouldn't quit." *Ugh.* I try my best to remain calm and professional, dispassionate and cold like a fish. I keep stumbling, however, every time Jerry puckers his lips to sip his tea and raises his eyes to watch me over the rim of the cup. It's almost as if he is trying to arouse me on purpose. *Yeah, right.*

"I wanted time to figure things out, but he keeps sending me harassing texts." I talk about the scare at the grocery store. "This morning, I was going back to work after two days off for recovery."

Jerry interrupts, a note of concern in his voice. "What do you mean by 'recovery'? Did he hurt you? Were you assaulted?"

His intent look is disarming, and I feel my cheeks brightening. I nibble at my lower lip before I say, "Um, things got a little rough, but that was before I told him to stop. I can't exactly say that what happened after that was an assault. It's what he's doing now that I called about." I scrub my hands along my thighs. There's a gleam in Jerry's eye that makes me nervous about what he's thinking.

"Until I saw my car, I was going to try to work things out with him. I'm not sure I have a choice now. I'm concerned for my safety."

Detective Jarvis is even more of a cold fish than I am. "You say you know the man and you were having sexual relations with him. What's his name? And what are the circumstances of the incident?"

She says "sexual relations" and "incident" as if she's making an accusation. I'm guessing she's not sympathetic. *Is she like this with all women in trouble, or has she just taken a particular dislike to me?* Compassion doesn't seem to be her strong suit. She'd be more effective making some gang-banger sweat in a dank interrogation room. At least she's not assigned to the Sexual Assault Unit.

I tell my humiliating story in vivid, albeit brief, detail but make it very clear to Detective Jarvis that I'm only providing background to Dillon's stalking and that I am not reporting an assault. I can't in good conscience do that to Dillon. The picture of him in handcuffs, being stuffed into a police cruiser and branded for life as a sex offender makes my eyes water and stops my heart. I pinch my inner thigh to snap myself out of that horrendous vision.

I am completely staggered by Jerry's reaction to my story. He is solemn for the duration, and his body language remains open, reserving his judgment. When I drop the bomb that I was at a club and engaged in a scene with Dillon St. Laurent, my poor heart leaps into my throat. The look he shoots at me slams me against an invisible wall.

His blue eyes flash and white fire scorches my body. His nostrils flare as he snorts up a quick hit of oxygen. My pussy weeps and my nipples pop in recognition of a Dom aroused. So much for avenging angel; this guy is more likely an Alpha devil. Right now, I just want to cry. The stress is all too much for me to handle.

My palms sweat profusely, and my stomach twists like someone is trying to pull it into taffy. My voice, however, is remarkably stable. I'm putting up a good front even though I feel like dying. I dig deep and square my shoulders, hold my head up, and barrel on through until I'm finished.

I give them copies of all the incident reports that I have and show them copies of the receipts from the hotel, Jessica and Dr.

Jefferson, and then I show them the texts on my phone. Showing them Dr. Yuri's report with the photos was the hardest part. It's bad enough having Detective Dreamy see my naked, damaged body. He, at least, doesn't react beyond a rapid flicker or two of his long lashes. It's Detective Jarvis who rattles me the most.

Throughout my narrative, I catch her pursing her lips. She makes little *tutting* sounds of disapproval, stabbing me with sharp stares as she makes her notes. Women are supposed to stick together. I wish we could have that sisterhood kind of bond, but I'm as mistaken in this hope as I was with Steffie.

Based on the timing of her gestures, it's clear she's not on my side. She likely thinks I got exactly what I deserved and that I'm wasting her time. She's green, no more than 25. How comforting it must be at that age to think that you have the whole world figured out, that everything is black and white and not shades ... *I am so not going to make a reference to that book right now.* Her puckered lips make me think she must be a prude to boot. *Now who's miss priss?*

"Well, I suggest we don't bother with the stalking charge. We have more than enough evidence to have him arrested for sexual assault. We can also add in a charge of unlawful confinement."

"No! Oh my God, NO! You can't arrest him. I agreed to let him tie me up and spank me. He just got a little carried away."

"Ellen, back off. You're upsetting Miss Piper," Jerry warns.

"Why? This woman was abused. Aren't we here to protect her? The law is very clear; there is no such thing as consensual assault."

"Don't presume. Ask her what she wants." He sounds like he's trying to patiently teach her something. I wonder if she's just coming up against BDSM for the first time. She glares at me.

"What would you like us to do then, Ms. Piper? You don't seem to be all that upset by Mr. St. Laurent beating you silly. I just don't understand why some women seem to get off on that." In my head I hear "slut" in Jed's accusing voice, and I see red. I fly out of my chair in less than half a second. I groan as clothes pulling on my abrasions remind me that I'm still not 100 percent.

"What does how upset I am have to do with anything? You're here to help me, not judge me. Show some respect." *This is hard enough for me as it is. Where does she get off making it worse?* Boiling-hot anger fizzes through my veins, rendering me a mad woman wanting to rip her head off. I'm like one of those tightly restrained maniacs who could snap at any given moment. My rant has more attitude to it than volume as I let her have it.

"Besides, just because I can keep my shit together for a few minutes instead of falling apart and blubbering like a baby, it doesn't mean that I'm not upset. You have no idea how long and hard I've cried. You don't know that I'll probably throw up the moment you leave. You might not guess that I wedge a chair under my front and back doorknobs at night because I'm terrified that Dillon will try to break in. But I'm not scared because of what happened at the club."

I'm shocked that that part feels true; the rest is an exaggeration because she's pissed me off. I would have cried harder and longer if I'd given in to sorrow. I do feel nauseous though, especially because of where she's heading, and I have been barricading my doors.

"I'm an intelligent woman, Detective Jarvis. I'm the Chief Librarian at the state School of Law Library. I understand about evidence and the law. But I don't think church or state have any business interfering in my sex life. That's not what you're here for."

Evanya is coaxing me to chill. I know I'm spiraling out of control. I can see it happening but can't pull back. I haven't snapped yet, but maybe the hard-ass is getting the picture about how "upset" I am.

"Erin, breathe. Just relax and breathe." Jerry's warm, firm hand pressing on my shoulder changes my state instantly. My mouth closes as my head tips forward and my hands clasp behind my back. I breathe slowly and that helps me to settle down a bit. I'm looking at the floor as a blow of realization socks me in the gut. *Domination and submission. Hand on shoulder, steady command. Just like Dillon does to me when he's trying to manipulate me.*

Now I snap. I'm all flailing arms, swinging wildly to knock Jerry's hand away. As they say, if looks could kill, Jerry would be lying flat on his back right now with a black hole between his eyes, smoke curling above the mortal wound. "Don't touch me! Why did you do that? I don't need you to ..."

Jerry cuts me off before I blurt out something inappropriate. "Erin, I apologize. You were agitated, and you've been through enough already. I just wanted to calm you." He flicks a quick look at Detective Jarvis, and I catch his drift. *He knows that I know about him. What is he thinking right now?*

All the wind drops out of my sails. I plop back down in my chair. An embarrassing, loud *phhtt* like a juicy fart escapes from the cushion. *Perfect! Where's the trap door to swallow me when I need it?*

This is turning out to be far worse than I anticipated. On top of I-want-to-hide-under-a-rock degradation, I'm dealing with a moralist who wants to burn me at the stake and crucify Dillon and a Dom who wants to subjugate me. I wonder what kind of karma I am dealing with here.

Jerry glowers at his partner, arms folded tightly across his chest, until she swallows hard and offers an insincere apology. *Does she know he's a Dom? How does he punish her when she's bad?* My skin tingles, and I bristle when Jerry slides his chair across the gleaming hardwood toward me. Waves of heat and desire shimmer in the void between us as he faces me squarely.

"Erin, Ellen needs some lessons in tact, but her question was fair. Have you considered what you want, how far you are prepared to proceed beyond this interview?"

"I honestly don't know. I care about him. I could probably drop it if it wasn't for his threats." *God, what a mess. The worst part is that I'm really mad at Dillon for screwing up the good thing we had.*

"I just want to feel safe. The ironic thing is that, in many ways, being at the club has been safer than trying to figure out the vanilla dating scene. Out there, you never know what kind of creeps you're going to meet or what risks you might be taking. The club has a structure, rules, support and oversight. We agree to treat each other respectfully, to honor boundaries. Safe, sane and consensual. He blurred a line. But now that he's pursuing me, I'm scared.

"I'm not looking for revenge; that's not who I am. I just need to be certain that Dillon won't hurt me. I want the stalking to stop."

"You're right, Erin." Jerry places a hand lightly on one of mine. It is rough and tanned, and twice the size. It makes mine look dainty. His tone is appeasing and soothing.

"You should have been safe at the club. You should have been able to trust him to respect your safeword." His eyes contain none of the coolness of their frosty color as they sweep over my face. They are as warm as a summer sky.

"We have to investigate now that you've called us in, regardless of what you decide down the line. We've got your statement, and we'll check this guy out. We'll talk to the witnesses and see if they're going to stick to their stories." What he means is that there is a reason that the club is private, and I'm threatening their secrets.

"I suggest you be careful who you talk to from the club."

"Yeah, that much I get. Steffie Harris, the owner, isn't very happy with me. She was verbally abusive when I went to see her on Monday. I don't expect that you'll get a warm welcome from her."

I tell Jerry that I've only spoken to three other people from the club. I tell him about Lacey, using her alyce alias, and my lawyer friend. I don't reveal Jim's name in case Jerry knows him in a professional capacity. When I mention Master Ronan, storm clouds gather in his eyes, and a dark scowl blows across his face.

"Be careful with him, Erin. Christophe may not be the friend you think he is. Don't set yourself up to be hurt even more." His gruff voice and stern look send chills down my spine. He must know Christophe since he used his first name. Jerry doesn't elaborate.

I wonder if he knows Dillon, too. I've not seen Jerry at DYKKC, but I know the community is pretty insular and tightly connected. *If he does know Dillon, would that work in my favor or against me?*

Detective Jarvis stands; Jerry follows closely. She says, "We've got all we need for now, Ms. Piper. We'll investigate what happened at the club and talk to Mr. St. Laurent about not harassing you. But think long and hard. You don't have to take his abuse." Her feet are spread wide in a stance that says she's ready to pick a fight. Her face is pinched like she's trying hard not to start one.

"It's clear that you don't approve of the choices I've made about my sex life. That's my business, not yours. Regardless, I still have a right to due process and to be safe. I don't agree with the route you want to go, but I can't do nothing." A sudden wave of grief swamps me. Tears stream down my face as the stress takes its toll. I drop to my chair with a thud. *That's what I did.*

"What is it, Erin? Tell me." Jerry's tone is soft and careful but also firm. I shake my head quickly.

"Look at me, priss. Talk to me." My conditioned response when his thick finger lifts my chin is to look up at him and tell him everything. My voice sounds far away, even to my own ears.

"Sir, I tried so hard today to not have a meltdown, but I just did nothing." Jerry takes in a full breath and scrunches his face in a hard blink. I cock my head and look at him, trying to puzzle out his reaction. *Oh, I called him Sir. Yes, Sir. Anything you want, Sir.*

He has to clear his throat a couple of times before he says, "I don't understand, Erin. Explain."

"When I went to the club, it was to explore, to find out who I am. I'm confident at work, but that's not who I was the rest of the time. I let others steal my belief in myself. I'm a good person, but I always thought I had more inside me that I couldn't reach.

"I worked hard to find out what I'm made of and what was holding me back. Despite your warning, Master Ronan has been a big part of my self-discovery. I found an inner core of strength. Now, I ask for what I want and need. I feel empowered. The last couple of months, for the first time in my adult life, I have been truly happy. I had a place to belong to, people who cared about me."

All through my monologue, Jerry holds my hands, rubbing his thumbs over my knuckles. He maintains unshakable eye contact—the Dom stare. I don't doubt that he is listening to and cares about every word I say. Detective Jarvis sits quietly, her hands in her lap.

"That's something to be really proud of, Erin. I can see how strong you are. So why are you crying?"

"I'm not strong at all. What really hurts is ... I let him defeat me. It's not what he did to me; I'm alive and my body will heal. That doesn't really matter to me. But he couldn't hurt me where it counts if I didn't *let* him. Dillon was just a catalyst for what I did to myself.

"I freaked and gave up. I didn't relax into the scene and try to enjoy it or submit to my Top. But I didn't keep protesting and fighting for myself either. I did nothing. I checked out and went numb. I gave him all my power, but not in an equal exchange. I threw away all my hard-won gains as if I had never made them. I let him break me, and I'm not sure he was even trying to." Admitting my failure out loud just destroys me.

"Don't you see? I can't do *nothing*. I have to do something, but I don't know what the right thing is. I don't want him arrested. Can't you just warn him?" That last thought comes out on the tail of a long, mournful sigh. I'm as exhausted as if I've been up for 72 hours straight, and it's not even noon yet.

Jerry's cool, cool appraisal penetrates into me. I feel completely naked, and not in the way that feels exciting and promises the fulfillment of dark desires. I have never felt more vulnerable and exposed in my life. For some reason, I want this man to see me, and it scares me that maybe he does. I know I've helped create this mess, and I don't like what I see. *What does he see?* My hands are shaking with the need for his approval, and I can't seem to stop.

"Of course, we'll tell him to back off and, hopefully, that will be enough. I can be pretty persuasive. We won't do anything more serious for at least 24 hours while we poke around a bit. You can decide later if there's a need to go further.

"We can help you with the paperwork to file a restraining order against Dillon if it comes to that. It will let him know you're serious, and he won't be arrested unless he breaches the order. Give that some thought, okay? We'll call you tomorrow."

With that, they make their way to the door. Jerry hangs back and puts his hand on my shoulder again as he leans in and speaks in an oozy hush against my ear. "You're not collared?" I shake my head. "I left my card on the table. It has my personal cell number. If you need to talk to someone who's not a member of DYKKC, you can call me ... anytime." He squeezes my shoulder to make his point.

I look up into his hypnotic gaze. "Th-thanks. I'll think about it."

"Don't think about it too hard. Just call. Be careful, priss." I'm bowled over by him calling me by my club name. Obviously, I mentioned it. It's presumptuous, perturbing and pretty freaking awesome. I hate the name, but, the way Jerry says it, all dark and soft as smoke, I'll let him call me that and whatever else he wants. And I'd likely do whatever he wants me to do.

I watch Jerry's spectacular rear end, hugged and shaped by his trousers, as he walks down my front path. His ass could be named one of the great Wonders of the World. "Holy hell. What I wouldn't give to see that butt naked. Stop it. Stop it. I need to stay away from men, and he's a man. Oh Lord, he most definitely is a *man*."

Now that that's over, my adrenalin crashes. I splutter and splatter all over my kitchen. After 20 minutes or so of replaying the interview in my mind, I scrape myself up and head to bed for a nap. This emotional struggle is hard, but I do feel a little better. *I stood up for myself.* The detectives will talk to Dillon, and he'll back off now and let me catch my breath. *Maybe then I'll be able to fix this.*

I take just one muscle relaxant to help me sleep and to ease the tension that built in my body during the interview. As I drift off, my hands rove across my skin, only, in my mind, it's those gigantic, strong hands of Jerry's that caress and tease me. When one hand finds its way down between my hot thighs, my lips curl into a smile as I whisper his name. "Jerry Vaughn. Detective Dreamy, the Dom."

< ♂ + ♀ >

The name flashing brightly and buzzing nastily on my phone wrenches me out of a particularly sweet vision of Jerry's luscious body stretched out above me as he rides me hard. *Steffie Harris.* What a rude awakening.

"You stupid bitch. You're going to pay for calling the cops." She cusses a blue streak as she rips viciously into me. Man, that woman has a foul mouth. Too bad she didn't heed my warning.

No one could accuse Steffie of being subtle. She doesn't veil her threat when she tells me to drop it. No warnings of bodily harm, just a trashed reputation and finding myself in a living hell. I wonder if Jerry rubbed her the wrong way. If it wasn't him, I bet Detective Jarvis rattled her cage. Speaking of cages, I bet Ellen's eyes popped out of her head when she saw Steffie's office décor.

Then Steffie pulls the rug out from under me. "We don't need your toxic influence around DYKKC, priss. Effective immediately, your membership is terminated. A lifetime ban. I never want to see your fat ass in my club again. And stay away from Dillon. You've done enough damage."

I gasp and flounder, sucking air like a fish thrown up on the beach. The shock is suffocating. *She thinks I'm the one who has done the damage?* I blurt out, "Fine. Victimize the victim, Steffie, but you'll pay for this. Don't think I'll keep quiet."

I disconnect and plaster a fake smile on my face. I'm sticking up for me. Evanya *tutts* at me. I don't know what her problem is. I've just claimed back another piece of the new, strong Erin that I had found before this nightmare with Dillon began.

Jim has sent a couple of texts wanting to know what happened and asking if I'm okay. I probably should have contacted him after Jerry and his prickly partner left. I answer that I'm fine and haven't made any decisions yet. 'Steffie is pissed and making matters worse,' I tell him.

'Don't worry. Will deal with her.'

'No need. Won't be seeing her sad ass anymore. She banned me.'

My phone rings instantly. I have a brief conversation with Jim. He says he'll fix it; I tell him not to bother. I'm pretty adamant that he not get involved any deeper. The situation is way out of hand, and Jim's and Christophe's interventions aren't doing me any good. He hangs up in a huff. Doms just don't like being told what to do.

"If I really do want to fix this myself, why am I disappointed and pissed that he didn't show up when I told him to stay away? If I was really important to him, and he had a backbone, wouldn't he have arrived at my door anyway, put me in my place, and saved me from my stubbornness?" *I don't really want to be the tough one all the time. I want someone to take care of me once in a while.*

"Now you're starting to get it," says Evanya. "You've got to let someone in. You've got to let a man be a man." I'm confused.

"Wait a minute. What kind of lame advice is that coming from a higher self? Shouldn't you be telling me to quit whining? Shouldn't you be telling me that they're messing up and that I'm perfectly capable of taking care of this myself, that I don't need a man?"

"Yin and yang. Yang and yin. Male and female. Black and white. Hard and soft. Hot and cold. Strong and yielding. Energy flows. Meditate on it. That's all I'm saying."

Evanya has really lost it, and I sure don't feel like meditating on anything right now. A frenzy of laundry and scrubbing bathrooms distracts me from the craziness until dinner. In between chores, I assemble a big pan of lasagna. I'm resorting to comfort food *again*, but I'll worry about my hips tomorrow.

I stretch out on my soft, ultra-suede couch and eat dinner in front of the TV. A movie and a couple of glasses of a spectacular 2008 South African cabernet sauvignon help me while away the hours until it's time for Christophe's video call. I'm kind of dreading talking to him. Just like Jim, he's not going to be happy that I was on my own with the police. But, unlike Jim, he wasn't here to do anything about that.

On the other hand, I'm absolutely dying to hear his reaction when I mention that Jerry is the investigating detective. I need more dirt on that story. There's something big there. I can feel it.

< ♂ + ♀ >

Chapter Seven – Angel of Mercy

Wednesday Evening, September 19

Just as I expected, Christophe's reaction is overly protective but also, surprisingly, overly possessive. He went ballistic when he heard what Dillon did and was mad at Jim for not being with me when the police came. "Did you say Jerry Vaughn? Shit. Is there someone else they can send to take your case?"

"What's the problem?" He immediately starts to backpedal. His face blanks, and he says, "It's nothing, priss. Don't worry about it."

"Come on, tell me what the deal is between you two. He had the same reaction when I told him you top me. Except he came right out and warned me about you." I sit back and wait to see whether it will be an ice storm or fireworks from my tight-lipped wolf. *Two can play your game of evasion, buddy.*

"What did he say?" The words are forced out of his mouth, each syllable clipped, flat and cold enough to freeze a cup of water in the Sahara Desert. *Icicles it is.*

"Just that I should be careful. So, what do I need to know, Christophe?"

"Nothing, priss. It was a competition for a woman's attention. He's a sore loser. Now drop it. Tell me what Vaughn is going to do." He has warmed up a couple of degrees but is still playing it super cool. *Why doesn't he warn me about Jerry in return?*

"They're doing a preliminary investigation. I haven't made any decisions, but Steffie pissed me off and might force my hand. She tore a strip off me today, and then she banned me from DYKKC."

"She did what? Look, don't worry about it. I'll deal with her."

My laptop wobbles on my knees from the force of my hand hitting the couch. "You will not! Jim said the same thing. You both need to stop intruding and making a mess of things. You two don't have a clue what subtlety is. This is my problem, and I'll handle it."

"priss ..." I glare at him. "*Erin*, we both care about you. We're just trying to protect you and make this difficult situation easier for you." His tone drops very low and becomes soft and sweet. "It worries me knowing you're on your own, but you don't have to be. Please, let me help." I've never heard Christophe plead before.

"I know you care. I appreciate it." I sigh. "I know it's hard for you Alpha types to do nothing. The best thing you can do for me is be my friend, my rock. Just tell me I'll be alright. Please don't go behind my back trying to fix things and make me regret telling you about this." I'm cooling off, and I'm worn out again. I don't want to fight with him. I don't want him fighting my battles for me either. Despite what Evanya wants, I can't let him inside my life that far. I just want his reassurance and affection.

"I'm sorry, sweetheart. I'll let it go. But I meant it that you don't have to deal with this all on your own. I'll be on a plane tomorrow. I want to hold you in my arms until you feel safe again. I miss your pretty, golden eyes and sweet, red lips. I need to feel your hot, soft body cuddled up next to mine."

He sounds so innocent, as if we hadn't been squabbling about his heavy-handedness only a few moments ago. *Wouldn't it be heavenly to be in his arms, the object of his tender mercies?* If I'm not mistaken, I actually hear longing in his voice. *Can I do it, open up that much?*

"Christophe, I miss you too. But this is not about you and what you need. Please don't come home. You've got a job to do, and I'd feel guilty taking you away from that. I have to be the one to fight to get back what I lost that night. I need to do this, and you have to let me."

"Do you miss me, sweetheart?"

How can I deny it, especially when he's calling me "sweetheart" again? "Yes, I miss you. It would be nice to have a friend at my side, but don't come home. Just call me again soon. That's what I need most right now."

"Are you sure? The minute I get there, I'll kiss you until your knees go weak and you fall into my arms. I'll pick you up and carry you to bed. Then I'll slowly undress you, kissing every inch of your soft, creamy skin as I reveal it. Oh, you like the sound of that, don't you, priss?" *No shit, Sherlock.*

He's like a dark wizard, using black magic and seductive incantations to conjure an intense response from my body. I can only sip shallow breaths, and my eyes have fluttered closed. My fingertips trace my lips, trying to soothe his hell-fire kisses. An involuntary sigh heaves loud enough for him to hear. *God, in only ten seconds, he's got me gagging for him.*

"Yes, that's it, sweetheart. Feel my hands on your sexy body. Caressing you, squeezing you. Every touch followed by a kiss and a lick." Flames of desire are what are licking me, and they're licking at my pussy. *Good Lord, have mercy.*

I curse him for being a demonic fiend, but on my screen he looks like a sexy god. Such sweet words and smile have a sinful effect. The memories and fantasies of Christophe, Master Ronan, teasing and pleasing me are just as real as if he was sitting beside me now instead of half a world away. And, ohhh, the things I want to do to him, for him.

"Touch yourself the way I touch you. Undo your buttons, slowly. Show me your snow white skin. That's it. So beautiful. My fingers want to trace along the lace of that pretty pink bra. Do that for me now, sweetheart. Sooo good. Hold your beautiful tits and squeeze them, massage them. Yeeeesssss. Pinch your nipples. Hard, priss. I want to see them poking through the lace."

It doesn't matter that technically it's my hands that are on me; I feel *him*. My nipples ache, needing more from him. My pussy is weeping, waiting for his fingers and his cock. Gentle sighs turn to desperate moans.

"Take off your bra, priss. Show me your pretty tits. Ohhh, yeah. Such a handful, so firm. I love how high and proud those perfect beauties sit. Work them for me. Make them jiggle and bounce. Chérie, you're killing me." His French accent is stronger, sexier now.

He doesn't usually say much once we get to this point. I love the words, even if he sounds far away. I smile and a deep, throaty groan rumbles from between my pouty lips. I crush the girls together, mashing and mauling them roughly. I love when Master Ronan does that to me. My neck unlocks and my head drops back as my hips gyrate and grind my butt into the couch.

"Sir, please." My tortured cry reveals the depth of my longing for him, my desperate need to have his lips pulling on my nips.

"Stand and take off your pants. Show me your gorgeous pussy. Show me how wet you are for me, priss. Do it now." I obey his fervent command without hesitation. I open my eyes to get my bearings and look at my screen. *Holy Shit!*

They say the camera adds ten pounds. Well, it also adds inches. His medical scrubs are off, and a naked beast sprawls across my screen. In front of me, larger than life, is the image of Christophe's imposing erection. It's long and strong and pointing right at me.

In the artificial light of the digital glow, his usually purple head looks almost black. And menacing. I lick lips that are parched by want. The thought of wrapping them around that silky, dark helmet revives me and makes my mouth water. The tip of my agile tongue imagines sweeping away the drop of pre-come dribbling from his slit on the other side of the screen. His flavor is fixed in my cell memory. God, he tastes yummy, sweeter than any man I've had the pleasure of pleasuring.

"You're dripping, sweetheart. I bet you are so hot. Stick your fingers in and take your temperature. Tell me how hot you are."

"Oh, Master. Ohhh, God. I'm scalding my fingers. It feels like I'm dipping into a steaming lava pool. I'm so hot for you, Master." It dawns on me that I'm calling him "Master." It's an indelible reflex.

"Sweetheart, my sweet baby. I want to sink myself deep into you, drown in that heat." Christophe's words are heavily laced with lust and end with a long, raspy growl. That sound always makes my nipples tingle like they're hooked up to a live current.

My breath draws in short, ragged pants and sweat trickles down between my breasts. My hips sway and rock as I jam my fingers as far into my tight channel as they can extend. My eyes fly open as the first stirrings of my orgasm unwind in the remotest corners of my sex. Like I'm in a wet dream, I stare at Christophe's huge hand wrapped around his huge penis. He is stroking himself the way I want to be stroking him.

"Master. Please. Your cock looks so beautiful. I want it so much. Please, put it in me. Please, Master." I'm whimpering like a needy child begging for candy. And I do *need*. My PC muscles clench like a vice grip tightening, frantic to grasp his glistening, rampaging shaft as it jams into my slick core again and again, threatening to break me into a million pieces.

"Yes, priss. Keep pumping your fingers. You're incredible, pretty baby. Fuck, I love to hear you moan like that. I know you're close. Come for me, priss. Come now."

On cue, a wildfire rages between my legs, scorching my inner thighs, incinerating my fingers sliding in and out of my molten depths. My spine lengthens and arches, flinging my head backward. My hips buck uncontrollably, and my whole body jerks and dances in an ecstatic seizure.

"Christophe!!! Oh my God! Christophe!!!" I don't shout, I scream his name. I've never screamed his name during my climax. But something has changed. What we're doing is different. Where we're doing it is different. I feel *him* inside me, the man and not the mask. The connection feels real and solid—and more than domination.

I regain my faculties just in time to witness his release. Loud, feral grunts blare from my speakers in time to jets of come pulsing from his cock into his hand. Blurry resolution or not, I can see every one of his muscles displayed on my screen rippling in vigorous contractions.

On his final spurt, he snarls out my name. The vibrations of that one sound tickle my ear drums, and I register strains of lust, affection, need and something else that I'm not willing to define right now. Whatever it is, it's enough to send me over the cliff again.

We both collapse at the same time, panting like we've each run a marathon. Sweat shines on his chest and a single drop hangs on the tip of his nose. I look at my own chest and see a healthy sheen and a rivulet running between my boobs. We stare silently into each other's eyes; the shushing of static and our labored breaths are the only sounds. Minutes drift by before either of us speaks.

"I'm coming home, sweetheart. I'll be there soon." His voice is full, expressive. *Sweet, stubborn S.O.B.*

"It means a lot to me that you want to, Christophe. You have no idea. Stay, please. I don't need the karma from asking you to come home. Can you call me again, like this?" My voice is barely louder than a whisper. I'm choked with emotions that I can't even name. I want him, and I don't want him.

"Alright, I give in, but, baby, I'm not happy about it. I'm going to tan your hide when I do see you. I'll text to let you know when my next break is. Be well. Know that I'm with you and you're not alone, sweetheart." He blows me a kiss and touches his fingers to his computer screen. I do the same.

"Be safe, Christophe. I miss you." The emotion is too much for my lonely heart. A whirling tornado rips through me, one of longing for deep connection, regret for keeping my distance, gratitude for his affection, and denial of my own. The screen goes blank, and I crumble.

As I put my clothes back on, I replay taking them off. *Wow! Wow!! Wow!!! Did that just happen?* I've had phone sex before, but cybersex is a first for me. I text Christophe and tell him how hot I think that was. He replies, 'Ur hot, not just the sex.' *Yeah, so is he.*

"Damn, I want to do that again with him. But next time, he's got to cover his laptop in plastic wrap or something. I want to see him gushing when he comes, not have the action hidden in his hand." *Did I just say that?* What a dirty thought, freakish even. I know other people do things that are way more twisted than that, even broadcast it live on the internet, but that was a new adventure for me. Christophe is always leading me into new territory.

"How could I ever have thought that Dillon was my favorite?" Christophe is the one who arouses me and gets my body humming at a frequency the others can't raise me to.

"Why did I insist that he not come home? Having him here to hold me, make love to me, take care of me, isn't that what I've been fantasizing about for months? Isn't that what you want for me, Evanya? What the heck is my problem?" The wise one is notably silent. She doesn't pout—that would be beneath a higher self—but she's not above letting me stew when she's trying to make a point.

I pour myself another glass of wine and gulp the whole thing down. I don't even taste the notes of black currant and roasted fig. When I discovered this exquisite wine last month, I dipped into my savings account to buy two cases. I had never been that indulgent before, but it's just that good. I drain the rest of the bottle into my glass and sit down to sip and savor it this time.

"What am I going to do about you, Christophe?"

I pass out on my comfy couch with too many emotions, too many sensations, and too many questions swirling in my wine-soaked head and in my dream-filled heart. I wake in the dead of the night, dreaming I'm Goldilocks trying to find a comfortable chair. One's too big, and one's too small, but there isn't one that's just right. I stumble off to bed, feeling like I don't fit.

Chapter Eight – Fifth Circle of Hell

Thursday Evening, September 20

There's a crisp chill and the ripe smell of harvest hanging in the air tonight. The days are getting shorter and the nights longer now that autumn has arrived. This is the perfect weather for running. My body is delirious to be well enough to do this again. Out on the street, I feel like I could keep striding for a full marathon if it would take me away from this place and all my troubles.

$< \male + \female >$

My first day back at work hadn't started well. An apoplectic Steffie paid me a surprise visit. Apparently, harassing me by phone and banning me from DYKKC wasn't enough for her. She needed to embarrass me in front of my staff as well. She was at least vague enough that no outsider could catch on to what her tirade was all about. That was important to me because I couldn't get her away from the Reference Desk and into my office.

The gist of her complaint was that both Christophe and Jim had called her *again*. Christophe, the hard-headed ass, was particularly rough on her. "I don't like being threatened, Erin," Steffie hissed. At least she didn't use my alias. I wish she would have told me what Christophe's threat was, but she wouldn't.

"I've already told both of them, several times, to stay out of it. I have no control over those two, and you should know that. I can only control myself. And here's what I'm going to do. Coming here this morning, airing this in public, was a big mistake. One that you will pay for. And, Steffie, that is not a threat. I will make good on it." In fact, it was just a threat. I was bluffing again, but my patience with Dominants was running out. Being a submissive doesn't mean being a doormat. I stood my ground.

She swung her hand back, winding up to slap my face. I caught her wrist before she could connect. I called to one of the librarians cowering behind the stacks, asking if she saw what Steffie had tried. She did, as did several other people, some of them lawyers.

I wanted Steffie's loud mouth out of my peaceful library, so I kept up the pressure. I stepped up and put my mouth to her ear. My voice was cold and calm, unwavering. "If you wanted me to keep this quiet, you're making it increasingly difficult for me to do that. I suggest you get out of here before I call Detective Vaughn to file assault charges against *you*. That will definitely bring your dirty laundry into the open."

"I'm not afraid of you or Snapper." *Who's Snapper? Jerry?* Steffie shook me off, took one look at the ice in my eyes, and strutted out. My staff crowded around me like cowboys circling the wagons the second she was gone. They all wanted to be sure I was okay. I told them I was fine and that they should get back to work.

My Reference Head, Jillian Ferris, wasn't easily put off; she saw my hands shaking. She wanted a private conversation with me in my office. Jillian is a mother, highly perceptive and instinctively protective. It took me ten minutes to convince her that there was nothing to worry about. When I told her I was taking an extended lunch, she almost started in again.

It wasn't hard to decide on my course of action. I texted Jerry as soon as Jillian closed my office door. I told him I wanted to file the restraining order against Dillon because he wouldn't stop with the threats—as I arrived at work my phone had dinged with a new one. He wanted to see me 'or else.' I also wanted to file a complaint against Steffie for her attempted assault. My anger raged at full steam, and, against my nature, I wanted swift retribution.

Jerry met me on the front steps of the police station. His smile was bright and sexy. He lingered when he shook my hand, his fingertips sliding along my palm as he finally released me to take me inside the station. My body's reaction to seeing him again was unexpected and visceral. The cleft below his smile called to my tongue and distracted me from focusing on the latest with Dillon and what Jim and Christophe had done to set Steffie off.

My eyes wandered as I told my Detective Dreamy about also being kicked out of the club. I was both annoyed and impressed by his honesty when he admitted that he might have been partially responsible for Steffie's reaction, although he didn't say what happened during his interview with her. When he apologized, I couldn't tell whether he was actually sorry about me losing my membership. He gave me that Dom stare, all murky and mysterious. And penetrating. The way my nipples smoldered, I thought he was shooting laser beams at me. He told me that everything would be fine, that I'd be fine. I did believe him about that. The covert way that he squeezed my knee under the table sealed my trust. And stirred my desire.

I had already filled in the paperwork for the Civil No-Contact Orders from an online form and handed the stack to Jerry so he could check them over before I took them to the County Clerk's Office. He warned me that there weren't sufficient grounds to file against Steffie. I'm glad he talked me down from that ledge. I admit that my response to her was a tad rash.

My jaw dropped when he promised to call in some favors to have the papers served on Dillon by dinner time. They must be some pretty big favors because it looked like I wouldn't have to appear in court to get the temporary order done. I'll still have to appear in two weeks if I want to make the order permanent, but I've never heard of being able to bypass the system like that. *I wonder why he would go to such lengths to pull in those favors for me.*

< ♂ + ♀ >

I jog in place while I wait for a traffic light to change. It's kind of a metaphor for how I feel right now—stuck in place, waiting for some signal telling me I can resume my normal life. I know I'm impatient. It's only been a few days since this mess blew up.

Dillon and Steffie don't seem to be willing to back off. And Christophe and Jim are still meddling and making things worse. Of course, I'm not blameless either with Steffie. I did give her a hard time this morning. I'm just glad I didn't make the situation worse. It seems I've got a long road ahead of me. Even if all the nonsense stopped today, I've got a truck full of emotional baggage to handle.

Usually when I jog, each footfall that connects with the earth channels a little packet of negative energy out of me. It washes me clean, reinvigorates me, helps me feel alive and happy. The opposite is happening tonight. I imagine each pounding step as a kick to someone's head. It's not like me to have dark, violent thoughts, but that right there is some of the baggage I'm going to have to handle.

I wasn't anticipating such a battle with Steffie. It's an added stress I don't need. *How can the woman be so cold?* She teaches that safewords are sacrosanct. It's a basic principle of BDSM. I expected more support. Well, I did get that, just not from her.

Christophe and Jim have been supportive alright, but they've gone overboard with Steffie, pushed her too hard, and that's why she's attacking. They're both sooo going to get an earful when I get home. I plan out the speech I'm going to give them. It's about them backing off and letting me control my own life. *Boundaries.*

I round the corner, and home is in sight. I've got my power playlist pounding in my ears—Tina Turner, Aretha Franklin, Chaka Khan, Cher, Patti LaBelle. They're my heroes, all strong women singing about taking charge of their lives. I'm on top as the Mistress of my own universe again. I open my front door just as Aretha belts out her plea to be respected.

"Aaaiii!" I'm barely two steps inside and being propelled forward. A hefty hand snakes around to clamp my mouth shut. A solid, powerful chest barrels into me and laminates me to my closet doors. In my tired and not-fully-recovered condition, I can't break free no matter how hard I struggle. Ice water runs through my veins as terror swamps over me.

"priss, hold still. I need to talk to you. You can't keep putting me off." *Bastard.* I knew I recognized his tangy aftershave. I let myself go limp. Just as Dillon eases his hold on me, I shove and twist hard.

When his hand slips off my mouth, I scream, "Fire!" No one comes when you cry "rape." This is one time I'd be grateful if Mr. Bilson butted in. It only takes Dillon two seconds to regain control of me. He's so freaking strong.

"Why did you have to do that? Now look what you've made me do." I don't understand what he's talking about. Then the bitter taste of a ball gag fills my mouth as Dillon shoves it in and secures it behind my head. In just a minute, maybe a minute and a half, he has me roped rodeo-style.

"This is making me crazy, priss. Everything is such a fucking mess. You should have answered my texts and not run away from me. You won't cooperate, so now I have to make you listen. But not here. You're coming with me." I thrash like a captured crocodile, but I'm wrestled by a pro. My eyes expand to popping-out-of-my-head proportions when he picks up a big hockey bag. The madman folds me up and stuffs me inside. It's a tight fit—I'm not exactly tiny—and I'm securely bound. I have very little wiggle room. *First assault, now kidnapping. This ass is going away for a long time.* If I wasn't insanely angry right now, I would probably go back to being scared.

Before he zips up the bag, he says, "I'm sorry, Erin. You have no idea. I didn't want to have to resort to this, but I've been pushed beyond my limits." His voice is thick and warbly. Salty tears cloud my vision, but I can see that his cheeks are flushed almost purple and his forehead and upper lip are slick with sweat. Then the metallic *click click* of the zipper closing, leaving only a small air-hole opening, signals my descent into a lower level of hell.

As he carries me away, he calls out, "Bye, Erin. Thanks for fixing my equipment." My front door slams. I'm in motion, swinging. Then he puts the hockey bag, with me in it, on the back seat of his SUV. The slamming of the door signals his clean getaway.

< ♂ + ♀ >

During the drive, I kept trying to convince myself that Dillon would never really hurt me. When the car stopped and I knew we had reached our destination, the fear rushed back in to slam me at full force. My poor heart couldn't take the stress, and I passed out. Now awake, I pull on the leather cuffs binding me spread-eagled to the four solid, wooden posts of a king-size bed. I'm in a dark, masculine bedroom. *This must be Dillon's house.* He's pacing at the foot of the bed but stops dead when he realizes I'm awake.

"priss, don't worry. You're safe. I promise I won't hurt you. I just need you to listen. Please, baby. I know I've gone too far. I'm sorry, but I had to do something. I can't make things right if you keep shutting me out and running away. I had to make it all stop."

He steps close to me and eases himself down beside me on the left side of the bed. I jerk to get out of his way, but I can't move more than a couple of inches. Dillon strokes my hair and shushes me. Then he removes the gag. My jaw is frozen, and I have to work to get it to relax.

"You're right, Dillon. This has to stop. Let me go."

"I will. I swear. priss, I know you're scared and angry. But you have no idea what's going on. Fuck, everyone kept saying all kinds of shit to me. Except you, and you're the only one I needed to hear from. I didn't know what you were thinking. I was worried about you and about us. I couldn't lose you. I guess I went a little crazy." This is a very different man from the one who was cold enough and detached enough that he could bundle me up and cart me off like a piece of luggage. He's unraveling.

"I'm sorry for everything that happened. Are you okay, baby?" My answer is a torturous stare.

Dillon takes a very long pause, his eyes trained on his fingers skimming along my elbow. "I get it, Erin. I don't blame you for hating me. If you're wondering about my face, I guess I deserved it. They broke in here last night while I was asleep and dragged me out of bed. They threatened to kill me, told me to stay away from you." Then I see what I didn't notice before. Dillon's lower lip is split and his left eye is puffy. He lifts his T-shirt. His entire upper body is mottled with angry bruises as black as his shirt. The hilly pattern of red and purple welts on his back reminds me of the underside of an egg carton. *Oh, God! What the hell happened?*

I'm beyond shocked. *What other damage can't I see?* I recoil from the ugliness, instantly nauseous. My next instinct is concern and empathy. I can't imagine how much my big, beautiful bad boy is suffering from the battering to his ribs, back and vital organs. I know how agonizing my own small bruises were, and they were nothing like this. It's bad, really bad. No wonder he's come unglued.

"Oh God, Dillon. I'm sorry. No matter how angry I am, you don't deserve this. I'm sorry this happened to you. It makes me sick ... that someone would do this because of me. I could never do this."

I wear the pain of his injuries on my own body. The sight hurts me physically. I can't watch boxing or even football because the violent hits send shockwaves of sympathy cascading through every part of me. It's why I can't watch a lot of what goes on at DYKKC.

The more I think about it, imagine heavy fists pummeling into his soft flesh and hard muscles, marring his beauty, damaging him, terrorizing him with unforgivable threats, my gut wrenches and bile bubbles up in my throat. I know how strong Dillon is. It would have taken an army of brutes to do this to him.

"I know you wouldn't, Erin. You're too sweet, too kind for that. There's only one person I know who would do it."

Christophe. Yesterday I thought I might be falling in love with him. Today I'm reminded that he's a ferocious beast. All my strength and willpower drain from me as the impact of this latest betrayal assails me. This was a vicious, criminal attack on Dillon, as well as a blatant disregard of my right to make my own decisions. *How could Christophe think I would be okay with this?*

My eyelids clank shut like the metallic ringing of a closing prison door. Tears leak from the corners of my eyes and roll down into my ears. Tears of regret for what happened to Dillon. And tears of loss ... because I *will* lose Christophe over this. I'm tired, bone weary, fed up with being manipulated, used and stripped of my free will by the men in my life. I want out, out of all of it.

As if he heard my words, Dillon's hands are at my right wrist and the ripping sound of Velcro® separating fills my ears. Dillon places my arm at my side and carefully rubs and eases the tension in my joints. In moments, I am free of all the restraints. I lie still, relatively comfortable now, sunk deep into the fluffy duvet and soft mattress. No thoughts, or feelings; my head and heart are barren wastelands.

Dillon lies down beside me, curling toward me, and rests his head on the flat shelf where my left arm connects to my shoulder, my shoulder meets my chest. His nose and mouth sit directly over my heart. Moist breath blows across the top of my breast, warming me through my jogging top as he speaks.

"I truly am sorry, Erin. You'll never know how much. I should have stopped sooner, the instant you said your safeword. I took the game too far. But please believe me, in my mind, I *was* still playing. I thought you were, too. You calmed down when I sweet-talked you and kissed and caressed you. I made sure to ask if it was okay to continue. I was so relieved and happy when you didn't say no. I honestly thought you were into it, that you changed your mind."

"No." I don't remember him asking me for consent. This changes everything. *Damn. I've screwed up badly.*

"Baby, I made a horrible, horrible mistake. I'll never forgive myself for hurting you." His left hand drops from his hip to my bare belly. My muscles twitch and then warm to his gentle caress.

"I felt sick when you looked up at me with your sweet, honey eyes and asked me not to ... rape you. I could never ... do that to a woman ... not to you. I regret that you thought that for even a second ... If I could go back and change it ..." *I wish you could, too. I wish I could change what I did. I'm so ashamed.*

Something stirs inside my heart, the most fragile spark of tenderness. Dillon sounds like a lost little boy, not a proud and strong Dom. I don't recognize this man. *What could lay him so low?*

"Erin, I know why you won't talk to me. I don't blame you. I'm a monster. I like to ... hurt women. I don't know where it came from, but there's a darkness in me that I have to keep on a short leash.

"I'm not like The Squire or Ronan. I've watched you with both of them. I've seen how much you laugh with Jim, how much fun you have with him. I can't remember when I last laughed like that. My life isn't a lot of fun. I'm not trying to excuse any of what I did that night or since. It's just the way things are."

He pulls his hand from my belly and clutches it to his own heart. His words are strangled by distress. I can feel him; it's actually more than distress—he's really suffering.

It would be easy to say he deserves to suffer, but I don't like to see anyone in such agony. After years of spiritual training, it's my nature and first thought to be compassionate, usually. Except that my wounded human self is at war with my higher spiritual self ... and winning big time. Evanya, that better part of me, is nattering inside my head. She's rooting for me to triumph in the end. I hope I can turn things around and do her proud.

"I'm not as smart as Christophe. I watched your last scene with him. The problems you were having with your boss. I was amazed. How you transformed. You were glowing. Shining with confidence.

"I was in awe, how he helped you get there. He knew just what to say and do. Like a psychologist. I don't understand feelings like that ... not well enough to take the risk ... taking a sub or myself into unknown territory." Dillon's childlike voice has dropped to a muffled murmur, speaking in stops and starts, reaching for every word.

"I stick with the scenes I know how to run. The bottoms I play with aren't that complicated either. They don't want much from me other than for me to boss them around. And to hurt them until their endorphins kick in and they get their hit of pleasure. I should have stayed away from you, Erin. Should never have started anything.

"You caught my attention your first night at the club. When Jim stripped you in Purgatory a week later, I saw how scared you were. I knew he had no idea how special the gift was that you gave him. I was angry to see that player's collar on you." *Jesus. I didn't realize. He was the one slapping his bullwhip against his hip.*

"But, when I saw the desire in your eyes, when I was servicing Steffie ... and your tears when you thought I was angry with you ... that was all it took. I had to have you. I wanted to hear you moan again, needed to hear you call me Sir. Needed you on your knees offering me your softness and your sweet submission. Even though I knew right then that you are too good for me, too pure." *I don't know how he can think I'm pure, not with all that I've done.*

His right arm remains trapped between us. His fisted left hand drops from his heart, brushes across my middle, unfurls to cover my right hip entirely, seeking the comfort he desperately needs. I can't give it to him but can't push his hand away. I even take some comfort from the heavy heat and connection between our bodies.

"If you like my softness, why are you so harsh with me? Why were you so rough that night?"

"I told you. I know how much you give and how strong you are. Jim doesn't have a clue. Every time I push you harder, I'm amazed by what you will withstand to please me. My life has been so fucked up the last six months. It feels like everything is being taken from me, and I have no control over it. That night, more than ever, I needed your full surrender. I'm sorry I was a selfish prick.

"When I asked if you wanted to use your safeword, I hoped you would, that I'd finally found your limit. When you didn't, the rush of you wanting to go even further for me was so thrilling. I'm sorry I hesitated when you did say red. I wanted you to change your mind. I needed you to want me no matter what, and I missed your cues."

I wondered every time if he was toying with me, trying to break me for sport. I thought it was an ego trip for him to play with the tender sub and make her cry. And, yes, I still went back for more. *But he said he doesn't want to lose me. He wasn't trying to break me.*

"Is that why you were so angry with me?"

"Angry? Oh, I wasn't angry, baby, I was on fucking fire for you."

It wasn't just a game. He really wanted me. Me! I wish he could have asked for what he needed. I could have been sooo good to him, would have given him anything, done anything for my beautiful bad boy. It's sad that he's hiding under his role of being a bastard. It sounds like he really believes there's something wrong with him. But he's far more perceptive than he gives himself credit for.

My head cuts in and tries again to shut down my compassionate heart. *I. Will. Not. Open my heart to him this easily.*

"Erin, I didn't understand what you were feeling, the dark place I pushed you to. I tried to put myself in your shoes, but Doms don't always understand how vulnerable a sub can feel. I couldn't figure out why you were so mad at me. I knew I had screwed up somehow, but I did stop. I figured we should just be able to talk it out.

"I got a taste of what you were dealing with when those bastards came for me last night. I had no control over what they did to me and to my body. I didn't know how far they would go. I'm supposed to be this big, scary Dom, and I was fucking terrified. It only took a few seconds, long enough for me to disregard your safeword, and I did that to you, didn't I? I took away your control and scared you so bad. And what I've been doing since ..."

A patch of coolness slowly spreads across my chest. Dillon's hot tears are dripping, turning cold before they land on my skin and trickle into my cleavage. If I let it, this could kill me. It rips me apart when I see a man wounded enough to actually cry. He really gets it, really feels my pain. I could forgive him, except for one thing.

"And, yet, you did it to me again tonight."

"Yes." The single word is almost imperceptible. I'm only sure he spoke because of the puff of air on my breast.

"I'm sorry. I snapped," he chokes out. "You wouldn't talk to me. People think I raped you. Snapper came to see me yesterday and reamed me out. I hurt from the beating last night. Then the new guy I hired at work stole one of my clients. Steffie went off on me because she's worried about the cops. Next thing I know, some asshole was handing me a restraining order." That's a heavy enough load for anyone, but I get a sinking feeling that what hit him the hardest, what has broken him, is me not talking to him.

"I had to talk to you. Everything was such a mess. I'd made such a damned mess. And I didn't know what to do. It was wrong. I was wrong." Dillon presses his hand hard into my hip each time he says the word "wrong." He knows it, feels the guilt, the remorse.

"I'm sorry things are hard for you. I really am. But you have to stop harassing me, Dillon. You can't keep making things worse, for both of us. You have to give me space. I want to do the right thing. And I wish I could just talk it out with you right now, but I can't. I need to be able to figure things out without you or anyone else breathing down my back. Please leave me alone while I try to figure out what the right thing is.

"I know that will make you feel like you have no control. You're going to have to deal with that. I would never deliberately hurt someone else, especially not you. Unless you keep pushing and back me into a corner. Do you understand?"

Dillon takes a long pause before he says, "I do." He lifts his head and looks me in the eye. "I *do*. I'll respect that. I respect you, Erin." That sentiment hits my heart. *Damn.* I don't want to let him in there again. God, the way he's looking at me, I wish I could just throw my arms around the back of his neck and kiss him with everything I've got. The problem is that what I've got right now isn't much.

"I'll take you home. I'm sorry for the whole kidnapping thing, but thank you for listening. It's more than I deserve. I won't bother you again. I promise. I'll wait, and I'll accept whatever you decide I have coming to me." I stare into Dillon's deep, blue eyes and see the truth swirling around with his pain. He means what he says. Still, I can't be with him anymore—both of our emotions are too raw for me to handle—and I insist on taking a cab. I'm shivering cold in my skimpy jogging clothes. Dillon gives me a pair of black sweats that I have to roll up at the waist and a gray hoodie that hangs on me like a sack.

We stand together on his front porch, not touching, neither of us saying a word. I make him go inside when the cab pulls up. I can't have him watch me walk away while he's thinking how much he's hurt me. Not when I'm thinking about how much I've hurt him, and how I'm not yet ready to make it right even though I know I should. He's put his fate in my hands. Based on my recent actions, that might not be a smart thing for him to do. I know I'm screwed in the head; I just wish I knew why and what to do about it.

< ♂ + ♀ >

I'm home; I'm safe; and I can't stop crying. My body is not just trembling, it's vibrating. My teeth click together, and I might just bite my tongue off if I'm not careful. My body shuts down all of a sudden and tightens up.

I'm hurtling toward full-blown meltdown. Fetal position, thumb-sucking, bed-wetting. *Dammit.* I was just starting to feel like myself again. *Why did Dillon have to push me back over the edge?* I can't handle this on my own. Without even thinking, I pluck Jerry's card out from under the sunflower magnet on my fridge.

"Jerry. It's Erin Piper. Something ..." I can't get the words out. Shock squeezes my throat closed. I suck hard for every breath. I'm shaking so bad now that I can hardly hold the phone in my hand.

"Are you hurt? Should I call an ambulance?" I assure him I'm physically fine. "I'm there in 15 minutes. Hang on, Erin." He doesn't give me time to protest.

All I can do is wait, nearly catatonic. It seems like only 30 seconds later that a loud pounding on my door startles me. I have to mentally command my muscles to move. I peek through the living room window to be sure it's Jerry. I'm both relieved and dejected. I hate that I have to ask for help. and I'm glad that there's one man willing to step up and take charge of me when I need him to.

One quick look at me and Jerry knows I'm in rough shape. He wraps his arms around me. They *are* perfect for holding me. I didn't want to find that out this way. Violent shockwaves rock me again; my knees buckle. Jerry scoops me up and carries me to the couch.

"I've got you, baby girl. I've got you." *I've got you.* Three simple words with profound meaning. They start to seep into the cracks in my weary soul and fill me up.

"I'm sorry, so sorry." My words don't come out clearly. It sounds like I'm babbling under water. I am; I'm drowning in my own tears.

"It's alright, baby. You're alright. Tell me what you're sorry for, Erin." He strokes my cheeks with a feather-light touch and combs his fingers through my hair. I lean into his fingers and rub my head along him, just like a kitten begging for attention. Jerry cuddles me up in his lap. The soothing warmth radiating off him melts me.

"I shouldn't have called this late. I know I should be stronger. I just didn't know what to do. I'm sorry."

"I told you to call anytime, remember? I'm glad you did, priss. Why don't you tell me what happened?" He grips my shoulder and gives me a little squeeze of encouragement. If Jerry wasn't lending me his strength and commanding me, I wouldn't be able to talk about my latest terror. I have to give the man credit for being patient and not flipping out as I unravel the story in fits and starts. If the tables were turned, I wouldn't be as restrained listening to what happened. *Ooo, restrained. Freudian slip? Damn, I'm sick.*

He holds me upright, one hand on my back supporting me, the other across my knees comforting me. I am more grounded in his arms, more in control of myself, no longer shattered, merely fractured. The more I talk, the more I am able to let go of the fear. I can't even look him in the eye when I begin. By the time I finish, I have turned to face him, no more shaking and no more tears.

Jerry relaxes back on the couch, pulling me into a full embrace. There's nothing friendly about the gesture; it is a lover's embrace.

It's inappropriate behavior for an officer of the law. Yet, his arms clasping me tight feel so right. Wrapped in his warmth, I let go.

"I know how powerless you felt before, priss. How are you handling this?" That sexy voice sluices over me, flushing away the last bit of tension in my body. Except for the sexual tension slowly amping up in the most sensitive parts of me. I stretch out like a cat under a sunbeam and drag myself all over him, chest to chest.

"I'm doing better now, thanks to your intimate interviewing technique. Do all victims you question get this up-close-and-personal attention?" I continue to get up close and personal with him, rubbing more body parts of mine against more body parts of his in tiny, incremental movements. I think I'm being subtle and sly.

A rumbling chuckle precedes a quick swat on my behind. "Naughty girl." His left hand remains where it lands. *Ohmygod! What am I doing?* I try to wriggle away, but Jerry clutches me to his chest with his right arm. His left hand slides around in slow, sensual circles. *Oh, please don't stop that.* "Talk to me, baby girl."

"I think I was in shock when you arrived. I'm much better now. I was really scared and incredibly angry when I woke up at Dillon's. He did himself a big favor when he untied me. If he had kept me prisoner while he talked to me, I wouldn't have listened to a word. Now that we've talked, I'm not as scared of him." *And I know it's not all his fault.* Time and distance from him eases the threat level back down. And Evanya has been making progress as she chatters away in my head. Being in Jerry's arms doesn't hurt either.

"Don't let him off the hook so easily. He crossed too many lines and broke too many laws. He violated the restraining order, and then he committed a felony. He really kidnapped you; that wasn't roleplaying. This is serious. Don't let him talk his way out of it."

"Do you really think I'm that much of a pushover?" Hurt grips my heart, and I strain to break out of his arms.

"Shhh. Of course, I don't. Relax, pretty girl. I think you're incredibly strong. I just mean that you sound so ... settled." He flattens me against him, his hand pressing my head against the solidness of his chest and the softness of his steel gray, brushed cotton sweater. His heart drums out a loud and steady beat that is music to my ears. I inhale his cologne. That spicy scent with the citrus top notes stirs up my carnal instincts.

"I'm far from settled. I'm just not freaking out anymore. I walked out of his house on my own two feet, unharmed. That's a big win right there. I listened to him and held my own. That's win number two. But just because I have a little more understanding about what drove him, it doesn't mean that I am anywhere close to forgiveness." I sigh, trying to push back tears that are threatening again.

"I have to be honest about my part in all this. I don't know what I'm going to do, but it doesn't involve Dillon going to jail.

"My feelings are all muddled up. I need time to untangle what the three of them have done, and Steffie, and what I've done as well. Whatever course I take has to be right for me."

"Good girl. I'm going to call in a forensic team to dust for his fingerprints, in case you change your mind. I'll say you had a suspected break and enter. If you want, those prints can show he broke the restraining order, and we can bring him in for that."

"Okay, but it won't be necessary." I've made up my mind, at least about that. It feels good, and Evanya approves.

I snuggle in closer and snake a hand up to the nape of Jerry's neck. My happy fingers dance along the edge of his hairline. I smirk ever so slightly when I hear his breath catch. Jerry brushes his lips against the top of my head in a light kiss. If I wasn't dealing with the most traumatic experience of my life other than my parents' deaths, this would be perfection.

"No big decisions tonight, Erin. We'll get the fingerprints, and you'll have options. Just stay here in my arms for a while longer before I make the call."

I love how he's being supportive but isn't trying to push me into anything. Although, there is one way I would love to have him push me or, rather, push into me. His in-control attitude has me wishing he would take control of my body and just plain take me.

I want him to take me hard, to hammer away all the hurt, to show me who's in charge. I can't deny that when he put his hand on my shoulder yesterday morning I didn't even think about submitting to him. There was no need. I could kneel at this man's feet and be completely happy. I only fought surrendering because he caught me by surprise while I was trying hard to be self-reliant.

We lay together, just petting each other. I stroke all over the side of Jerry's head and neck with my nose and chin. His rough stubble stings. I close my eyes and listen to his even breathing and strong heartbeat. I can't stop purring like a contented kitten.

I almost drift off to sleep, but I don't want to miss a second of being in Jerry's arms. The sexual energy has dissipated, replaced with companionable closeness. *This is where I'm meant to be.* It's an utterly ridiculous statement and feels shockingly true.

$$< \male + \female >$$

It's already after midnight and the forensic team is just walking out the door. I need sleep, but there's one more thing I have to talk to Jerry about before he leaves. He bundles me in his arms as soon as the door shuts. He freezes when I say, "I talked to Christophe last night ..." Jerry clears his throat but doesn't say a word.

"He was as unhappy to hear your name as you were to hear his. What's the story with you two?" *This is a test, Jerry, a big test.* He steps away from me but tangles his fingers with mine, pulling me onto the couch beside him. He takes a long pause to collect himself.

"I was a member at DYKKC. Actually, one of the founding members. So, yes, if you're wondering, I know all these characters you've been dealing with. Three years ago, I brought a woman that I had been dating for a couple of months to one of the theme nights. She was willing to explore, and I thought we had a great time. Toward the end of our scene, I noticed Ronan standing in the corner. His eyes were glued to her, to her ass to be precise.

"When we went back a week later, I made the mistake of leaving her alone in Night Moves for two minutes while I went to the men's room. He was talking to her when I returned. A Dom doesn't address another's sub without permission. He smiled at me and left right away, but I watched her watch him as he walked off.

"I wasn't very smart. Before we left, I told him to stay away from her because she was important to me. He saw it as a challenge.

"Three weeks later, my girl and I had another good night at the club, and I thought things were cool between us. I dropped in for a meeting with the DMs a few days later and found him doing a scene with her. I don't know how or when he got to her, but he did. He just gave me a smile and a nod when he saw me and kept right on fucking her. I walked up and whispered in her ear, 'We're done.' And she let him keep right on fucking her."

I can tell by the way his voice tightened up that he still has an emotional charge on this. I am very impressed that he manned up and shared such detail, especially after Christophe's one-liner. "Was she important to you?"

"I don't know. She could have been, but he saw to it that it never happened. I saw them together again on the weekend. A week later, he was already done with her. She wanted to come back to me, but the damage was done. I couldn't trust her or him. He's a user, Erin."

"Thanks for telling me the truth, Jerry. All Christophe said was that it was about a girl. I'm sorry that happened."

"It was about a month later that I quit." His voice is thick with emotion; I have no idea what he's feeling beyond deep pain.

"It must have been a bad situation for you to quit DYKKC. I know what it's like to be cut off from the community. I've only been into this for six months, and I just got kicked out yesterday, but already I feel the loss knowing I can't go back. It must have been like losing your family."

There's an awkward silence between us before he says, "There was a bit more to it than that for me ... but you haven't lost everything. You'll still have your lawyer friend and Ronan."

"No, I'm done with them. I'm pissed at both of them for sticking their noses into this mess and causing me even more grief with both Steffie and Dillon. I know you warned me about Christophe, but I could never have imagined he would do anything as vile as what he did to Dillon. Dom or not, he's a doctor, for Christ's sake. He's supposed to do no harm. I can't trust him anymore. Trust is important to me, too, Jerry.

"As soon as you leave, I'm texting them to stay out of my life. I'm exhausted from all their Dom drama. It's going to take time to get my head straight and heal. I don't think I want to find another club. I might walk away from the whole scene altogether."

Jerry's eyes are wide and bright. Again, I can't tell what he's thinking, and he doesn't say anything. Just looking at him, trying to figure him out, a restless heat stirs in me again. I really want to know him, in the biblical sense. My claws come out, and I knead my paws along his chest and belly. This mischievous instinct to groom him, to lick his luscious body all over, kicks in.

My tongue just can't help itself. It slips between my lips and takes a quick, short swipe along the outer edge of his ear. Jerry stiffens but doesn't say anything. My tongue ventures further and licks his earlobe. I give just one sneaky suck. Jerry's breathing deepens, and his chest rises higher and falls further, but I'm not meeting any resistance. My tongue, which clearly has a mind of its own—because I am brain dead at this point—grows even bolder.

I slide broad, long strokes along that sensitive junction and the area surrounding where his ear, jaw and neck converge. Jerry moans softly. The rest of my body decides to get in on the action and wiggles around on him again, only not as subtly this time. As my tongue continues to lick, my pelvis grinds against his crotch. I can feel that he's got a hefty load of steel in his pants.

"Jesus, Erin." *Ohmygod! What the 'f' am I doing?* I leap off Jerry and off the couch.

"Oh, God. I'm sorry. So sorry. Forgive me. I shouldn't have ..."

Jerry grabs me and pulls me back into his lap. "Shhh. It's okay, Erin. There's nothing to be sorry for. You just surprised me."

"But I am sorry. You've been nothing but nice to me. You've given me support and comfort. And, here I am, throwing myself at you like a hussy, taking advantage of your kindness." I'm beyond embarrassed; I'm deeply disturbed by my wanton behavior.

I'm not prepared for Jerry's howling laughter. "You're taking advantage of me?" He laughs again, really loud. Walking-through-the-bar-with-your-skirt-in-your-pantyhose level of disgrace burns a hole in my gut.

"Oh, priss. Here I thought I was taking advantage of you. You're too precious." Add toilet-paper-stuck-to-my-shoe humiliation.

Jerry places a lingering kiss on my cheek before he wraps me back up. "No apologies. It's good having you in my arms. We both feel it. It's late, and tonight is not the best time to explore this." He pushes his right index finger against my trembling lip and adds, "But we will, baby girl." Then he kisses my forehead. His words sound like both a promise and a threat. Everything inside me clenches.

He stretches his long body and pulls us both off the couch. "I better go. I've got an early start in the morning. How about you? Are you going to work?"

"Yeah, I can't afford to lose another day over this bullshit. What? Don't look at me like that. I'll be fine. I really appreciate you coming tonight. Thanks for all your help and for the company. You've been great. Sleep well." *Great, I'm jabbering like a simpleton.* I feel so awkward after acting like a horny cat.

Jerry touches my cheek and flashes me a smile that is colored with what looks to me like sadness. I can't even begin to imagine what that's all about. All he says is a simple "good night." I close the door behind him and slump against it. My teeth chatter like winter has already set in. The cold is just the absence of Jerry.

When I turn around, I'm confronted by the mess. Black fingerprinting dust is smeared all over the front entryway, even into the kitchen and on every doorknob down the hall. It seems a fitting metaphor for the rest of my life right now. All because of a jackass named Dillon, and that beast named Christophe. And a jerk named Jim, and the bitch named Steffie. *What a screwed up menagerie.*

I'm bone weary, completely sapped of the energy to do anything to make myself feel better. I leave the mess and go straight to bed. I don't even chant with Deva Premal. *I'll live to fight another day.* Tonight, I just want to wallow in my sorrow. *You're such a frigging Drama Queen.*

The last thing I do before I go to sleep is send two almost identical texts. 'Bastard. U couldn't respect me & had to be a hard ass. U have no idea what u cost me. Don't ever contact me again.' The first one goes to Jim for his screw-ups with Dillon and Steffie. In the text to Christophe, I add, 'Can't forgive what u did to Dillon. U r dead to me.' I turn off my phone, knowing I've taken the coward's way out. I pull my knees up to my chin and slip into the oblivion of dreamless sleep that is the hallmark of absolute exhaustion.

< ♂ + ♀ >

Chapter Nine – Atonement

Saturday Morning, September 22

I take full advantage of a bright Saturday morning and let myself move at an unhurried pace. Calmness, tranquility and stillness are on my agenda for today. I've lost my center, have traveled light years away from it, and really need a break so that I can find it. I can't take much more of this being at odds with the world.

Before I can do any meditating or journaling, I'm gripped by a gnawing hunger that needs attention. I didn't feel much like eating last night after getting home from a miserable day at work. I put on the kettle for tea while I cook myself a scrumptious omelet for a very late breakfast. I stuff it with cream cheese, green onions and a few juicy shrimp. Some leftover asparagus tips would have been the perfect addition. Instead, a light sprinkling of chopped tarragon picked fresh from my herb garden behind the garage completes the filling and satisfying dish. I think I'll have to be content with simple pleasures like this for the foreseeable future.

I think longingly of my latest creation hanging in my workroom closet but decide against putting it on. That would be a simple pleasure, but today is not the special occasion I'm saving it for. It looks like it could be a while before there will be any special days if yesterday's events are an indication of the trajectory my life is on.

A barrage of texts from both Jim and Christophe started dinging the moment I powered up my phone. I deleted them all. Jim, to my dismay, showed up at the law school library and caused a minor scene, ranting on about not understanding why I wouldn't see him and accusing me of being ungrateful. That was the most worked up I had seen Jim get about anything, but I couldn't explain with an audience. It could get very uncomfortable for me at work because he comes in a couple of times a week to do research. I had to put my staff on notice to intercept him and keep him away from me.

As bad as that whole spectacle was, the worst came at noon, and I was pretty much a zombie after that. The bizarre scene plays out in my mind like a B movie. I flop over in my chair; my forehead bangs smartly on the kitchen table. *I'm such a trusting fool.*

$$< \male + \female >$$

Jerry surprised me at the library with an invitation to lunch. We walked to Mercury Diner just off campus. I warmed to his touch as he guided me along the sidewalk. Jerry kept the conversation light by asking me about the law school and my job. We arrived at the diner just before the lunch crush began and were seated at the last booth by the sunny, front window. After ordering our burgers, Jerry reached across the table and brushed one thumb across my cheek. My shoulders rolled in an involuntary twisting shake. It was one of those woo-woo things, a subtle nudge from the universe telling me to pay attention.

"You look beautiful today, Erin, but tired. I'm sorry I kept you up so late last night. I bet you didn't get much sleep, did you?" A tender smile curled at the corners of his mouth, and his head dipped slightly. If I had let my imagination run away with me, I could easily have thought he was going to kiss me, but my imagination is usually better than reality. His plump lips remained on his side of the table.

I told him my fatigue was frazzled nerves from Jim's outburst. "Jim? Not Jim Burton?" When I said he was the one, Jerry fell against his seat back, forcing the air out of his lungs. He propped his elbow on the melamine table top and lowered his head so that he could squeeze the bridge of his nose between his index finger and thumb. The sun streaming through the big, plate glass window bounced off his silky hair. It looked like he was under a spotlight, which was appropriate because the whole nose-tweaking thing seemed like a diva kind of move.

"Geez, Erin. You do know how to pick 'em, don't you? First, you get into a dangerous situation with an animal like Dillon. Then you put your trust in a hound dog like Christophe. Now you're telling me your other friend is Jim Burton, a phony if I ever met one."

I was gobsmacked by his disdain. "What are you talking about?"

"The Squire is no Dom. He's a playboy who likes to get a little edgy and play the role, but he doesn't know the first thing about being a real Dominant. You couldn't have picked three more unsuitable characters to introduce you to the lifestyle. You really are naïve, aren't you, priss? No wonder you're in so much trouble."

My knuckles turned white as I gripped the table. I had to restrain myself from ripping his tongue out. I was down to my last nerve, and he had just pinched it. Until my scene with Dillon and the fallout from it had brought out the worst in all of us, those three men had been very good to me, better than anyone I had dated in the vanilla world. Jerry was wrong; there is an infinite number of "unsuitable characters" who could have taken advantage of my vulnerability and abused me. It's too easy for a sub to end up with a woman hater who uses the title of Dom as an excuse to be cruel.

I have not a shred of doubt that Dillon, Christophe or Jim would never purposely hurt me. Some of the things they've done may be bad, but they are good men. It's one thing for me to complain about my own friends, but I couldn't let the arrogant ass whine about them. And I certainly couldn't let him insult my intelligence.

Jerry started to speak again, but I thrust my palm toward his face to shut him up. I breathed in deep and rapid pants in and out of my nostrils until I found my calm center. Well, at least, a modicum of temperance. *Do all men have a 'Stupid' switch that flips on when you are the least prepared for it?* I was disillusioned by this side of his personality, and it was an immediate deal breaker because I was running at a near zero tolerance level for bullshit and bullies.

I slapped my palms on the table, gave Jerry a single, firm nod, and pushed my way out of the booth. I spun on my heels and took a step toward the door. Jerry's command was low and menacing. "Sit down, Erin. Where do you think you're going?"

His imperious tone raised my hackles, and I reconsidered walking away without an explanation. I whipped back around and glowered coldly at Jerry before easing back into the booth. I leaned forward and answered his question, spitting the words out ever so slightly louder than a whisper.

"First off, I will not talk to you about Dillon again unless I'm speaking to your badge and your partner is present. Case closed. Secondly, I get that you have a bias against Christophe, but, except for what he did to Dillon, he was good to me. Thirdly, Jim is the one who introduced me to DYKKC. I owe him a debt for that.

"I'm not the babe in the woods that you seem to think I am. I know exactly who Jim is, and, when I scene with him, it's for something specific that only he can give me. I never would have had the courage to join the club and explore if it wasn't for him. I don't want to hear another disparaging word about any of my friends. I may be on the outs with all of them right now, but I'll likely forgive them, at least Jim and Dillon anyway.

"Now, as for what you just had to say about me, I can't begin to tell you how disappointed I am. My whole world has been ripped apart in a matter of days. I've been barely keeping my head above water, judged or betrayed on almost every front. The last thing I need is your condescending criticism while I'm trying hard to remember that I'm a good person and deserve to be treated better than I have been.

"I would expect such an insensitive attitude from your cold-hearted partner. I could deal with her telling me that everything that happened to me was *all my fault*. But you, after you supported me and held me last night, I believed you were on my side. I hoped maybe we could be friends, maybe something more than friends, but you've just kicked my sorry ass back into the real world and proved to me that, indeed, the only person I can count on is me.

"Quiet, Jerry. You've said more than enough already." He foolishly tried to get a word in while I was on a roll. "I'm glad I found out who you are quickly. It'll save me a lot of heartache later on. You're no different than the three you just ridiculed. I'm done with you, with all of you, and the whole BDSM scene. I can't take this chest-thumping crap anymore, when a man thinks he is right and has life all figured out just because he has a penis."

I slid out of the booth with a good deal of grace, but Jerry grabbed my wrist. I leaned in close and barked into his ear. "If you follow me out of here, I'll make sure you'll wish you hadn't. No one is ever going to mess with me again." He wisely did not come after me.

$$< \male + \female >$$

I am sooo over men, especially domineering men. Regardless of whether I'll forgive my three Tops and be friends again, they let me down and hurt me. And now Jerry, too, before anything even got started between us. God, it stings how quickly that all blew apart. I didn't even get a kiss out of him, let alone have any of my silly, schoolgirl fantasies fulfilled.

Someone with as much meditation training as I have should be able to diffuse these emotional outbursts better than I've been doing. Of course, I've been meditating a lot less since I joined DYKKC. I've been avoiding looking too closely at what I've become, what I've been doing. I hate that my reactions are so automatic and defensive. It's a childish way to behave.

Some days, living in my childhood home without my parents sits heavily in my heart. Their absence is an acute ache, especially right now. I feel like an abandoned orphan and want my mom or my dad to hug me up and tell me that everything is going to be okay. Not that I could ever tell them why I hurt so much. I have to remind myself that I'm strong and can do anything when I know what I want. What I *don't* want is any more of this drama.

Maybe I had been on a short fuse with Jerry, but his tone lit a fire under my ass. I couldn't help but explode because, to be honest, he's right. I am naïve. I can hunt down an obscure legal precedent in minutes, but I hadn't known how to find my own G-spot until Jim found it. I can choose the best employee for my team with a few, insightful questions, but I've had the worst luck choosing men. I didn't like Jerry rubbing my nose in my sexual inexperience, but I have a ton of experience protecting my heart. Safe is what I want.

Why did I ever think I could handle these strong Alpha males? Maybe I should just join an ashram.

"Grrr! Enough wallowing." I push up off the table and shove my chair back. I need to get out of here before the walls close in on me. There won't be too many beautiful days like today before the snow starts to fly. It's the perfect excuse to get out of town and put some distance between me and all this crap.

I toss a few things into an overnight bag and then search for the phone number of the guy who rents cabins on the lake. It's late in the season, and the added bonus of privacy along with lots of fresh air, warm sunshine, a peaceful lake, sweet-smelling pine trees, a cozy log cabin, and an outdoor fire pit really makes me smile. That's my idea of a perfect getaway. The simple pleasures of life.

My doorbell rings just as I'm about to make the call. My stomach drops into my shoes. Before I even have any idea who's on my front porch, I wish I was already gone. There is an ominous, black pickup truck at the end of my driveway that I don't recognize. I angle my sight line through the blinds to see who's leaning on the bell.

"Erin, let me in." My brain concedes there's no point in trying to shut him out. From my body's reaction to seeing Jerry on the other side of my screen door, I would be fighting a losing battle against my hormones.

He fills the door frame as he sweeps in, blocking out the sun and turning my little foyer as dark as twilight. Somehow, as he maneuvers us around to let me close the door, I end up plastered against the cool wood, perfectly centered in the frame. He stands three feet from me, so it's not his body that flattens me against the door. It's his aura, his potent male energy. I'm shaking like a timid mouse facing the sharp teeth of a devouring predator.

Jerry sees my overnight bag and asks if I was going somewhere. I'm only a little bit ashamed that I can't muzzle my inner bitch.

"That's a brilliant deduction, Detective. Yes, I was going to the lake because, for the second weekend in a row, I feel the need to escape from overbearing little boys pretending they are grownups."

My guess at the expression on Jerry's face would be frustration. He huffs out a big breath and hangs his head. He takes another few breaths, either to think of what to say to another bratty outburst I can't suppress, or to buy himself time to calm down before plowing on with whatever his agenda is. I'm not going to apologize.

Jerry's head glides up and locks into place; our eyes are level. "I find myself in treacherous waters with you, Erin. As a public servant, it's my job to protect you and help you in any way I can. I take that responsibility seriously. What's dangerous, what's kept me awake every night since we met, is how I feel when I look at you.

"You're so beautiful and precious. My protective instincts go haywire with how much I want to keep you safe. I lost control yesterday; you make me lose control. I ... *never* ... lose ... control." He steps closer, looming over me as he barks out the last sentence. My nips prickle from the charge of male sex that sparks from him. He sounds bewildered, like he can't believe his reaction to me. What I can't believe are three words. *Beautiful and precious?*

"I know you're angry with Christophe and Jim and now with me, but I understand them. I may envy their connection to you, but I feel their need to make this all go away for you. I let what I know about those three get in the way of what I know about you. You can take care of yourself; you're capable of doing what needs to be done. That doesn't stop me from wanting to do it for you anyway, from shielding you from more hurt." Yeah, those words change everything. *Did he say that he envies Christophe and Jim?*

I'm frozen like a marble statue, no heat in my skin, no flexibility in my joints until Jerry lays a noticeably shaky palm on my shoulder. His touch mobilizes me. I loosen up, rising on my toes, pressing myself into his hand. There is no process to the conclusion I arrive at; I just know instantly that I need Jerry to touch me, everywhere.

"My words were careless and hurtful. I acted like an ass. Please, forgive me, Erin." His need and vulnerability are etched in the hard lines on his tight face. His apology is sincere. When I say yes, relief erases every crease. A broad smile carves new, sexy lines around his tempting lips. I lick mine and anticipate pressing them against his.

I'm only marginally disappointed when he envelopes me in a crushing embrace instead. He holds me for long minutes—the only movement is the in and out of our breath—until the world feels like it's spinning in the right direction again.

It's not until this moment, when it feels like the laws of physics have corrected themselves, that I realize how off kilter I've been since I walked away from him. I knew something was wrong in the cosmic order, and I thought it was Jerry and how he insulted me. That wasn't it. It was me and how easily I walked away from him. I guess that's what the universe was warning me about with that nudge at the diner. I almost paid a heavy price for my pride. *Thank God he came back. Imagine that, a Dom who doesn't back down.*

Jerry kisses the top of my head and speaks softly into my hair. "Thank you. Come with me, priss. I have something I want to talk to you about." He weaves his thick fingers between mine and clasps my hand tight as if he never intends to let go. At least, that's what a giddy voice inside my head is begging for.

$< ♂ + ♀ >$

Chapter Ten – Commandments

Saturday Afternoon, September 22

I tag along behind him as Jerry leads me to the kitchen table and pulls out a chair for me, turning it at a right angle to the table edge. When I sit, he drags a chair for himself in front of mine. The shudder of the rubber feet scraping across the floor sends a corresponding shudder through my bones.

The laws of physics haven't quite resumed normal operation because the time-space continuum warps. In an unblinking stare, I watch as, in slow motion, Jerry folds his long, hard body and settles his yummy ass on the seat cushion. He positions himself with his legs spread wide. Then he grabs the edges of my chair and hauls me up until my knees are trapped against the front of his chair.

In this time rift, my breathing has stalled at the top of an inhale. My lungs start to burn, needing release and intake of oxygen. The shock of Jerry's heavy hands pressing on my knees triggers the vigorous expulsion of stale breath and gasping for fresh air. I see Jerry's lips part and his tongue move as he speaks.

I have time to formulate the thought that, based on his masterful arrangement of my entrapment, he either needs me close to him for what he is about to say, or he thinks it's going to make me want to run. *Oh God, maybe I should be scared.* Then O_2 molecules begin again to circulate in my brain, and the time warp smooths out.

"I have a proposal I'd like to make." *Damn.* "I think I have a way for both of us to get what we want." *Ohmygod.* "I want to protect you, Erin, take care of you, and help you get through this difficult time." *Shit.* "And you've cut yourself off from the BDSM community with no way to get your needs met." *Hell!*

"Are you listening, priss?" I must have a vacant look on my face because Jerry grips my chin and tugs. Oh, I don't like that he's calling me "priss," not anymore—even if he is using his sexy, melt-my-insides voice—but I nod my head. I'm not capable of coherent speech. My balled-up hands rest on my thighs at my hips. I dig in hard to try to anchor myself. I can't afford to let my mind spin out of control; regardless, it begins to whirl as he reveals his proposal.

"Good girl." *Here we go.* "I'm offering my services to be your Dom while you heal and try to regain some sense of safety and normalcy." *Services, like he's some kind of man whore.* "We'll sign a contract for a specific period of time." *Business-like, just like when I hire a temp.* "We'll clearly define the responsibilities we'll each have, and what limits we have so there will be no misunderstanding." *Sounds civilized.* "For the duration of our contract, I will be your wise Master and you will be my obedient slave." *Sounds barbaric.*

"Do you consent? Say something, priss." *I'm mute.* I could probably speak if I could unglue my tightly pressed lips. However, if I do pry them loose, the questions swirling in my brain would fly out faster than the speed of sound. And lost in the midst of all those crazy thoughts would be the one word I want to say. *Yes.* I already want to call him Sir, *have* already called him Sir, but I have to force myself to hold my ground throughout this.

"Jerry, before I say anything about your proposal, I have to be honest with you about how much I detest the name priss. It's what everyone at DYKKC calls me, except for Jim., and I don't want to be reminded of that place. It's also insulting in its inaccuracy." I am simultaneously steadied and tipped off balance by both of Jerry's hands bracing my knees again.

"I see. What does he call you, and why?" I tell him the name and say that it's a perfect way to describe our relationship.

"I told you I scene with Jim because he gives me something the others don't. Fun. No complicated emotions or mindfucking games. Taking me to my limits of sensation but not really stretching them. I can always relax and escape with Jim. Our sessions usually ended because neither of us could stop laughing." Jerry's face is stony still and void of any clues to his thoughts or emotions.

"Well, I won't be calling you playmate, for obvious reasons. But what we will share is deeper than a fun romp. Until I come up with a suitable name, I'll call you Erin or sub or slave as I see fit. Now, what about the contract?" Jerry betrays a little hint of hope with that question and something else he's holding back.

"I am … intrigued. Before I put my trust in you and agree to something as serious as binding us together by contract, I need a clearer picture of how you see the Master/slave relationship. I know it's different for everyone. I want to understand you and what you'll demand of me." No matter how cool and sophisticated I try to be about this, the raised pitch and tremor of my words destroy the image I want to project. The crazy dance my hands are doing on my thighs also gives me away.

Jerry slides his hands from my knees and drapes them over my jittery hands. He lifts both of them, pries the fists open, and kisses each palm in turn. That does nothing to calm my nerves, especially when he scoots forward to the edge of his chair. His crotch is snugged tight up against my knees, and the heat wafting from his chest is as oppressive as if that part of his anatomy was also huddled against me. Cool is a long-abandoned pipe dream. Jerry does not relinquish possession of my hands when he continues. *Possession. Will he want to collar me? Will he be the one I let do it?*

"For the length of our contract, you will be under my exclusive protection and care. I ask you to place your trust in me, bend to my authority, and allow me to make certain decisions for you. And we'll negotiate scenes to help you work through your recent ordeals."

Jerry's tone is matter of fact until he says, "You need someone on your side who has your best interests at heart." He lands a butterfly kiss on the tip of my nose. My nose says yes. So do my eyes, ears, cheeks, chin, throat, shoulders, breasts and every other body part down to the tips of my toes. Except for my lips. I can't make that word pass them yet.

The kind of scene he's talking about sounds like something that Master Ronan would have done for me if he was here, and if I would have been able to let him do it. Jerry fades from my awareness for a moment as waves of regret push and pull at my heart.

I owe Christophe a lot for the sessions that opened me up, for the raw emotion we shared. I truly miss him, and it hurts that I've had to cut him out of my life. I shutter my misty eyes to keep Jerry from seeing my tears and my love for another man. And how deeply his betrayal has cut me.

"In all other interactions between us, you will unconditionally follow my lead and guidance without hesitation; you will obey my commands respectfully and without question. You will trust me to do what's best for your healing and your happiness."

Jerry's authoritative tone wrestles my attention back. *Do I really want to give someone this level of control over me?* I'm not sure. The trouble is that I can't ignore the pleasurable, slippery feeling between my thighs. I waggle my butt, pushing it in a circular motion into the seat cushion; I'm not sure whether I'm trying to relieve or fan the flames of desire licking at my swollen labia and twitchy clit. Jerry's open palms slap down soundly on my thighs, making me gasp in alarm and from a little bit of pain.

"Sit still, Erin. Are you paying attention? Understand that there will be consequences for disobeying me, even partially." I swallow hard, but my mouth is as dry as soda crackers. All my fluids have apparently relocated south. As does my blood when a smug smirk crawls across Jerry's lips.

He is obviously aware of how turned on I am right now. I'm guessing that he's guessing that he won't have to press too hard at the negotiating table to get what he wants, whatever that is. He hasn't said.

"Yes, Jerry. I get healing, happiness, and having my needs met. That sounds incredible, but it seems pretty one-sided in my favor. It doesn't sound like I'd be much of a slave. What do you get out of this arrangement?" I'm not trying to be a smartass. I really want to make sure this works for Jerry in a way that I can not only agree to but willingly participate in.

"I will have you under my exclusive command, protection and care. Knowing that you're safe is something I want, and I only trust myself to do it. Knowing that you trust me and will obey me is important to me."

His voice softens, becomes wistful. "It's been a long time since a woman has had that kind of faith in me." Jerry drags his fingertips along the edges of my jawbones, first one and then the other. "Your words stung yesterday when you said you were disappointed in me and that you could only rely on yourself. It was hard to watch you walk away. I want you to learn that you can count on me."

Those are not hollow words. The strain in his normally brilliant eyes is evident. Anxiety rolls off him in waves. His genuine hurt and frankness catches me off guard and slams into my gut. It resonates, and I feel it as deeply as he does. I can't imagine what it is costing a proud Dom like him to be open and forthright with me. I appreciate that he's not hiding or playing games. I believe him, but I'm still baffled as to why it matters to him in the first place, why my opinion of him and my trust would be important.

"It hurt me, too, to walk away from you." It's my turn to deliver a butterfly kiss to his nose. Just when I think we're getting into sappy territory, the kind booby-trapped with emotional quicksand, Jerry flips everything around.

"And sex ... hot, kinky, dirty sex. I get that, too, and lots of it. Whenever I demand it and however I want it. That will be the first clause in our contract." We both fall apart into fits of hearty, lusty laughter. Our bodies jiggle and wiggle together in a way that is impossible to ignore. Belly laughs spread and connect chest against breasts, knees tight to crotch, nose beside nose, forehead touching forehead. Then lips slide along lips, tongue dances with tongue.

Our first kiss. All the frustration, temptation and passion that has been building in me floods out of me and flows into him. I feel the same wash of need, desire and lust spill out of Jerry and rush into me. We delve into each other, testing, tasting, teasing. Nothing has ever felt as good as the softness of his lips pressed against mine, until they become hard and demanding. *God, that's so much better.* He is so hungry and eats my mouth voraciously while his fingers clutch and dig into my shoulders. Every cell in my body sings, filling my soul with music as beautiful as an aria sung by an angelic choir. I have never been moved more by a kiss.

Jerry slides one hand up to tangle in my hair at the nape of my neck and the other along the slope of my left jaw. He directs our kiss, guiding my head as fluidly as if it were a piece of cork bobbing in a goblet of sweet wine, moving me about so that his tongue can explore every surface and pocket of my mouth. He stuffs his thick tongue down my throat. I could accuse him of being as clumsy as a teenager, except I know his movements are purposeful. He's raiding, looting, taking everything he can get. I give myself over unreservedly, no control, only capitulation. I follow where Jerry is leading us, instinctively, intuitively, innocently.

Our bodies melt into each other, chests pressing, limbs tangling, and hands grappling. Jerry revs me into overdrive as he pushes back to free my trapped legs, slides his hands under my butt, and hauls me up onto his lap. We can't get any closer to each other unless we remove the barrier of our clothing. *Holy hell, this is HOT!* Literally. I'm sweating because the bonfire under my butt—fueled by highly flammable hormones—is burning me to a crisp.

Sign me up, mister. Master. A good, strong man to depend on, protection and caring, therapy sessions with fringe benefits, giving my respect, trust and obedience to a man who not only deserves it but craves it, and lots of hot, kinky, dirty sex. And, I hope, thousands more kisses like this. I'm not sure I'll survive the sex if just his kisses are this devastating, but I've never had a better offer.

I'll take the risk. Those are all things that I want right now, need as much as I need air. And I really *need* air right now. Mine is stolen from me. Jerry drags it right out of my lungs as he breathes me into himself. His kiss might very well kill me. Then he forces the air right back into me, mingled with his own breath.

Holy shit! I've never had a kiss like that before. Sharing our breath, our life force. That exchange feels like a contract right there. Okay, speaking of contracts, I'm ready for this. I'm dying for this. I press my palms against Jerry's hard-muscled chest and separate us. I have a moment's pause when I acknowledge to myself that I'm about to give myself, enslave myself to a man I met four days ago. It's rash, reckless. And I don't care.

Jerry stares into my eyes for a few beats of my riotously thumping heart then snaps his head back and forth in a quick shake. The feral glimmer in his eyes recedes. It's like a curtain of discipline descends and closes off that untamed part of him. Remarkably, I want to see more of that dangerous wild thing. It's remarkable because I am terrified of the power of the beast within him and dread what I'm in for should he ever be fully unleashed. At the same time, I don't want to be denied that peril.

$< \male + \female >$

It takes me a few moments to regain my mental faculties—a particularly challenging feat to accomplish while wrapped around a portable incinerator. The sex-crazed look might have left his eyes, but the steely determination that shines instead is just as fierce. With my brain reengaged, I put on my manager's cap to approach this in a business-like manner. There are a few things I know about contract bargaining. I won't give a blind agreement-in-principle until I have some idea what specific terms I'm getting into.

"Jerry, I'd like to talk about the contract, negotiate before rather than after making my decision. Where do we start?" His right hand whips up lightning quick. He cages my chin with a crushing grip, forcing my mouth open and pressing on my bottom teeth with his fat thumb. I don't know why that move has such a powerful effect on me. *Lordy, Lordy.*

A tingle shoots up my spine and smacks me between the eyes, blinding me. Another shoots into the heart of my sex and explodes into a mini orgasm. He sends another energy surge down my transmission lines, causing a brown out in my power grid. *So much for thinking straight.*

"Good girl. Thank you, Erin. This makes me very happy that you want to do this." I haven't signed anything yet and try to correct him. He does it himself. "That you have the courage to explore the possibility." I couldn't have said anything anyway with my mouth still pulled open. He's *introducing me to the mastery he will have over me, over my body—over everything if I'm not careful.*

Submission. I want this; I need this; I need him. This is why I forced myself to pass through the Gates of Hell, otherwise known as the front door of Devil You Know Kink Club. I know that everything is a big mess right now with my three Tops, but I have no regrets. I still care about each man for who he is and what we've experienced together, but there are three of them, not just one.

Each Top knows that I bottom for the others, and I know that they each top with other bottoms. Our times together have been amazing, at least for me, but we can't go very deep when our energies and attention are divided. I can't fully submit to any one of them because of the others. We all lose in that situation.

What will it be like to be exclusive? To serve one Master? To give myself to him alone? Jerry crushes his lips possessively against mine, biting hard on my bottom lip and then soothing the sting with gentle swipes of his tongue. If that's a preview of what's to come, exclusivity is going to be a very good thing.

< ♂ + ♀ >

Sitting in the living room with my laptop on the little pull-down desk in my oak entertainment unit, Jerry opens a browser window and navigates to a BDSM site I've never seen. I ask him to bookmark it for me. He snickers, and I'm sure I hear him whisper, "Good girl." He saves the page before he reaches back to pinch my right nipple, hard. My vaginal muscles clench, hard. He prints two copies of the template contract he wants, and we return to the kitchen table.

"Come sit on my lap, Erin, while we do this. It will be easier if we're not trying to read over each other's shoulders."

I'm not buying it. He's not trying to make anything easier for me; it's just the opposite, in fact. He is establishing his dominion over me. I'm the helpless little girl, and he's the big grownup with the authority. We're definitely not meeting at the bargaining table as parties of equal strength. I'm not complaining. I'm not about to protest the disparity in our power ranking because I have another chance to get up close and personal with the fabulous body I've craved since we laid together on the couch Thursday night.

We shift around until we both get comfortable. *Okay, this may be more of an issue than I thought. Holy smokes.* And I do mean smoke, as in smokin' hot. Just like when we kissed, everywhere our bodies touch, even in places where there's no contact, I'm burning up. It's like I've climbed onto a bed of coals instead of a man. I reach with a shaky hand for the glass of water I poured while we were getting the contract. I take a big gulp in the hope of cooling down a degree or two to prevent my brain from overheating and frying.

I've only indulged my kinky side at DYKKC, and all my scenes have been on an *ad hoc* basis with the same three Tops. We just had a chat before we began, and all our agreements were verbal. In the six months I've been at the club, not one of the three has shown any interest in changing our free-agent arrangement. Christophe hinted at it this week, but I don't think it would have even occurred to him if Dillon hadn't stepped out of line.

Jerry met me only four days ago and already wants to lock me into an exclusive contract. And he wants me to have faith in him. A lump as big as a watermelon lodges in my throat. A couple of tears sneak past my defenses. While the concept of a Master/slave contract isn't foreign to me, I've never done one of my own. I don't think this should be too hard to work out, though, because I've gotten pretty familiar with what my soft and hard limits are.

It's funny. Going over the list of options, I'm like a little girl on Santa's lap telling him what I want for Christmas. I don't have to worry about whether I'm on the *Naughty* or *Nice* list; Jerry has called me a "good girl" more than once today. I have to remember that old saying about being careful what I wish for—because I'm going to get everything, exactly as stated, once it's in the contract.

Jerry doesn't balk at anything I add or delete, and I'm agreeable to all of his amendments. I'm actually relieved because he adds some hard limits that I never would have thought to specify, like no children or animals, no urine or scat, and no blood play or body modification. I add no taking pictures. It's only a short discussion to negotiate punishment. I falter for a second or two before I grant him more leeway than I gave to the others, only drawing the line at caning. I even agree to the use of whips knowing that I have the ultimate control with my safeword. Christophe is the only one I have allowed to use a suede flogger on me, and he knows how gentle he has to be. I hope I don't regret my concessions. Jerry's not exactly hiding his intention to push my boundaries.

Every time we make a change to the contract, Jerry has us initial both copies like you do when altering any official document. This one isn't legally binding, but it reflects the integrity of our promises to each other. My logical mind understands why he has me initial as we proceed rather than at the end. He obtains my assent, layers my acquiescence by degrees, and desensitizes me to the magnitude of my surrender. My logical mind doesn't comprehend how effective his strategy is against my heart and soul. I happily yield to it all.

We discuss medical conditions and STDs; we're both healthy and clean. We talk about contraception; I'm on the pill, and Jerry will use condoms. The process is all very easy, if you call signing your life away easy, until, under the heading "The slave Will Not," I add, "participate in any public nudity or sexual activity" and "share her body, clothed or undressed, with anyone other than the Master." Under the heading "The Master Will Not," I add, "purposely humiliate the slave in public" and "require the slave to interact with anyone other than the Master during a scene."

"Do you want to explain, Erin?" It's not a question.

"I guess that's the best way I can figure to say that, when we're running a scene, you and I are the only ones present. I won't share and won't be shared in any manner. Also, before I got tossed from DYKKC, I was thinking of cutting back on the time I spend there. I'm already tired of the exhibitionism. I know that everyone thinks I'm a prude. That's why they call me miss priss.

"I'm not. It's not that I can't get naked in public, it's just that it never did much for me. Well, that's what I would have said before all this shit happened with Dillon. Now, the idea of being nude or in a compromising situation with others watching is repulsive to me. I get that that's ironic because an audience might have prevented me getting hurt in the first place if someone had intervened.

"Before, my concern was about privacy; it was an intimacy issue. Now, I would feel too exposed and vulnerable. I may choose to confront those issues later, but I'm not going to agree to it during our short contract. Can you accept that, Jerry?" I await his answer with bated breath. It's pretty ballsy of me to even ask for such an indulgence.

"I think you've got enough to contend with as it is. I want to help you and stretch you, not break you. Is that a hard limit?"

"Yes, Sir." *Already with the 'Sir.' You're so easy.* Still, I've earned a sultry smile from Jerry. I want more of those, lots more.

"Good girl. Anything else?"

"Not that I can think of. How about you?"

"I'm good. Remember, we can make changes to this if we need to and if we both agree. Let's sign this and make it official." Jerry puts his signature on the page without hesitation and hands me the pen. I take a few deep breaths to get my hand to stop shaking. Then, I go for it. *Gulp.* It only took about half an hour for me to agree to sign my life over, body and soul, to a near stranger.

"Good girl. Thank you for trusting me and for trusting yourself. I'll do everything I can to make sure you don't regret your decision. I'm really proud of you for taking this step. You've been through a difficult time, and I know it takes a lot of courage for you to do this." His praise pumps up my heart and strokes my pussy.

Jerry plants a delicate kiss on my cheek and draws me into a tight embrace. I feel like I've died and gone to heaven. He is such a man, and I feel like such a woman in his strong arms. I snuggle in and take full advantage of his advances. I draw in a satisfying breath, savoring his sexy cologne and that scent that belongs only to this man. It's musky and something else I can't describe. If power had a smell, it would be the intoxicating fragrance that oozes from Jerry's pores. With each breath, I feel a pulse of heat and a prickle racing through my nipples.

The biggest surprise to me, other than Jerry being here in the first place, is that he hasn't taken advantage of the inequity of our roles. I assumed the contract would be more one-sided. In the erotica I read, the Dom bastard mercilessly extracts debasements from the sub that I can't imagine any sane woman agreeing to.

I expected Jerry to demand total surrender, especially since the term of our contract is short. It expires when I feel I have emotional closure on what Dillon did or one month from today, whichever comes sooner. *I wonder why he insisted on such a short time. Maybe he's not really as interested as he says.*

"I've given a lot of thought to this contract over the last few days. I would like to start right away. I'm not presumptuous, just well prepared. Expect that from me, sub." *Hang on. He's given it a lot of thought?* I didn't think that he just showed up on a whim, but that sounds like he's more than just interested. I'm also confused by the considerate tone he uses with me.

"Help me prepare by telling me what happened with Dillon and how you felt." He kisses my cheek and speaks softly in my ear. "I know it will be hard. Be brave, sub. Don't leave anything out. I need to know everything so I can help you without making mistakes."

His smoky voice is hypnotic and irresistible. We whisper in each other's ears as I recall for Jerry all the pleasurable and painful details, answering his incisive questions. Our hushed conversation is disarmingly erotic, like we are sharing our most private secrets. I share mine openly while Jerry gives his away with his queries. *How can someone flatten you and build you up at the same time?*

"I'm ready to start tomorrow, sub, as long as there is nothing you can't clear from your schedule." *Oh my. Am I ready to start this soon?* If he's telling the truth, Jerry has been thinking about this for days; I've had like five minutes. It strikes me that he must have been thinking of this soon after we met, maybe even that day! The idea is as frightening as it is touching. This would be where that phrase "be careful what you wish for" comes into play.

To be honest, it *is* what I wished for. *Do I really want to put this off? Not on your life!* Hot man, hot sex, and healing. I can't think of a single reason to wait.

"Tomorrow would be excellent. Thank you, Jerry."

He leans closer and nuzzles into my neck. He traces along the curvy edge of my ear with his nose. "Good girl. Thank you for being so agreeable. From now on, you call me Master." He strokes my hair and tangles his fingers into it, yanking on a few strands to correct my slip. Then he pulls back and cups my face in his hands.

Oh my! I had noticed before that his hands are big, but they are truly massive. I wonder if that means that his "equipment" is proportional. I've lain across his body, and I'm sitting in his lap. He does feel big, but tight jeans make good camouflage and hold things in pretty well. Maybe he's got more under the hood than it seems. *Hope springs eternal.*

A lazy smile meanders across his lips as he gazes at me. His glacial eyes should be cold, but they radiate great warmth, warmth that melts my defenses and has me willing to do whatever he says. I probably shouldn't fall so easily at his feet after everything I've been through; I should be a little more careful, but I couldn't care less.

Even though I never thought Dillon or Christophe would hurt me the way they have, I *know* this man won't. My intuition tells me he's a good guy through and through. And Evanya is a raving fan. It's a no-brainer to throw caution to the wind. *Didn't I say just a couple of hours ago that I'm finished with men? Never say never, I guess.*

"Your day will be yours tomorrow until 5 pm. Do whatever chores or run whatever errands you want. Do something nice for yourself as well. I guarantee you that, while we'll ease into things and the play tomorrow might not be too intense, the emotions you'll be dealing with will be. Do you understand, sub?"

"I do, Master."

"Good. Give me a key to your front door. Go get it now." *Okay, that's unexpected.* While I'm pondering this development, Jerry is holding his hand out, palm up, waiting for the key.

"Now, sub." I'm already such a sucker for his velvety-smooth voice. I don't stand a chance of being able to resist anything he asks for. I climb off his lap and retrieve my spare from the junk drawer beside the stove. In the absence of his warmth beneath me, a chilling breeze on my butt alerts me that my agitated pussy has leaked her juices right through my jeans.

Head and eyes lowered, I place the key in the center of his palm. Jerry closes his big mitt over my fingers and pulls me back onto his lap, steering me with his other hand so I straddle his left leg. I tense my muscles to fight back my urge to grind against his meaty thigh.

"Good girl. Thank you. Just a couple more things and we'll be all set. Okay?" I nod and gulp to suppress my nerves.

"Although I'm going to trust you with a great deal of freedom tomorrow, I still expect you to follow my demands to the letter. You must leave here by 2:00 and return at precisely 5:00. There will be tasks for you to complete before I arrive at 6:00. I will not tolerate tardiness or laziness. Do you understand?" The instructions, and his sincerity, are clear; I just have no idea what he's up to. I nod again.

"Good. One last thing, sub. Follow the grooming instructions in our contract before you leave. You won't have time later. Do you understand?" I nod, except this time he makes me respond verbally.

"Well, that's it then," Jerry says. We sit in uncomfortable silence for a minute or two. It seems that neither of us knows what to do next. Then Jerry's eyes sparkle and gleam. I know that look from my experience with a wolf, a coyote and a panther—the predator is in pursuit of his prey. *What kind of animal is hunting me this time?*

< ♂ + ♀ >

Chapter Eleven – Temptation

Saturday Afternoon, September 22

"Perhaps we shouldn't wait. I'd like to play a little bit right now. You need to learn to follow my commands, slave. And I think you should give me a sample of what I've bargained for. The scent of your hot pussy has made me a little hungry, and you've been a bad girl and left a wet spot on my leg. You owe me some of that." *Could I possibly be more humiliated?* But Jerry's steady stare relaxes me. If he's not embarrassed, then I won't be either.

I don't need any further discussion. I'm ready for this, ready for him, ready to serve him. I lower my head and place my hands in my lap, waiting willingly for my Master's first command.

"Please strip for me." *Wait a minute. Since when does a Dom say please?* Jerry has been pleasant and polite all day, but he has me indentured now. This is where he's supposed to turn coldblooded. *Where is that Jekyll and Hyde transformation to exacting Master?*

I look up slowly, searching his face. He still looks like a Dom. His jaw is firmly set, and his eyes smolder with what looks like determination. I can't mistake that he is the one in control; his aura of authority is palpable. The phrase "walk tall and carry a big stick" springs to mind, but I'm relieved by his respectful manner.

"Would you like music, Master?" I'm going out on a tenuous limb saying even one word, but I want to reward his kindness. I hope we can both use this time to learn about each other. He certainly opened my eyes with his negotiating style when we settled our contract. *Could he be a strict but just Master rather than a bastard?*

"Why not? Put on a good show for me, slave girl. And no more talking unless spoken to. Understand?"

"Yes, Master." His steely stare speaks volumes.

I walk to the bay window in the living room to close the blinds. Jerry orders me to leave them open. I ask for permission to speak and quickly explain about Busybody Bilson next door. Jerry wants to see my body by natural light, so he angles the blinds to block prying eyes but not all the light. I gesture toward the coffee table, indicating that he might want to slide it away from the couch to give me some room. He frowns but does it.

The music has to be sultry and sexy for this performance. I've only got one chance to make a good first impression. My only option is something by the über-sexy Bryan Ferry. I pop in the Roxy Music *Avalon* CD, an oldie but a goodie, and skip ahead to "To Turn You On." I hit the CD *Repeat* button before hitting *Play*. The whole album will make a great soundtrack for whatever goes on after my clothes come off.

Be bold. Be bolder than you've ever been. I've only stripped like this once before for my college boyfriend. I couldn't get into it, and he didn't seem too impressed. I was crazy nervous then and that was with flattering, subdued lighting in the bedroom. Here I am in the middle of the living room with sunlight streaming in, and I can't hide. Still, I'm more relaxed because this time I don't have the same old insecurities about my body. I really want to please this man, and, if I can trust the wild look in his eyes and the tense set of his jaw, he's going to like whatever I do, no matter what. Still, I want to do my best for my Master.

As the first haunting beats and chords of the song begin, I breathe slowly, stretching my lungs to maximum capacity. I drop my shoulders, loosen my hips, and unlock my knees. As I start to sway to the rhythm, I turn from the stereo and lock eyes with Jerry. I curl my lips up in my best attempt at a come-hither smile. I seriously hope it doesn't look like a sneer instead.

I sashay leisurely toward him, running my fingers up my midsection to just beneath my breasts. As my left hand slides up and onto my left breast, kneading it roughly, I extend my right index finger, landing it dead center on Jerry's chest. I apply feather-light pressure as I push him back; he retreats without resistance and lowers himself slowly onto the seat when his knees make contact with the couch.

I turn away and walk a few steps, jiggling my wide derrière as I go. When I circle back around, I throw another wicked smile and lick my lips. I swing my hips and wave my arms in a slow, seductive dance. My whole body writhes like a sinuous snake as my hands roam along my skin, clutching, massaging, pinching and caressing. Every now and then a moan or a sigh passes my lips.

While I'm teasing and pleasing my own body, I take careful note of the changes in Jerry's. His breathing rate is more rapid and shallower. I catch the occasional flaring of his nostrils as he takes in a deeper breath to replenish his deficit of oxygen. His pupils are so open that a mere trace of his beautiful blue irises shows. If I look closely, and I am looking very closely, I can catch a faint twitching on the left side of his strong jaw. *Got him!*

A thin sheen of perspiration glistens along that space just under his straight nose and above his plump upper lip, now dark with the beginnings of a heavy 5 o'clock shadow. I sooo want to lick that sweat off him, feel the rough stubble on my tongue, but I stay with the task at hand. Then I look down and almost lose all focus.

My magnificent new Dom is sporting a very eager erection that is straining to break past his zipper. Yes, his impressive hard-on is evident even through those tight jeans that I suspect are hiding the true nature of the goods. I'd dearly love to give that bulge a helping hand, and a hand job, but I have to keep dancing.

I twirl around and face away from Jerry and glide my hands around and around the ripe globes of my bottom until I can regain my composure. *Shit, Erin. You're shaking your money maker for a virtual stranger. WTF?* I tell that prissy voice in my head to "shut the hell up," and I get back to business.

I begin disrobing, slowly, so slowly. Jerry's grip on the arm of the couch is tight enough that he could snap the bones in his fingers. His expression is strained like I'm torturing the poor man. Not that he's complaining. He's following every movement I make. The intensity of his scrutiny is more than a bit disturbing.

I really wish I was wearing something sexy, but at least my fuchsia cotton shirt has buttons that I undo with great flourishes. When I pull the shirt open and let it slip off my shoulders, Jerry licks his lips. *Good Lord. He looks like he wants to eat me. That's not a bad thing, is it?*

I cup my heavy boobs and lift and separate. I let my head fall back, and I give myself over to the pleasing sensations as I squeeze each plump breast and pinch each dusky nipple through the diaphanous lace of my pale pink demi-bra. A roaring groan from the couch brings my eyes back to look at Jerry.

"So beautiful. Take that bra off *now*." I reach behind my back and unhook the fasteners in two seconds. My hands rise up and leisurely slide the straps down as I sway closer to Jerry. When I let the bra fall to the floor, my 38D beauties dangle just out of arm's reach of a now panting beast. *Please, please, please touch me.*

"Magnificent. You're killing me, sub. But, remember, this is just a sample, a taste. No touching for either of us."

He's the one killing me. For spite, I lean closer as I shimmy and shake my girls. That elicits from him a rumbling growl that starts from the base of his spine and burbles to his crown. That sound bleeds from his every pore and flows over me, blistering my skin. *Yay!* The first growl from a man is always the sweetest and most satisfying. And the most devastating. My knees dip as the sound waves crash into me. I'll remember this growl forever.

"Enough. Jeans. Now." *Oh my. Impatient are we?* I must be more talented than I ever knew.

A little voice peeps up in my head. "Silly girl. Did you forget? When you're a brat to a Dom, there's always payback, and payback is always a bitch." *Oh no!*

No more fooling around. The song is almost over, and I want to be naked by the last note. I unzip my jeans and circle my hips as I shuck the soft, faded denim. I carefully step out and stand straight. My feet are already bare, so the only scrap of clothing on me is my pale pink thong, now transparent, drenched with my juices.

Jerry nods toward my mound and his direction is clear. I hook my fingers into the thin strips of elastic on the sides and tug at my panties until they land on the floor, just as the music fades away. Jerry clears his throat, and I smile coyly at him in all my naked glory.

After adjusting the swelling in his jeans, Jerry stands and walks toward me. He is so tall, and so large, and his energy field is so strong that he inhabits all the space in the room. I am stunned, immobile but for the pounding of my heart.

"You are a truly beautiful woman. Your body is a work of art." I see him staring at the traces of my injuries as he circles around me. He starts to speak but stops himself.

A moment later, Jerry presses his lips to my ear and whispers. "Your body should be worshipped, not battered and broken. I promise I'll take good care of you, baby. I know what you're worth." His steamy breath sets off ripples of grasping need in all my girly parts. His low, crooning tones vibrate deep in my heart. I hold my breath and screw up my courage. *I. Will. Not. Cry.* Sweet Jesus, that is *the* single most amazing thing anyone—man or woman, parent, friend, teacher, colleague, lover or stranger—has ever said to me.

A girl could fall in love with a man who says things like that if she's not careful. But I can't afford to let my heart go there. I've only got a month with him at the outside. This is an agreement between two consenting adults for sexual gratification and power exchange. We're not dating. Nonetheless, I'll make the most of every second.

Our contract says, "Beyond any negotiated scenes, the slave shall make herself available to the Master and grant him full access to her body in any manner he desires, at any time and place." I conceded when Jerry crossed out the words "within reason." The whole contract is beyond reason. Still, the part about giving Jerry access anytime, anywhere, anyhow sounds reasonable to me. He did say he wouldn't ask me to miss any work—and he won't make any decisions regarding my career—but I'll gladly take time off if he as much as hints at it. I want everything and every minute he's willing to give me.

< ♂ + ♀ >

Jerry takes a step back and lets his fingers skim over me about an inch away from my skin. His almost-but-not-quite touch still singes my flesh. As if she's trying to extinguish the blaze, my pussy dribbles fluid down my thighs.

"Sit in the armchair over there, sub, and spread your legs for me." *Awesome. Here we go.* Once again, I'm astonished at how easy it is to bare myself to this man. In my old life, I would never consider being this ... loose ... with a man that I haven't even gone on a date with. Yet, I have this piece of paper that says I belong to Jerry, my Master. Along with all the restrictions that will come with that obligation comes incredible freedom. I'm free to give in to my desires and my needs in a way that I've never been able to do before —not even at DYKKC.

I am keen to obey, and I follow his direction until I'm settled in the pose he wants. I recline with my knees bent and my feet planted at the outer edges of the chair cushion. Then Jerry kneels between my legs and has a good close look at my moist pussy. I've actually surpassed moist; I'm sopping.

A loud purr rumbles in the back of my throat when Jerry puts his head between my legs and inhales deliberately and deeply. "Nice. Rich and earthy. I want to spend hours licking up all that wonderful cream, but no touching today." I stop purring instantly and let out an agonized groan that is met by a sadistic chuckle. *Yes, payback is a bitch, and her name is Denial.*

Jerry returns to the couch, stretches out like a lazy lion, and issues his next command. "Play with yourself, sub. Show me what pleases you. Show me what makes you moan, how to touch you. I'm not promising I'll do any of it, but show me anyway."

"Yes, Sir." I say it with enthusiasm, letting him know I really like that command. I know he's just pretending he won't please me. I am so turned on and so happy right now. I can almost forgive Dillon and maybe even thank him because, if it wasn't for his boneheaded actions, I would not be enjoying this man today. Talk about screwed up silver linings. *The universe moves in mysterious ways.*

I do my best to show Jerry how the girls like to be made love to. Except I can't show him that I need to have his sensual lips sucking my nipples, that I want his tongue to lick and swirl and his teeth to nibble and nip. Then my hands head south.

I drag my long, pink nails along my skin, delving into all the tender places along the way. I brush my palms along every exposed inch. I tickle down my sides and across my belly, raising a trail of goosebumps on the path of my progress. My fingers twirl in my neatly trimmed, soaking wet curls. I pry apart my folds to give Jerry an unobstructed view of my swollen clit and tight little slit.

I swish my fingers through my slick juices then hold them out in front of me. My curled digits glisten in the sunshine spilling through the blinds. Jerry, in one fluid motion, pushes himself off the couch. His lithe body slinks up to within inches of my knees. Electricity crackles up my arm when he grasps my hand.

"You are no priss. You are a wicked vixen."

"Yes, Sir."

"Yes, what?"

"Yes, Master."

With a devilish glint in his eyes, he slowly pushes my fingers between his lips and into his hot mouth. His rough tongue swirls as he sucks and licks me clean. The sound of his pleasure tickles my fingers while his heated gaze tickles my clit. I answer his moan with one of my own.

"God, you taste as sweet as honey." My temperature spikes. I just know my whole face is crimson. He pulls my fingers out of his mouth with a loud pop. He gives my fingertips a quick kiss and then drops my hand. The lion turns and saunters back to the couch.

"Don't get me wrong, baby. I'm looking forward to sinking my dick between those glorious cheeks of yours tomorrow, but I wish the scene script had me going there first." He points unabashedly at my pussy. His boldness unsettles me, and I try hard to swallow past the golf ball wedged in my throat.

"I want you spread out underneath me as I thrust hard and fast into your slick pussy. I want to watch your pleasure painted on your face as I slam into you. I want to see your perfect little mouth open as you scream and call me Master. I want to look into your eyes and see my reflection shining back at me as I possess you."

I gasp and struggle for breath like an asthmatic in the throes of a vicious attack. Tears spring to my eyes and spill down my cheeks. *That's why Christophe never felt like my soul mate. He never looked in my eyes when he was buried deep, only during aftercare. That's why I was anxious to get to that part of our time together.*

And Dillon only ever took me from behind. Even Jim, when we were playing and laughing with each other, never made direct eye contact when he was inside me. *None of them wanted to see me when I was the most open. How could I have missed it?* Stark reality is a sharp, serrated blade that tears my heart as it stabs into me.

Jerry launches off the couch and is kneeling in front of me in a flash. He wipes away my tears with the pads of his thumbs. "What's the matter, baby?"

I shake my head.

"Tell me, sub." His voice is only a fraction firmer this time, yet it is an unmistakable command.

"Please, Master. Don't ask me to say it now. May I wait to tell you after our scene tomorrow? Please?" He pauses while his eyes search mine.

"Very well. Don't think that I will forget."

"Oh, no, Master. Thank you. I'll be happy to tell you tomorrow. I'm just too raw to do it today."

"You're welcome. Hush now. There's one more thing I'd like to do if you'll allow it."

"Of course, Sir. Anything." *If I'll allow it?* It doesn't matter what it is, I'm in. He's made a huge compromise for me by granting my request so easily, so I'll gladly give him whatever he asks.

"So eager to please your *Master*. Where do you keep your toys, *slave?*"

Gulp. "In a bag under my bed, Master."

"I'll be right back. No touching. You know the rule, even if it's not explicitly written in the contract. Until we're complete, your pussy belongs to me, and your orgasms are now mine. When we're together, you *will not* come until I say so. And you *will* come when I command. Even when we're apart, you *will not* come unless I say so. And you *will* come when I order you to. Understood?"

"Yes, Sir."

"Yes, what?"

"Sorry. Yes, Master." I've got to do better at remembering the proper honorific. Master needn't have been emphatic about my orgasms though; I understand only too well. They don't call it orgasm control for no reason. I'm surprised by the sigh of approval that surges through me as his words echo in my heart. "Your pussy belongs to me." *Sorry Susan B.*

Sitting here alone gives me too much time to imagine what's going to happen. I don't know whether to worry or rejoice that he's gone for my toys. Thank goodness Jerry returns quickly. *Oh, oh.* He's brought the whole knapsack.

"A person's toy collection says a lot about them, don't you think, sub?" He rummages through the contents of my pack. There isn't much there. I wasn't very adventurous about taking care of my own pleasure before DYKKC, and I haven't had time to build my collection since.

I've got one purple silicone dildo, large but not King Kong large. One vibrator, a basic model that gets the job done. A set of three, linked, silicone ben-wa balls. No cuffs but a half dozen silk scarves. One pink satin blindfold. A pair of rabbit fur mittens, a couple of feathers, and a pink, nylon mesh, exfoliator puff. My toy bag says I'm into sensation play rather than impact play.

Then Jerry unzips one of the pockets and pulls out a small, red satin pouch which he pops open. He slides out a long, 18K-gold chain with a diamond pendant on the end. It's my hip necklace. "Who gave you this?"

"A present to myself, Master." He nods. He's pleased with that answer. I know what possessive men are like about women wearing jewellery from another man.

"Who do you wear it for?" *Bingo.*

"Only for myself. I haven't worn it for a man, if that's what you're asking, Master."

He shows his teeth under a knowing smile. "Would you wear it for me, baby? Will you put it on and not take it off until our contract is completed?" Just like a collar. *Possessive? YES. And I like it.*

"I would be happy to, Master." He wraps his hands behind my waist, winding the delicate, glittery rope around me, fastening the clasp below my navel. I lean in, trying to steal the touch he's been withholding.

"Stand for me. Show me." I stumble when I get up. I hadn't noticed that my legs had gone numb from sitting in the same bent position for so long. Jerry catches me and, for the brief moment before he releases me, I have found paradise in his arms.

"Forgive me. I should have realized." He chafes each leg in turn with his colossal hands and then sits back on his heels to take a look. His finger bats at the sparkling diamond hanging just at the edge of my pubes. "Very sexy. I like." He grabs my hips, rearranges me in the chair, and returns his attention to my toy bag.

In another pocket he finds the pair of nipple vices that were a gift from Dillon, the ones he used to torture me *that* night. *I'll have to get rid of those. Maybe Lacey will like them.* Jerry notices my grimace and raises an eyebrow to question me. I explain, and he puts them in his pocket without a word. I'm grateful I won't have to deal with them anymore. *Tough luck, Lacey.*

He chooses to work with the vibrator. For the next 20 minutes, he tests my "responsiveness" as "research for tomorrow's scene." The man knows how to use a vibe for maximum devastation. What a relief that my wand massager was in my bathroom.

"Are you close, baby?"

"Not yet, Master." I twist and moan and purr like a happy kitten. I love to move my body. As I wriggle and stretch, I can diffuse the sexual tension building in my body. It helps me last longer. Energy flows deliciously instead of building up to a massive explosion. Even so, Jerry raises the stakes, luring me to the edge as he slides the tip of the vibe right over my quivering clit. I hear Bryan singing "To Turn You On" again as Jerry presses down the vibe while he inserts first one and then a second crooked finger into my slippery sheath. My breasts jut forward, bowing my back. My chest expands as I pant like I do when I jog five miles. I wail out my elation. *Now I'm close.*

And, suddenly, I'm not. Jerry turns off the vibrator and drops it to the floor. He snags a handful of my hair and pulls, bringing me close enough for our noses to barely kiss. His heavy lids drop closed. He sniffs sharply and blows a hard, hot breath across my face. "Erin ..." *It's the first time he's called me Erin since signing the contract. He's even started calling me baby.* I'm thrilled he's having a difficult time maintaining his composure and has forgotten about the no-touching rule. The slide of his fingers probing my core was exquisite. It seems that he's lost his control around me again.

"You are stunning when you're on the edge. The way your skin flushes pink and shimmers with perspiration. Beautiful. When you wriggle and writhe under my touch, it's sexier than your striptease was. Your whimpers and moans are like sweet, seductive music. Your eyes flicker and shine like a candle flame. I can't wait to see you fall over the edge and come apart for me tomorrow."

Wait a minute! "To-tomorrow, Master?"

"I'm just tasting today, remember, sub? You can serve me the whole damn buffet tomorrow. And, no, you do *not* have permission to touch yourself or use your toys. I want you begging me for relief." He regards the pleading look on my face and laughs maniacally. He could give me six orgasms between now and 6:00 tomorrow, and I would still beg him for more. *Yes, that bitch's name is Denial.*

Jerry's name could be Serpent, tempting and teasing me like this. He stands and tips my face back with one finger on my quivering chin. He freezes me with his ice-blue stare.

"Sweet, beautiful Erin. Leave by 2:00 tomorrow; be home at 5:00; and wait for me to arrive at 6:00. I'm leaving now, but you must stay. Stay here in this chair, just like this, open and wet and trembling. And in need of me. Don't move, slave, until you hear my truck drive away." Jerry's lips are firm against mine, and he forces my mouth open to flick his tongue against mine. His sharp teeth bite down on my lower lip before he pulls away.

"Stay!"

I am positively choking on unrequited desire. The second he is out the door, my head drops forward—my spine has dissolved and my neck is a limp noodle. His truck peals away from the curb. I'm sure he does it so I can hear him leave. I crumple into a heap, jiggling jelly-style. He said there would be no touching, but I can *still* feel his fingers probing inside my juddering vagina. I better stop thinking about it, or I'll come, and that's not allowed.

OhmyfreakingGOD. If that was just a taste, I'm in biiiiig trouble tomorrow. But it's just the kind of trouble I need. *Oh, yeah!*

A long walk, a cold shower, and a couple of shoot 'em up movies on cable did nothing to distract my restless pussy during the long, cold night. I just hope that Jerry is suffering as much as I am. It's midnight, and I push *Send* on a text. 'You're a mean one, Mr. Grinch, Sir.' The bastard texts back, 'That's MASTER Grinch. Only 18 more hours to go My pretty slave. :) '

Chapter Twelve – Resurrection

Sunday Morning, September 23

I'm up at dawn, marveling at the sun painting the world with bright hues of rose, mandarin and gold. This daily miracle is a sign of renewal that always gives me hope. After the bleak week I've had, the message sinks into my being, reminding me that I am alive and life is good. And that things can change for the better in an instant.

I head out into the fresh morning, the air infusing my body with vibrant energy. Tulku, the *Transcendence* CD, fires into my brain, adding to my joyful mix of bliss frequencies and positive vibes as I jog through my neighborhood. I haven't felt this jazzed, this elated, in a long, long time. I'm like a new woman.

Thanks to this upbeat mindset, the morning flies by surprisingly quickly as I clean the house from top to bottom. Then I clean and pamper myself from top to bottom. I hop into my car at 11:30. The one bright spot in my horrible day Friday was coming home to find that the nasty epithet had been cleaned off my rear window. I had hidden the car in my garage but hadn't yet mustered up the energy to remove the paint myself. I don't know who did it or how they got into my garage. I am just grateful to be able to drive again.

Citrus Grill is my favorite Vietnamese restaurant. It's near the law school, but I've come here for lunch instead of going to the one closer to home. It's worth the longer drive. I treat myself to a big bowl of sate beef soup. The broth is rich and super spicy with loads of rare beef. I squeeze in extra lime juice and savor every spoonful.

My afternoon is incredible. I spend a few hours cruising my favorite craft supply stores, sourcing new baubles and materials. Then I hit the used bookstore for a delightful hour of browsing and score a real gem—a pristine 1928 pirated copy of D.H. Lawrence's *Lady Chatterley's Lover*. It's a beautiful volume from Florence, Italy, bound in red cloth with an art deco label on the spine. It contains the original manuscript, not a revised or censored edition. It sets me back $215, but it's worth every cent. Now there's only 45 minutes left to get home. My stomach is queasy from nerves, but I'll stop at the deli for a quick sandwich. I think I'm going to need the energy.

$$< \male + \female >$$

My hands are shaking as I stand at my front door. I haven't felt this discombobulated since the first night I went to DYKKC. My mood is a blend of adventurous, lusty and fearful. My tongue sticks in my mouth; it's gone completely dry with want for getting naked with Jerry. But I'm also anxious about confronting the hurt I suffered at Dillon's hands as he helps me deal with that.

"Is that what he has planned for tonight? He hinted at it when he talked about—how did he put it?—sinking his dick between these glorious cheeks of mine. How will he do the scene? What's his style? Will he tie me up and talk me through it like Christophe does? Or will he have some other tricks to help me get my head straight?"

How will we each act and react, and what will the outcome be this time? I've learned from my scenes with Master Ronan that every script will take on a life of its own once you're into it and the power exchange starts to flow between Top and bottom. What happened with Dillon is a case in point, although that was more of an abandonment of my power than an exchange. I could stand here for another hour going through the Who, What, Where, When and Why questions of what will happen and not get any closer to an answer. I don't have that kind of time.

There is an envelope taped to the front door, my name printed on it with heavy, black marker in bold, masculine script. My fingers reach up tentatively and brush across my name. Just from this quick physical connection, I can feel Jerry here with me. I am suddenly immersed into the scene in a way that is more real than before. *He wrote my name. He taped the envelope on the door. What was he thinking while he did it? Is he as anxious and excited as I am?*

I carefully unstick the envelope and cross my threshold. I'm in such a hurry to read what's inside that I want to rip it open. Instead, I take my time to prize the flap up carefully to preserve it. Whatever is inside, this is going in my scrapbook. "Welcome home, Erin. You've only got one hour. Go straight to the kitchen table for your first instructions. Follow them all without delay. Before you know it, I will be at your door, and we can begin."

I hastily kick off my shoes, hang my jacket, and dash to the kitchen. A striking, red crystal vase containing a bouquet of exquisite, long-stemmed, red roses graces my table. I stumble, and my hand flies to my chest, resting over my heart. His romantic gesture throws me for a loop. *I thought this was just about sex and control.* I'm confounded but grateful. The roses are gorgeous.

A cute card with a picture of a little boy and girl holding hands stands beside the vase. The message inside reads, "Sweet sub. Enjoy the beauty and fragrance of these roses. Let them fill your senses and arouse your passion. But don't linger long. I'll be with you soon."

The tips of my fingers gently caress the velvety petals, a red so dark they are tinged with near black. These are no supermarket flowers. I know Jerry has dropped some serious coin on them because the scent is rich and heady. As the perfume fills my lungs, my whole body vibrates with life, sighs and then relaxes. Then it heats right back up when I notice another envelope and my ben-wa balls on the corner of the table.

"Drop your drawers now and put these in My hot pussy, slave. Then close all your blinds and light the fire. Go to your bedroom and dress in the clothes I've laid out. Wear something naughty underneath. There is another set of instructions on your bed."

"OMG. This is so much fun. It's like a sexy scavenger hunt." It's exciting to follow Jerry's commands, and I'm touched by the thought and preparation he has put into this scene. It's way over the top of anything I could have anticipated or need. *I totally love it.*

I'm already super slick, so it's a snap to insert the pleasure balls into my tight vagina. My PC muscles grip hard to hold the balls inside. My clit is buzzing, and I have no idea how I'm going to keep myself from coming. I'm going to take one look at Jerry when he walks through the door and lose it.

I close the blinds, and I'm just about to light the fire, which Jerry has already stacked, when the doorbell rings. My heart leaps, and my chest tightens. *No, no, no! He can't be early!* I crack the blinds. Mr. Bilson is on the landing. I need to ignore him, but he's ringing with one hand, and his other hand is banging on the door. I pull my panties and jeans back on and fling the door open.

"What can I do for you, Mr. Bilson?" My tone is totally bitchy.

"Are you alright, Erin? I saw a man go inside your house while you were gone this afternoon. He came out later, but I was worried. Should I have called the police? Were you robbed?"

"No, Mr. Bilson. Everything is fine. He's a friend of mine. I knew he was coming and gave him a key. Thank you for looking out for me, but I have to go. I'm in a hurry and expecting company." Despite trying everything I can to get rid of the pest, short of flat out telling him to f-off, he wastes ten minutes of precious getting-ready-for-Jerry time with a lecture about me giving keys to strangers and preaching other safety tips. As soon as I slam the door in his face, I grab my cell phone and start typing furiously.

'Sorry. I'm so sorry Master. Please forgive me Master. I'm not going to be ready on time. I'm so sorry Master!!!!' I hit *Send* and wait nervously, my heart pounding, an ocean of tears swelling. Maybe by giving him lots of warning he'll go easy on me. *As if!*

'Warned u not 2 b late sub. What happened?' *Warned? Oh, I wish I could hear the tone in his voice. Just how pissed is he?*

'Sorry Master. Nosy Ned saw intruder in my house. Came to check on me. Couldn't make him leave. I tried so hard Master. I'm sorry Master.' I hope I've said sorry and Master enough times that he understands that I really am sorry. At least he knows about Mr. Bilson and how annoying he is.

'Guess intruder was Me. Lol. I forgive u sub. How late r u?'

'10 minutes Master.'

'Will see u at 6:10. Is My pretty slave wet for Me?'

'I'm dripping Master.'

'Good. Now go. :D '

I am so relieved that I almost pee my pants. I high-tail it to the bathroom to wash the nervous sweat from my body and swish a toothbrush around my dry mouth. Vigorous brushing gives my hair a healthy luster. Jerry put in our contract that he wants me to let my locks flow free, but I think about the braid I wore that night with Dillon. I start to secure my mane with a leather thong when I remember Jerry's "consequences" for even partial disobedience. *Yikes!* I dodged a bullet on the tardiness, but I doubt he'll forgive another screw up. I fluff my hair up and let it spill down my back.

I skid into the bedroom and am confronted by more attacks against my efforts to remain calm. *Ohboyohboyohboy.* The sheets on the bed are turned down, ready and waiting. On the bedside table is a small pile of condoms, ready and waiting.

"Okay, girl. Stay focused. One thing at a time." Jerry has laid out a bubble-gum-pink silk blouse with pearl buttons and a café-au-lait satin skirt that skims my curves and ends at mid-thigh. It's classy, not slutty. I like that he's chosen what he wants me to wear, and I love that he's chosen so well. I dash to my work room and bring out the hanger with my newest masterpiece, the "something naughty." I'm glad I waited to wear it. This is the perfect occasion.

"Shit! The fireplace! Damn you, Bilson." I hustle out to the living room, strike a match, and set it to the crumpled newspaper. I say a prayer of gratitude that the fire catches right away and is roaring in only a minute. The dancing flames illuminate another pile of condoms on the sheepskin rug, ready and waiting. And my toy bag, ready and waiting. Jerry must be a Boy Scout, always prepared.

I speed back to the bedroom and have to stop to take a breath. Then I dress carefully, getting all my parts in the right places. I reach for the envelope on the pillow. My hands are shaking like I'm a heroin addict going through withdrawals.

"Don't forget that sexy perfume you wear. And put your hair up like you wore it for him. Then go to the front door. Put your bare toes on the tape on the floor. Stand with your spine straight, hands clasped behind and raised to your mid back, head bowed. Be still and wait for Me, slave." The note is signed, "Master." Submissive stance or, at least, Jerry's version of it. I groan about braiding my hair, but at least I have my answer about his plans for tonight. The mention of tape on the floor has me perplexed.

I haven't yet been able to embrace the deferential posture and what it represents. To me, there's a big difference between passively letting a man do things to my body and openly displaying my submission to him, my complete surrender to his mercy. Each of my Tops had their own variations on the submissive stances that they expected me to assume. I would pose as directed, but I could not fully embody the intent of the stance, partly because I belonged to none of them, but also for reasons unique to each of them.

I didn't mistrust Jim, but I didn't have the deep-seated level of confidence that would allow me to give myself fully to him. He's too much of the trickster coyote, hiding behind humor and playfulness. His focus is never what I would call Rottweiler intense. That's when a Dom is keenly tuned in to every breath, every twitch of muscle, and every sound of his sub. He can almost read her mind from the clues that her body sends. That level of engagement is beyond Jim, and I don't think he was particularly bothered about my emotional surrender as long as we both had Screaming O's.

Even with my big, beautiful bad boy, I always held something back. I found his hard edge exciting, and I sometimes wondered what would push him over it. I guess I found out. The realization that I was always at odds with him nearly floors me. Even when I thought I was pleasing him, I was trying to control him and keep him in check because I was also terrified of that edge that I loved. *Oh, Dillon. You must have felt that. I'm sorry.*

The only man I've come close to trusting enough to relax with and give almost total control to is Christophe or, rather, Master Ronan. He has that Rottweiler intensity. We understood each other, or so I thought. I knew he would never be only mine, but I thought that when I was with him I had his undivided attention. An energy flowed between us, each giving and receiving at the same time to the same depth—except for the part of him that he hid, the part that couldn't look at me when he was inside me. I guess I understand why a Service Top would need walls. He is, after all, the one who taught me about boundaries. I see now that he didn't let me in any closer than anyone else, that he has that same level of focus and attention with every sub he is with. *I guess I wasn't any more special to him than any other bottom, even the male ones.* This new insight somehow makes his betrayal worse.

I must be crazy to go down this road again. After how all three of them let me down, it's ludicrous to put my physical, mental, emotional and spiritual welfare in the hands of another man. Yet, I've already done it; I did right from the first sight of him. What I'm about to do with Jerry should be completely different than anything I've done with any of the others, even Master Ronan, because, as soon as Christophe and I walked out of the club, we severed our connection, and we each took back our power.

When Jerry subdued me in my kitchen during our first meeting, I bowed to him, not because of conditioning and brainwashing, but because I had a natural response to Jerry's authority. He won't have to train me; I already belong to him—even if it's only for a month—and not because of a trifling piece of paper. Our bond feels like a sacred contract.

I felt power cycling through us yesterday as I gave him my body and my trust, and he gave me his complete attention and guidance. He did not take that back from me when he left. Even now, I still feel that connection and give and take between us.

I settle myself at the door. It's only 6:05. I drape my braid over my shoulder, letting it slither into my cleavage. I obediently pose my body for my Master as he directed. With my fingers laced, when I raise my hands to the middle of my back, I have to thrust my breasts forward to achieve a comfortable stance. *Cunning devil.*

I have five excruciating minutes to wait. They are the longest five minutes of my life. I'm going to be a woebegone wreck by the time he opens that door.

"Snap out of it." That sounded like I was channeling Cher from *Moonstruck*, but it's Evanya weighing in on my distress. "You're a grown woman. You're smart, sexy and strong. You're beautiful, and he wants you enough to negotiate 'unlimited access' to you. Remember, he thinks you're a vixen and not a priss. Now, breathe!"

I do my meditation breathing—in through my nose for the count of four, hold for the count of four, out for the count of four. The minutes tick by, and I drop into a trance-like state, rising to a higher plane where the world is beautiful, bright and shiny. I even chant softly. I'm relaxed and ready. After feeling like I wanted to just curl up and fade away not too long ago, I'm alive and excited about this new stage of my life. Until I hear the rumble of a big truck pulling into the driveway ... and then silence. When I hear the door slam, my heart slams up to tickle my tonsils.

Chapter Thirteen – Ascension

Sunday Evening, September 23

The doorknob creaks as it turns, and the movement releases a flood of tears that splatters down my face. I can't staunch the flow nor name the emotion behind it. My knees knock and rattle, and my eager beaver gushes. Despite my confidence-boosting pep talk and calm-inducing breathing, I panic. *This is really happening.*

A breeze hushes over me as the door swings just inches away from my downturned head. *That's why the tape.* Master is a director, setting the camera perspective, placing his subject, his slave, framing the scene, exactly as he wants to view it.

I can only imagine the impact on him, opening the door to find my total acquiescence on display for him. He rests for an eternity at the threshold, motionless. I can't even hear him breathing. *Do I measure up to his anticipation? What need have I answered for him?*

I wish I could look up and see all of Jerry as he stands before me. What I do see in my own limited field of vision is tight, black leather pants and Jesus sandals on the sexiest male feet. The strong scent of leather blended with the zest of his cologne and "eau de Jerry" is an intoxicating cocktail. My teeth twitch. I need to sink them into something, preferably a hunk of naked man.

I keep my head hung low as Jerry, my Master for the next month, circles me. He hasn't said a word yet. From the corner of my eye, I see him slip off his sandals, open the closet, and hang a black leather jacket. *Sweet Jesus.* I just about pass out when I get an eyeful of his praise-worthy ass molded into those tight pants. *That's what I want to bite.* Oh, I want to bite his ass so bad.

Those naked toes, perfectly manicured, come to rest directly in front of me. He's close enough that the heat and animal lust blasting off him make me sway. Jerry studies me like the predator that he is, fixating on his quarry. His x-ray vision cuts right through me. My nipples pop up high in response to his perusal, all that sexual energy sniping at me. My pink pearls ache and yearn for Jerry's lips and tongue, but especially for his teeth. *That's where you can sink your teeth, Master.*

"Hello, slave." His impossibly low, bass tone punches right into my solar plexus, and I flinch. His fleshy thumbs skim my cheeks, sweeping away my tear stains, but he doesn't question their origin.

"H-h-hello, Master." *Stammering, like an idiot. Smooth move, Erin. Can you be more unsexy?*

I jump when his huge index finger, with a nail as big as a nickel, flicks off his thumb and stings one of my swollen nips. "You look beautiful in that outfit, as I knew you would."

"Thank you, Master." *I've pleased him.* Relief and pride wash over me. I want to be a good slave. I want to make him smile.

He flicks the same nipple with savage precision three more times in quick succession. Each sting shoots straight to my pleasure button. I clamp down on the ben-wa balls, and they roll in my core. "But didn't I instruct you to wear something naughty underneath?"

"Yes, Master."

"Why are your breasts naked? Have you been a bad slave? Do I need to punish you so soon?" Three more snappy strikes. My poor little nipple is on fire. And it feels bloody amazing.

"I did wear something naughty, Master. At least, I hope you'll think it is when you see it. It's special, just for you." Another three ruthless pings and a harsh tweak. I'm so close to coming. *It's too freaking soon to be this turned on.* I have no idea how I don't keel over dead from a heart attack. My little blood pump is pounding like a pile driver, trying to bust through my ribs to leap into his hands. My heart seems to know that's where it belongs no matter how valiantly my head tries to deny it.

Jerry grips my chin with an uncompromising and almost cruel force as he tips my head back. "Let's go take a look then, shall we?" His frigid stare locks onto my doe-eyed gaze. *God, please don't let him be angry or disappointed.* I'm hanging on to my tears, but a shaky feeling inside signals that the clouds in my head are about to open up again and pour.

He grabs my ponytail and leads me to the fireplace and the sheepskin rug. As we walk, I finally see that above his waist Jerry is wearing only an open, black leather biker vest. Bad-boy style. *Shit, double shit, and triple shit.* I guess, after the hell I've been through this last week, maybe I deserve a stupendous reward like this.

This man is my miracle and beautiful beyond anything I could have imagined. His upper body is the most perfectly sculpted work of art. His muscles aren't pumped up and enhanced by steroids or supplements. He's an all-natural male. You can tell, just like you can tell when a woman has implants.

His hairless pecs and abs look like they have been chiseled from marble. *So very lickable.* His dark brown nipples stand pert and almost as large as mine. *So very suckable.* His torso is a roadmap of veins laid over those rock-hard muscles. *So very traceable.* There are two thick veins running south down below his waistband. Good blood flow means ... *Oh my. Thank you, lord, thank you, thank you.*

I let my neck swivel loose as Jerry wraps my braid around his fist. He gives a purposeful tug that wrenches at my roots. The sting is oh so delicious and prompts a gentle cry from the back of my throat. Jerry's handsome face, dark with desire, hovers just above my own. My breath hitches as I realize he's going to kiss me, and it won't be a friendly peck on the cheek.

He stabs his thick tongue between my lips, invading like a conquering Goth. He ravages my mouth with a hunger that is out of control. He bites down on my lower lip and sucks hard. I surrender my bounty to my new ruler, completely relinquishing my will. Abruptly, he untangles from my locks, drops my head, and steps away. I'm left dazed, amazed. I am stupefied, struck mute.

When my eyeballs finally uncross, I look at Jerry and imagine hot, blue flames dancing in his eyes. In an instant, he morphs from a jetfighter pilot screaming at Mach 5 to a Zen Buddhist monk meditating serenely. Jerry's face is sober as he undoes my blouse at a leisurely pace. He unhooks every button before he spreads the fabric wide. When his eyes flash wild and bright, I know I've been redeemed. He nearly tears the delicate silk in his haste to get a good look. The zipper of my skirt is down with no fanfare, and he has me stripped in five seconds flat.

"Erin, where did you get this? It's incredible. *You're* incredible." His fingers slide slowly over the inch-wide leather straps of my harness. He is completely absorbed and enchanted, so focused on me and what I'm wearing that he doesn't notice he just called me Erin. But I notice. Maybe I'm setting myself up for a huge fall, but a small spark of hope flares up in the center of my chest.

"I made it, Master." I can't disguise the pride in my voice as I reply. I dyed leather straps cranberry red and cut them into various lengths, affixing brass O-rings, rivets and buckles to create a woven masterpiece. The polished brass fittings glint and glow in the flickering firelight. Four strips, joined by O-rings, circle each breast. At the top, straps buckle over my shoulders and connect to a band that spans across my back, buckling under my arms. Another band of leather circles my waist, buckling at the sides. Short straps in the front connect the waistband to the breast straps. From O-rings at the side buckles, two long straps drop across my midriff, snake between my thighs on either side of my mound to connect over my perineum. A single 5/8" strap runs up my butt crack and connects to the band at my waist, buckling in the small of my back. The supple leather has hand-tooled embellishments in a rose pattern with Swarovski crystal studs in the center. It's a rugged restraint as well as a work of art, if I do say so myself.

"You made this, Erin? Really?"

"Yes, Master. I wanted a special, sexy treat after everything bad that's happened. Do you like it? Is it naughty enough for tonight?"

My answer is a soul-sucking kiss. Jerry crushes my body into his, one arm across my shoulders, the other crossing down my back so his hand can grab my naked butt and grind my pelvis on his.

"Spin for me." He growls low and long as I turn 360°, letting him see my body all strapped up. The diamond dangling from my hip necklace sparkles below my navel in the V of the midriff straps.

"That is so sexy, baby. Is it strong?" I say it's very sturdy.

"On your hands and knees, slave." I drop on command, my knees sinking into the soft sheepskin in front of the lively fire. Jerry grabs hold of the harness at the two O-rings in the back. He hoists me up into the air. I'm on top of the world, ascending into heaven.

What a surprise. What a thrill. I've never worn one of my harnesses for anyone, so I didn't know how the straps would snug up, digging into me and bearing my weight evenly as Jerry turns and swings me in a circle. He laughs uproariously; booming thunder fills the room. *I'm flying! This is freaking amazing.* No, FUCKING *amazing.* I can't stop giggling like a schoolgirl.

"Oh, Erin. We're going to have some fun with this, baby." I can't remember a happier moment in my life. Jerry is genuinely delighted, and I did that for him. I've surprised this amazing man and pleased him. *He growled at me, for me.* I have to fight back tears again. *He called me Erin again, and baby.* I wonder if there is even the slightest possibility that I might become more than just a short-term slave for him. *Look at all the work he's done, and the roses. Doesn't that mean something?*

"But let's get on with our scene, shall we, sub?" And there's my answer. We're back to "sub." He sets me back down on the sheepskin rug, and I come crashing back to cold reality. Thankfully, the warmth from the fire banishes the instant chill.

"Yes, please, Master."

"Do you call him Master?" I quickly shake my head when I see my mistake. We're in a scene, and Jerry is Dillon. Keeping it straight when to call him Master and when to call him Sir is becoming quite a chore. "On your knees, sub." I settle myself where he points.

"Spread wider for me." I'm more than happy to oblige. "Good girl." He steps in front of me and presents his package to me. Right in my face is a big bulge, held snug by tight leather. *Ohhh!*

"Suck me, sub." Jerry's voice is as restrained as his family jewels. His words are husky with need.

"Yes, Sir." Like there would be any chance that I would say no. I've been dying to get Jerry's cock in me, anywhere. I lick my lips in anticipation as I reach up, unsnap the fly, and unzip the zipper. His rod jerks like a crazed bull lunging to bust loose. *Commando! Yes!*

"Mmm. Mmm." I can't help the hungry, yummy sounds I'm making for the succulent sausage jutting toward my face. I carefully extricate his treasures and yank his pants down. Jerry clutches my braid for balance while he steps out. I kiss my way up to claim him.

"No hands. Grab your waistband behind your back and suck me now." Jerry, the demanding Dom now, barks out his orders. A thrill rushes across my skin, but, damn, he's robbed me by not letting me hold his impressive shaft in my hand and stroke that velvety skin.

I lick the glistening drop of pre-come on the tip of Jerry's purple head with a broad stroke of my flattened tongue. *Tasty.* Then I slurp that tip into my greedy mouth. It's humungous, slightly larger proportionally than any cockhead I'm familiar with, and I've seen quite a few dicks around DYKKC. I sure hope that Jerry is capable of starting slow, or else this monstrous appendage is going to cause me some serious damage. Ohhh, but how freaking amazing he'll feel slamming into me once he's got me ready.

Right from the first lick, Jerry starts thrusting his hips toward me. *Not so slow after all.* I pull back slightly as he pushes forward, trying to warm him up a little with licks and shallow sucks, and giving myself time to adjust to his girth before swallowing him deep. Jim taught me how to deepthroat on my second session with him at the club. *Thank you, Jim. Jerry's going to be a very happy boy in a short while thanks to your tutelage.*

I've never enjoyed giving head more than right now. Jerry's shaft tastes like it's been dipped in honey, and his juices are as robust as fine wine. His musky scent invigorates my senses. I'm a drunken mess, riding on a power high because he growls like it's his first time getting a blow job. And it's because of me, what I'm giving him.

Now that I'm giving myself over completely to pleasuring my Master-for-the-next-month, even though I have to pretend that he's someone else, my own pleasure surges in tandem with his. My gift to Jerry is a gift to myself. *Isn't this what a power exchange is supposed to feel like?* I want to make him feel as powerful as a god. He already looks the part; he should feel it too.

Jerry is tugging on both of my ears and pumping more urgently; I'm ready now to let him go as deep as he wants. As nervous as I was while anticipating this scene, in this moment, it's easy to relax and create an incredible experience for my Master. My throat angles and opens wide for him. My muscles slacken, and he slides his steel all the way in until my nose is almost resting on his belly. I couldn't possibly take him any deeper from this position.

Jerry groans, except it's more like a roar. "Fuuuuck, baby. That feels amazing. Your mouth is magical. Oh, God. Thank you." *Wait, okay. Mr. Manners again.* I'm not sure I'll get used to this, but it's way better than being treated like shit by Dillon.

What a rush! I can't afford to lose my cool now, or I'll suffocate. I need for Jerry to do his part, too. He's a Latin dancer rolling his hips to the sultry beat of sensual music. His enthusiastic erection could really wreck me if he breaks his slow, steady rhythm. Jerry's even-paced breathing now has a pronounced hitch each time he grinds out a feral grunt. My chin bumps against his huge, heavy balls that have hardened and pulled up. He's close. *God, I can't wait to watch his control break.* I suck a little harder to hurry him along.

"I'm coming. Don't you dare waste a drop, sub. Swallow it all." I'm so thirsty, craving all he has to give me when he lets loose. Jerry tugs on my braid to anchor me before he slams into my throat as deep as he can go. *Oh God.* My shoulders curl and my stomach clenches as my gag reflex kicks in. No! My heart will break if I have to pull back before he comes. Then I feel the hot, thick fluid sliding straight down my throat. His cock swells even bigger as he shoots jet after jet of come.

"Errrrinnn!" Jerry's hips buck, but he hangs on tight to my braid as ecstasy wracks his body. His muscles twitch and dance; waves of pleasure ripple through him as he empties himself in me. I want to taste him, need to taste him. On his last spurt, I pull back slightly so some of his seed spills into my mouth. *Mmm, sweet and fresh. Lord, thank you.* I won't have to embarrass either one of us by spitting.

"Baby," is all he can croak out before his knees buckle, and he drops to the floor, toppling us both into a pile on a cushy cloud of sheepskin. He grabs one of my straps and hauls me like I'm a sack of potatoes until I'm pressed against his chest. *I love spooning.* Jerry drops tickling kisses on my shoulder as he palms my breasts, shooting me sky high. I could float here in this dreamland for days.

"You're very talented, little slave. It's been a long time since anyone's been able to deepthroat me." *I don't doubt that. It was a* challenge, *albeit one I will gladly accept again.* "You didn't tell me that was part of the script. That was naughty. It was a nice surprise, but I'll have to punish you for withholding information I asked for." Jerry's sigh has a note of something that pulls at my heart. Being a romantic fool, I'd like to think it's more than disappointment.

I can't let him misunderstand, not to avoid punishment because I'm pretty sure that's a given, but because I want him to be happy. "It wasn't, Master," I squawk. My throat is a little tender.

"Wasn't what?"

"In the script, Master. I have never done that with The Saint. Only twice before, with the one who taught me. That was special just for you, Master." I don't dare mention who my teacher was.

Jerry chomps down possessively into my left shoulder in that tender spot at the base of my neck. *Ow.* He's marking his territory, staking his claim. Dillon bit me once, and I didn't like it. I added "no biting with the intent to mark" onto my list of hard limits. It stings and burns beyond description, but I don't care. Jerry can bite me, mark me wherever the hell he likes.

"Mine," he says. *Yes, Sir. All yours, Sir, for as long as you want. Which is only one month. Bloody Hell.*

"Thank you, Master." *His. If only.*

< ♂ + ♀ >

Damn. I should have kept my mouth shut because the soap bubble we've been floating in pops, like Jerry suddenly remembered that he's supposed to be a Dom. He pushes me away and snaps, "On your knees, sub. Forehead to the floor." I'm there in an instant. Soft lamb hairs tickle my eyelids closed. I can't see, but the rustling in my toy bag perks me up. The familiar cool sensation of lube oozing down my crack alerts me to what's next. *Isn't he jumping ahead?* I draw in a deep breath to ask for permission to speak, and his palm lands a snapping crack on my butt.

"No talking. Don't make me punish you." Okay, he remembers that part of the script. "If I hurt you later, it will ruin the pleasure for both of us, so I'm getting you ready, sub." I relax and breathe. I push to widen my sphincter and let his finger in. I gasp in delight at the slight bite as he slides in. He starts to poke and probe, and I just can't help swaying my derrière. I freeze when he swats each cheek.

I don't own any butt plugs, but a sizable rubber one knocks at my back door. Gentle pushes and coaxing words get that baby worked right in. Jerry checks in to be sure I'm doing okay before he proceeds. I'm doing more than okay. With the ben-wa balls in my vagina, both my channels are deliciously full now. A flood of sensory stimulation pushes me close to the line I don't have permission to cross. What sweet, sweet torture.

This is how it's meant to be. Jerry is exactly the kind of Master I've been waiting for. He's in control of himself, and of me. He's patient and considerate, yet I have no doubt who's the boss of me. It's just the right balance for my tastes.

It SUCKS to have an expiry date on this arrangement. *How hard will it be for me to say goodbye after a few weeks? Hell, what about by the end of this scene? If it's this good now, how high will I be flying by the time we're done, and how far will I crash when he leaves tonight?*

There's a dark, empty place inside me that hungers for a man to care enough about me to keep me bound by his side. That's why I love my harnesses. My sense of belonging to my Master dissolves as he unfastens all of the buckles. As an answer to my pout, he says, "The harness will get in the way of the ropes and hurt you, sub." I know Jerry's being kind. I'd chance it, but he's the one in charge.

I let go of my disappointment, focusing on what Jerry is doing to me. As he tugs at the buckles, the leather strips creak and dig into my tender body. I would embed them into my skin if I could, make them part of me. Even so, Jerry setting me free is one of the sexiest things I've ever experienced. *I'm a gift unwrapped for his pleasure.*

"That was so hot, baby. Taking you out of that harness was hot." He nibbles on my earlobe as he croons, "But I can't wait to strap you back into it." *Did he just read my mind? Oh, yes, Sir. Strap me up, restrain me, have your way with me. Keep me.*

This scene couldn't be more perfect than it is right now. Jerry is a thoughtful Master, not a bastard like Dillon. He used scratchy jute to tie me up with, but Jerry binds me in cording as soft as corn silk. He fulfills the spirit of the scene, but these small details give me the confidence to drop all worries about what is yet to come.

Jerry racks up brownie points at a rapid rate. I could kiss him, if I could reach him. He is maddeningly out of range because he just cinched me up and settled me in the armchair to begin the torture of my poor pussy—her gnawing hunger for him pains me. How unfortunate that she won't be satisfied anytime soon.

Like actors rehearsing a play, we go through the motions, adhering to the script of my night with Dillon, but adlibbing here and there, building excitement and releasing tension, advancing toward the climax. Except Jerry denies my climax time and time again. Just as I scramble up to the point of delirium, he tears me back down.

I know we're following a formula to get me to a particular goal, but this is more than a game. Heaven has granted me a miracle, and

I'll be damned if I'm going to waste it. I appreciate every second, every nuance. I savor each moment in the moment. Like this moment when Jerry's gaze weighs heavy on my pussy, adding to the pleasing pressure of his probing fingers.

In the next moment, everything changes. Snaps and crackles draw Jerry's attention from his task, and he is captured by the mesmerizing fire. Uneasiness settles on me like a heavy shroud. *Is he just playing his part, or has he already lost interest in the scene, in me?* His nimble fingers continue to pinch and penetrate robotically, albeit in shallow thrusts because the ben-wa balls block deep entry.

Jerry's actions don't pack the same punch when he's distracted. Still, persistent repetition takes its toll. *Oh, yes.* Gripping tension radiates from deep in my womb, and I resort to panting breaths to stave off the impending release. My foundation of sanity is rapidly slipping away. His head swivels back toward me; a hard frown mars his handsome face. He pulls his slickened fingers from my sex. The slap he lays on my inner thigh snaps through the room. I huff and puff to restrain the bad word I want to shout at him.

"Do. Not. Come. You know the rules, sub. What will I do if you come?"

"Punish me, Sir." Our words are straight from the script. Now I can relax again since we seem to be back on track. Except relaxing is the worst mistake. The ben-wa balls and butt plug conspire against me, pushing me back to the orgasm launch pad when Jerry slips his finger down and presses circles over my perineum.

I sink my teeth into my bottom lip to choke off the curse that flies up my throat when Jerry's whole hand thumps brutally on my mound. "You're so easy, slut. Can't you hold on longer than that?"

"Ugh." *Oh, shit.* Jerry pushes my emotional hot button with deadly precision. I screw my eyes closed, and my lips quiver. Jerry is speaking, but all I hear are Dillon's and Jed's voices mocking me in stereo. Panic dances at the edge of my awareness; tears lurk in the corners of my eyes. Then I hear my own voice above the bullshit. *I am not a slut. I am not a slut. I am a strong, sexy woman. I have every right to give in to pleasure. I am passionate, not perverted.*

I won't let those bastards defeat me again. I stretch and fill my lungs to ease my tension, and a forgotten, locked door opens in my soul. My strong words of affirmation cross over that barrier and work their way into my psyche. I am *a strong, sexy woman. Pleasure is good.* I force back my tears and gather up all my courage.

When I open my eyes, I know there's a new light shining from them. Jerry has been watching me closely. His head bobs in a quick nod. *He sees it too!*

"Good girl." I damn near fall apart when Jerry lays a soft kiss on my lips and then repeats into my ear, "Good girl." I remember getting gold stars from schoolteachers for giving correct answers. *Jerry just gave me a whole box of gold stars.*

I don't have more than two seconds to bask in my success before I hear the evil buzz of my wand massager. Strong, sexy woman or not, that thing will be his weapon of my destruction.

It's near impossible to not climax with that implement toiling away to force my collapse. With the ben-wa balls and butt plug working in tandem, I don't stand a chance of hanging on to any sense of rationality. The real kicker is the sight of the bare-chested Adonis sitting in front of me, doing the things he's doing to me. I'm kind of a visual gal, and he really is a tasty feast for my eyes. *I'm doomed!*

I catch an evil glint in Jerry's eyes before a curtain falls, and they go blank. He rests the wand head just above my clit. *Whew! That's tolerable.* I concentrate on my flow of breath, and I'm doing okay. Jerry turns when the fire pops again. With his attention elsewhere, his hand drops, and the wand head slides onto my clit.

Stars burst behind my eyes, and I'm right on the brink. I press my lips together with all the strength I can conjure. I force air in and out of my nostrils in short bursts. A moan starts from the base of my spine, rolls to the top of my head and rattles around my brain. Nothing exists except for that moan.

Until my brain is jangled by a powerful yank on my hair. But I'm yanked back to the present and out of the danger zone.

"You almost came, didn't you, slut?"

"Yes, Sir." That's it. End of answer. Nothing superfluous.

"But you stopped, didn't you, sub?"

"Yes, Sir." That's all he needs to know.

"Good girl." Another surprise kiss. It's the best kiss *ever.*

This is where the script gets some new pages. Lesson learned. "Yes, Sir. No, Sir." That's all I'm allowed, and that's what I agreed to. No need for punishment. It's up to me to uphold the rules. That's a big responsibility. This scene is flowing smoothly with me keeping my end of the bargain. I'm proud of myself, and it seems Jerry is proud of me, too. *We both win.*

I'm already at close call number four. I honestly didn't think I would make it this far. It's not from lack of trying on Jerry's part to push me over the edge. He persecutes me with the same fervor that Dillon did. Plus he has added the extra toys. He certainly is dedicated to his craft. Regardless, I've crossed every hurdle so far. I hope I can handle whatever his next test is.

I really hate the sound of my own wand. Once again, Jerry lays the head just above my swollen clit. *I'm cool. I can do this.* My pep talk works until Jerry pushes the massager on top of my clit, on purpose! The blue sparks flying at me from him ignite my ire. *So he is a bit of a bastard after all.* I use the same tactics as before—pressed lips, snorting breaths, deep moaning. I'm able to hang on by a thin thread.

"Hold on. Don't come, sub. When can you come?"

"When you're in my tight, fuckable ass, Sir, and only when you give me your permission."

"That's right. You're so beautiful, sub. You look like you have a fever—bright red flush, glistening shine of sweat, watery eyes, runny nose. You're a mess, a sexy, hot mess for me." Jerry smiles faintly and sighs. He closes his eyes like he's lost in a dream.

That's when it happens. That despicable wand drifts below my clit and onto my slit. I'm not sure how I never knew that that is "my spot." It's not too intense like the battering of the wand vibrating directly on my clit. It's not too far away and tickling mildly like when it's placed just above my clit. *Goldilocks, it's just right.* Pleasure, not pain. Pleasure that's irresistible and seductive. The pain I've been able to withstand. But this bliss, I can only give myself to it. I want to sooo bad. I. WILL. NOT. DISAPPOINT. MY. MASTER. I pitch the script out the window and improvise.

"Intermission, Sir. Intermission." *I'm allowed to use my safeword.* I'm *supposed* to use my safeword if it will preserve the scene. Jerry and I chose our own safewords when we negotiated our contract. During a scene, "intermission" means "yellow," or pause and check in. "End scene" means "red," or full stop. "Exit" means an immediate termination of the contract.

"What's the matter, sub?"

"Sir. I can't take any more of this. I'm sorry, Sir. But I can't hold back even five more seconds." I drop my eyes and hang my head.

"Good girl. Thank you for telling me. I need to know your limits." Mmm, such a sweet kiss he lays on my lips. *How will I live without his lips?*

Jerry drops the wand on the hardwood with a clatter that triggers in me a sigh of relief. His whole face is relaxed and open. He asks if the ropes are hurting. I answer "play on," our version of "green." Warmth flows over me as his gaze wanders over my body.

"I've been waiting too long to bury myself deep in your beautiful ass." He growls, and I gush. "Are you ready for me, sub?"

"Oh, yes, Sir." I hope he can hear that, not only am I ready, I'm willing and impatient. His laugh rumbles like distant thunder and reverberates along my skin. Every nerve in my body zings. I hope I don't combust before the part where he thrusts inside me. I'm wild with wanting his cock.

Jerry lifts me in his strong arms and carefully turns me around, laying me across the chair with my collarbones resting on one padded arm of the chair and my bound legs butting up against the other. Even with my knees sinking down into the soft cushion, my behind is raised high enough for Jerry to have easy entry from the side of the chair. The best part is that my head hangs free; I won't need to be visiting Dr. Jefferson again.

Rough, ardent hands surf across my back, breasts and belly, soothing me, arousing me, frustrating me. The swipe of his palms over my behind is almost enough to do me in. More cooing and coaxing, and, before I know it, the butt plug is out.

The ripping of a condom wrapper signals that it won't be long before I get what I want. The squelch of lube squirting rings in my ears, and the slide of coolness energizes my entire being.

"God, you're so damned amazing. Hang on tight, sub." I've been stretched and loosened and prepared for nearly an hour, the longest I've ever survived orgasm denial, and it still stings when Jerry spreads my cheeks and spears the head of his hard-on into me. I gasp and squeal like a stuck pig.

"Intermission, Sir."

"Does that hurt, sub?"

"Too much, Sir. You're too much for me, at least with the ben-wa balls still in me." He laughs and reaches underneath to pull on the string to extract them. As each of the three balls pops out, explosions ricochet through my womb. The last one almost blasts me into the stratosphere.

"Thank you, Sir." I float my words to him on a soft sigh.

"Good girl. Brace yourself. I'm going to fuck you hard. And when I'm ready, I'll let you come." His wicked words and steamy breath in my ear are like a shot of epinephrine; my heart jumps and pounds out of control. Jerry grabs my tits and hangs on for dear life, leveraging himself as he glides first his tip and then his rock-hard shaft in my back hole with steady pressure. I try to push him out, and that lets him slip in easier.

"Aaaahhhh!" *Help me, Jesus. Iamgoingtolosemyfreakingmind!* I can't believe he's in, all of him, all the way in. Every blessed long, fat inch of him.

"Shit. You. Are. So. Hot. And. So. Tight. I've. Never. Felt. Anything. So. Fucking. Fantastic." Each word is a percussive grunt at the end of a piercing stab of Master's tool. A few more like that and I won't be responsible for my pussy's reaction. I've never felt so full, so possessed, so whole. This feeling is much more than physical fulfillment. *I'm in big, big trouble.* My heart is messing around where it doesn't belong. It needs to stay out of this, or we'll never survive once he's gone.

Jerry grants me mercy and releases one breast, which he was squeezing to mush, but drags his hand down to take up residence between my thighs. His manual manipulation skills are so good, so evil, that I'm about ten seconds away from the point of no return. My loins are on fire and pent up desire strains every muscle to the max. My grumbles match his grunts.

"Come for me, sub! NOW!" He shouts that last word, deafening me, as my channel stretches further to receive his swollen, throbbing missile. I let my mind and body go loose and surrender to the orgasm that has been building forever. Pleasure overtakes us, and we scream each other's name as Jerry bangs into me one last time and detonates. I feel his endless pulsing, but his liquid heat is insulated and slightly cooled by the condom. Safety, but a little less sensation—a necessary but disappointing trade-off.

I am done in and about as solid and stable as chocolate pudding. Jerry is the same and melts all over me, spreading his full bulk on me. Squished, and squashed, and satisfied. I don't care that the ropes are tight. It doesn't matter that my legs have fallen asleep. I'm not complaining that I'm flattened by this hulking hunk who is so gratified that he doesn't have the strength to hold his weight off me. *Surely this is heaven.*

It's a completely different finish than the last time I played out this scene. No punishment, pain or soul-destroying terror. Only pleasure, sensuality and soul-healing happiness. This is a big win for me and cause for celebration. But I realize it's also a flagrant illustration of my failure.

Chapter Fourteen – Contemplation

Sunday Evening, September 23

Jerry's bones seem to have reformed, far too quickly for my liking. I was warm and cozy with him pinning me to the chair, but I immediately miss the pressure of him in me and on me. Still, I'm relieved big time as the ropes start to fall away from my aching limbs. Pins and needles ravage my arms and legs as pinched nerves release and blood flows freely through my veins again.

Before I'm fully coherent, Jerry gathers me up, wraps me in my fuzzy, fleece throw and deposits me on the couch. My eyes won't focus, but the tenderness in the sweep of his fingers across my jaw tells me everything I can't see on his face. When he cradles my chin and kisses me softly, I break apart. *Stupid heart. I don't want to hear your crazy notions that this is the man we need. He's out of our league, and he's not going to be around for long. So shut it, now.*

Jerry still hasn't made a sound, but loud pops fill the room and sparks fly as the log he throws in the fireplace catches alight. His perfectly proportioned ass sways as he struts to the bathroom. If I could trust that there's more between us than the contract, I'd be playful and bold enough to say something about the stellar view. It's killing me to hold back anything from myself or from him.

He prowls back toward me after stopping in the kitchen for a bottle of cabernet sauvignon. The wine is not one of mine, but it's a very good Chilean vintage. In his other hand is a platter of fruit, cheese and crackers, and chocolate. *I can get into the sex and the sensation, but why is he laying the seduction on so thick?*

Jerry opens up the blanket and thoroughly bathes my privates with a warm cloth. He scoots in beneath me, pulling me up against his still heaving chest. He unwinds my braid, buries his head in my fluffed up tresses and breathes me in. *The way he takes care of me, so intimately ... Can I pretend he's my boyfriend, just for a minute?* Jerry's concerned voice kills any hope of staunching my tears.

"Thank you, sub, for letting me do this for you. Are you okay?" *Shouldn't I be the one thanking him?* I'm sunk if I speak, so I throw my arms around him and burrow into his armpit. Maybe he'll be satisfied with a nonverbal response.

"Mmmmm." I go crazy for the sensation of skin against skin, that scrumptious friction of two naked people colliding. I shift and rub my body over Jerry's, nuzzling his face with my nose in that kitty cat way I like.

"That feels nice, sub. Tell me, did the scene work for you? Did you have any insights?" *Okay, I can do this. Disengage gooey heart, bring analytical brain back online.*

I draw strength from some unidentified reservoir in my gut. "It was my fault. What happened to me was my fault, Master." My heart, still running in the background, rouses out of hibernation and lays me flat. Uncontrollable sobs seize me. Jerry holds me tight.

"Hush, kitten. Take it easy. Just breathe, baby." Jerry waits a few minutes for my crying jag to subside before he speaks again. "Would you feel better if I strapped you back into your harness?" *Does he know me that well already? Or is he really asking for what he wants?*

I can't describe how eminently right it feels being back in my harness, especially with my Master snugging me up in it. I don't know what it is about a few scant strips of leather that is so sexy. If I could wear only one item of clothing for the rest of my life, this would be it. I might as well be naked, yet I feel safe and secure.

The way that Jerry ogles my body and skims his palms over me sends spirals of lust through my whole being. He snags the two straps under my breasts and yanks me hard against him. A zing of desire zips straight to my clit when he growls in my ear. "You look so damned good in this thing that you make me hard." *Yes, indeed, he is verrrry hard.* "Let's finish our conversation. Then I'm going to take you to bed so I can finally bury myself in your wet pussy." *Yes, indeed, it is verrrry wet. And you can have my pussy anytime you want. Right now, in fact.*

"Now, tell me why you think that what Dillon did was your fault, sub." Jerry settles us on the couch and shifts us around until I am straddling his lap, both of us sitting eye to eye.

"I failed my Top, Master. I broke the rules before he did, and I pushed him too far." I lower my head in shame. Facing Jerry head on is unbearable. He thwarts my evasive tactics by gripping my chin and holding my face up to the light so I can't hide my culpability.

"That sounds a bit simplistic. Tell me more."

"I was angry at Dillon for his shitty mood. Instead of trying to make him feel better or cutting him some slack, I was a brat to him. I forced him into disciplining my sassiness and bringing out the clamps. That was the first point our scene went astray. If I had kept to my allowed responses, like I did with you, he may have been able to stay on course."

"I know Dillon, remember? He likes to inflict punishment. Saying thank you was a minor offense. But, in the mood he was in, he would have found another excuse to serve up the pain." I shake my head, telling him he's letting me off easy. He stills me with his firm hold on my chin. "Is there more?"

"Warranted or not, I didn't submit to my Top's punishment, Master. I kept antagonizing him and questioning his authority."

"Safe, sane and consensual, baby. Bottom or not, you have a right to question when your Top is not acting responsibly. You don't park your intelligence at the door when you engage in a scene. Understand, sub?" Jerry's words and tone are strict. His fat thumb pressing on my lower lip while he speaks is as effective in subduing me as his hand clamped to my shoulder was on the day we met.

"Yes, Master. There's more." He nods as if to say that I should continue.

"I was very confused at the time, but you helped me see tonight that my biggest sin was coming when I didn't have his permission. I should have used my safeword before I came, at least called yellow and warned him instead of waiting until the situation was already out of control. I could have saved us both a ton of grief. It was my responsibility to maintain the flow of the scene, and I failed."

Jerry's hand slides from my chin to palm my cheek. "Good girl. I'll agree on that. I was proud of you tonight, sub. I know it can be hard, can feel like you've failed when you have to use your safeword. It takes courage and strength to admit when you've hit your limit. You protected us both. You gave us both an opportunity to act with honor. I have no idea whether it would have made a difference with Dillon, but you acted with integrity and allowed me to maintain my nobility." *Nobility? Wow, that word has weight.*

"Unlike him, I don't like to be obliged to reprimand my slave for disobedience. I have more than enough of being the disciplinarian and enforcer at work. Thank you for not putting me in the position of having to do something with you that I don't want to do."

"You're welcome, Master. I'm glad I realized in time. Oh!" A light bulb flashes above my head. Jerry stares and waits patiently. *Oh, God. Can I say it out loud?* My heart is itching to spill it all; it likes sitting on my sleeve. My head asks for a bit more caution.

"Master ... I know what made the difference tonight." My heart wins again. I try to drop my head and my gaze to make it easier for me to confess. Jerry waggles my chin again and shakes me up.

"I was desperate to not disappoint you—it was *imperative* that I not disappoint you—and the right response flowed when I made you my priority." *Stupid, meddlesome heart. You had to make me say it.*

"Desperate?" I'd like to wipe that smug grin off his face, except it's damned sexy. I like that he likes that I was desperate for him. The wicked gleam in his baby blues ensnares me, his willing captive.

Jerry is a different kind of predator than my panther, coyote, and wolf. There is something about the way Jerry moves, the way he speaks. He's in a class all of his own—Master is a mighty lion. A picture of him as a proud and laudable king, the king of the pride, flashes before my eyes. I think of Simba, except that's too lame and tame to consider for more than a half second.

"Y-y-yes, Master. I wanted to be a good slave for you. I didn't want to let you down. I had to set aside any concerns about my own agenda. But, with Dillon, I was a bad sub. I was thinking only about myself instead of my Top. I've been angry with him for being preoccupied and letting his mind wander that night. I'm ashamed to say I was hurt; I thought I wasn't good enough to hold his attention. So I couldn't stay present either. I let my emotions run away with me, and we both got hurt." *And I robbed him of his chance at nobility.*

"How do you think things would have ended if you trusted him?"

"I did trust ... Oh! Oh, I've never trusted him the way I trust you, Master." I know it's true the moment I blurt the words out. That's why I tried to keep that bit of control with Dillon. I'm gonna cry again. *You had to make me admit it, didn't you, Jerry?*

"You honor me greatly, sub. Thank you," he whispers. Eyes flash. Lips crush. Tongues parry. Teeth gnash. Hands grope. Bodies press. We both lose ourselves in the carnal response to our profound emotional revelations. We are naked, body and soul.

Regaining composure, Jerry first, of course, he says, "Erin, listen to me closely now. Yes, I called you by your name. We need to step outside of this scene for a minute. This is important.

"A man lives by a simple code. By virtue of his strength, he is a leader and protector. He has to hold himself to a high standard of discipline that allows him to fulfill his responsibilities in the world.

"A *man* never hits or hurts a woman or child when in the throes of anger. There is never any circumstance that could justify such an action. That kind of violence is called assault, and it's punishable by law. It's very different from benevolent discipline and correction or erotic torment. Losing control to that degree, or using his superior strength or his position of power to commit that or any other act of aggression, a man can no longer call himself a man." Jerry's words bear down on me and wrap me in a blanket of comfort that assures me I have found refuge in his arms. He means every syllable; I believe that code is ingrained in every fiber of his being.

"And the moment a woman closes her heart in anger or fear, she is no longer a woman." *Whoa!* I'm not sure where I found those words—they are probably Evanya's—but I don't doubt their truth as they sound in the space between us. Jerry's arms enfold me like a suit of armor. That is the only shield I need. *God help me, my woman's heart is open and undefended before him. I love this man.*

Jerry pulls back. The energy between us stretches like an elastic cord. I don't know exactly when it happened, but we've forged a resilient connection. Our physical separation doesn't feel to me like a loss, and the bond between us is just as strong. Jerry cradles my face in his palms and drags his thumbs across my cheeks. *Does he feel it, too?* The desire flaring in his eyes is tempered by what feels to me like respect, maybe even appreciation. His insistent but tender kisses send trickles of lust flowing through me—and waves of affection and love.

"Erin, just as a man has a code, so does a Master or a Dom. Our needs should never be more important than our submissive's. We exchange power, not steal it. We never knowingly push a sub too far beyond her limits unless we are selfish, a true sadist. And when we give a sub a safeword, it becomes an unbreakable vow to do no harm. No matter what happened during your scene, Dillon broke his vow to you. When he violated his pledge of safety, he committed a moral offense. You are *not* responsible for that.

"I know you have a kind heart, but that doesn't absolve Dillon of his responsibility or release him from blame. It was not your fault that he compromised you. Or that he harassed you. Or that he kidnapped you. There are no excuses for his behavior. He is answerable to you, if not the courts, for his offenses. Whatever help you need from me to get what feels like justice to you, you have it. Without question, or reservation, or limitation."

"You really mean that, don't you?" The answer is written all over his face and communicated by his touch. My eyes water again.

"I haven't had this level of support in a long time, someone on my side no matter what. Not since my parents died. Jerry, I can't begin to tell you how much that means to me. Thank you seems inadequate." With his reply, Master takes us back into our scene.

"There is a different dynamic between a Master and slave in a committed relationship than between a Top and bottom who play together occasionally at a club. As short as it is, you and I are bound by contract. That's a solemn commitment.

"As Master, I expect more of my slave. I'll be stricter in most things, but more forgiving in the rest. I will take what I want from you but will also give you more protection and care, and more of myself. If something is troubling you, you have to talk to me. We both have responsibilities to fulfill to ensure we each get our needs met and honest communication is the most important one. I think we're doing well so far, don't you, slave?"

The mature woman of just moments ago has fled the room. In her place is a pre-pubescent ninny, the kind who would swoon because a teen heartthrob *maybe* smiled at her way back in the 25th row at a crowded concert. *He thinks we're doing well.* I smile like a giddy fan-girl, crushing on Jerry big time.

"Yes, Master. Really well, Master." *Except for the part where my optimistic heart is already daydreaming about a honeymoon with the Lion King. That's definitely not a good thing.*

We sit side by side on the couch awhile, feeding each other nibbles from the snack platter and sipping wine. I'm more relaxed than I've ever been; the wine just makes me more floaty and flowy.

My fuzzy dream state doesn't last long. My still waters start to ripple, then churn, then rage, disturbed by the greedy way Jerry sucks my fingers each time I bring a morsel to his lips. It isn't fair. He's such a tease. He probably thinks he's a smooth seducer; I think he's mean to work me up so much and not do me right away.

We try to set aside all heaviness and aim for light conversation. Jerry asks about my home and some of the things he sees, like my artwork. Talk about home leads to questions about my parents, and Jerry holds me close and kisses the top of my head while I talk.

Seeing that I'm getting sad, he changes the topic by asking what kind of music I like and what hobbies I have. *Just like we're on a date.* Jerry is very curious about my recent interest in leathercraft and is anxious to see my other creations. He absent-mindedly grabs at random straps of my harness. Each time he pulls, he seems to be entranced by the way my body sways. For me, every little playful tug he makes tugs something inside—a frayed nerve connected to my clit, or somewhere deeper in my core, a delicious memory of our scene, or a fragile heartstring. In a flash, play time is over.

$$< \mars + \venus >$$

Jerry clinks down our wineglasses, sloshing drops of cabernet onto the coffee table. Leaping off the couch, he brusquely clutches my back straps. I squawk and squeak as he lifts me into the air. He carries me toward my bedroom, stalking down the hall that seems to stretch endlessly before us. When, at last, we near the bed, with the covers all turned down, ready and waiting, my majestic lion swings me back and launches me onto the bed. *I'm. Really. Flying.* All my breath bursts out of me, along with my ability to speak, as I land in a heap. *OMGOMGOMG! This is so hot.*

I try to scrabble my way upright and over to the far side of the bed. But a fierce beast pounces on me, growling like a savage, jerking on my straps to maneuver me beneath him. Blue eyes aren't meant to look feral, but Jerry's do. They glow with animal lust. I'm both a frightened little kitten and a cat in heat. We rough and tumble all over my king-size bed, rolling and pinning, biting and licking, sucking and pulling. Unleashed and uninhibited, we wrestle with each other in a wild battle. Jerry's superior strength wins out, flattening me into the firm mattress, immobilizing my arms and legs with all his weight bearing down on me.

"Stay!" he commands. My Master's piercing stare sticks me to the bed. I know how a butterfly feels with her wings pinned down for scientific examination. He shifts his bulk and towers above me on his knees, reaching for one of the condoms that are ready and waiting. *Oh goody, oh goody, oh yes!* I lick my lips as I watch him roll the sheath over his hard length. I can't wait.

I don't think there's a more glorious sensation than the glide of hard penis into soft vagina. There is nothing to compare it to, no simile descriptive enough. The combining of masculine and feminine energies in the shared goal of pleasure, completion. The colliding of angles and curves in an artistic arrangement. Ebb and flow, advance and retreat, possessing and surrendering. How can the phenomenon of that exquisite motion be done justice by the composition of mere letters and spaces on a page or words floating in the air?

I've experienced the wonder and magic of intercourse before, had mindblowing sessions with my three Tops. Nothing, however, could prepare me for Jerry sinking himself home inside my love vessel. Home it is. He's the one who belongs there. My heart already knows. Now my body knows. My soul knew long before we met.

In the soft glow of lamp light, I see tiny images of my awestruck face glinting off the glassy surface of his eyes. *Does he see himself reflected in mine like he wanted?* I've never given so much of myself, or received as much in return. I am a goddess in the thrall of this god. I don't care if I crash and burn tomorrow; tonight I am making love for the first time. I won't hold back even a scintilla. We stoke each other's passions until we explode in a dazzling conflagration of heat and light, hollering each other's names as we flare.

It seems to take hours for the flames to die down to glowing embers, but I know it hasn't been that long. "What is it that you wouldn't tell me yesterday, my little slave girl?" The abrupt disturbance of the comfortable silence jars me out of my reverie. *'slave'? Was all of that closeness and connection and outpouring of heart energy just an illusion created by a skilled Master?* It's shocking how one tiny word can fling you hurtling back to earth.

"Jerry?"

"Yesterday you cried when I told you what I wanted to do to your pussy. I've waited patiently, *slave*, for you to tell me why."

"I don't understand." Now he waits quietly. "You called me slave. Not Erin. Hasn't the scene ended?"

Jerry throws a heavy leg across mine, imprisoning me. "This is new for you, sub, so let me explain again. You contracted to be my submissive, my slave, for a certain period of time. I will call you sub, or slave or any other damn name I like. When we're alone and relaxed, you may call me Sir. During scenes, when we're fucking, or when you're being disciplined, you will call me Master. At any other time, you will wait to follow my lead. Do you understand, sub?"

"Yes, Sir." I guess I do understand his rule. It's the rest of it that I'm having trouble with. It feels like Jerry is putting a wall up that doesn't feel right after what just happened between us. I don't like the distance.

"Now, tell me why you cried, sub." There's a stern, impatient edge to his tone. It still takes me a moment to find my voice.

"You said you wanted to see your reflection in my eyes when you were inside me." I have to pause, and the next part is barely a whisper. "None of them ever looked in my eyes."

Jerry rolls on top of me. His eyes lock with mine, not wavering, not even blinking. I wish I could read the expression on his face. Long minutes pass like that before he speaks. "Oh, baby. How could they not look, not see you? They have no idea what they missed. Seeing your passion and your pleasure beaming from you is a gift I treasure. It was a thrill and an honor to witness that split second when your eyes glazed over and you started your fall over the edge, knowing I'm the one who brought you there and pushed you over. I'll never forget that moment."

Crying. Like. A. Big. Baby. Just like that, the walls crash down again. His shifting moods make me dizzy. All I know is that, this second, I am very happy.

"Hush, kitten. Let's brush our teeth and call it a night."

"Sir? You're not leaving?" My bright tone couldn't be more obvious. I'm more than pleased that he might actually be staying.

"You did some powerful work tonight, sub. I'm your Master, not your Top, and it would be irresponsible to leave you alone before you feel grounded again. I promised you protection, emotional as well as physical. I need to be here for you if you experience sub drop. I won't let you refuse aftercare like Dillon did. You've already learned the problems that can cause."

"Oh." My dead tone could only be construed as dejection. *He's fulfilling a duty to make sure I don't get depressed after an intense scene.* That thought alone is enough to drop me down. *I am nothing more than an obligation.*

"Besides," he says with a mischievous smile, "you granted me full access whenever I want. I just might want to ravage you and dip into your tight little pussy a time or two more before we go to work in the morning." *Alrighty then. That's more like it.*

"Yes, Sir!" My sensible, rational mind is freaking out; my stupid, open heart is over the moon. *Don't read too much into it; he sooo wants me. You're a responsibility; he sooo wants me. It's only temporary; he sooo wants me.* Only time will tell.

< ♂ + ♀ >

Chapter Fifteen – Penance

Wednesday, Morning, September 26

The ping of an incoming text pulls me out of my dream of sailing through the air toward a crash landing on a gigantic marshmallow. '2nite at 7. Wait at yr door like b4. Wear only harness. Have special treat for My slave. Make sure u r wet. NO COMING.' *Damn, I'm wet already!*

What a great way to be woken up. But not as great as it was to wake up Monday morning with Jerry in my bed, dipping into my cunny as promised.

< ♂ + ♀ >

He was spooned up against my back, one hand grabbing a boob, the other stroking my clit. My top leg was pulled back and locked into place by one of his, opening me up and giving him the free pass he claimed as his right. I jumped up out of REM sleep as the fat crown of his morning woody split me open and penetrated deep into my already wet heat.

Jerry rocked into me slow and steady, for all of maybe 30 seconds until he knew I was awake. Then he shifted into hyperdrive and hammered away until we both screamed, each shouting a different expletive. He dragged me to the shower as soon as I could breathe again and sponged my body and shampooed my hair. His attention to the task dissolved me into a puddle of goo; I worried I might wash down the drain with the soap suds. Leaving the house that morning, leaving him, was the hardest thing I've ever done.

An hour later, the sexting started. Naughty little messages like, 'Put honey in My tea. Tasted like yr sweet pussy.' And 'Pinch yr nipples slave girl. Do it hard.' And 'I'm so hard thinking of yr ass.'

Just after lunch came the message I was expecting. 'Slide yr benwa balls deep in My hot pussy slave.' When I arrived at work, I had found them in my purse as I was putting away my car keys. That started a flurry of wicked commands and obedient replies until five minutes before quitting time. My Master told me to take the ben-wa balls out before leaving. Then all communication stopped.

I was frothing at the mouth by the time I got home. I couldn't wait for him to call or come over to put me out of my misery. But there was no call. Nothing. By 9:00, I was so horny that I climbed on the arm of the couch to get a bit of relief. I slid my mound back and forth over the curved arm, sending me into dangerous territory. I was walking with one foot in heaven and the other in hell. I had to stop when I got too close to sliding into full release. *Bastard.*

I realized that Jerry hadn't specifically said I couldn't initiate contact, and I was tired of waiting. My little fingers got busy texting. 'Not touching self but riding couch arm. Need to come sooo bad. Really close now.' I wanted to see what kind of rise I could get out of him. I knew he would punish me if I came, but what would he do for teasing him? *What kind of penance will he demand?*

None. After climbing the walls for another hour, I gave up. He must have had a good laugh knowing what he was doing to me. I got ready and climbed into bed, sad and angry to be sleeping alone like almost every night of my life. I hate my empty bed and his absence made it worse. I played meditation music to help me contemplate kindness instead of ways of causing Jerry bodily harm. I repeated the CD a couple of times, so it was near midnight when I fell asleep.

Like I was a marlin caught on a deep-sea fisherman's line, I was dragged up from the depths of sleep by the ringing of my phone. Before I could mumble, "Who is it?" I heard, "Put two fingers in my pussy, slave girl." It wasn't until later in the morning that I realized Jerry had said "my pussy" like he had in his texts. *His property. Hell, yeah.* At the time, I didn't think; I just did as he ordered. It was no surprise that I was already wet. Maybe I was *still* wet.

"Pump your fingers hard. Make my pussy feel so good." The one thing I did notice was that his voice was just as groggy and thick as mine would be if I had tried to speak. Jerry ground out a series of short commands, just one or two or three words each, leading me along a twisting, steep path up the mountain. I was about to drift over the edge when he yelled into the phone. "Stop! No coming, sub." He chortled in a way that resonated evil merriment. "That's your punishment for riding the couch without my permission." I growled and spat out the f-word.

"Language, sub. That will be ten strokes when I see you." *I doubt he means caressing strokes of his talented fingertips, but will it be his hand or something more fearsome making good on his sentence?*

"Get some sleep, kitten. I imagine you've had a restless night." Then there was nothing but dead air. He had already clicked off before I could call him a smug shit and earn another ten strokes. My phone rang again at 6:30 yesterday morning. That time he guided me to take a leap off the cliff and fly. I would have lost my mind if he hadn't allowed me some respite. What was even more satisfying was hearing how very pleased he was that I had made "his body" happy.

"His body" wasn't at all happy as last night ended with my legs twisted like a pretzel, trying to squeeze the tension from my loins again. Because of all the texts he sent during work hours, I turned my phone off yesterday afternoon to get some work accomplished. Besides, I kept catching my staff staring at me. They were probably wondering why my eyes would cross every five minutes.

When I walked out of my office, I turned my phone back on. There were several messages from Jerry. He was incensed that I had blocked his access to me, but I had done it as a matter of self-preservation. I texted an apology to him anyway. He texted back his "correction," a command to get in the elevator and rub between my legs and moan.

A couple of law students were in the car when the door opened. I waved them on and texted 'no' to Jerry. I couldn't do what he wanted, but I knew that going through the motions in an empty car without an audience wouldn't satisfy his demand. He told me not to argue. I reminded him our contract prohibits public humiliation. The alternative he offered was another ten strokes across my ass. I repeated my 'no,' and that was the last I heard until bedtime.

The sexting resumed and Jerry sped me along the race track, telling me where to touch myself and how, but he wouldn't let me cross the finish line. If this is going to be his *modus operandi* for the next month, I am going to be a sleep-deprived mess. I might actually beg to end our contract early if he is going to be such an unrelenting pussy tease. Before crawling into bed, I set up a unique ringtone for Jerry—"No Sleep Tonight" by the Faders.

$$< \male + \female >$$

Just reading Jerry's latest text has me wet in anticipation of tonight, just like he wanted. I know I'll stay this way until he arrives, especially since he didn't give me any relief this morning. I know which harness I want to wear next for him. It's not as strong as my newest one because the fasteners are snaps instead of buckles, but it really makes a statement. My whole body, except for my legs, will be encased in strips of leather forming diamond patterns.

Again, my breasts will each be outlined by four strips of leather, black this time, connected by brass O-rings. A strap at each of the top points of the diamond shapes above my boobs and across my shoulder blades is riveted to a heavy, black collar. Since it's my own collar, I have no concerns about wearing it for play tonight. Smaller diamond patterns continue down each arm, ending in O-rings that slide over my middle fingers. The diamond that terminates just above my clit and the one that sits at the top of my butt crack are coupled by a length of heavy grosgrain ribbon. It holds everything together and is easier to clean than leather is when saturated by pussy juices. It also sinks into tight crevices in a way that is both maddening and exhilarating.

Jerry hasn't sent any texts today, other than my wake up call, but it's been impossible to concentrate on work without someone directly in front of me needing a solution to a problem and forcing me to pay attention. I'm useless here, so I slip out an hour early to miss the heaviest of rush hour traffic.

I while away the time before his arrival by following my Master's grooming instructions–showering, shaving, and slathering myself in the organic, vanilla-scented body lotion he couriered to me at work this morning. The note in the package said, "Wear this for Me tonight. You'll taste as good as you'll smell." I shudder and hope that he'll taste every inch of me that I spread it on.

My stomach is churning, but I force myself to eat a light dinner of last night's leftovers of grilled salmon, steamed broccoli and rice pilaf. The carbs will give me energy, and the protein will give me stamina. A shot of orange brandy for dessert warms me nicely all over. I line my toes up on the spot by the front door with two minutes to spare. It's just enough time to regulate my breath and get in the correct stance.

$$< \male + \female >$$

My nipples burn as hot as a volcano spewing lava while his key turns in the lock. The breeze from the door opening and closing cools the nubs into hard pebbles of basalt rock. All I can see with my head down are Jerry's dark blue jeans and brown suede loafers. His icy hands shock me as they slide over my arms. Those big hands curl around the O-rings under my boobs and drag me brutishly against his chest. I simply adore the way he manhandles me. The air whooshing from my lungs when we connect forces my head up. He claps his hand firmly on top and bends it back down. The gesture overtly establishes his primacy.

The only sound I hear is the groan I can't suppress when Jerry pinches my nipples and then crushes my breasts together. He grabs my collar and drags me toward the couch. Without a word, he slides the coffee table out of the way, sits down, and pulls me across his lap. My bare ass is presented to him. I could lie here for hours enjoying his palms sliding over my goosebumped skin. But I know that he is warming me up for something not nearly as pleasant.

"Twenty strokes, sub. Let's get them over with so I can give you your surprise. What are the first ten for?"

"For swearing, Master."

"Good girl. What are the other ten for?" This question is trickier.

"For turning my phone off, Master."

"Yes, slave. That was a huge mistake, but your first option for correction wasn't a spanking, was it?" He shows his disappointment in me by the tone of his voice. "You rejected both options available to you. Instead of obeying in a way that wouldn't embarrass you or using your safeword, you dismissed my authority and flat out defied me, *twice*. I think that earns you a bonus ten strokes." *Shit.*

"Your ass is going to be crimson by the time I'm finished with you." I can hear his smile about that part of it. "I will count each stroke, and you will thank me for it. Then you will ask me for another. Do you understand, slave?" I said I did. This is my penance, asking for, volunteering for punishment.

I don't doubt that Jerry is going to have a little fun turning my skin red with the first ten strokes. Swearing is a minor trespass. It's not in our contract, just something he's decided he doesn't like, and I guess I was a bit of a brat. But I've failed my Master by making him pile on the additional 20. I remember what he said about being the enforcer at work. Guilt rides roughshod over my heart because I regret turning him into that.

The first smack of his open palm sounds more painful than it is. It's not nearly as hard as Dillon whacks me, even on his first slap. *I can handle this.* Still, I squirm across his legs as he counts, "One."

"Thank you, Master. May I have another, please?" Dillon taught me the appropriate response, although he made me do the counting as well. The next five swats come hard and fast, on alternating cheeks. I don't have time in between each one to say anything, but I do squeak out my thanks at the end and request more.

"Good girl. You look so pretty in pink." His crooning is as soothing as his hands circling my stinging flesh. The next four slaps come in pairs on each cheek. "That's your first ten, sub. No more swearing, or you'll get double next time."

"Yes, Master. Thank you. Please continue." I detest the sharp sting of the ass whacking, and each swat had an unnerving extra consequence. Every jiggle of my cheeks worked the harness ribbon tighter over my slit and deeper into my butt crack. I have the ultimate wedgie, a combination of both pleasure and pain.

I can tell precisely how upset Jerry is about me turning off my phone because the next ten smacks are as hard and fast as Dillon's wallops. My bottom is blazing out of control. I could use some of that fire-retardant foam they spread at the airport when a plane is coming in for a hard landing. My tears drop silently in heaping spoonsful, making a big wet spot on the couch cushion. I've already almost reached my limit. I don't know why I thought Jerry would go easier on me than Dillon did.

"You will not turn off your phone again, slave. Full access is what you agreed to in the contract. This is a serious breach." Jerry's really mad. There's an electric hum rattling in his voice box. He squeezes my tender bottom as he growls out his words. It hurts so much that I can hardly keep myself from sobbing out loud. I'm glad it hurts. I deserve the pain. I'm mad at me, not him, for bringing this set of smacks on myself.

"I'm really sorry for making you angry, Master. I promise it won't happen again."

Jerry slides an arm under my hips and lifts my butt in the air. Then I'm rewarded by the best feeling in the world. He blows refreshing, cooling air over my scorched skin and covers me in tickling, butterfly kisses. He also runs his finger under the ribbon between my legs to ease the torque against my sensitive flesh. I squirm, this time in delight that he wants to soothe me.

Jerry is strong and quick. The next second, I'm spinning around, and half a second after that my nose is pressing up against his; I'm looking into his eyes for the first time tonight. Sitting across his lap, my butt hangs off the edge and dangles in the cool breeze.

"slave, I said a man never hits in anger. As mad as I was about you not keeping your end of our agreement, I was more upset about you preventing me from fulfilling my responsibility to you. I did not express anger with my hand tonight; I've already let that go. But just because I'm no longer angry, it doesn't mean I'm not determined.

"Tonight, I needed to, if you will excuse the pun, *impress* upon you the gravity of what you did. You are under my protection, girl. Dillon is still a threat, and we need to be able to communicate with each other in case he comes after you again. You might not have time to wait for your phone to power up. I almost went to the library to make you turn it back on. I had to tell myself you would be safe at work, but I was nervous the whole time. Please, don't make me worry like that again."

Now I can't stop the tears. *What a shit I am to cause him such genuine concern.* I was selfish, not a good slave at all. A little bit of distraction on my part is not worth putting my Master through that kind of stress. I bury my head in the crook of his neck as I cry. His white T-shirt is soaked. I hope I've not stained it with mascara.

"I do have to take some of the blame here. I admit I was having too much fun tormenting you. It's been a while since I've had a slave of my own. It was selfish of me to interfere with your work time. I'll make you a deal. I won't pester Erin as much at work, and my slave never turns her phone off again. Okay?" Jerry has me wrapped up tight, talking to me with his face buried in my hair. I'm shaking so bad. *Wait. It's not just me. It's Jerry, too.*

"It's a deal, Master. I didn't realize the repercussions. Thank you for helping me understand. And thank you for being honest, about everything." I gotta respect a Dom who isn't too proud to admit his errors. I'm already pressed up hard against Jerry, but I need to get closer. I seriously love this man, and I want him all over me, inside me. And I want to be all over him. My fingers weave into the thick locks of his hair; my fingernails scrape along his scalp; the rest of me rubs and ripples against his body. I move in that instinctive way, like I have feline blood flowing in my veins.

"Mmm, that's nice, very nice, sub. Let's finish your correction. Then we can get to your treat." *Rats.* "I'm tempted to go easy on you, but I can't. It seems you haven't learned your lesson.

"You defied your Master. You didn't like what I told you to do, and you wilfully said no. You disrespected me. I thought that after Sunday's session you had realized a better course of action than conflict. I'm disappointed that I was wrong about that."

"Oh, Master. I didn't mean any disrespect. I just couldn't do as you asked. I didn't think ... We weren't in a scene. I was confused. I didn't know I could use my safeword. I'm sorry, Master." I hang my head in shame. Bile erodes the back of my throat. I'm feeling a little nauseous and quite wretched. Nothing could have made me feel smaller than knowing I've let him down. He wanted me to get the point about using my safeword. Now, I do. But I really am confused. *When do we get to be just Erin and Jerry, two regular people having a conversation? He's taking this slave business so seriously.*

Jerry captures my chin, and he tilts my face toward him, forcing me to meet his indomitable stare. "Every demand I make puts us in a scene, 24/7. At all times, you will respect me and obey me. For the length of our contract, you are my slave, and you are always under my authority. When I give you a command, you will follow it. If you can't, then use your safeword. I will not tolerate insubordination."

A strange and complex blend of emotions overcomes me. I'm not doing a very good job of keeping myself in check. I need to sort this out. "Permission to speak, Master?"

"Unless you are going to ask me to continue your spanking, permission is denied."

I look at him with big puppy-dog eyes; I'm not faking them. All this emotion inside me is going to burst in a messy way if I don't get to talk about it. I continue to implore him with my gaze.

"What is it, sub? Tell me what the problem is."

"Thank you, Master. It's not a problem really, just something I need to say to help you understand, to help myself, too." Jerry uses the straps of my harness as leverage to pull me up to straddle his legs. I'm grateful because the pressure eases on my prickly bottom. The only problem is that he snugs the ribbon roughly against my clit again. I have to force myself to ignore the extreme stimulation.

"Master, more than any man I know, you deserve the respect you ask for. I'm disappointed in myself that I acted thoughtlessly. You are right to expect better from me. And you are right to discipline me." As I start to put words to the feelings, my depth of understanding grows.

"I've seen Masters mercilessly beat their subs for no reason other than for the pleasure of causing pain and to make someone else less than who they are. And I've seen bottoms bratting during scenes, deliberately provoking their Top to get the spanking they craved and keep the upper hand. It was all a twisted game to them."

My hands rest lightly on Jerry's shoulders. I slide them up so that just the very tips of my fingers glide along the angles of his jaws. "I can't be a part of that. And I've never believed in corporal punishment. Violence doesn't instill respect, only fear. But it feels different with you. Why is that, Master?"

The desperate need to have that question answered howls at me from deep inside my mind. My response to his beating makes no rational sense to me. The answer is there, but it's trapped.

"There are sadistic Doms and bratty subs who selfishly push for the high they need without regard for the person they are playing with," he says. "They subvert the exchange of power between a Top and a bottom. Those Doms do damage to their sub's psyche with their mindless brutality, and they lower themselves to the status of tyrant or beast, denying themselves the genuine devotion of their sub or slave. The bottoms deny their Top the privilege of being in control, being a leader and guiding their sub. In return, they deprive themselves of the chance to be brave and let go of control, and of the reward of being taken care of by their Top.

"Sometimes, sub, what we do *is* just a game, a role played for wicked fun. But this is a valid lifestyle, and when one player is insincere in a scene, we both lose out or get hurt. But, when both players are strong and true, and if we have each other's best interests in mind, we can experience a deep sharing that is very spiritual." *God, yes, I want that, Master.*

Jerry untangles his fingers from my leather casing, slips his hands underneath the straps, and strokes both hands up and down my spine. A billion soda bubbles burst along my skin where he touches. The little explosions compound until a drawn out note of pleasure erupts from my lips. I let my hands fall back to his shoulders so I don't collapse.

"If you are against punishment, sub, why did you let Dillon spank you?" There is an aberrant note of uncertainty in Jerry's voice, like he really doesn't want to know the answer, but he just can't help asking anyway.

"I saw how rough The Saint was with the others. I knew I didn't want that, couldn't handle that level of pain, but I did know that there was something I wanted from him that I couldn't get from either The Squire or Master Ronan." I really don't like bringing other men into this intimate moment with my Master. Using their aliases is the best I can do to keep them out.

"It was a submissive's concession to her Top. I thought he wouldn't want anything to do with me if he couldn't at least do that." My voice turns progressively shakier as the words tumble out.

"Well, it seems like you made a fair trade with him. And there's always the happy bonus of how good it feels." A weak smile barely lifts Jerry's lips. A *fair trade*? No! Oh, God. I've compromised one of my long-held beliefs—that love and sex shouldn't hurt, shouldn't be bad or dirty. I bargained that away to get something else from Dillon that I can't even identify. *Did my lack of clarity set me up for what happened?*

"I've never felt that, Master, when the pain turns to pleasure. To me, it's just a myth. There was no bonus, just a price to pay so I could play." Even to myself I sound like a sad, little girl.

"You mean that right now your bottom doesn't feel wonderfully warm?" Jerry clutches my chin and angles my head back. I can't bear his keen inquiry and have to close my eyes. "Look at me, sub. Answer me." It's plain to me that I've disappointed him again. He probably thinks I'm too weak, "breakable" as Dillon calls it. *I can't lie to him. I'll just have to find a way to live with his rejection.*

"I'm sorry, Master. It just hurts—bad. I guess I'm too soft." Jerry huffs in a breath and wraps his arms around me. He rocks us for a few moments before he speaks. His words come out in a crackle like shattering ice.

"So, letting me tan your hide is a price you think you have to pay for being with me?" *Oh, God.* How selfish I sound. I shove myself out of his tight embrace and drop to my knees at his feet.

"No! No, Master. That's not what I meant at all. It's different with you. Truly. I'm grateful for your discipline. My butt hurts something fierce, but, after the first ten smacks, something eased inside of me. I meant it when I said thank you." Jerry's searching stare continues to penetrate my heart's defenses.

"The second ten whacks hurt a lot more, but, at the end of it, my heart felt lighter. I was grateful for the relief from whatever had made my heart heavy." I close my eyes and pause. I ponder that heaviness, like a mini meditation, and get the answer I was looking for. *Shit!*

"What was that all about, sub?" Jerry sees the evidence of my realization on my face. I can't tell him that the weight was believing that whatever I do or don't do doesn't have consequences, doesn't matter, that I *don't matter to anyone.* I used to think Dillon was just using me and didn't really care. Jim said he wanted to comfort me, but he didn't argue when I said no. And Christophe said he was going to come home but let me convince him to stay. They didn't care enough to figure out what I really needed, despite what I said.

Jerry knows, and he's willing to give it to me, whether I like it or not. When I walked away from the diner, he came back and forced me to let him in. He didn't abandon me to deal with my heartache on my own. And he's working *with me* now, helping me directly, instead of meddling behind the scenes. *Do I matter to you, Master?*

I can't tell him the truth. It's too soon to lay my heart bare. If I say anything at all, he'll know how much I love him. That's not part of the friggin' contract, and I can't burden him like that. Or expose myself to such hurt when he pulls away. He's waiting for an answer.

"I'm just grateful that you helped me understand about keeping my agreements." *That'll do. It is true, just not the whole truth.* "I get down on myself when I sometimes don't follow through on what I say or break a promise. It doesn't happen often, but I get really mad when it does. This was a good lesson for me. Just like the next ten strokes will help me remember about using my safeword."

Jerry's smile is broad but still a bit hesitant. I know he knows that I'm not lying. He's also not convinced that I've told him everything. He's pretty perceptive that way. His experience as a cop has probably taught him how to recognize when people prevaricate.

"Oh, now I get it!" The answer I wanted smacks me between the eyes. "It was always punishment before, me making up for doing wrong. But you called it 'correction' a while ago. It's more than just semantics; it's about intent, isn't it? When The Saint spanked me, I thought it was all about him taking payment for whatever injustice I had done him, or for what I didn't give him. And because it turned him on to see how far he could push me." *Would it have felt different if I had known what I know now about his needs?*

"But you're helping me correct my weaknesses. This spanking is for my own good. You really do want to help me, don't you? Thank you, Master!" I'm babbling like I'm five and my best birthday wish just came true. Before my brain grows up, I reach up, cup Jerry's face in my hands and lay a big smacker of a wet kiss on his lips.

"Oh, Master. Please, may I have my last ten strokes? And can you please go just slow enough so I can thank you after each one and ask for another?" *I must be an idiot, but his correction says he cares about me. That he wants me to be my best me.*

Jerry's reply is sprinkled with light-hearted laughter. "Don't misunderstand. I'm not exactly turned off by the sound and feel of my hand hitting your splendid ass, or the sight of the fire-engine glow on your plump cheeks. And a sub should do as her Master asks without sass. But, yes, each strike serves a purpose for your benefit. I think you've learned the lesson I was trying to teach you, kitten. Enough now. I'm anxious to get to your treat."

Oh, no. No way am I going to let him deprive me of the relief I'll feel when he has corrected me. I'm not Catholic, but I imagine this is what confession is like. As long as the penitent feels true remorse and makes atonement from the heart.

"Master. You assigned me a total of 30 strokes. Are you going back on your word, Master? If you go easy on me now, Master, how will I learn to trust your authority, Master?"

"That's a lot of 'Masters.' Are you bratting now, sub?"

"Oh no, Master. I just want to be sure you know that I'm ready for the correction I need, Sir."

Jerry's laugh is full and rich, and trembles up from the base of his spine, shaking us both with the force of a quake emanating from the very center of the earth's core. Faster than you could say, "Present your bottom," Jerry has me laid across his lap.

We set up a steady rhythm. *Smack.* "One." "Thank you, Master. May I have another?" *Smack.* "Two." "Thank you, Master. May I please have another." By the time he finishes, tears are streaming down my face, and my nose is runny. My rear end is hotter than the sun, but my heart is as warm as banked embers. I will never again forget to use my safeword before conflict breaks out.

Jerry slides out from underneath me, leaving me stretched out on the couch, ass up. "Good girl, kitten. Wait here." *When did he start calling me kitten?* I'm not sure, but I like it. The endearment feels uniquely personal. My heart throbs in my throat while my butt throbs at the same pace. Jerry returns with my bottle of aloe vera.

"I'm sorry that hurt so bad, kitten. This should help." He smears thick gobs of the gel all over my screaming cheeks. The instant cold is a relief; the smoothing action of his gentle hands is pure bliss. *Wow.* This part of his spanking feels incredible to me—the warmth of my Master's nurturing care after the fact.

My heart spins out of control when he drops a line of kisses down my spine, from the nape of my neck to the cleft between my cheeks. I feel his heart beating in his lips as he lays them on me. I remember what he said, that my body should be worshipped and not battered or broken. This feels like worship, and regret for the battering. *I don't want to ever give him cause to do this to me again.*

Jerry helps me stand. The softness of his brushed cotton T-shirt is heaven on my breasts. The contrasting scratchiness of his new jeans is heaven on my midriff and thighs. "Let's have a glass of wine while we wait for that goo to soak in. And we can talk about your treat. Okay, kitten?" *Okay by me, Master.*

Chapter Sixteen – Genesis

Wednesday Evening, September 26

"Have you ever been collared?" The question flies at me out of left field. We're standing side by side, facing a blazing fire that Jerry has just lit. The Australian cabernet is as bold as the question, but far more smooth. He strokes his finger along the collar around my neck. "I know this is part of your harness, but have you ever let a man put his collar on you, sub?" I know the flickering flames in his eyes are just reflections, but the heat that flares out and washes over me is entirely too real.

"I'm wearing my hip necklace for you, Sir." I'm waffling on the truth again. I just don't want to bring another man into the room with us again. He swings the dangling diamond pendant, tickling my tummy. My brain struggles to process messages of longing sent by all of my girly bits while trying to keep the rest of me functioning. He presses his question, and I have to answer.

"Only once, Sir. My initiation night at DYKKC, with The Squire." Jerry wants all the gory details, like how I felt about t, and why it was only once. I tell him how surprised I was at first that I didn't resist when he fastened the collar on me, and how my attitude changed during the following week. I also tell him that I would only ever allow it again if I could fully trust the Dom to shoulder the responsibility. My body jerks as he switches gears on the fly and makes my head spin so fast that I might need a neck brace.

"Come nuzzle against me the way you do, sub." He deposits our glasses on the mantle and tugs on the straps covering my forearms, tucking me into his shoulder. His fingers slide as slow as molasses down my sides until they grip my hips. The throaty command Jerry issues is more like an invitation to paradise. "Purr for me, baby girl. And rub your beautiful body all over me." *Purr, purr, meow.*

"That's it. God, I like this soft side of you, sub. You make me feel so good. Feel how hard I go when you go soft." I stretch up onto my tippy toes to grind my mound into Jerry's crotch and am rewarded with a prize-winning cucumber poking back at me.

"Meow, Sir." I bury my fingers in his hair and cradle his head for leverage as I hoist myself even further up Jerry's washboard abs and rock-hard chest. I've got one leg twined around his solid trunk and strain to get the other up as well, all the while tickling his ear with the tip of my nose and lapping at his upper jaw with broad strokes of my juicy tongue. In my wide-open posture, I'm getting him even wetter as I smear my cream all over his jeans.

In a surge of passion and strength, Jerry digs his fingers into my hips and lifts me. My other leg finally winds around him like a clinging vine curling up a telephone pole. *Thank goodness.* I've now got the purchase I need to do what I've been aching to do for ages. My hands roam across shoulders as wide as a bus, along traps and delts and over triceps and biceps as hard as cabled steel, and snake around and along a spine as straight and strong as a mighty oak.

This is no idle journey; it is mission critical. At last, I find my target. My hungry fingers bunch up the hem of Jerry's T-shirt. I pull and twist and inch that shirt upward. *I need skin.* The need is a powerful addiction that engulfs me, a wraith inhabiting my soul and taking control of me. With a bit of cooperation from the object of my obsession, the shirt sails to the couch. Now my nuzzling flips from teasing to tormenting as my little, pink tongue seeks newly exposed territory. My relief is fleeting; my hunger for the salty, tart flavor of his skin is insatiable. *Who the hell am I right now?*

"kitten, you drive me mad." *Purr, purr.* "If you keep that up, we'll never get to your treat." His already sexy, deep bass has dropped another octave into the impossible-to-resist range. My tongue and lips and teeth step up their campaign and expand their exploration, seeking out undiscovered erogenous zones.

Between licks and nips, I ask, "This isn't it, Master? You mean there's something better than tasting you?" The laugh that reverberates through Jerry's chest crashes into me. Each "ha" is a depth charge exploding in my emotional waters. My heart is about to be blown apart. Before I die, I need him inside me one more time.

"Master, please. It's not my place to ask, but I need you. I really, really need you. Please, Master." My voice drips with desire and desperation. My nipples scream for attention, and my pussy howls to be filled.

No verbal response. My man is all action. He clearly needs this as much as I do because he doesn't tell me I've overstepped my bounds or make me be more specific or make me wait. Jerry lowers us onto the sheepskin and plonks me onto my knees. *The wild beast is loose.* If the ravenous look on his face is any indication, I now have no doubts that I am indeed going to die. *He's going to eat me alive and fuck me to death.*

Jerry moves like lightning, and his jeans whip off in a blur. He rolls on a condom just as quick. One second later, he reefs on my harness and tosses me onto my back. My butt prickles as it hits the ground, but the sting doesn't last long because Jerry throws my legs over his shoulders, lifting my ass completely off the ground as he rams into me in one fluid movement.

I couldn't be quiet even if Master commanded me upon threat of severe punishment. His rampant thrusting forces the sounds of ecstasy from me against my will. He is equally vocal. This is the kind of intercourse I love—hard, fast, deep, unrestrained, all-consuming. Every ten strokes or so, Jerry yanks on the straps of my harness or my limbs and rearranges my body in an athletic ballet to gain a different angle of entry, to go deeper, or for leverage for even rougher humping. *Gotta love a man with strength and stamina.* Three words are on my lips; my heart begs me to let them loose. I *can't. I can't. I can't. But I wish I could.*

My eyes sting as sweat flies from Jerry's forehead, nose and chin, raining over my face. My jaw is clacking, gnashing, needing to bite, but I can't get my teeth near any sensitive spots. I have to satisfy my compulsion to mark my mate by scratching and digging my claws into his chest and shoulders.

My world turns topsy-turvy; the beast pitches me over onto my knees. In an aggressive move, he pins my chest and shoulders to the rug. He's a raging lion subduing his lioness, draping his body like a cloak over mine and sinking his teeth into the crook of my neck. He snaps sharply, my scream wailing out more like a gruff roar above the sounds of the slapping of belly striking against butt and slurping of cock sliding in pussy. The savagery of our coupling is as ancient as all life. *Fuck. Buck. Wrack. Wreck.*

"Give me more, Master, please. I need more." Jerry picks up his right knee and plants his foot solidly on the floor. He wraps one arm around my waist, locking me in place, raising me to the right angle for him to impale me with all the power he's got. Each devastating impact shunts me ever closer to oblivion. We're both panting wildly, spurred to madness by primal forces beyond our awareness or understanding, caught in a mating ritual not yet done with us.

"Christ, sub. I'm gonna come. Come for me, kitten. Come hard around my cock." His other arm slides between my trembling legs, laying fingers like red hot pokers along my most sensitive skin, branding my clit and labia. He tweaks my bud ruthlessly. His touch flings me into the void in a free fall with no tethers or nets. My body slams into a wall of sensation at break-neck speed. The contact illuminates my world in a burst of glittering stars, revealing a host of shining angels circling my head. Another collision plummets me back to earth as he thrusts, grunts and disintegrates over top of me. I'm ripped, ruined, raw, replete.

I think Jerry is broken, or at least temporarily incapacitated. The only sign he is alive is that he groans every time an aftershock ripples through my vagina and grips his overwrought penis. His unresponsive bulk crushes me but is a blessed burden I gladly bear.

"Wow, Master. Now *that* was a treat. Wow. Thank you." The tone of my praise and gratitude is a little flat, like me. Jerry moans and struggles up onto his forearms. He tilts his hips forward, trying to remain buried inside me. One final, massive tremor from deep in my core spits him out. We both sigh our disappointment.

"That wasn't it either, kitten." Jerry lifts and rolls me onto my back. He chuckles like a very happy man; his broad smile coaxes those three words back to my lips. I need to tell him I love him. I'm saved from ruining everything by his full lips capturing me in a robust kiss. We haven't kissed very often, but when we do, he really rocks my world. I don't care anymore what his treat is; all I want is to lie here in Jerry's arms with his lips fused to mine.

When Jerry comes back from the bathroom, I'm lying on my side sipping my wine. He squats and kisses and caresses my behind. When he lies down beside me, he says, "You asked me what I wanted from our contract."

"Well, I'd say you just got some of your hot, kinky, dirty sex, Sir."

"Yes, kitten. I did. Do you like it when I call you kitten?" He waltzes his fingernails along my upper arm, shoulder and over the tops of my breasts. His attention is focused on the goosebumps springing up in the wake of his finger dance.

"Actually, I do, Sir. It feels right. It's easy and fun to think of myself as a playful kitty."

"The world I see every day is pretty bleak, sub. There's not much in my life that is soft and sweet like you. There is something very feminine and feline about you that I respond to ... What I want is for you to be my kitten, to be my pet." Jerry gets up and retrieves a bag from the front entrance. He sits in front of me, cross-legged, and I match him. The ache in my butt is now a warm reminder of Jerry's interest in my growth.

Jerry reaches into the purple plastic bag and pulls out a furry, black headband with cat ears on it. Then he brings out a bra and panty set of tiny triangles of black fun fur held together by thin, black strings. The outfit is adorned with pale pink, satin ribbons. Attached to the back of the panties is, of course, a long, black, furry tail. His hand disappears into the bag once more and comes back out with a thin, pink leather collar.

"I know what you said about collars, sub. But, for as long as our contract lasts, will you wear my collar and be my pet?" My first instinct is to say an immediate and adamant yes.

"What exactly do you mean, Sir?"

"When I tell you to put on this gear, you'll become a pussy cat. You won't just play a role. You'll move and act like a cat, no words unless I give you permission to speak, no doing anything for yourself that a kitten can't do. I'll take care of you ... and play with you. I'll be your Master in a way that I'm not now." I've read about this kind of thing. The phrase "sex kitten" has a whole new meaning.

"Sir? You know that cats are independent creatures, don't you? They can't be trained like puppy dogs can be." He nods. "There's no disciplining cats."

"Well, you won't get any spankings when you're my pet. But there are other ways of correcting bad kitties." His smirk is less than innocent. I get the feeling that he would very much like for me to be bad. I shiver at the possibilities. But, oh, to unleash my inner feline. To be free to be the animal I am. To give in to instinct. To let go of the conventions of civilization and live wild and unbridled.

On hands and knees, I burrow into Jerry's chest and lick one dark nipple. Then I pounce, tipping him onto his back. I only have the upper hand for but a second before I'm rolled and flipped. Jerry strokes my chest and tummy, and my hands and feet rise into the air, pedaling and begging for more. "Meowww."

"I'll take that as a yes. Thank you, sub. I know I've asked this for myself, but I think this will be a treat for you as well, won't it?"

"Meowww." *It is indeed. He knows me so well.* It feels natural. Indulging curiosity, moving with feline grace, living for pleasure and play, frolicking like a frisky kitty, cavorting like an untamed lioness. In most circles, pet play is meant to be demeaning, making the sub or slave less than human. I can't see it that way. Jerry is giving me a gift, giving me something more rather than taking away.

"Let's get you out of this harness and into your kitty gear." Jerry's jaw twitches with each snap he pops. "Damn, sub. It's still sexy as hell taking you out of this. But it's almost a shame. If this one didn't have a collar, I might be tempted to leave it on." The cogs in my brain immediately start turning, dreaming up a new design.

Jerry is just as turned on by dressing me in my new costume as he was by taking off my harness. A fine tremor unsteadies his hands as he buckles the pink collar around my neck. His eyes bore into mine while he does it. There is much unsaid between us, but my heart hears every word. Jerry kisses me again, at first tentative and tender, then confident and crushing as he lays me back down. He brushes his hands over me, tangling in the fur on my breasts.

"Every pet should have a name. Did you have a kitty when you were a child? Yes? What did you call it?"

"Velvet."

"Mmm. That's just perfect. Soft. Downy. Silky smooth. Just like you. My velvet." I'm in awe of how strong Jerry is in this vulnerable moment, in his need for what only I can give him. My whole body cries out for him. I arch and slump under him as his hands rove over the plush bra and panties. I am fascinated by his fascination.

Jerry gathers me in his arms and whisks me off to the bedroom, cooing and fussing the entire way. He handles me like I truly am his precious pet. In this moment, I cease to exist as Erin and embody the essence of velvet that resides deep in my soul. *This is who I am.*

Chapter Seventeen – The Dominion of Darkness

Friday Morning, September 28

My life has never been as magical as it is right now. The past two days have been a realization of all my best fantasies. Actually, that's not true; Jerry has pleased and teased me in ways I never could have imagined. After midwifing my birth as velvet, he spent the rest of the night switching between playing the rascally tomcat and the majestic lion. When he left yesterday morning at 5:00, it felt like he tore my skin off and dragged my guts with him, even though the psychic cord joining my heart to his remains strong.

What helped me survive the separation was our flirty sexting throughout the day. Among the racier messages, Jerry told me to clear my weekend and be available for him. He has plans and won't tell me what they are. I don't dare hope that I'll spend the whole weekend with him. That would send me over the edge of bliss. He also ordered me to get into full kitty gear as soon as I got home yesterday. When I thought about putting on my ears, tail and collar, all I could think about was hours of playful petting, sensual stroking, languorous licking, and sultry sex.

My Master arrived at 5:30 last night with a silver rope chain that he clipped to my collar as a leash. He also brought little, white fur mittens that force me to curl my fingers to get into them. Then he buckled them around my wrists so I couldn't slip them off. They restricted my dexterity to the point where I was unable to do very much of anything for myself, and that was just the way he wanted it. It was all part of his "Master" plan.

Jerry stripped to his briefs and sat us on the kitchen floor. He brought a variety of scrumptious finger foods for our dinner. I had no fingers, so he hand-fed me, making a deliberate mess, smearing and dropping food all over us. Licking each other clean was so hot. After eating off every part of each other's bodies, Master washed off our residual stickiness in a hot bath. He pampered me, gave me a vigorous towel rubbing, and put me right back into my kitty gear.

I couldn't stop purring. That is, until I had to go to the toilet. I danced around until Jerry got the message and removed my bikini bottom. I was mortified when he watched and wiped my bum. It's such a private act, and no one has seen me go since I was potty trained. I let Jerry stick his tongue in my vagina and his penis in my anus, expose myself to him in shameful ways, yet I freaked when he dabbed a bit of toilet paper on my butt. Because, in that moment, I realized how completely reliant velvet is on him for her well-being, even in my own home. He makes me need him. *Master, indeed.*

We were both clean and pink from the warm bath when Jerry cuddled me up in his arms and carried me to bed. It was another almost sleepless night of cavorting under the sheets. Jerry spent long minutes tickling me with my tail, softening me up and riling me up. He splayed me out, like I was taking a good kitty-cat stretch, and then fucked me slow and steady until I came for the fourth time since he arrived. That was just the warm up for the hard pounding he gave me from behind. That time, we both fell apart, growling and howling before we drifted off to sleep, tangled in each other's limbs.

"On your back, now. Spread for me, slave." Those are the words I woke up to this morning at 6:00. I rolled and obeyed in a hurry. I was tired and sore, and I'd never felt better in my life. Jerry kissed the living daylights out of me while he lined his joystick up to make love to me. In my mind and heart, everything we have done in the last few days has been making love–the contract is all but irrelevant to me as impetus for what I do. No man has taken my soul to the heights and depths that Jerry has, into the realm of sweet bliss.

Jerry was suited up and ready to go, but, despite how much I wanted it, my poor bruised pussy couldn't take him. I yowled like a cat with her tail caught in a slamming door. "Well, slave, I'll have to find another place to put my morning wood." My wicked grin matched his as he removed the condom and slid me to the middle of the bed, looming over me, prodding his hard length at my face.

We may not be getting particularly creative with our positions yet, but the passion is absolute heaven. It's what I want and need. I have no complaints, and, since Jerry is the one in charge and directing all of our time together, it seems he has no complaints either. It's a little scary how compatible we are. I'm thinking and feeling things I shouldn't be thinking and feeling, especially when I have no idea what he's thinking and feeling about me. This morning, I'm just too freaking happy to care.

It was 7:30 by the time we were showered and Jerry was on his way. He had brought a change of clothes with him and didn't have to leave as early as yesterday. I had some time, so I lingered over a pot of tea, replaying the last few days. Two weeks ago, I felt like I had stumbled through the Gates of Hell. Now, the happiness and love flowing through me have lifted me out of the Underworld.

I particularly remembered when I said to Jerry that a woman stops being a woman when she closes her heart in anger or fear. It's harder for me to hang on to all the resentment, hurt and blame over what happened with Dillon. I'm almost ready to completely forgive him. I'm not sure what to do about Christophe, but I can't be mad at Jim anymore. He's been too good to me to cut him out of my life just for going a bit overboard in trying to protect me. He didn't answer my call, so I sent a text saying 'I'm sorry' and asking him to call so I can apologize properly. I'm still waiting to hear from him.

The other person I can't be angry with anymore is Steffie, despite her banishing me from DYKKC. She really flipped out on me, but I threatened everything she's worked hard for. Just like I flipped out when Dillon threatened everything I had worked hard to become. She needs to do something to make sure the safeword rule is enforced at the club, but that's no longer my concern.

I'm having a hard time focusing on work again today. I'm used to Jerry's heat now; I live for it, and I'm freezing up without him. My heart is still warm, but the rest of me is frigid without his touch. That he has this kind of effect on me is both good news, and very, very bad news.

Before I joined DYKKC, I was able to go for weeks and not think about sex or miss it. Once I became a member, one of my boys would fill me up every week or two, and I'd be good for days. Now, I can hardly manage 15 minutes without a dirty image or thought passing through my brain, or a gnawing need chilling my body in Jerry's absence. He is a very bad influence. *But he's so damn good.*

Sexting keeps me going again today. In most of his texts, he calls me sub or slave. But sometimes he calls me velvet. During our roughhousing, there are times when he is not my Master; he is every bit the animal that I am, my ferocious lion. *He should have a name for his lusty alter-ego. Rex is Latin for king, but he's not a Rex. Regis! Yes. It means kingly.* I text my theory to him, and I'm delighted that he approves. *Regis and velvet.* "Regis and velvet sitting in a tree, K-I-S-S-I-N-G. I love it."

It's goofy, juvenile thinking. And I have a matching goofy, juvenile grin spreading from ear to ear. I prefer to think of this giggly feeling as innocent, childlike delight instead of childishness. I'm happy and fuzzy warm again. Jerry sends another text that makes my heart pound and melts my body through and through.

'velvet My pet. Regis yr King commands u 2 rub yrslf. Come 4 Me.' In the heightened state I'm in, I achieve his naughty objective almost immediately.

After the pressure release, I convince Jerry to leave me alone while I work. Somehow, I keep myself together throughout a staff meeting. We discuss a new online search portal for all things legal that the Associate Dean wants to purchase. We consider whether it would be worth investing in the tool to replace the resources we currently use. I listen to the staff feedback, grateful that I've got such talented people on my team. Reviews say this software has too many bugs in it. We all agree that sometimes new technology is not superior to doing things old school. Jillian will prepare a draft recommendation that I will edit and submit to the A.D. Sitting back in my office chair, I remember the Silent O I gave myself only an hour ago.

As the clock ticks toward 4:00, I debate leaving early. I'm itching to start the weekend because my need for release builds anew. Jerry's text convinces me to wait it out. He won't be over until later tonight and says I should have dinner and go for my run. That's great news because, although Jerry has kept me super active, I've missed jogging all week. I need the outlet to take care of some of the sexual tension in my body.

$$< \male + \female >$$

I've got my groove on, and I'm singing along with Etta James to "I Just Want to Make Love to You." That's what I want—to make love to Jerry, to give him all my lovin', to take care of him, to serve him, to have him make love right back to me. I'm floating on a cloud after an awesome run, wrapped up in my own little world, distracted by romantic notions, dreaming of scenarios that I have no right to imagine. I slide my key into my front door lock. The anticipation of what Jerry has up his sleeve and when he'll show is killing me.

I'm just about to turn to close the door, but my feet lift off the floor. A gloved hand clamps over my mouth. An arm as thick as a boa constrictor squeezes around my waist. *Not again!* The door slams shut; I'm slammed against the closet doors. *Damn. That hurts.* I struggle with all my might.

"Hold still, bitch." *What the hell?* The growl in my ear is definitely Jerry's. The rumble is pure menace. My blood rushes as cold as a glacial stream. "You've run from me too long. You're going to pay for that. And you're going to listen to what I have to say." Each word he spits is drenched in malevolence. *God, I hope this is our next re-enactment and not something else.* We haven't talked about this or negotiated anything. *Do I trust him?*

Jerry's chest presses his full weight into me, plastering me to the closet and sparking deep fear in my psyche. This caustic contact smears a chemical burn along my back. All I'm able to move is my legs; I kick out for all I'm worth. I connect a good one to his shin. I'm rewarded with a dull grunt. Then I groan at the sounds I hear. I recognize the metallic pop, a snap clicking open on something leather. The scraping swish becomes immediately identifiable when a sharp, cold point lightly pricks my jaw. *Holy shit! He's got a knife.*

Now I know what a real panic attack is like. I can't stop shaking. I'm hyperventilating and fast losing my ability to think like a human. They say our primal instinct is to fight or flee. They almost always forget to mention the third option—freeze, like a deer in headlights.

"Remember your safeword, sub. Be brave, but use it if you need it." It's barely a whisper. *He's just thrown me a lifeline.* My breathing slows. If he's playing a role, he's good at it. *I bet he plays the bad cop.*

"If you don't stop struggling, you're going to get hurt. I'm not messing around." I can breathe a little easier when he unwinds his arm from my waist. But that free hand goes to his pocket at the same time his other hand snicks the knife back in its sheath.

"Open." *Damn.* He stuffs a ball gag into my mouth, and I suck on the bitter tang of rubber. Jerry fastens it tight, stretching the corners of my mouth. He's being far rougher than Dillon was when he did this. I don't get it. *It's like he's determined to drop me in the deep end.* His plan is working because I'm fricking terrified. I've never seen this savage side of my noble lion.

"We need to talk, but not here. You have a choice. It'll be easier for you if you cooperate. Or, do things the hard way and resist me. It's up to you. Either way, you're leaving here in that." He points to a folded up hockey bag by the door. No big surprise there. '*Cooperate,*' *like he wants my complicity in my kidnapping.* For some reason, that's harder to deal with than having no choice.

He digs into his pocket again. Lightning shoots up my arms as he wrenches them behind me and secures them with a plastic zip tie. I saw a video online about how to break free of those, except Jerry's a cop and knows how to layer my wrists to prevent that.

There's a persistent alarm clanging in my ancient, reptilian brain. I can't help my reaction, no matter that my evolved, thinking brain tells me I'm safe. Sweat beads on my forehead as thick as condensation on a can of ice-cold soda on a hot, humid day. Stress chemicals course through my veins and sting like cobra venom. I twist and contort my body; I'm a wild animal trying to escape a hunter's trap. I spin and come face to face with my attacker.

This is make-believe, right? Regardless, I'm flushed with dread—perhaps more so than when Dillon came at me for real. Because I see the same callousness in Jerry's eyes that I heard in his voice. He's not pretending. He *is* the beast, unrestrained and ready to maul and mangle. I gush fat tears that splat on the floor with the force of Niagara Falls. My knees wobble, almost toppling me over. While the rest of me is immobilized, my heart pounds against my chest cavity as the beating muscle tries to make a break for it.

"On your knees, face down," Jerry barks. His eyes are inky balls of black ice. His breathing is deep and steady, restrained. I've never faced such cold fury before. He is elemental evil. I don't want to, *can't*, think about what he's tapping into to be able to sink down to the state he's in and to generate the ominous current sparking in his aura. I shudder at the image of Dr. Frankenstein's electrical conductors breathing life into a monster. *He won't hurt me. This is not who he is. He's my Regis.* I wish I could believe my brave words.

I dally too long, trying to settle the tempest of fear raging in my innards. Jerry swoops in behind me, a menacing raven grappling my shoulders, driving me to the ground. He gathers the coil of sinister rope lurking beneath the hockey bag and snakes the cord around me, hogtying me securely. I'm as rigid as a corpse, frozen by deathly panic and the locking bonds.

"Hang in there, kitten." Another wisp of a lifeline to cling to just when I need it the most. The timing can't be a coincidence. It's how I know that Jerry is deep in Dom space, tuned in to me as if he is under my skin. *He won't hurt me.*

I just can't seem to relax into that thought. It's still scary as hell when he hooks his hands into my bindings and stuffs me into the bag—and leaves me. I should be relieved when I hear his heavy boots thudding down the hall to my bedroom. Instead, my heart feels abandoned. Agonizing minutes later, he returns and tucks clothes, my makeup case and purse around me to pad out the bag.

I'm lying on my side and watch him in my peripheral vision as he crouches and leans down to me. He wraps my ponytail in his leather-clad hand. He studies my face then drops his gaze to my neck. My pulse must be throbbing furiously enough for him to hear as well as see. The taut lines of his face soften, barely, but I'm alert to every nuance now, as keyed in to him as he is to me. *Kiss me.*

God help me, but desire flares in my pussy and spirals all the way through me, pricking my nipples to attention. It's a sick thrill to be this helpless, at his complete mercy, aware that he could do any number of nefarious things to me, but *almost* certain he won't. He is just a hair's breadth from my cheek. His hot breath steams me, and his lips tingle against me even though he hasn't touched me yet.

"We're leaving now. Don't cause any trouble. Because, when we arrive, no one will hear you if I make you scream." His hiss is the most vile sound I've ever heard. And scream I do. With the ball gag in my mouth, my keening is impotent as a cry for help. The bastard knows my suffering, and he breaks eye contact and zips up the bag anyway. The chance to use my safeword or signal has passed. I'm in this as deep as I can go. And the hole is dark, and dank, and dismal.

My primal mind is shrieking at me. *I'm going to die. Or worse.* I can't hear my heart or Evanya above the ear-splitting screeching. I feel upward motion; my captor takes me to the truck he must have hidden down the street. The swaying cocoon quickly lulls me into a false tranquility. *Clunk!* The door opening jacks me back up. I'm weightless for a moment, then my brain squeals as I'm tossed on the seat, the jarring impact wrenching every muscle and joint.

Mr. Bilson calls out to Jerry before he closes the door. I guess the unnecessary roughness was because he had to get me out of earshot in a hurry. My survival instinct, that directive to fight, kicked in too late. I can't yell loud enough around the gag to breach the soundproofing of the truck, and I can't struggle at all. Jerry quickly dispatches Mr. Bilson. *No hope of rescue.* How easy it is for him to get away with this. My heart freefalls and lands with a thump. Unable to scream, I'm reduced to feeble whimpering.

The emotions and hormonal cocktail swirling through me have stripped me of my strength. But above my sniveling, I can finally hear Evanya's soothing, dulcet tones. "He told you to 'hang on, kitten.' Remember, you're still his kitten." I boo hoo uncontrollably in relief and release. Her gentle, melodic words start to seep into my consciousness like a hymn, bolstering me ever so slightly.

< ♂ + ♀ >

Chapter Eighteen – Deliverance

Friday Night, September 28

I jolt when the truck dips and rocks. Jerry is in. He doesn't speak but forces a ponderous out-breath from his lungs. He slides the hockey bag around on the seat so my head is beside him. Dragging the zipper down, he finally opens an air hole for me. He reaches in and his warm, bare hand caresses my cheek. His thumb rubs gently over my stretched and slobber-covered lips as he sighs again.

The engine roars to life, and we're on the road to who knows where. With no music keeping time, the silence stretches for what seems to be an hour. In reality, it is probably only 15 minutes of stop-and-start, in-town driving before Jerry slows down. He puts the truck in park but doesn't kill the engine. "No one can hear you now, so I'll take off the gag, but I warn you to keep quiet. Don't sass me. Don't test my patience." I *wouldn't dare.* All I hope is that, after this is over, Jerry will explain why he's being such a bastard.

Before the gag comes off, he cinches on a fur-lined eye mask. I regain one sense but lose another. Jerry has to force my mouth open to get the gag out because my jaws have locked. He massages my muscles and joints brusquely, wiping away the drool as he works. His hands hurt but are effective. Jerry's touch is a small mercy, but, in my agitated state, it feels to me like the greatest gift. My stomach flutters with something other than fear.

Jerry drives for another ten minutes or so. Every little bounce and sway tosses my stomach around like I'm on a rollercoaster. By our straight trajectory and the speed we're moving, I know we've been on a freeway. We slow down to a crawl and turn right. After a couple of minutes, we turn right again. Gravel crunches under the tires. A *country road.* The ride is bumpy but short. So, *maybe a long driveway.* The vehicle is silent now except for the ticking of metal contracting as the constant heat of the engine dies.

What happens now? I'm nervous but also relieved because these ropes hurt, and the zip tie has rubbed my wrists almost raw. Whatever Jerry has planned, I just pray it involves cutting me loose. I'm airborne, swinging along in the hockey bag, keeping quiet as a mouse. All my other senses are filling in the data my eyes have been robbed of. We're through a door, across a big room. There is only silence, except for the echoes of Jerry's footfalls telling me we're going down a short hallway. Then we descend. *A basement?* A heavy door creaks. The scents of leather, oil and sweat assault me. *Oh God, a dungeon.*

I can't stop myself; I whine. With a quick pump of his arm, Jerry shakes the bag, tweaking my strained body. Then he sets the bag down. The give and the softness underneath me suggest I'm on a mattress. The *click click* of the zipper unzips something in me–trepidation, with an undertone of erotic stimulation.

So far, despite the fact that it's way more intense than my original kidnapping, Jerry has stuck to the script. That means I'm about to be cuffed to the bed. With Dillon, I felt nothing but straight-up fear when I woke up restrained. This time, I have the chance to process what's happening as Jerry unpacks me from the bag and lays me out on the bed.

The pop and scraping sounds precede the knife slicing off the zip tie. My breath whooshes out as my wrists fall off each other. Jerry loosens the ropes only enough to free my wrists completely. He's gone only a moment; water gurgles from a nearby tap; he settles on the bed; cool terrycloth bathes my wounds; warm lips kiss away the pain in my wrists and my heart. *Another lifeline.* I wish Jerry would say something, anything, but this will do for now.

Jerry makes quick work of undoing the rest of the ropes. His strong hands massage and chafe my aching muscles and joints. It's not enough to make me feel good, but he does ease some of the tension. I just want this to be over. I want his hands to keep working me over, to pleasure me. I need for my Regis to play with his velvet, not for this cold terrorist to toy with me and manipulate me.

As if I've got no more strength in me than a baby has, I'm spread, limbs stretched and shackled to the bedposts. My closemouthed abductor kneels beside me, then crawls over me, straddling my hips before he lays flat on top of me. His full weight pulverizes me, embedding me into the fabric and springs of the mattress.

"Now I can do anything I like to you, take my payback in any manner that suits me." His resonant voice, right at my ear, jabs into me, flinging divergent shivers of doom and delight into my belly. This push and pull of polar opposites is taking a heavy toll. I don't know how much longer I can hold back from begging him to spare my life or to make me come.

My head jerks down into the mattress as Jerry sinks his teeth into my tender earlobe with a vicious chomp. Then he gnashes down on the vulnerable spot at the base of my neck. He suctions hard and long. Nasty gnawing on my shoulder stings me just before he tries to take a chunk from the ripe flesh at the top of my left breast. With each peck, I arch and strain into him, gaining a little more lift as his attack and his weight shifts and descends. The plump swell just below my navel is his next snack, then the sensitive skin of my inner thigh just above my left knee. Each mouthful he takes is clearly meant to mark me. Each wound throbs, contracting my vaginal wall. *The pain that pleases.*

"You stripped me of my dignity, Erin, my ability to set this right. So, I'm going to strip you." The first thing to come off is my blindfold. *He wants me to watch what he does to me.* Jerry withdraws what I now see is a big-ass hunting knife. My focus is locked on the glinting point as he slides it under my jogging top from the neckline down to the middle of it. The blade splits the fabric as if met by no more resistance than air. A few more razor cuts and scraps of ruined material fall off me. The top didn't give me much coverage as it was, but the frigid air turns my skin as bumpy as bubble wrap.

Jerry then turns his attention to my jogging shorts. Each slice of the knife rockets another payload of adrenaline into my blood, enhancing every sense. I'm juiced up on a cocktail of endorphins and cortisol and probably about ten other natural stimulants. I'm scared out of my ever-lovin' mind, but I've never felt so incredibly alive. *Is this why people jump out of airplanes and run with bulls?* This close to death, I want to cling to life, to seize it. What a rush!

If Dillon had even just shown me a knife, never mind if he had actually used one on me, I would have been screaming my face off at him. But it's Jerry who pulls my shredded shorts from under me. The line between fear and excitement isn't just blurred, he's completely eradicated it. Who cares how this relates to past events? I'm totally centered in the moment and what's happening with Jerry, with my Master, in the nasty role he is playing for me.

His raging power is imposing, and totally awesome. I should feel small and insignificant, dwarfed in the face of his potency and might. The ironic thing is that I no longer feel helpless at all. Power sparks and surges through me. *I am his muse.* I am moved by the extraordinary knowledge that I can inspire and arouse such passion and intensity in my Master, even if that passion is dark. To know that he would go to such lengths and work so hard to free me of my sorrow, would push me right to the extreme edge of my tolerance, makes my grateful heart beat wildly.

The flashing of the knife jerks me back to harsh reality. I'm down to my black sports bra and plain cotton panties. A quick flick of the blade snaps my bra open. Two more cuts at the shoulders and a few on my panties, and I am completely bare. The ravenous look in Jerry's eyes traps my breath in my throat. I spit the air out when ... Jerry strips. Huh? Keeping his clothes on while I'm naked would have been another reminder of his dominance. "Now there's nothing between us, Erin. Let's sort this all out." I'm still cuffed to the bed, so there is that between us, but I get his point.

< ♂ + ♀ >

What I see in front of me finally filters through to my overtaxed brain. Jerry is covered in bruises and abrasions, just like Dillon was.

"Master, oh my God. What happened?" I blurt without asking for permission to speak. *Damn, what if this isn't pretend?*

"There's no need for formality now, Erin. You can call me Dillon. Three wise guys broke in here last night and gave me a very pointed message. 'Stay away from Erin.' Well, I've got a message for you, priss. Don't fuck with me." He advances toward me, climbing back on the bed, and I'm no longer sure what's real and what's pretend. Animosity rolls off him and plows into me, leaving me gasping for breath. *Shit. He can't. He wouldn't. Oh God, don't hurt me.*

"Dillon, please. I didn't do this. I would never do this. I couldn't hurt you like this."

"I know that, and we both know who did. But you did hurt me this much, Erin. You just can't see the marks. You think that accusing me of being a rapist wasn't a swift kick to my balls? You think that every text you ignored wasn't a punch in the face? You think that when you tried to have me banned from DYKKC you weren't sticking a knife in my back? That when you went to the cops and filed a restraining order, that wasn't a bullet in my heart?"

I stare at Dillon/Jerry, trying to separate who is who. Hell, it doesn't matter. I just have to respond.

"Maybe I can make you realize just how much you've hurt me," Jerry says. I see him, like in a slow-motion replay, pull his hand back in a fist. *Not a freaking chance, buddy.*

"Stop it. Stop it, Dillon. Maybe I did hurt you. But have you conveniently forgotten what you did to me? You nearly did rape me, asshole. You certainly raped my mind and stole my freedom of choice when you ignored my safeword. Excuse me for getting all bent out of shape and needing a bit of space to recover from that." My words shoot at him as quick as machine gun fire and as loud as cannon fire.

"We entered that room together, Erin. We negotiated the scene together. I followed the script that we agreed on. Tell me how I took your freedom of choice when you willingly consented." Dillon/Jerry sounds as angry as I am. *These aren't Dillon's words, so is this what Jerry really thinks, how he judges me?*

"We were so close to the climax, Erin. I was just keeping the scene in play. Lots of subs say no when they mean yes."

"But you were with *me*. You know I'm not like the others. As hard as you pushed me to *my* limits, when did I ever use a safeword with you? Or when did I ever *pretend* to not give my okay? Never! Don't you think it might have been important to know why I was using the safeword for the first time?

"The minute I said yellow, you should have stopped to talk to me. Maybe we could have worked things out and had a happy ending to the scene. But the second I yelled red and told you to untie me, you should have done exactly that. *Why* I used my safeword doesn't matter. Anything after that would have been rape."

"You make it sound like I'm some kind of criminal. We were playing, Erin. You consented. It was a game you wanted to play."

"I wanted to play with The Saint, not whoever was in the room that night. You weren't in there with me, and I needed it to end."

"I might have zoned out for a bit, but after I spanked you for coming, *like we agreed*, we were back on track. We had both worked hard to get to where we were. We both deserved the reward.

"You looked so beautiful with your bright red ass waiting for me. I had kept you on the edge for so long, and you were so wet and so close to coming. I wanted to hear you moan in ecstasy like you do when I'm buried deep inside you. It was my gift to you for being such a good girl.

"I asked if you were okay, and you didn't use your safeword again. I didn't know anything was wrong. And the worst thing was that you wouldn't let me help you during aftercare. Why couldn't you relax and let me give you what you wanted, what you needed?"
OH MY DEAR GOD.

"End scene, Sir. End scene." I can't let this go on any longer.

"What's wrong, sub? What just happened?" Jerry looks and sounds anxious. He leans over and unbuckles my right wrist.

"Oh, Sir. Nothing is *wrong*. Absolutely nothing. You're a genius! I get it. I totally get it. Thank you." I'm beaming and wrenching to get free. My hand latches onto his shoulder so I can make eye contact with him. I want him to set me free, but I can't help myself. I stretch as far as I am able and lay a big, fat kiss on his mouth. I'm stunned when Jerry pushes me back down and re-cuffs me.

"I don't know what's going on with you, sub, but I'm not finished with you yet. If there is no problem, then we'll continue."

"But, Sir. There's no need. I understand what you were trying to get me to see. And, boy, what a relief. I know now what I have to do to make amends and move on. Thank you, Sir, Master. Thank you so much." It's all clear to me, but Jerry's brows are furrowed in grooves deep enough to plant potatoes.

"Hmm. Why don't you enlighten me and tell me how much of a genius I am."

"Master, please let me go first. I did use my safeword."

"That's to be used when you're in pain or too uncomfortable to continue. You don't look like you're hurting to me. And you admitted nothing is wrong."

"Okay, there is something. It's just too painful for me to let you continue to be this nasty brute. I know that's not who you want to be. And, honestly, I can't take any more drama. My poor heart is going to explode if you come at me again with that mother ... Pardon me, Master. That exceedingly large and frightening knife."

Jerry huffs and scowls as he uncuffs me. I can tell he thinks I'm topping. Well, too bad.

"Spill it." He barks at me, but then he starts to massage my aching muscles and joints. He continues as I speak. I almost lose my train of thought as he works his magic.

"Master, you're a master of reverse psychology. You really pushed my buttons and made me explode. I got to spew all the toxic emotions and unresolved thoughts I was still holding on to. I was stuck in my own pain and creating a world of hurt for everyone."

"Really? This is fascinating. Continue." I could drown in the sarcasm dripping from his tongue.

"When you first came through my door, you really scared me. Then, when you pulled the knife, I almost made a mess in my drawers, and I don't mean wetting them. When I look at Dillon's actions in comparison to how merciless you were, it's clear that he wasn't trying to hurt me. Even as far as he had been pushed, all he wanted to do was get me alone so he could talk to me. It was a bit extreme, sure. But ..."

"Sub ..."

"I know. You're right, Master, but you've said it a couple of times now. I wouldn't let him make things right. He should have talked to me once he got through the door, but I know how distraught he was, and I doubt I would have been very cooperative if he wanted to sit and have tea." I'm just motoring along, not letting Jerry get a word in as I gush enthusiastically about my astonishing insights.

"Anyway, that whole monologue about safewords and him wanting to get us to the prize at the end of the scene. So inspired, Master. I guess I didn't really believe him when he poured his heart out in front of me. But when you pulled the reverse attitude, it was like shining a light on the truth. There was no crime; he didn't have the *mens rea*. He was deep in scene space. Not exactly Dom space, but immersed in the scene nonetheless."

"The *mens rea*?"

"You're a cop, so you know what that means. The guilty mind. He had no intent to hurt me. I accused him of being too far gone to see what was happening, but so was I. I didn't see that he truly was just trying to play out our scene." I suck as much air into my lungs as I can fit, lifting my shoulders and expanding my ribs to the max. I let all my breath rush out, feeling totally cleansed as it dissipates.

"Sheer brilliance, Master. I can't thank you enough. Now, seeing the root of Dillon's actions, and owning my own mistakes, I can forgive everything. I'll drop the restraining order on Monday, and then we can both be free." Jerry stops massaging me and just stares with his mouth open slightly.

"That isn't exactly what I was going for, sub. That isn't *at all* what I was going for. I meant to show you that Dillon is dangerous. You need to understand how much he could really hurt you."

I shake my head and smile at him. My poor, hard-boiled cop. "That's just the thing, Master. He's not, and he won't. You're going to tell me again that I'm naïve, aren't you? I'm just not willing to suffer anymore, or have others suffer needlessly. Dillon would never deliberately hurt me. We both suffered because of an unfortunate miscommunication, and because I wouldn't talk to him. I see the truth and can let go, leave all the pain in the past and move on."

Not many people understand my willingness to forgive. They see me as weak. My relatives can't believe I forgave the trucker who fell asleep at the wheel and killed my parents. No one sees my acceptance of the way things are as strength. That's why I don't talk about it much, but there are eternal truths much deeper than we can fathom from our human perspective. My soul set out a dramatic test for me two weeks ago to see how much I could forgive a lover. Since then, I've been floundering without that connection to my spiritual core. I'm excited to have found my way back.

Jerry's face tightens; hard lines score his forehead and ruin his luscious mouth. He doesn't share my enthusiasm. "I don't get it, Master. Isn't that what you wanted for me, to be free, to be healed?"

"Of course, sub. I guess I'm the one who doesn't understand. I'm glad you think I've helped, even though I'm not sure what I did."

"That's okay. We can talk more about it later. Right now, I'd like to express my deep gratitude and appreciation. How may I do that, Sir? How may I serve you, Master?" I allow a soft smile to grace my lips but lower my head and eyes. He's given me so much, worked so hard to bring me relief, that I will gladly give him anything he wants. Even everything I have and everything I am. His gift is more precious to me than he will ever know.

"Come here, sub. Perhaps we both could use some aftercare." He takes my hand and pulls me close against his chest.

"Be careful, Master. Your bruises." Jerry laughs as he swipes his hand across his abs. Makeup!

"Oh, Master. You really did go all out for me, didn't you? Thank you." I snuggle close to Jerry, thrilled to be enveloped in his strong arms, absorbing his heat. We lie like this for the longest time, both content to do nothing but breathe together, to fall in sync with each other. *I love this man. It feels like he loves me. Should I tell him?*

"If you really want to thank me, sub ..." Shivers leapfrog up and down my spine in response to the rich melody of his words and anticipation of the invitation he is about to make. "Get on your hands and knees. Stick that beautiful butt of yours up in the air for me. I want to bury myself in your ass, not because I'm pretending to be someone else, but because you want to let me in."

"Oh, God, Sir. Yes! Please, I need to feel you inside me. My ass belongs to you, Master." Quick like a bunny, I'm in position, quivering with want and desire. Jerry strokes my peaches and leans down to take a bite of each one. Then he wraps himself around me, nuzzling at my ear. "Thank you, baby."

< ♂ + ♀ >

Jerry took great care making love to my whole body before he made glorious love to my behind. We both sprawl out on the bed in the afterglow, boneless, unable to move.

"Master, if that was supposed to be me thanking you, why am I the one floating on a cloud?" I think it would be safe to call him Sir at this point, but, after the way he just owned me, I think Master is the more appropriate term.

"I'm right there with you, sub. I guess that's what you call a win-win situation."

"May I ask, where exactly are we, Master? Is this your home? Or are we at a club?"

"I guess you could say it's a bit of both. We're on my land about ten miles south of town. My house is a separate building a little closer to the county road. This building was originally a feed barn toward the back of the property. When I left DYKKC three years ago, I visited all the other clubs within 50 miles looking for a new community. I didn't like anything I saw and started flying solo.

"About a year later, a few buddies who were as dissatisfied as I was with the local scene came up with the idea to renovate this place and create exactly what we wanted. I carved a plot off my deed and five other guys bought in. I own 51%, and they own equal shares of the rest. Their buy-in paid for the renovations when we flattened the barn and rebuilt." I'm surprised that Jerry is being open about this. I let him ramble because I realize how little I know about him. I want to learn as much as I can before he clams up.

"There are six dungeons below ground, one for each of us, completely sound-proofed. So, even if anyone else was here, no one would hear you scream, little slave girl." I'd be a little bit frightened by that remark if it wasn't for the playful lilt in his voice and the lazy way he rolls over to latch his lips around one of my nipples. If I was to scream now, it would be an ecstatic cry.

"The ground floor has a kitchen-dining-bar area, a large social area kind of like Purgatory, communal showers, and a traditional man cave with a pool table, foosball and a big-ass, hi-def TV and entertainment system. For manly sports only. We don't allow porn, sub." *Yeah, right.* He continues to tease my nipple with his fingers.

"On the second floor, we have two offices and six playrooms for guests or for subs who are a little skittish about dungeons. Are you skittish, sub?" Not *with him keeping me distracted from the purpose of this large room.* He suckles hard on the same nipple again as his inquisitive fingers slide down between my thighs. When he tweaks my clit in a vicious pinch, I know the answer he wants to hear.

"Yes, Master. I'm a bit nervous. It's my first time in a dungeon." Really, the room is not much different from Playroom No. 8 at DYKKC and has some of the same equipment, toys and implements. Except that the walls and floor are made of stone, there are no windows, and we're underground. Oh, and right now we're the only two people here. Funny how that all adds to the fear factor.

"I haven't brought anyone down here since the first weekend it was ready for use." Jerry's voice sounds far away. He's not merely wistful; he seems haunted. *Almost two years?* He searches my eyes while I search his. Sometimes, I see things intuitively, almost psychically. I can't be imagining this—I catch a fleeting glimpse of a ghost trapped in the murky depths of his pupils. I want to know his story so I can help him banish whatever specter has him captive. I have no doubt that he is being held hostage by someone or something tragic. I also have no doubt that if I try to pry right now, Jerry will shut down instantly.

Jerry lifts and shifts until he's lying on top of me, his hips wedged between my legs. He bears most of his upper body weight on his elbows, but his belly and hips force me down into the mattress. Unsheathed and uninsulated, his penis is as hot as a jalapeño. He's still recovering from me thanking him, but that flaccid mass cuddled against my slit feels divine. I'm having thoughts I shouldn't have, careless thoughts.

Jerry brushes my hair from my cheeks, pulling me back from my fantasies of having him bare inside me. He opens his mouth as if to speak but snaps his lips tight. *Ask me; I'll say yes.* Instead, he presses his puckered lips to mine for a second before he slides his rigid tongue as deep into me as he can reach. The growl rumbling in his core travels up his throat. The energy streams from his tongue, turning it into a living vibrator. A quick pulse in his groin signals that he is coming back to life, and it brings my fantasy back to life.

"Come on, sub. I'm starving. Let's go upstairs and get something to eat." That's why they're called fantasies; they have no basis in reality. *Pity.*

Chapter Nineteen – Desecration and Destruction

Friday Night, September 28

Jerry boosts me up the stairs ahead of him, fondling my butt as we ascend and cross the hall. He really is an ass man. I explode in a fit of giggles as I burst through the door and into the kitchen. I have no advance warning when I careen into the middle of a huddle of nearly naked men; my own laughter had drowned out the loud guffaws circling the room.

Cheering and jeering and whistles assail me from all quarters. Panicked, I throw an arm across my chest and a hand between my thighs as I turn to flee back downstairs. I smack into a hard wall of flesh. I'm sandwiched between a pack of hyenas and a lion.

"Who's the rabbit, Snapper?" "Hey, Buddy. Nice ass on this one. I bet you like that." "Bring her closer. Can we touch?" "Show us her tits, Snapper."

"Manners. Don't run away, sub. Turn around and say hello to my friends." Jerry claps his hands onto my elbows and half lifts me as I kick and scuffle, and he walks me backward into the melee.

"Intermission, Master. Intermission." As I raise my objection, or at least try to, Jerry spins me, exposing me, presenting me to his buddies. He has me pinioned, molded against his unyielding frame. With my wings clipped, flight is impossible. A big, strong man is a godsend unless he's using his might against you.

"Behave, slave. Stop struggling. Relax, kitten. You're safe. These are good people. Let me introduce you." Jerry starts off as the authoritarian but switches his approach mid-sentence. Soft and reassuring words do not excuse his behavior. Even if those words are whispered in a hot, humid hush into a sensitive and susceptible ear. I hate saying my safeword again; and I hate it even more that he's put me in a predicament where I *really* need to use it.

"Intermission, *Master*." I throw a lot of weight behind the word "Master." My mood rapidly ramps up from startled, to upset, to mortified and, from there, to pissed right off. Then all the way to cold resolve. I've said my safeword twice now, and he's still deaf to it. I'm standing here in the buff being visually dissected by crass strangers. And I can't believe he's doing nothing about it, can't believe another Dom is breaking the safeword rule.

Even though I've forgiven Dillon in my heart, my tolerance level for hurtful behavior is pretty low. Right now it's nada, zip, zilch. Forget three strikes; Jerry is out right now. I bypass "end scene" and go straight to terminating our contract.

"Exit!" I jab my elbow hard into his gut and stamp on his foot. As I break free from his imprisonment, I break apart inside. My heart is crystal shattering on marble tile. I'm the one running away, but he's the one who has abandoned me. *How could he withdraw his protection so casually? How could he break my trust so easily?* As I fly down the stairs, his friends call after me to come back.

I hit the last stair as I hear and feel the heavy thumping of big feet. I make it inside the tiny bathroom but can't get the door shut as Jerry catches up to me. I lean all my weight against the door, but I'm ridiculously outmatched. Jerry crowds in. The only place for me to go is to sit on the throne. Oddly, I don't feel regal and radiant.

I can't tell if Jerry is angry, hurt, embarrassed or confused. "Exit? Really? What just happened, sub?"

I glower. And glare. And stare him down. Actually, I stare him up since I'm sitting on the can. "Our contract is finished. Stop calling me sub. You don't deserve that fealty from me. You forfeited your rights to anything from me." His face is blank; his voice is mute.

"Go read your copy of our contract, Jerry. Then tell me you can't figure out what's going on. I actually didn't need to say exit because you already breached it, ripped it into pieces, and then ran it through a cross-cut shredder."

Genuine bewilderment washes over his face. *In-cred-i-ble.* He rubs his hands over his chin and then runs them through his hair. He crumples against the wall, shoulders stooped and knees bent. His cluelessness pushes my button that says, "All men are stupid."

"Did you not sit me on your knee and spend half an hour negotiating the terms with me? Does our agreement mean so little to you that in only a week you've forgotten my biggest concern? You blow past my most stringent hard limit and don't even notice? Unbelievable."

"Language, sub." *You're. Kidding. Me.* I am more than done with him. I shoot off the toilet in a tirade and get right in his face.

"You just can't help yourself, can you? Are you going to paddle my ass again for swearing? In the middle of a major bust up, you're going to chastise me for using the f-word? Try to focus on what really matters here, Jerry." In the quiet, my words ricochet off the walls like an avalanche echoing through a deep canyon. I have to take a breath.

"I do know what's in our contract. What I do not understand is your reaction. You agreed to obey me without question and to give me full access to your body to do with as I please. We just had a very edgy scene. You were incredibly brave and had no trouble trusting me to direct it without any negotiation. Then we shared the aftercare, so intense and beautiful. Now you freak out because I want you to say hello to my friends?"

"Our Master/slave relationship was a solemn commitment, or so you said. You promised me your protection. What you agreed to was no public nudity. No public humiliation, Jerry. You signed your name to that. It was a hard limit you said you wouldn't push.

"Not only did you not shield me from your friends, but you ignored my safeword and put me on display for them. You whored me out to them for their entertainment. That's not protection."

"You're being ridiculous, Erin. They're my friends. All I asked of you was to meet them, to be sociable. You need to be comfortable being naked around strangers if you want this lifestyle. That was for your benefit, not for them."

"Of course it was for them. You weren't thinking of me. You broke another of my hard limits when you let them take pictures of me. If it's not for their entertainment, then what? Their profit? Are they going to sell them to some porn site?"

"Pictures? What are you talking about?" A soaring eagle with its talons sunk in the hide of its precious dinner couldn't clutch any tighter than he's gripping my shoulders.

"You didn't see them clicking their phone cameras?" In half a second, I'm dumped back on the toilet and left alone in a very empty and quiet room. Jerry is gone in a flash.

I pick myself up and plod along into the main room of the dungeon. It's fitting that I'm in a torture chamber. I get myself all tangled up struggling into my jeans and T-shirt that I find right next to the scraps of black fur in the hockey bag. As I jiggle up my zipper, I topple over onto the bed, whacked and wasted.

"An accountant, that's what I need. A nice, steady, stable bean counter. Or a school teacher. A kind-hearted and trustworthy teacher. He doesn't have to be exciting. He just has to respect me and be good to me. I could settle for that. Exciting is too much trouble, too much heartache." Heaving waves of sorrow curl and break over me, right down to my toes. My knees bend up almost to my chin as I turtle into a protective shell. Sorrow envelopes me like an obscuring black cloud.

"Is this what my life is to become?" I remember lying on a bed just a week ago with a despondent Dillon curled up against me. He had the same listless tone and the same disbelief at how his life had turned completely upside down. My eyes water as compassion for him floods through me. If he feels even half as pitiful as I do, then he must be wholly deflated. *I have to apologize as soon as I can.*

"His situation is different though, isn't it? He's responsible for the mess he got himself into. He has no one else to blame." It's only five or six seconds before I answer my own question.

"It's no different at all. You're responsible for your life, your own messes, too, Erin. Dillon did what he did and that's on him, but don't forget your part in his pain. As for this debacle, you're the one who stepped out on the wild side in the first place and played around with things you had no business playing with. What on earth did you think you were doing? As soon as you get home, you're going to delete all that trash off your e-reader. You're just not cut out for this shit. Stick to the life you know."

The fist of misery that has a death grip on my heart squeezes hard, wringing out all the crazy hopes and dreams I've indulged in.

$$< \male + \female >$$

"No worries, sub. That's all taken care of. All photos have been deleted and none were emailed, so you can relax." Jerry sounds upbeat, cheerful. He must think he's fixed everything. The bed dips and his hefty hand tries to roll me over. I shrug out of his grasp and scoot out of his reach.

"Sub, why are you dressed?"

"Because you're taking me home." My words are as flat as my crushed heart.

"I don't understand. I didn't know, but the photos are dealt with. The guys know what they did was wrong, and they left. You don't have to see them again. Let's go back up for something to eat."

"Thank you for seeing to that." I pull myself up and face the man I once respected. It just about kills me. "Tell me, Jerry. If they hadn't taken the photos, would it have been okay then? Okay that you paraded me in front of them? That you ignored my safeword?"

"I told you I would push your limits. The guys weren't supposed to be here, but it was a good opportunity to challenge your aversion to nudity. It's my decision what is in your best interests. Don't forget that you're my slave. As your Master, your growth is my responsibility. You're shaking, and you're blowing this all out of proportion because you're suffering sub-drop. Come here, sub. Let me hold you." He grasps my hands, trying to pull me into a hug, and pleads with his eyes even if his words are not exactly conciliatory. I *wish I could just forgive and forget.* I tear away from him.

"Sub-drop? Been there. This isn't it. This is betrayal. I trusted you to help me cope and move beyond some very traumatic events, and you didn't take a misstep. You've put me through unbelievably tough situations and done it with sensitivity and care. I can't say enough how very grateful I am for that. I could forgive you for this, except for two things. Public nudity is specifically prohibited by our contract, and you broke your unbreakable vow.

"Less than an hour ago, you pushed me hard until I went ballistic about Dillon not respecting my safeword. Then you turn around and do the same thing to me.

"You condemned Jim, Christophe and Dillon. And you called me naïve for associating with them. Maybe you were right about me being naïve because I dove in blindly with you, trusted you without a second thought. But it seems I've gotten mixed up with yet another man just like them, one who doesn't think I'm smart enough to have a clue about what's best for me, or that I deserve to have a say in how to handle my fears or anything else in my life. It seems I just can't find someone worth trusting." Jerry's about to speak; no doubt he will try to justify himself, so I keep going.

"You told me that as my Master you would hold me to a higher standard. Well, as your slave I'm holding you to a higher standard. You made me believe in you. You said we could renegotiate our contract, and I might have done that if you had just listened. You let me down at the first true test. It kills me that you proved me right, that I'm the only one I can count on."

Jerry drops my hands. He looks gutted. That would make two of us. I roll off the other side of the bed and gather my things. I'm conspicuous about leaving my velvet gear in a pile on the floor.

I don't know where I find the steam to propel myself up the stairs and out his door. I'm just dying. *How can I walk away from the man I love? But how can I stay?* Evanya is warning me to do just that, to stay and not run away again. But, thanks to Christophe's lessons, I know where to draw the line.

Jerry is quiet the whole drive to my place. I'm huddled up, staring out the window, seeing nothing, only vaguely aware of the route we're traveling. When he parks in my driveway, he kills the engine and twists his whole body toward me. The cab of his truck is cavernous, but he fills his half and mine when he leans forward to brush his fingers across my tear-stained cheeks.

"Erin, don't end things like this. Don't walk away again without talking after a scene gets messed up. I'm still your Master for three more weeks. We can get back on track. I made an honest mistake, but I thought I was helping. I would never want to hurt you."

"Huh, that's what Dillon said, and you told me not to believe him." It's a spiteful thing to say, but it's out of my mouth before I can censor it. My heart is spurting blood all over the space between us, and I just don't care if he bleeds a little, too. *Why should I be the only one hemorrhaging like a hemophiliac?*

"That's not fair, Erin. You can't compare how he hurt you to what happened tonight."

"Can't I? What happened to your Dom code? You're the one who drilled it into me how important it is for me to use my safeword. Remember how red my ass was from that lesson? I called for an intermission. We could have stepped back and negotiated, revised our contract, but you made the decision without me. Just like I thought Dillon did, you stole my right to choose, but at least he stopped when he realized I wasn't alright.

"You lost your nobility tonight, Jerry, in one stupid act of arrogance. You have no idea how much that hurts me. I'd like my key back, please." I stick my hand out, palm open and waiting. I wish I could hold my head up high as I wait, but I can't get through this if I have to look at him.

Jerry's sigh is strangled, like maybe there's a landslide of boulders crushing his chest. It would only be fair because that's how I feel. He fiddles with his key ring until he finally slides my key off. The metallic jangling is as foreboding as the clanking of a knife being sharpened. The thrust of the blade hits my heart when he presses the key in my palm and captures my hand. He whispers one word, "precious." A single sob booms from deep in my belly. A flood of tears as corrosive as sulfuric acid eats away at my face.

I float out of the truck and through my door. Funny, I usually associate floating with dreaming, but this is my worst nightmare. I expected it to hurt when our contract expired in a month; I could never have anticipated this end and outcome after only seven days. Seven days of heaven desecrated in one moment.

I collapse against the door as soon as I close it. My knees lock, and I just lean like that famous tower. It's probably five minutes before I hear Jerry's truck pull out of my driveway. My knees finally give. I wail out my grief for at least half an hour in a big heap where I landed. When I start to retch, I crawl to the toilet. It's just the dry heaves; my body is trying to hurl itself inside out, and why shouldn't it? My whole world has been turned topsy-turvy, tossed upside down, *again.*

"Stupid heart. I told you this was too good to be true. Funny, though, how we were both wrong. You thought he was perfect, and I thought I wasn't good enough. I deserve better than this. Damn, this hurts!"

My tummy has stopped rolling and pitching, so I make my way to my bedroom, staggering like a wino who's just sucked the last drop out of his bottle. I tear at my clothes, barely able to get them off with hands that hardly function. The pendant of my hip necklace knocks against my shivering stomach. My clumsy fingers can't manage the clasp, so I just pluck at the chain until it snaps. I'd laugh at the metaphor if it wasn't so damned depressing. The knife in my heart twists, finishing me off.

As I bury myself under the bedcovers, I'm hit by a crazy feeling of déjà vu. Naked, numb, broken, and betrayed. Wrapped up in a blanket. *Where's my DM to the rescue? Who's going to help me now?*

Chapter Twenty – Out of the Desert

Saturday Morning, September 29

"Erin, move your ass." "No. I just want to stay in bed." "Move it, Sweet Cheeks. Don't let him do this to you." "But I don't want to." "Not good enough." "I don't have to be anywhere until Monday morning. I cleared my schedule, remember?" "So? You can't just roll over and die. Don't just hand him that power." "Ouch. Low blow, Evanya. You know that's the hardest part of what happened with Dillon." She doesn't always fight fair.

"I'll be strong on Monday. Just leave me alone." I yank the covers over my head. I ignore Evanya's butt-kicking, even though I know she's trying to stop me sinking too low. I'll pull myself together, later. It's only fair to take some time to wallow. Last night was the death of a dream that deserves to be noticed, and mourned. After all, I've lost the love of my life. I have no doubt that he is "The One."

For a couple of hours, I drift in and out of sleep, and bouts of tears, and long tirades of expletives. I drag myself out of bed when the phone rings. Of course, I'm hoping that it's Jerry and dreading that it's Jerry.

"Hey, Lace."

"What's up, girl? I haven't heard from you since we talked on Tuesday. Then I heard last night that Steffie banned you. What the hell is that all about? You okay?"

"Not really. Things aren't good right now." Sniffles lead to moans, which lead to gut-wrenching fits of blubbering.

"I'll be there in half an hour." I tell her not to bother; she won't take any argument from me and shows up as promised.

"What the hell, Erin? You look like shit. This mess with Dillon has really knocked you out, hasn't it?" I tell Lacey that I'm not busted up about that anymore, that I've forgiven him. We sit in the kitchen, and I spill everything about Jerry.

Lacey is speechless at first. She sets aside her cup of tea and pulls a bottle from my wine rack. It's only 11:00. She knocks back a whole glass and pours more without offering me any, not that I want it. She plops down in her chair and says, "You and Snapper together, huh? Wow. I heard he was at DYKKC investigating, but I couldn't have seen that one coming."

"What does that mean? You obviously knew Jerry before he left the club. Tell me what I don't know about this man."

"You know I love you, so please don't take this the wrong way." She swallows another huge gulp of wine. "I can see the appeal you have for someone soft and easygoing like The Squire. You're the perfect plaything for him. But I could never figure out you with Master Ronan and The Saint.

"You're the most vanilla of all the subs. And yet, both of them came looking for you. At first, I thought they were just trying to break you, but everyone knows that never happened. You've stayed strong. You even got Dillon to keep your sessions closed.

"Those two luuuv to discipline, mercilessly. You've seen what they're like with other subs. They are very talented with paddles, crops and canes. But the way they wield a whip ... Their skill in flogging and flaying is a sight to behold." Lacey licks her lips, lost in a dream. A sad smile quirks the corners of her mouth. She takes another big swig of cabernet and puts her hand on my shoulder.

"That kind of skill doesn't just happen. You can't just pick up a bull whip and start whacking away at tender flesh. It takes lots of practice and a very good mentor." She tips forward and hisses in my ear, "Who do you think they learned from?

"Want to know why they call him Snapper? It's not just the explosive sound his whip makes when he cracks it." Lacey sidles up to me again, her wine-soaked breath steaming at my ear. "He can take the brattiest, most insubordinate sub and bend her, break her, snap her will like a twig ... in just one session."

My abs clench, and my intestines twist and take a swan dive, flopping onto my uterus. *My Regis!* He wanted to worship my body. Not abuse it. He wanted to guide me. Not break me. But that's what he does to other subs.

"I don't get it Lacey. So, he's not just a Dom? Not some guy who just wants me to call him Master? He's like a real Master?"

"Not *just* a Master. *The* Master of the whole Eastern seaboard. He used to teach most of the classes at DYKKC. People would come from miles around to watch his sessions and to learn from him. He had three protégés, Ronan, The Saint, and his last one was Tuck." Lacey flounces back in her chair and stares into the bottom of her empty wineglass.

The penny drops, thudding in my heart. "There's more to it than that," Jerry had said when he talked about Christophe and leaving DYKKC. Not betrayed by a random Dom, but by his own protégé.

"I understand now why Jerry quit the club. How crushing, and humiliating, to have someone who was no doubt like a son or brother to him turn on him the way Christophe did." My heart is already broken, but this revelation batters it to a bloody pulp. Except, this time, it's hurting *for* Jerry and not because of him. *Oh Christ!* The rest of what Lacey said blows me to pieces. *Three apprentices, and I've been with two of them!*

"That's just what put him over the edge. Something happened, and he changed long before that." Her voice drifts off as her eyes glaze over and fill with tears. WTF?

"What happened?"

"It wasn't just Ronan's betrayal." She's haunted, speaking to me from somewhere in the past. "He tried to save someone … who couldn't be helped." Lacey is in deep. I've never seen her like this, and it's breaking my heart. I cup my hand and stroke her cheek, crooning as I speak, trying to be as sensitive as I can, but I can't leave her stuck in whatever dark place she's in.

"Lacey, sweetheart? What is it? Why does what happened to Jerry hurt you?" Lacey's head snaps toward me. Comprehension about where she is dawns, and her eyes nearly pop out of her head.

"Oh, God. What am I doing? I can't do this. Leave me alone." I try to catch Lacey's arm as she springs out of her chair, but she dodges me and bolts with her fingers dug in her purse, retrieving her keys.

"Lacey, wait! You can't go. You've been drinking."

"Don't stick your nose where it doesn't belong, priss." I'm hot on her tail, but she throws a hip check at me that would have thrown a hulking hockey player through safety glass. I tumble to the floor, and she's gone before I can recover.

"Oh, Lacey. Be careful, girl. Angels, protect her." I close the door and shuffle to the kitchen. The bottle of wine calls my name. I snatch it up and take a couple of long pulls before I collapse into a chair. The look on Lacey's face was pure terror. I can't begin to guess what that was all about. And I don't know what to make of the little bit that she did tell me.

Regis. What happened to you? Why did you give everything up? And what on earth would a major Master want from a priss like me?

"It's been a long time since a woman's had faith in me" is what he said.

"God, help me. What have I done?"

$$< ♂ + ♀ >$$

Hunger pains finally pull me out of my meditation. The clock says I've been sitting here for almost an hour and a half. All that time, and I don't feel any closer to knowing what to do about Jerry. I do know, however, what I'm going to do about Dillon. I send him a text telling him I'm dropping the restraining order on Monday. I ask if he would meet me. A message pings back immediately, and we arrange to meet at Sandler's Deli for a late lunch.

When he walks through the door, my eyes flood with hot tears. *My big, beautiful bad boy.* Flying out of my chair, I dash across the room and fling my arms around his neck. We both stumble, but Dillon holds me tight and steadies us.

I was going to stay strong; I was all set to tell him I was ready to forgive him. What do I do instead? "Oh, Sir. I'm sorry. I'm so sorry. Please forgive me."

"Hush, priss," he murmurs as he wraps his fist around the braid I wove just for him. He kisses the top of my head and pulls my braid to tip my head back for a kiss on the lips. "Let's sit." Dillon spins me around, dropping both hands to my hips, and he pushes me in the direction of the booth.

My butt hasn't even hit the seat when a menu lands in my lap. The waitress isn't looking at me; she's all eyes for Dillon. I can't say I blame the girl. Being hurt and angry, I'd completely forgotten how handsome and magnetic he is. In his firm Dom voice he says, "Thank you. I'll call you when we're ready to order." Her smile falters, but she obeys his command. *Did she have a choice?* My creaming pussy knows the answer.

"I can't imagine what you have to apologize for, priss, but let me start." Dillon lays himself bare for me, reiterating his apologies from the night he hauled me to his house. I open myself for him, letting in every word and emotion he offers. His remorse echoes my own.

I thank Dillon and begin my own apology for not using my safeword sooner, for letting my emotions get in the way, for the horrible things I accused him of, for not listening, and for cutting him out of my life. My eyes lower and my head bows as I make my last apology. "And, mostly, Sir, I'm sorry for not submitting to you and to your authority. I always held a bit of myself back. I failed you, failed us both. I'm so sorry." I cry in silence, but my body shakes as my chest puffs like a bellows trying to revive a dying fire.

"priss, stop. This is not your fault, baby girl. The success of our scene was my responsibility. I was the Top. I failed you."

"No, Sir. I will not let you take the blame for this, at least, not all of it. You couldn't have done anything more than you did. I was in sub-drop, and I didn't realize how deep I had crashed. I should have let you give me aftercare and talk me down. If you'd had a chance to remind me that you'd asked if I was okay ... I'm sorry I freaked so bad." I put my hand on his to press my point. Warmth flows up my fingers, speeding along until it settles in my heart. Dillon flips his palm over, encasing my hand in his. He gives me a strong pull.

"Come here, baby. Sit beside me." He slides me along the bench seat until I'm practically in his lap. He cups my face in his strong hands and kisses away my tears. The tenderness in the brush of his lips against my cheeks melts my bones as surely as if the man was the spring sun thawing a winter's worth of ice and snow.

"Thank you, baby. It's not necessary, but I accept your apology."

"You're welcome, Sir."

"How about you stop calling me Sir, and I'll stop calling you priss. We're not at DYKKC. Let's just be two friends trying to work out a terrible misunderstanding." When he coils his arms around me, I burrow my nose into the crook of his neck. What a relief to not have that wall of hurt between us.

"What changed, Erin? I thought you would never speak to me again after my last stunt."

"I had a bit of help." If I'm truly sorry, I can't hold back from him anymore. I tell him about Jerry and our contract. Dillon flinches and stops breathing. "We did some roleplaying so I could work it out."

"What does he think of you being here? You know you shouldn't be speaking to me without his permission. I won't do that to him." He pulls us apart, and the cool air between us mimics the chill that's settled on our conversation.

"I know what happened with Christophe. I wouldn't do that to Jerry or to you either. He doesn't know I'm here, but he has nothing to say about it because I ended our contract." I don't go into much detail but tell him how Jerry was the one who broke the deal first and that I couldn't stay with him.

"I understand, Erin, really. It was stupid of him, but you walking away from Snapper would have been a heavy blow for him. Did I tell you that he was my mentor?"

"Jerry told me what happened with Christophe, but Lacey was the one who told me this morning about his three apprentices. Then she wouldn't tell me more about Jerry. She flipped out and ran out of my house. What was that all about?"

"It's not my story to tell. You'll have to ask Lacey or Jerry. Talk to him, Erin. If you can get past what I did, you can work it out with him." When I drop my head, he lifts it back up and arches his left brow at me.

"I can forgive you, Dillon, because I love you. I can't forgive him ... because I fell *in love* with him. I miss him so much already. It's killing me, but I can't trust him. If I can't trust him, then we have nothing." *If I can't trust him with something as harmless as nudity, or as important as my safeword, how could I trust him with a whip, or my whole life?* That's an especially troubling thought after what Lacey has told me about Snapper.

Dillon gives me a big bear hug and then opens up the menu. He said he doesn't understand people, but he's smart enough to know I can't talk about Jerry anymore. Lunch conversation is sparse, and the silence between us is warm and comfortable. As we part, Dillon gives me a long, lingering, *friendly* kiss.

My heart lifts a bit now that this friendship is rescued, even if the rest of my relationships are in tatters. It's too ironic that the only person I can talk to now is the one who set this maelstrom of pain and misery in motion.

$$< \male + \female >$$

Friday Night, October 19

The last three weeks have been the loneliest of my life. Even when the big rig plowed into my parents' car and stole them from me, I had other family and friends to be with me at the beginning of my grieving. Jim still won't return my calls and neither will Lacey. Jerry and Christophe have given up calling me. I can't go to DYKKC because those devils no longer want to know me. And I can't tell my vanilla friends about anything. Dillon is the only one speaking to me.

The worst pain of all is the distance I'm keeping between me and Jerry; my resolution not to let him back in is steadfast. I haven't been in my work room, can't stomach even looking at my collection of harnesses, let alone make a new one. I had my hip necklace repaired, but it sits in its red satin pouch in my toy bag. Even that has been abandoned; my orgasms still belong to Regis.

My days are filled with work. I've thrown myself into exercise, running five miles five times a week and spending an hour in the gym before work every day to get myself out of my house and away from my lonely bed. On weekends I take a yoga class both mornings and again both afternoons. Because I have no appetite, I'm eating less. I've lost 18 pounds this month, and my curves are not quite as rounded. I almost miss that extra padding that I used to curse. But I am very proud of my muscle definition and fitness level. My reading is restricted to biographies or the classics—no erotica downloads.

"Screw it! I've got to stop moping," I declare. Evanya was right when she said I can't just roll over and die. "I'm taking my life back."

Now that I know I am a kitty, I'm going to have to find another Master who is looking for a fur ball who will purr in his ear. I know there isn't anyone at DYKKC I could call to be that for me. I have to move on. Maybe it's time to check out the other club across town.

I groom and dress with care. Most of my clothes are loose now, so I choose a purple satin corset that I lace tighter and a black leather miniskirt that used to be too close-fitting. A garter belt with black fishnet stockings and silver stilettos complete the outfit. I know I look hot. I even let myself get excited, in a good way, about my night out. "Maybe I'll find some new friends."

< ♂ + ♀ >

The moment I step into Belladonna Gentlemen's Club, I get a nervous vibe that perhaps the rumors I heard about this place are true. I don't think there are any gentlemen here. I bypass the strip club and head straight to the playroom. It's a black hole. The culture is completely different, totally hard core SM, no diversity of tastes. I realize how unique DYKKC is, how inclusive. davey and his Mommy wouldn't be welcome here, neither would any of the Goths or Trannies. I bet this crew dine on tender subs and devour vanilla cream for dessert. I am sooo in way over my head.

Before I can get back to the coat check, five scary looking Doms circle me. Each is dressed in black leather vests and pants, with heavy, black boots on their feet. Two have shaved heads; two have long, shaggy hair and goatees; and one is wearing a black balaclava.

The predators smell fresh meat. They try to overpower and intimidate me, constantly circling and making me dizzy. They argue over who is going to have me, as if I have no say in the matter. Then a very handsome, very hot man comes to my rescue, pulling me from their clutches and over to a shadowy corner.

"*Eres muy hermosa, niña.* So beautiful. I apologize for those boors. My name is Amancio. I am the owner of this club. Tell me your name, baby girl." His eyes, as dark as bittersweet chocolate, never leave mine or blink as he dips his head to kiss the back of my hand. He keeps a firm grip, holding me captive as the sharp tip of his tongue paints wet circles on my skin. "Your name, little one?"

I don't know what to say, and not just because of the way he made love to my hand. What name do I give? "playmate, Sir" is what pops out. I lower my head, my gaze on the floor, and see the expensive, black leather shoes on his gargantuan feet. *Oh my!* A long, elegant finger lifts my chin. On the journey back up, I spy a very conspicuous bulge in his charcoal, pin-striped trousers.

"Sit, playmate." Amancio gestures to a cushy, scarlet couch. His crisp, white dress shirt, open at the neck, contrasts brightly against his dark, Hispanic skin. The fit of Egyptian cotton over his sturdy shoulders and trim waist is impeccable, body-hugging but with no straining or gaping as he lowers six feet of exquisite sinew and bone to sit beside me. Our thighs are less than two inches apart.

His aura of power is weighty, prodigious for someone who is probably as young as I am. Evanya is shouting warnings at me, but I have already figured out that there is something hinky about this guy. Up close, the razor-thin mustache and sharp goatee cast a forbidding pall over his otherwise refined face. His manner is the opposite, as smooth and enticing as his silky, black hair that is pulled back in a filigreed silver clasp. His actions are considerate, welcoming, but his brilliant smile never shines in his eyes. His gaze is hard, probing, and so are his questions. I get the very distinct impression that he is sussing out my weaknesses.

Despite the alarm bells ringing loud in my head, I almost fall for his Jedi mind tricks. He keeps his voice a monotone as if he is trying to hypnotize me. He strokes my cheek when he praises me, and he presses my knee or squeezes my arm when he expects a concession from me. The leisurely conversation twists in circles while his fingers trace spirals up my thigh. He is weaving a spell to ensnare me. It's not that hard to trap me because it's been a very long, dry month, and my body aches to have my thirst quenched.

He slips his hand inside my corset and pulls out a breast, and I don't gasp—I sigh. He sucks my nipple into his mouth and bites down, and I don't flinch—I moan. He slides two fingers under my skirt and straight into my juicy sex, and I don't pull away—I purr.

"Come with me, precious," he whispers to me. *precious. That's what Jerry called me. I need to be someone's precious.* Heartache compromises the strength of my defenses, and I crumble. I would do anything to be someone's precious.

What saves me is a little look. He has pulled me to standing, sliding a well-manicured hand up underneath my skirt to grasp one of my naked peaches in a possessive hold. I am swaddled in a hazy fog of sensation and need. I peer up to smile at him in appreciation of his touch. Just in time to see him give an almost imperceptible nod and flick his eyes to the left. I follow his sight line from where he had been looking to where he indicated, from the posse of five beasts to a curtained doorway.

Tornado warning sirens blast in my head. I realize I've been set up, played like the naïve, trusting fool I am. *Sonofabitch.* I slap his cheek and shove him back onto the couch. I run with the roar of his laughter chasing behind me, stopping at the front door just long enough to grab my keys and phone. I make it out in one piece and hurry to the safety of my car. I only get a couple of blocks before swerving into a drugstore parking lot. My body's going into shock, shivering like I've got hypothermia. *I need help.* My phone drops from my numb fingers and back into my purse three times before I can hold on and dial.

There is only one person I can talk to, and I have to get through Steffie first. I have to tell her where I am and why I need Dillon. I'm surprised she actually tracks him down and puts me through. A long 25 minutes of waiting drags by. When he arrives, he pulls me out of my car and cuddles me until I stop shaking. Once I'm calm, he buckles me into his SUV and slides behind the wheel.

He chews into me right away, clearly not so sympathetic of my predicament. "What the hell were you thinking? What kind of dumbass goes to a new club on her own? Don't ever do that again."

"I'm sorry. What am I supposed to do? I have no one to go with, and I can't go back to DYKKC. You all opened me up, and now I'm completely shut out. I feel like a pariah wandering the desert. I've lost the life I had, my new home, my new family. I can't go back to being just a dull librarian." I get his point, really, but hearing my pathetic response out loud makes me incredibly sad.

"You still can't take risks like that. You have to find someone you can arrange a safe call with. It's less risky to tell a friend where you're going and to ask them to be available if you need help, and to worry if you don't check in on time. What if I couldn't be here for you? What if something happened and no one knew where you'd gone?" Again, he's right.

"I want you to promise me you'll never go there again." I tell him I've learned my lesson and begin to recount what happened. The mention of Amancio's name sets off an explosive reaction that almost ends with him running the car off the road.

"Never again! You stay away from that man. Promise!" I do. His alarmed attitude is confirmation enough that I have dodged a bullet. I'm fine this time, but one of these days my appetite for kink and the risks I take to get it just might get me into some serious trouble. *Idiot. When are you going to learn, slut?*

$$< ♂ + ♀ >$$

I'm grateful that Dillon is not content to just drop me at my door. I don't want to be alone with memories of that terrifying encounter, or my self-loathing. We make a toasty fire to chase away my chills and sit beside each other on the couch, each with a glass of wine. We really don't know much about each other because most of our interaction at DYKKC revolved around whatever scene we were doing. What a treat it is to just talk to my friend.

I knew that Dillon is the regional sales manager for a company that sells energy-efficient windows. I didn't realize that he chose that company to work for because he's very involved in sustainable living and the green movement. I really like that about him.

As a matter of fact, the more we talk, the more I find out that I really like the man. His family is obviously important to him, based on the number of stories he tells about them. He wraps me in his arms and holds me when I tell him about my parents. He acts so tough and menacing, but, really, he has a very kind heart. A thought flits briefly through my mind that I now know more about Dillon's life than I do about Jerry's. Then I let that notion float away as I focus back on the man I'm snuggling with.

Somewhere along the way, this amazing man stopped trusting himself and believing in his value. He could give any sub so much more than just the endorphin fix she is looking for if he could stop hiding behind the sadist mask. I don't mean to suggest for a moment that he set aside his talents for punishment and discipline. What I see doesn't involve that.

If Dillon could forget the *role* of being a Dom and allow himself to simply be a strong man who craves control and an outlet for his masculine power and leadership, and if he could allow a bottom to drop the *role* of being a sub and simply be a strong woman who craves a firm hand and an outlet for her feminine softness and submission, well, how off-the-hook fantastic would his sessions be? He thinks he's not as much fun as Jim or as intuitive as Christophe, but that's because he's hiding who he is—a decent man with a strong heart and a kinky mind. I wish I could find a way to show him that.

Every now and then, when he thinks I'm not looking, I catch Dillon staring at my breasts. I suppose I should have changed out of my corset and into something more respectable, but I'm enjoying his attention. His hunger may as well be written on a billboard for how blatant it is. I'm kind of surprised he's not looking at my butt instead. He's always enjoyed playing with the girls, but I thought he was an ass man through and through. Who knew?

This time, the spell coiling its tendrils around me is laid with no warning bells. I want to succumb to it, to submit. Dillon heads to the kitchen to get us another glass of wine; I follow right behind. When he sets the glasses on the counter, I take his hand and lead him to the front door. Fixing what broke between us, healing both of us, is all I can think of in this moment. I don't know if anyone else could understand what I'm about to do, but I have to do it for us.

< ♂ + ♀ >

"The last time you were here, it wasn't a very happy time for either of us. Whenever I look or stand here, I remember." We should have talked. I know how much damage I caused by shutting Dillon out, how I drove him to hunt me down here.

"Oh, Erin, baby. I'm so sorry."

"I don't want you to be sorry anymore. Change the memory for me, Sir." I let my eyes and head fall, and I lace my fingers behind my back. Even though we're friends again and have apologized to each other and forgiven each other, a scar remains that taints our relationship. I can't allow it to persist. I want to give this man what I couldn't give him before and erase that blemish.

"Erin, you don't have to do this."

"My name is priss. And, yes, I do, Sir, for both of us. I regret holding back from you, never giving you what we both needed—my complete submission. I offer myself to you tonight, *all* of me. I bow to you, Sir. How may I serve you?" The silence is overwhelming.

"Position One, sub." Dillon's voice breaks and crackles. I'm glad I'm not the only one choked up. As I fall gracefully to my knees, warmth descends on me like a mantle around my shoulders. Position One means to lower my eyes, bow my head, straighten my spine, lock my hands at the top of my butt crack, sit back on my heels, and spread my thighs wide. It feels right to be at Sir's feet like this, awaiting whatever command he chooses to make, yearning to give my best response possible.

"Suck me, sub." My beautiful bad boy is trying to be stern, but I hear the subtle traces of wonder and need coloring his order.

I am confident and rise boldly, kissing the swell in his jeans before I draw down his zipper. His rock-hard cock dives into my hands. "Sir," I murmur in a breathy sigh. He truly is magnificent. I worship his manhood, singing words of praise for his masculine beauty. I fondle his ball sac and then kiss his bright purple tip. When I lick and suck reverently, Dillon moans and spears his fingers into my long locks. I haven't had my hair down for him since the first night he claimed his right to punish me for interrupting his scene.

We have never been together like this. We've never been this intimate. Because, this time, I'm willing to be and do anything he needs to feel powerful, and treasured, and whole. A true exchange.

Dillon guides my head in his strong hands, placing me at the right height and distance for him to rock his hips and piston his twitching shaft into my receptive mouth. His fat cockhead hits the back of my throat in a steady rhythm.

His body tells me in so many ways that he's enjoying our dance— the primal groans and growls thundering up from his root, the waves of kinetic energy rippling through his muscles, the tangy beads of pre-come oozing from the slit in his ripe plum, the tenacious way he grapples my hair. And, still, he's holding back.

No holding back anymore, girl, for either of us. I tap one of his hands three times. That's one of our safe gestures that I'm to use anytime I can't say my safeword. It's difficult to speak with his silky shaft filling my mouth completely. Dillon's body tenses and stills.

"What is it, sub? What's wrong?" There's a nervous edge to his words. I think he's paranoid now, and I can't blame him.

"Sir. I can take all of you, if you wish it. If you would allow me the honor." I look up at him with pleading eyes. I need for him to take this pleasure. I remember the first time I took him in my mouth and how I thought of it as claiming my prize. But, if I am a good submissive, the prize should be his to claim.

"Christ, priss. You interrupted for that? Open wide, little girl. I'm going to fuck your throat. Swallow my dick, sub, all the way." The mock annoyance makes me smile.

I wrap my smile around him, at first taking in just the plump tip as I suck and swirl around the ridge. I lick and trace his pulsing veins with the point of my tongue. Then, as I wrap one hand around his massive member and steady myself with the other hand on his hip, I maneuver into the optimal position for blowing his mind as I blow his cock. I slide my lips over his proud warrior, inch by inch. I hum in appreciation as I suck back his earliest dribbles, as bitter and biting as sips of whisky, a prelude to the torrents of juice to come. Between us, we set a steady pace that drives him wild and still allows me to breathe occasionally.

The Saint's hefty sword swells and throbs as he plows into me like a rampaging Crusader. Each jab that he plants deep into my throat hurtles him closer to the edge of madness. I can sense his epic battle to remain on the side of good and not succumb to bloodlust. My prose may border on puce, but the high I'm on from how aroused Dillon is inspires me to effusive description.

Lifting only my eyes to meet his, I connect with my Top. He's watching me swallow him, watching his shaft disappear all the way in my mouth until his balls crush against my chin. His face is taut, pulled in the agony of ecstasy. The smile he tries to give me is a little twisted. *God, he's loving this. And he's so freaking beautiful.*

His eyes are flickering, like he's fighting to maintain eye contact with me, and to hold back his climax. My fingers cover Dillon's hands and slide them down to grasp the back of my neck. Then I let go, clasp my hands behind my back, look up with tears of gratitude glistening in my eyes, and give him a tiny nod.

I'm literally in his hands. *I belong to him, no matter the price.* I submit completely to his need. I will my body to relax into the potency of his lust. If I resist even an infinitesimal amount, he will harm me as he slams down my throat again. I don't give in or give up this time; I give myself over to *his* pleasure.

Dillon growls as he takes my throat without inhibition, his pace accelerating. Spit froths from my mouth. I want to watch him lose his control, but the edges of my vision blur. Three more lunges and Dillon hollers out a battle cry that shakes the earth and punctures my eardrums. He explodes in a flux of endless, pulsating jets of steaming come. As his thick seed gushes down my throat, I have to concentrate hard to loosen up and to not pass out from oxygen deprivation. I keep my cool, but all I want to do is shout for joy.

When Dillon pulls out, I'm both relieved to be able to breathe and bummed because of the withdrawal of his heat. I inhale slow, measured breaths; heaving gasps hurt too much. Dillon slides down the door, his hands still cradling my head. He kisses my forehead with such affection that he steals the very breath I have just fought to fill my lungs with. Unrestrained tears trickle down my face.

"Sorry, baby. Did I hurt you?" Dillon wipes away the salty tracks.

I shake my head to say no. "Thank you, Sir," I croak.

"Erin, you're crazy. I'm the one who has to say thank you. That was amazing, watching my dick disappear in your gorgeous mouth and feeling it slide down your throat. You're so very beautiful and amazing." If he is my almighty god, then his words make me feel like I am his great goddess.

"Thank you, Sir, for letting me be the one to give you such pleasure, to fulfill your command. It was a privilege. I'm grateful that you would allow me to give you service after all the hurt I have caused. I'm truly sorry, Sir." Over the top? Yes, but it's how I feel.

"Hush, now. No more talk about the past, or I'll have to punish you. I mean it, sub. It's over. All is forgiven, on both sides. Yes?"

"Yes, Sir." I think my smile could probably light up the whole night. At least it lights up the whole room.

"Come with me, sub. I'm not finished with you yet. Position Two in the middle of the sheepskin, facing the fire." I scurry so fast I almost skip to the spot he commanded me to. I kneel with my forehead pressed to the floor, arms straight in front of me, back bowed, thighs pressed together, and ass up as high as I can get it. He crouches behind me and slides my mini skirt up and over my derrière. His sweaty palms glide around in circles. *Yum.*

"Where is your toy bag, sub?"

"End of the hall, under my bed, Sir." Before he leaves, he swipes his index finger from my clit, through my juices and over my slit, and up to my back hole, which he prods but doesn't enter. "Mmm" is the only sound from him. The echo shoots into my sex; it ricochets around inside, hitting every nook and cranny. Dillon adds another couple of logs to the fire and heads off to get his booty.

When he returns, he plays out our last scene, with a few tweaks. When he poses me so that he can tease me and torture my pussy, he doesn't bind me. He orders me to maintain my pose. *Less painful, but more challenging.* My clamps are gone, so he pulls on each nipple with punishing suction and clamps my pink buds between his teeth until I bawl. *Just as painful, but short term.*

Dillon stays present the entire time, maintaining that Rottweiler intensity that makes me fret. As usual, he moves my body about like I'm a puppet, arranging me precisely as he wants for whatever he wants to do with me. I moan for him; I scream for him; I cry for him.

After teasing me, driving me to three near misses, he puts down the wand he's been wielding. "Back to Position Two, sub." He's had plenty of time to recover, and I salivate at the sight of his shaft fully erect and straining toward me. My heart aches for him to fill me. I rearrange myself on wobbly knees and present my ass while he rolls on a condom. Gobs of cool lube slide between my cheeks.

"Will you give me your sweet ass, sub?"

"Oh, yes, Sir. I give you everything. Take what you need of me. Use me as you wish."

Dillon pries me open with his inquisitive fingers, preparing the way for deep penetration. I'm so close to begging. He finally lines up his long, hard shaft and nudges steadily until his head pops right in. It hurts so good. I chew my lower lip and lean in for more.

In a few determined thrusts, he shoves his hard wood in me as deep as it can go. I pant raggedly as I process the sensory data bombarding my brain. He skims his hands over my body, squeezing my breasts as he kindly waits for me to catch my breath and for my sphincter to adjust to his baseball bat stretching me wide.

"Hang on, pretty baby. This is going to hurt. I need to take you hard." *Hell, yeah. Use me, Sir. Any way you want.* With no further preamble, Dillon harpoons his fingers into my hips and pounds into me at a steady but relentless pace. As I surrender to his hunger, as I focus only on my Top's needs, the slicing pain recedes. The more I give of myself to Dillon, the more I receive. The sounds of his desire and pleasure take me higher. My own moans and cries incite him.

Dillon stills inside me at the end of a brutal in-thrust. He leans over me and strikes my breasts simultaneously. My blood-curdling squeal rings out at the same time that my butt grinds against him to take his cock deeper.

"Oh, yeah. Again, sub? You want more?"

"If it pleases you, Sir." Now I understand how much he wants me to take this for him, to go beyond my known limits for him. I won't deny him. *This is what I didn't know I wanted from him. This level of submission.* Dillon's need for complete surrender had called to me, and I had responded but refused to admit my own need. I need to lose myself in him, give him everything, because he wants to take it, because he wants me, *all of me.* He rains dual blows on my breasts– three, four, five times. Dillon retreats, leaving only his tip in my ass.

"Such a slut, for me. You're not a priss when I'm wedged between your peaches, are you? Why is that, sub?"

"Because I am here to serve you, Sir. Your wish is my command."

"I wish to see my hand prints glowing red on your ass. Hold still, sub." He buries himself and stays deep while he maneuvers from side to side, giving himself room to land his hand as he thrashes away at first one of my peaches and then the other. The sway of his shaft inside me as he rocks from left to right to smack me is unlike any feeling I've had. It's like being filled to the brim by the pounding ocean, towering breakers rolling, ebbing and flowing, crashing upon my shores. I count for him, getting into the rhythm, and ask for more until I say, "Sixteen." The same number as that night.

"Such a good girl. Now, come for me. Squeeze my cock hard in your tight hole as you come for me." Dillon wraps his left arm around my waist as he pumps into me again. His right hand reaches around to rub circles around my aching clit. When he pinches hard, I scream and fall apart. Devastating tremors ripple through me. I clench Dillon's penis so tight that he can't move. Obscenities spew from his mouth as his jizz spews into me. This time around, we both get our happy ending and collapse in front of the fire.

"Thank you, priss. That was amazing, baby, the kind of scene I've dreamed about having with you." With heroic effort, I roll over and cuddle into Dillon's arms. My big, beautiful bad boy–tough, and strong, and real–has no reason to thank me.

"Thank you, Sir. That was amazing, the kind of scene *I've* dreamed about having with *you.*" Dillon smiles the warmest, most joyful smile I've ever seen on his face. When he presses his lips to mine, I melt and open fully to his possession.

< ♂ + ♀ >

"Come with me, sub." Back from clean up, Dillon extends one hand down to me. In his other hand he holds a couple of condoms he must have swiped from the box in the vanity drawer. He pulls me from the floor and wraps his arms around me for a tight hug before leading me to my bed. *Shit. My nerves are buzzing. This is new territory for us, and I don't know what it means.*

"Love the one you're with," Evanya says to me in a singsong voice. I'm with a beautiful man I do love. I have to put that other man out of my mind because he's not here. I won't let anything or anyone get between me and Dillon now.

I didn't understand before. I thought we never connected deeply, my Tops and I, because we weren't exclusive. Tonight I know it's because I was too afraid to allow it. I was the one who built the wall between us. I didn't know, or trust, that each scene could be a universe unto itself, the rest of the world ceasing to exist, if only I would relinquish complete control. I thought I had learned to do that with Jerry, but I didn't have a clue. I never dropped all my barriers and gave myself to him, for his pleasure, like this. I was too worried about the future to fully open my heart, thinking about how much I would hurt when our contract ended.

Dillon turns on the lamp beside my bed, bathing the room in a soft glow. The heat and hunger in his eyes sparks the same heat and hunger in me. We both need this, to wipe away any residual hurt, to open each other up, to help each other be more than we were.

The moment Dillon lays me on the bed, he spreads my thighs and pushes my knees up to my ears. He settles his mouth over my clit and flicks his tongue lightly across that sensitive bud. Then he swirls around it, expanding the arc before lowering his wet caresses over my slit. When his tongue dives in, my back bows and bliss sounds burst from my mouth. In just about 60 seconds, a record for me, I'm on the threshold, and I don't think I can hold back.

"Let yourself go, baby girl. Give in to it, give yourself completely to pleasure." What he says tweaks something inside, but I ignore it and let myself fly. Dillon licks and sucks and thrusts with his tongue until I collapse as quickly as a house of cards, utterly flat and ruined.

Dillon sheaths himself and lies between my legs, his cock dancing against my still spasming pussy. He leans over me, tickling my face as he brushes my hair from my eyes with his nose. His hands rest on my shoulders and push me into the mattress as his head dips and his lips claim my mouth. Lazy, languorous, unhurried kisses, sweetened with my juices, slowly blow my mind. His tongue slithers in and out, foreshadowing the other swordplay to come.

I am so befuddled that I almost miss the significance of the moment when he glides his erection over the entrance to my honey pot a couple of times before sliding it home. "Look at me, Erin," he commands. My eyelids flutter open, and his handsome face is shrouded in a dreamy haze. A vigorous thrust of his hips lifts me off the bed and clears my vision. *OhmyfreakingGod!*

"Eyes on me, baby." It'd be impossible to look away now. *What a rush!* Dillon not only makes love to me, chest to chest for the first time, he's plumbing my very depths. The love I see shining in his cobalt eyes pierces my heart. *Does he see love beaming back at him?*

Dillon's pace is slow but spirited. Each plunge and buck of his hips drives me into the mattress and then lifts me back off it.

"More!" I can't help my outburst. As *absofreakinglutely* awesome as his hip action is, he's too gentle. "Please, Dillon. Take more. Take me as hard and fast as you want." I do my best to communicate my consent with a look. I must have succeeded because he lets loose. So hard and so fast that I think he's going to pulverize my pelvis if he doesn't tear me in half first. His stamina is Herculean.

My orgasm slams into me like that same World-Series-winning hit that ripped through me the last time we were at DYKKC. This time, Dillon lets me ride it out, cheers me on, before he follows me over the fence. A deluge of tears leaks from the outer corners of my eyes and streams into my ears. I'm in the arms of my beautiful bad boy, loving the one I'm with. I don't know what this means for the future, but at least I'm not adrift alone in the world anymore.

Chapter Twenty-One – Revelations

Saturday Night, October 27

"Come on, Erin. It'll be alright. I promise."

"I don't know, Dillon. Steffie will freak if she finds out I'm there."

"I've already arranged it. You'll come as my anonymous guest. Wear a costume with a wig and a mask. No one will recognize you, especially with your new, smoking hot body. I'm teaching this class on the importance of safewords because of you. You have to come."

"I'm glad you're doing it. If it helps keep some bottoms safe, and some Tops, too, then I'm all for it. Especially if it helps restore your stature at DYKKC. I really regret how much my actions hurt you at the club on top of all the other pain I caused you."

"We said no more apologizing. Now, say you'll come. I'll pick you up so no one recognizes your car."

I ended that call on Wednesday by agreeing to give Dillon my support. So, here I am in carnival masquerade attire sneaking into forbidden territory. When I put on the purple bodystocking and peered in the mirror, I didn't look like myself. Dillon was right about that. The stocking hugged me and accentuated my figure in a way that is sexier than being naked. I was surprised and proud of myself for having sculpted my body the way I always wanted it to be.

The gold lamé cape around my shoulders shields me while saying, "look at me." My transformation is perfected with a Venetian mask, a red wig, and green contacts. I'm unrecognizable, and that gives me some comfort. I sure don't want to suffer Steffie's wrath.

The other person I don't recognize is Dillon. I just about had a heart attack when I opened my door and a bald-headed man stood on my porch. When I asked him what on earth he was thinking by shaving off his beautiful, golden locks, he said, "It's a symbolic gesture. Coming clean, starting over." I suppose I understand where he's coming from, but it's a bit extreme. I do have to admit that even though I will miss the way his hair drapes over his face when he looks down at me, the strong shape of his head and the openness of his face adds a new intensity to his physical presence.

Purgatory is packed tonight. I would love to believe that this many people really care about the topic. Of course, everyone is really here for the hot gossip. From what Dillon told me, there hasn't been a scandal this big since Jerry quit the club. I give Dillon's hand a firm squeeze to infuse a bit of courage into him.

A hush falls over the room as Dillon steps to center stage. His nerves disappear after the first minute as he gets into the flow of his speech. I'm really impressed with how open and honest he is. That takes real guts.

When he's finished, he receives a hearty round of applause. My heart warms knowing that he's accepted back into the fold. Then Dillon opens the floor to questions and things turn ugly in a hurry. No one is asking about safewords. The vultures are out for his blood, and sordid details. He does his best to deflect, trying to avoid answering questions about me. I appreciate his chivalry, but I'm not about to hang him out to dry again.

"If anyone has questions about priss, you can ask me directly." A collective gasp hangs in the air as I step up beside Dillon and remove my mask. He looks frantic, but I tell him I'm okay, and I want to set things straight. I shake the entire time I speak, but he holds my hand and rubs his thumb across my knuckles throughout.

Like Dillon, I am honest, don't hold anything back. I leave no doubt that my reaction to what he did was totally out of line and was about my own issues. I come clean about suffering from sub-drop and caution Doms and subs alike to watch for depression, self-doubt, guilt, anger, and blame. I'm surprised when Dillon admits to experiencing Dom-drop, although now I recognize that to be the truth. That leads me to end with a talk about the importance of communication and discussing things with your partner during aftercare when something doesn't work out the way you expect.

As we wrap up, both receiving applause, I look over the crowd and notice Steffie weaving her way to the front of the stage. *Damn.* There's no point trying to hide, so I march straight over to her.

"I apologize, Mistress Raidne. I'm leaving right now."

"The Saint told me he'd forgiven you. I didn't believe him. I appreciate you making things right for him tonight. You've got big balls for a sub, priss. You're welcome back anytime. I'll have the paperwork to reinstate your membership done on Monday." Steffie gives me a no-nonsense look and adds, "I'd rather have you here where you're safe. Stay away from Belladonna." She turns on her heels and merges back into the crowd. I never expected any of that, and I cough around a giant fur ball in my throat. Dillon wraps his arms around me and lays a juicy kiss on my lips.

The room is buzzing, and there's a swarm of people around us congratulating us and welcoming me back to DYKKC. Out of the corner of my eye, I catch sight of Jim. He glares at me and turns away. I guess not everyone is pleased to have me back. My heart hurts because my happy-go-lucky friend is still unhappy with me. I had turned into the kind of sub despised at the club—the one who unjustly blames her Top for her own insecurities and fears. I'd done it with Dillon; Jim deserved it least of all. He did nothing but try to help me. I wish there was a way to repair the damage I've done, but he won't come near me at work and won't pick up my calls.

Distancing myself from Christophe isn't unwarranted after what he did to Dillon. There's nothing I can do to reconcile with him anyway, even if I wanted to. He shipped out with DWB again five days after he got home. I was worried about him in Iraq, but this time he's gone to the Congo for three months. It's one of the most dangerous places on Earth, and that makes me extremely tense.

Jerry is another story entirely. Life has been excruciatingly painful without him this last month. I want him back, but I don't know if I can trust him to keep me safe.

I don't see Lacey tonight. I miss her, too. I don't care what all the drama and secrecy is about. I just want my friend back. Maybe if I ask nicely, Dillon will speak to her on my behalf and plead my case. It won't be as much fun being back here without her.

After 20 minutes of chatting with old and new friends, Dillon grabs my hand and pulls me toward the stairs. "Come with me, priss. I've got a room reserved for us. I had planned on giving you a reward for coming here tonight, but I'm going to have to start with some harsh discipline for unmasking yourself against my wishes."

"But that's not fair. I couldn't abandon you to the mob." *Jerk.* He'll use any excuse to warm my ass. Then I see the twinkle in his eye, and I realize he's teasing. I'm so gullible. My serious Dom is having fun with me, and that change in him means more to me than anything. *Maybe he really did shed a lot more than a hairdo.*

$< \male + \female >$

I'm still vibrating as I step out into the chilly night and wait on the sidewalk for Dillon. I'm buzzing from the thrill of being back with my DYKKC family. And, wow, that was some scene with Dillon.

The wind changes, and a different but familiar frequency of energy ripples across my skin. I look down the empty street, seeking the source. Jerry leans casually against a lamppost, bathed in a warm, pinkish glow. When what I see registers in my brain, my heart stops beating. My eyes sting from a spontaneous eruption of tears. The man is so handsome, his presence so compelling, that I want to run to him, throw myself at him. But I can't.

Jerry straightens his long body and takes a few steps toward me. I freeze. It kills me to have this self-protective reaction to him.

"Hello, Erin. It's good to see you. You look so beautiful tonight, kitten. Can we talk?" *Beautiful. kitten.* I'd resigned myself to never hearing those words from him again and never hearing that rich, deep tone that animates me, brings me to life. *Damn.* His voice is calm, and he's actually asking rather than demanding. He's giving me a choice, but he lets me know which one he wants me to make.

"What are you doing here?" My tone is more shrill than I'd like.

"I heard about Dillon's talk and thought it would be interesting to hear what he had to say for himself. I didn't expect you to be here, or for you to get up on that stage. I'm proud of you, Erin. Please, can we talk?"

"I, I, I ..." I stutter and stumble and can't force out either an encouraging word or a rejection.

"It seems you've forgiven Dillon. Give me a chance. Let me take you home so we can work things out. I've missed you, kitten." His first words are edged with anger, perhaps jealously, definitely pain. I can imagine it would have cut him deep if he saw me excited and all smiles going into the private room with Dillon, or coming out flushed and glowing. I'm glad we had the privacy curtain drawn and that he was spared having to watch me with another man. His voice softens as he says he missed me.

"I've missed you too, but I can't do this. I can't see you, Jerry. I trusted you, not just with my scenes, but with everything. You made it quite clear that you don't respect me. I don't trust you anymore." I lay it all out quickly and plainly. His shoulders drop, his chest caves, and his gut clenches. Just as if I had sucker punched him. *Why does it feel like I just punched myself?*

"So everything you said tonight was a lie? What happened to talking to your partner when something goes wrong?"

I blubber and hem and haw. *A hypocrite, that's what I am.*

"Erin, I made a mistake. Will you let me explain, make amends? I'm willing to accept any punishment you think is fit. But, please, talk to me." He's wounded alright, and not just his pride. The thing is, I have no interest in punishing him.

"What's the point, Jerry? Our contract would have ended soon anyway, and you would have been gone. I just saved myself the heartache of you leaving me."

"Is that what you think was going to happen? That I could just walk away from you that easily? Aren't you even interested in knowing what I have to say about that?" He steps toward me, a menacing scowl spread across his face. I hate that look.

"The lady said to leave, Snapper. Maybe it's best if you go." My heart leaps into my throat as my feet lift off the ground. I didn't hear Dillon approach. His arm wraps protectively around my waist and pulls me back in the direction of the club.

Jerry's ice-blue eyes flash before an Arctic blizzard blows over us. I can hear what he's thinking, and his ire is evident. *Oh God. I can't keep up this pretense.* I need my Master, need his lips, his tongue, his arms, his hands, his butt, his cock, even his sexy toes. I need his affection, his passion, his attention, his correction.

I can't stand Jerry being angry at me. And so far away from me. I'm just about to reach for him when he asks, "So, you've decided? You're with him now? Well, good luck with that. You deserve each other." What he says is petty and mean. My Regis is like that fabled lion with the thorn stuck in his paw. *Let me take away your pain.*

He doesn't wait even a second before he spins and storms off. My feet are paralyzed, but my eyes follow his rapid retreat. If I thought my heart was broken before, that was no more than the sting of a paper cut. As he walks away from me, he rips out my heart, slices it in tiny pieces, and douses it in vinegar.

"Are you sure you want to let him go, priss? I can't believe that the mighty Snapper would be willing to submit to your punishment. He must really want you back."

As the initial shock recedes and those words trickle down through my defenses, I shove and struggle to get free from Dillon. I race after Jerry, *my Jerry*. Just as I hit the parking lot, he tears out the far exit. *Oh, Hell. Why did I wait? What am I going to do now?*

Dillon doesn't need me to say anything as I stumble back to him. He can see the pain and the love written all over my face. I tremble when he cups my face in his steady hands. I can read the sadness in his ocean-blue eyes and feel it on his lips as he skims a light kiss over me. We both know this is goodbye.

"Don't let him get away, priss. Snapper is a good man. If you love him, you might need to find your inner Domme and beat him into submission. His pride won't let him give in easily now. Don't back down until you win. Be happy, baby."

Bittersweet. That's the word for this moment. Dillon is a good man, too. I will always have a place for him in my heart, but he's not the one I belong to. I fling my arms around his neck and give in to a morose sense of finality that sinks right down to my toes.

"Thank you, Dillon. I do love you." I bawl like a baby.

"I know, baby girl. I love you, too. I'll always be here if you need me." Our lips are drawn into a crushing kiss as strong as rare earth magnets clinging together in an inseparable bond. Our tongues do a last dance, a steamy tango with lots of flicks and dips and lifts. Our bodies follow the lead and wrap around each other, swaying to a sultry rhythm. If this is the last time I'm going to be in this man's arms, I'm going to make it count.

We gaze into each other's eyes, our hands on each other's cheeks. A loud squeal of rubber breaks the spell. I turn in time to see a big, black truck speeding away. SSHHIITT! Jerry must have circled the block. *Dammit. As if getting him back wasn't going to be hard enough without him seeing me suck face with another Dom.*

< ♂ + ♀ >

The streets were safer tonight because I took a cab home. I'm rattled from my run-in with Jerry and would have been a disaster behind the wheel if I had my car. I was seconds away from being back in Master's arms, but stupid pride and uncertainty did me in again. *What would it have cost me to stay and talk to him?* The price for shutting him out is utter emptiness. Now, I'm so freaking lost.

"How hard would it have been for Jerry to wait for me after seeing me with Dillon? How much must he need me if he would risk rejection yet again? How could I be such a callous bitch to him when that's not what my heart wanted? Not even my head wanted to deny him. What broken part of me stood passively and allowed him to slip away when he's the best thing to ever happen to me?"

There are so many questions to answer, but first I need to clear Dillon's essence off me and let him go. I add generous portions of Epsom salts and fragrant bubble bath to the tub. The haunting notes of a pan flute on Gabrielle Roth's CD *Ritual* slither into me. My heart cracks and my soul weeps as I slip into the water and wash my big, beautiful bad boy from the present to make room for another man in my future.

"What the heck is wrong with me?" I've made some monumental screw-ups lately. *Ha! That's putting it mildly.* My actions have defied logic, but smart people sometimes do stupid things. I've learned that the reason is simple—emotion trumps logic every damn time. Humans are not ruled by logic like fictional Vulcans are. Even when we think we are making a rational decision, there is an emotional need to which that logic speaks.

So *why did my actions tonight sabotage what my heart wants?* Obviously, I've got a conflicting belief, emotion or desire buried inside somewhere deep. If I can't uproot it, I'll keep making decisions that baffle me and block me from having what I want the most—a life with Jerry. *How could I be that stupid?*

"Stop beating yourself up, Erin. It won't solve anything." Evanya finally weighs in with her opinion. "Remember when you were studying compassion? You learned an important lesson about soul tests, didn't you?" *Oh, yeah. That's right. This screw-up is a soul test.*

I remember my guru saying, "It doesn't matter what anyone's stumbling block is, what their burden in life is, whether someone else judges it to be trivial and insignificant or devastating and insurmountable. That block is uniquely personal and is put there by our soul to test us."

Telling someone who is struggling to "suck it up and get over it" because someone else has bigger problems isn't always helpful or kind. There's no need for comparison. Pain is pain; we all have it, and that can be understood. But the content of our heart, the plot of our story, the path of our soul, what hurts us and how we heal it, that is different for each of us and that journey should be respected for what it is. Everyone has their own cross to bear.

My guru cautioned his disciples against judgment, but it's hard not to judge, and the one we're usually most critical of and the least forgiving of is ourselves. My soul has been pushing me toward a turning point and a better life. I have to believe that, be grateful for that, or none of this suffering makes any sense. I can condemn myself for my mistakes and cling to my pain, or I can forgive myself and figure out the emotion driving me. Now, I understand the email I got a few months ago from another of my spiritual teachers. It was about turning our wounds into a womb, using our hurts to nurture and give birth to a new way of being.

"What do I really want for my life? How do I want it to be different? And how do I want to be different?" There's no way I can answer those questions until I first answer the biggie, "Who am I?" Only, tonight, I think I should focus more on my human needs than the deep spiritual and existential nature of that question.

Who am I? I am a submissive, but without a Dom, I have no one to bow to or to serve. I am a kitty, but without a Master, I have no reason to purr. I am a warm, strong woman, but without a hot, virile man, I have no one to be soft with and love.

What do I want? I want my Master, my King. Regis, my lion. Jerry, my heart and soul. Life is Hell without him. I want the myth, Paradise, Heaven on Earth. Happily Ever After.

What am I willing to do to get what I want? Any damn thing I have to do. Jerry put himself on the line to help me after my crisis and again tonight at DYKKC. I can't walk away from him. I have to risk my heart and forgive him. And ask him to forgive me.

I spend the next hour soaking in the tub, examining everything I've felt and said and done, not just since things went wrong with Dillon, but all the way back to when my views about love and relationships changed, when Jed stole my innocence. I come to some very startling conclusions. When I stumble into bed, I'm a new woman, a woman with an open heart rather than a scared little girl who wants to hide. The world is a very different place.

Chapter Twenty-Two – The Promised Land

Sunday Morning, October 28

"Get up, Erin. Get moving. Stop wasting time sleeping." Evanya's voice inside my head rouses me from unconsciousness.

"Wha? It's 4:00 in the morning. Where am I going?"

"It doesn't matter what time it is. You're going to your Master's house. You can't wait. He can't wait. This is too important."

She's talking crazy again. "Are you nuts? You're kidding, right? It'll look like I'm chasing him. I've never chased a man. Besides, I don't think a Dom wants an aggressive woman who chases him."

"You're not chasing him. You're submitting."

"You want me to *submit*? To my *Master*? I'm surprised you approve of something so chauvinistic."

"Call it surrendering then, opening. Surrender your pride, and open your heart to love. Love no matter what the conditions are. Remember, in the grand scheme of things, it doesn't matter how things appear to be in your human life. I'm talking soul connection, eternity, big cosmic stuff. You know you love him and want to be with him. You've already decided. Put the man out of his misery. Now. He deserves that, don't you think?"

"Damn straight, he does." Now she's making sense. I roll out of bed, dress and climb in my car. There's little traffic on the freeway at this ungodly hour. Nonetheless, the drive to Jerry's property is interminable. I was in such a mindless state when he drove me home that I don't immediately recognize the turning off the county road. I go a couple of miles too far and backtrack a couple of times until I find his driveway. I don't want to wake Jerry before I'm in place, so I leave my car close to the road and tiptoe up the lane. My nerves rattle and snap, echoing the crunch of my feet on gravel.

"What if he turns me away the way I turned him away?" *Stop it.* If I let that kind of doubt get to me, I'll chicken out. I unbutton my coat, fold it, and place it on the rocking chair on Jerry's front stoop. The bitter night air shocks my system. I hope he answers the door before I freeze into an ice pop. All I have on is the cranberry harness I wore our first night and my hip necklace.

I ring the doorbell and arrange myself in Jerry's preferred submissive stance. And I wait. My goosebumps rise into peaks as pointy as my nipples. My teeth start to chatter, and I'm just about to ring the bell again when the porch light flashes on. Jerry opens the interior door and ... nothing. With my head bowed, I can't see his face and have no clue what he's thinking or feeling. *Oh, God! What if he has someone with him? Why didn't I think of that?*

Before I send myself into a full-scale panic attack, the screen door opens. Jerry grabs the strap under my breasts and pulls me into the living room. He sits on the couch, pulls on my harness and flops me over his lap. That's when I notice that he's wearing only tight, black briefs. The curly hair on his thighs tickles my tummy.

His first mangled words to me are, "How many strokes, sub?"

"Fifty, Master." It'll hurt like hell, but I'll take the pain for him.

"Twenty."

"I deserve fifty, Master. I've been very bad."

We dicker back and forth, me refusing to budge and Jerry raising the stakes by a few strokes. Then Jerry refusing to move and me lowering the sentence until we settle on 37 strokes.

"Hold still, sub." He catches me off guard by striking as he says "sub." I jerk a little but maintain my basic position. My naked body is still frozen, which tenses my muscles tighter than they have ever been. It's not the optimal condition for a beating. "One," he counts.

"Thank you, Master. May I please have another?"

"You're welcome, sub. But you needn't beg for more. I assure you, I have every intention of delivering your full punishment." I have no doubt, and he will be thorough. It doesn't escape my notice that he calls this "punishment" and not "correction." But that's what I want and what I need. In this case, he deserves retribution, and I deserve to pay the penalty. I'm the one who lost faith.

The next four blows are fast and furious as he counts. The following slaps make contact, one for every word that he grinds out. "You. Will. Not. Walk. Away. From. Me. Again. You. Belong. To. Me. I. Love. You. Erin." *He loves me? Oh God.* My tears suddenly have little to do with my aching ass.

My butt is hot enough already to melt steel, and I'm only just over half way. He continues without pause, the crack of his palm striking my tender flesh blends with his grunts and growls that sound suspiciously like "mine."

Each sting of pain, each lick of flame, burns the lessons of his punishment into my heart and soul—I was wrong to give up on us; Jerry loves me; I belong to him; I love Jerry; we belong together; and I can take 37 continuous whacks if I ever deserve it again. I doubt that I will.

Jerry turns me over to sit in his lap, letting my butt dip between his slightly spread thighs. He stares into my eyes, into my heart, into my soul. In the next instant, his lips are plastered all over my face in smothering kisses. My heart nearly stops when he slides his tongue across my lips and then plunges in. He devours me. He conquers me. He commands me. I am happy to be consumed. I am grateful to be possessed. I am willing to be ruled.

Jerry pulls back and takes a breath. I know the question he can't seem to ask.

"I was saying goodbye to him, Master. I care about him, but I'm in love with you. Truly. You are my whole world. Watching you walk away just about killed me, but I'm glad you did. You forced me to look into some very dark places that I didn't want to even go near, let alone analyze. Please forgive me, Master."

He peers deep into my eyes again before he says, "I forgive you, kitten. So, what did you discover that brought you back to me?"

God, it was hard enough to admit to myself. "I've danced close to the truth so many times in the last couple of months, even before any of this happened, but I could never quite catch it. I thought that what sent me over the edge with The Saint was him taking away my power, my ability to choose, by ignoring my safeword."

"It wasn't? You had such big breakthroughs during our scenes."

"Yes, I did. What happened *was* my fault. I sassed him and didn't submit to him; I didn't use my safeword soon enough; I gave away my own power. And I made it all worse by running away from him and not talking to him. Then I did the same thing to you. But I didn't know why I acted that way in the first place."

"You said you didn't trust him enough."

"It's more than that. I trust you enough. I said I don't, but I do trust you, and things still went wrong between us. I submitted to you the first time we met, and I think I fell in love with you the very next night when you dropped everything to come to me after I was kidnapped. But, in the end, I closed my heart to you. Because I didn't trust *myself* enough. I didn't try to figure out why until you left me standing in the street." I fidget because I'm afraid of what I have to say next. Jerry thinks I'm suffering a different kind of hurt.

"I know your butt stings, baby girl. Sit however makes you comfortable." I straddle his thighs, resting mostly with my knees on the couch cushions so my behind isn't touching. It'll be difficult to say what I need to when I'm this close to my Beloved's handsome face and the raging erection in his briefs. He cradles my head in his hands and kisses me slow and sweet, and I almost ditch my plan to tell him the truth so I can seduce him instead.

"It's funny how your mind will tell you whatever you want to hear when it's trying to protect you. The Saint primed me for my explosion, and my implosion, when he asked me that night at the club if I was a submissive. What really flipped the switch was when he told me to relax and let him give me '*everything I wanted.*' I told you that spanking was the price I thought I had to pay to get what I wanted, the wild sex and the screaming orgasms. I couldn't face who I had become, and I checked out. I unfairly blamed him for my own wanton cravings." A strangled cry forces its way out of me.

Jerry runs his hands up and down my arms as he says, "It's okay, kitten. You can do this." Not so fearless anymore, I still keep going.

"When you played out the kidnapping for me, you had a knife to my throat and were so menacing. I was terrified *and* turned on. Just before you carried me out of the house, I thought you were going to kiss me, and I wanted that sooo much. In the dungeon, I got so hot when you cut my clothes off me. When I stopped the scene and said I could forgive The Saint, I told you it was easy because I realized that he didn't want to hurt me. That is true enough, but my ego tricked me. It gave me an easy out to prevent me from going deeper into the real issue of what was happening, to hide my shame, even from myself." Here comes the part that will take all my courage.

"After I had made all those mistakes and lost everything, I still couldn't help myself. I really screwed up when I went to Belladonna. Amancio ..."

"You did what?!! What about Amancio?" Jerry is instantly livid and pulls hard on my harness. He gives me a good shake and snarls at me.

"I know, don't worry, Master. The Saint already raked me over the coals about that. I won't be going back."

"Why would you go there in the first place?"

"Because of who I am." That's it. I can't go any further. My tears are falling as heavy as rain during monsoon season.

"Where is this all leading, kitten? Tell me." It takes me a few minutes before I can compose myself enough to speak again.

"The night of my prom, my first time. Until then, I believed in the kind of pure love my parents had. My Dad was such a kind man. He was a hopeless romantic and worshipped my Mom. She was totally devoted to him. They were so amazing together, a real team. That's what I thought I wanted.

"What Jed did to me that night was what I accused The Saint of. He didn't wait for consent, took what he wanted and fucked me so hard it really hurt. And I liked it, at least the rough part. I was crushed when he told everyone I was a slut, when he said I begged for more ... because I couldn't admit to myself how dark and twisted I am inside. How could I like what he did?" My chest heaves, and I'm sure I'm going to have a fatal heart attack. The sound of Jerry's voice calms me down. His reminder to breathe helps even more.

"All these years since, I've known I'm just a dirty slut and did everything I could to pretend I'm not. You tried to make me think it's not true when you pushed me during the club scene. You wanted me to forget that word and know that it's okay to be sexy and to be submissive. It sure sounded good at the time. It was what I wanted to hear, and I tried to believe it.

"I knew you were wrong when I liked all the bad things you did when you kidnapped me, when a part of me liked that you held my arms and made me display my wickedness to your friends. The way they looked at me ... I love you, and the hunger in their eyes shouldn't have meant anything to me. I tried to blame my own dishonor on you. No, please don't say anything. Let me finish.

"That's why I went to Belladonna. I was easy pickings for Amancio because I couldn't control myself any longer. I needed to get dirty, and I thought anyone would do. Everything I've done just shows the depth of my depravity, the lengths I'll go to for a kinky fuck." I want to just breeze past that admission because the reality is too blunt, too humiliating.

"Amancio ... Did you? Did he?" Jerry can barely say the words.

"No! I was so scared. I ran for my life." The way he clutches me to his chest, crushing my ribs, makes me wonder for a brief moment about why both Jerry and Dillon react so powerfully to the mention of Amancio's name. Then I continue my confession.

"I know what I say next will hurt you, Master." *Deep breaths.*

"It's okay, love. If it will help you to get it out, and if it will help me understand, then go ahead." He's so brave, so trusting.

"I couldn't drive ... and called The Saint to take me home." Jerry's whole body stiffens. "When we were talking, I realized how much I love him, as a human being and a friend, and I had to fix the damage we both suffered. I learned that night what it is to truly submit. I had to set aside everything I needed and wanted, including how much I needed and wanted you, to give everything to my Top.

"I'm sorry, Master, that it wasn't you I learned that with, but I do know the difference. He was just my Top, not my Master." I'll never admit to a moment of uncertainty when Dillon was in my bed and gazing into my eyes. Jerry's eyes glisten as he tries to hide his pain.

"That was only a week ago. When I saw you tonight at DYKKC, I was such a fool for hesitating. I was ashamed of how much I had hurt you. And I was afraid of how much I needed you, and how much I would do for you. After learning what submission is, and admitting to myself that I'm a slut, I was terrified of how much of myself I would surrender to you if you asked, even if you didn't ask.

"Lacey and The Saint told me about Snapper and who he is. I knew I would lose my boundaries to that kind of Master, never have the strength to say no to him about anything. I knew, because I love you so much, how hard I would try to be what you need. I would suffer any amount of pain you wanted to inflict; I would bear any humiliation you wanted to subject me to. Ultimately, I was so afraid of giving everything I am to someone like Snapper and still not be able to give enough, not be enough for you. I was a cowardly child, Master." I avert my eyes, but Jerry won't let me escape.

"I don't know why a Master like you would ever want me. That doesn't stop me from loving you, Sir. I'm no longer afraid to give you my body, my heart, my life, my very soul. There is no one else for me, so I have no choice. I'll do or be anything you need. I submit to you as your slave, to do with as you wish. If you'll have me, Master."

My final words are nearly unintelligible as my desperation and total surrender supersedes any false modesty or fright. I'd rather just love him, but I'll debase myself if it's the only way to have him. I can't breathe without him. I've got nothing left to hide. I stand here in a firing range with a target on my heart, and he may as well shoot me dead if he no longer wants me now that he sees who I am.

"That's what you think of me? That I'm a cold, selfish bastard who would reduce you to a shadow of who you are?"

Jerry lifts me by my harness as he gets up. I can't read anything on his face or in his energy field except for disgust. He lays me on the couch, burning butt up. He unbuckles my straps and pulls off my harness before he abandons me and disappears. *I've ruined everything. He's gone to get something to punish me with. Probably one of his bullwhips. I certainly deserve that. Or clothes to put on me before he throws me out the door.* I bury my head into the corner of the couch and cry away every hope I had inside me.

"Stand, sub." I look up and recognize the black fur in his hands. I scramble off the couch and stand before my Master on legs barely steady enough to keep me upright. *Am I still his velvet?*

"Do you realize, sub, that when you judge yourself for wanting hot, kinky, dirty sex, you judge me for giving it to you?" His words smash into my jaw like solid uppercuts, knocking my head back and forcing tears to my eyes.

"When you insult and condemn yourself for offering yourself to me in spite of your fears about all the horrible things you think I'll do to you, you both insult my integrity and denigrate the value of the gift that you offer me." He's dancing around, setting me up for the knockout punch I know is coming.

"When you pretty much say you hate yourself for wanting to be my slave, you are saying that you hate me for wanting to be your Master. How is that love?"

And there's the right cross that knocks me to my knees. I've lost this fight, and I've lost him. I cry at his feet, in great shuddering sobs, while I wait for him to throw the black fur at me and walk away. I jump when something lands on my back. *Not fur.* It's Jerry's hand. He sits down beside me and strokes my back awhile before he grabs me by the scruff of the neck and pulls my head up.

"That's not what you meant, is it, kitten? You didn't mean that you hate me, did you?"

"N-n-no, Master. I love you."

"We're bound together. You can't denounce yourself without denouncing me. Do you see how that works?"

"Y-y-yes, Master." Little fingers of relief tickle my insides.

"How quickly you've forgotten me telling you that I know what you're worth. You're precious to me. I will not allow you to speak so disparagingly about my property again. Apologize to your Master for disrespecting what belongs to me, for saying such unkind things about my slut." Optimism now clutches at my heart.

In between sniffles, I mutter, "I'm sorry, Master."

"I didn't hear you. Speak up, slut. It almost sounded like you said you're sorry. Sorry for what?"

"I am sorry, Master. I'm sorry for thinking such bad things."

"About who?"

"About myself." He makes me be more specific. "About your slut." I almost choke on the word, but his smile sets my heart ablaze.

"That's right, *my* slut. My slutty kitty. On your hands and knees, pet." I'm in position before I even have a conscious thought to obey.

Jerry ties the halter top behind my neck and secures the fuzzy triangles over my breasts. He slides the G-string between my legs and knots it at both hips. Then he wiggles the mittens over my fingers and slides on my kitty ears. He holds out each piece and waits for me to kiss it and say please before he puts it on me. He ensures my unequivocal acceptance and submission. He had that before I walked in.

Finally, he fingers the collar. His hands shake, not with anger. I am transfixed, held captive by the evidence of his need. I'm not about to deny him a single thing, no matter what he asks of me. He draws in a few gallons of air and lets it all escape before he speaks.

"I gave up being Snapper a long time ago because I didn't want to be that cold bastard anymore. There's too much hurt in the world as it is. You are so beautiful, and soft, and kind. With you, I'm happy. With you, my life makes sense. I fell in love with you even before I knew you were a sub." I send him a quizzical look. Jerry dips his nose down to my ear.

"I knew when you called me an 'avenging angel.'" My knees buckle. *No. No. No. I'm going to die.* Jerry snickers softly and grips my hips to hold me up until I'm steady again.

"It's okay, velvet. I don't want someone you have to pretend to be or to not be. I love you just as you are. You are the perfect blend of sweet and tart. Of light and shadow. Of love and lust. I will always love you, take care of you, protect you, make sure your needs and desires are fulfilled. I'll do whatever I can to ensure your happiness. I *will* be your avenging angel. Will you be my angel? Be my pet? Will you accept my collar, Erin? Will you bind yourself to me for life?"

"Oh, God. Yes, Sir. My Love. My Master. You know I'm already yours. Forever." I'm a quivering hot mess of tears and hormones and emotions.

When the short, steel post slides into the notch, and the long end of supple, pink leather slides home through the guide loop, Jerry adjusts my collar so that the D-ring is centered in the front. He clips my silver leash in place. Jerry angles in toward my right temple, huffing hot, steamy breath into my ear. He chomps down on my earlobe and then takes a good hard suck. I shiver when he speaks in the sexy, smoky bass drawl that I can't resist.

"I'll sit you on my lap later today, kitten, and we'll negotiate the terms of our new contract. But, now, come with me, my love. Make me roar, velvet. And Regis will make you purr."

"Meow, Master."

< ♂ + ♀ >

I'm ready to start on making Master roar right where we are on the living room floor, but he has other ideas. With more speed than I'm used to from my lazy lion, he hops up, grabs my arms, pulls me up, and throws me over his shoulder in a fireman's carry. I squeal in delight like a happy little girl, until I get a sharp swat on my butt.

"That didn't sound very much like a kitten, or even a tiger. Have you forgotten yourself already, velvet? Am I going to have to show you how naughty kitties are punished?"

"Merrrowww." *Already? Didn't he just get finished telling me he wants to make me happy?*

"You're lucky that I happen to be on the verge of exploding. I need to be inside you right now, or I'd take the time to give you your first lesson in how I tame a wild cat."

Jerry takes giant steps and races us down the long hall to his bedroom. I'd like to get a look at his home, but it's hard to do upside down. Besides, there are much more important things to be looking at. I have a prime, close-up view of his splendid ass. I would love to sink my claws into his cheeks, but the damn mittens on my hands make my fingers curl up. I'm about to knead him with my knuckles when I'm dumped on the bed.

Oh, it's a big bed. It must be custom because it's bigger than a king-size. I feel tiny in this huge bed, and already my mind is calculating the surface area and how much room we have to play on. There's plenty of space for rolling around.

"Now, velvet, my wayward kitten. Since you have a habit of wandering off, I'm going to have to keep you tethered until you learn to stay where you belong." So, *no rolling around.* I don't even realize it's happening until after my wrist is wrapped in a leather cuff attached to a chain. I reach for it to pull the Velcro® apart, but the damn mittens confound me again.

Jerry is grinning like he's already won. Because, of course, he has. I hiss at him, and in two seconds flat my other wrist is bound. "Now, now, kitten. When you showed up on my doorstep like a mangy stray, I decided to bring you in because of your sweet, submissive disposition. What's with the defiance all of a sudden? Have you gone feral? Am I going to have to train you to respect your Master and put you in your place after all?" The gleam in his eyes tells me he would enjoy giving that lesson far too much.

"Your place, if you haven't realized it yet, velvet, is beneath me. I would have been happier if you had laid down and offered yourself to me, but I'll drill the lesson into you the hard way if I have to." *Drill me hard. Oh, sweet Jesus, yes.* I don't know what the hell is wrong with me. *Why did I hiss at him?* This is what I hurried all this way for so early in the morning. I better turn this scene around before it becomes something neither of us wants. I purr for all I'm worth.

"Hmmm. What makes you so happy now, pet? Is it that you're going to get a lesson? No? Or is it that you really do know your place?" *Purr, purr, purr, purr.* "Smart kitty. Is that a smile I see?" Jerry strokes my cheek with his fingertips and my smile spreads. He drifts his fingers across my lips, and I pounce. I open and suck as many fingers as I can capture into my mouth. I suction gently at first, and then I increase the force with which I pull him into me. My tongue swirls and slides and rubs against the pads of his fingertips and his knuckles. I moan and wiggle my butt while I look up at my lion with lust and longing.

Jerry's gaze flicks back and forth between my mouth and my eyes. He fixes me with an indecent glare as he says, "You seem to like to suck, precious." I nod and grin around his fingers. "Shall I give you something more substantial to occupy your mouth?" I open up and growl and squirm. *Yes, please.*

My mouth is empty for the short time it takes Master to strip off his briefs and straddle my chest. He spears his fingers into my hair and lifts my head a few inches. "Sweet kitten, here you go. Have at it." He drops my head on the pillow and grabs the headboard as he lowers his straining shaft to my mouth. I rise up to meet him and open wide. The instant my lips wrap around his penis, Jerry tenses, and my Regis roars.

I want to play, to tease and please him with my tongue, and suck him down like he promised I could, but Regis has a new plan. He thrusts deep again and again. In our position, he hits the back of my throat with his strong pump action. I gag reflexively and choking sounds fill the room as he slides in all the way. Drool bubbles from my mouth as he crushes his balls to my chin. His growls continue every few seconds, always on the advance, followed by a moan on the retreat. He truly fucks my mouth, wrests control from me, dominates me, uses me for his own pleasure.

I watch Regis's face and his reactions to his rutting. He fights for breath, gasping before each growl. His eyes are screwed shut and his jaws clench between roars. He looks like he is in horrible pain, but I know he is in terrible ecstasy. I can't wait for him to reach the point of no return and spill into me. I need my Beloved's seed in me, even if my mouth is the only place he would ever deposit it.

Regis lets out a frightful bellow, then pulls his twitching cock from my mouth and drops his weighty hands on my shoulders, forcing them deep into the pillow beneath me. His wide-open, ice-blue eyes are shining and locked to mine as he shuffles his knees backward and scoots down my body.

"Are you still on the pill?" I nod. "You and Dillon used condoms?" I nod. "Precious velvet, I'm going to take you bare, like the animals we are." I shake my head furiously.

"No? You dare say no to your King, your Ruler?" I shake my head wildly again. "Speak velvet. Explain your impertinence."

"No, Regis. Not like this, please. Not our first time. Not as Regis and velvet, not as Master and slave. Only as Jerry and Erin. I need Jerry to make love to Erin. I need my hands free to touch you. If you are going to grant me the gift of all of you, I have to give you all of me. I need every part of me to show you how much I love you."

"Oh, precious baby. You never cease to amaze me. We're going to have such a good life together. I promise." Jerry flattens his body over me and drives me into the mattress as he drives his tongue into my mouth. We feast on each other, him gnawing on my lips, me nipping at his tongue. It's not until I tangle my fingers in his thick, dark hair that I notice he has released me. My legs are already tangled around his. I plant my feet and push up. I grind my mound into his groin and howl when Jerry bites my bottom lip sharply.

He lets go of my breasts, which he had been macerating, glides his hands down my sides and wedges in under my butt. Pain floods through my lower parts, and I whimper.

"Still sore from your spanking, sweet Erin? Will you remember to never leave me again?"

"Yes, wicked Jerry. There is nowhere else for me to go. You are my home. You are where my heart lives."

"Oh, baby girl. Your pussy is where my cock lives, and it needs to be there now. Let's get you off your butt. That's not the part I want hurting when I make love to you, hard and fast." Jerry pushes up, untangles my legs and throws them over his shoulders. He tugs at the strings of my fuzzy thong to remove it and, in one punishing stab, he's buried to the hilt. *Sweet Jesus, he feels amazing.*

"Sweet. Jesus. You. Feel. Incredible. Erin. Oh. Baby. You. Are. On. Fire. And. So. Tight. Fuck!" Each word explodes from his mouth on the force of a thrust. Like he can't put a complete sentence together all at once. At least he can still speak. I'm having trouble even thinking. All I can do is grip his manhood tighter.

Jerry's hands are glued to my hips as he pounds away. This isn't the romantic coupling I was imagining, but I love it when Jerry loses control like this. Without the condom, the soft, smooth skin of his cock glides in and out of my slick and slippery channel in the most delicious way. His hefty girth stretches me to my limit but without the burn from the drag of latex on skin. No, the burn comes from his natural heat, no longer shielded away from my sensitive nerve endings. His steely rod is as hot as a branding iron. With each thrust Jerry marks me as his in a way that will never leave me. I will always feel him inside me, no matter how far away he is from me.

As my Beloved hammers away at my pussy, he hammers away at my heart, chipping away all the lonely years, all my self-doubt and self-denial, all the scars from heartbreak, all the walls erected for protection, all my fears of the future.

My lover, my life, pounds me until there's nothing left in my brain, and all I'm aware of is the swell of love expanding my heart. My eyes are shut tight. I should see only black, but a soft, pink glow floods my inner vision. The light intensifies, as does the color, deepening to rose. Brighter still, the hue turns to fuchsia. Brighter and brighter, the pink flows from shade to shade. A sound filters through the light show that has me completely captivated.

"Come for me, baby. Come now, Erin." Glittering stars of gold burst right between my eyes and shower down against a backdrop of purple plum. As my body shakes and quakes, ripples and rolls, a boiling, liquid heat fills me as my Beloved spills into me. I receive him; I welcome him; I'm wide open to him.

"Baby girl, I love you." The pink light fades, and I open my eyes to glowing, pale blue orbs inches from my face. *What a glorious sight.* We're lying on our sides—I have no idea when that happened—and Jerry is still planted deep between my thighs. His hot come seeps out, mingling with my own juices. *What could be better than the hot, wet, slippery evidence of our passion and love? Nothing.*

I circle my hips to revel in that silken sensation. The motion sets off little aftershocks that race through me, and I grip Jerry's cock tight. He's still hard, and he pushes deeper still, forcing a moan from me. I've never seen him look so peaceful, so content.

"I love you, too, Master." Jerry frowns, spoiling the angelic look on his face. He brushes a few strands of hair from my eyes so he can look closer at me.

"I thought you wanted me to make love to you as Jerry."

"I did. I do. But there's no point me trying to deny it, Jerry. You *are* my Master. You own me, body, heart and soul. I belong to you in every way. I always have, and I always will. Stop frowning, Master, and kiss me, please."

Oh, how he kisses me. It's one of his soul-sucking kisses. He draws the life right from my lungs. I feel like I'm going to die, until he forces his own breath back in. In a way that is an unmistakable display of supremacy, he shows me how even my breath is his to give. Yes, I'm in biiiggg trouble. My life is never going to be the same now that it is his to direct. And I couldn't be happier.

I feel Jerry throbbing inside me, thrilling me. He rolls me onto my back and pushes my knees up to my chin. He keeps me boxed up tight like a human package. I can't move at all, can't dance with him, but he bucks into me like a mad man, consumed by an impulse that drives him relentlessly to possess me. Heavy beads of sweat drip from his nose; animal musk wafts from his skin; sexual energy hums in his veins.

Jerry pauses, his cockhead pulled back to my entrance.

"My pussy," he decrees as he rams hard into me.

"Yes, Master."

"My slut," he proclaims as he thrusts deep three times.

"Yes, Master."

"My precious," he affirms as he kisses me softly and fills me completely on one long, sweet slide.

"Yesss, Master."

"Come with me, my love."

"Yes, my love."

Jerry lets go of my knees and wraps my legs around his waist. He plummets into me, all the way.

"Eyes open, baby girl. Let me see you fall." Four more pumps and a tweak of my clit and he gets his wish. I tumble from this world and fall into heaven.

"Are you mine, Erin?"

I don't know where the concentration comes from that lets me get the words out, but I tell him, "Yes, Jerry ... Master. I'm yours." As soon as the last syllable passes my lips, waves of love crash into me and knock me over and knock me out.

As I slip from consciousness, I hear him growl, "Mine. Finally mine."

Finally his.

< ♂ + ♀ >

Secret Reader Freebie

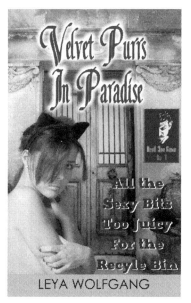

Thank you for reading Erin and Jerry's story. Just like what often happens with movies, I had more good material than I could use for this book. It would be a shame to waste all the steamy goodness, so I put it in an e-book called *Bonus Deleted Scenes: All the Sexy Bits Too Juicy for the Recycle Bin*. It's a special gift for my loyal readers.

Visit Devil You Know Kink Club at: **http://DYKKC.com/velvet-bonus/**. Type in the password to enter. It's the three words Erin can't believe Jerry says to her near the end of Chapter Nine (beautifuland_____). Sign up for the DYKKC VIP MEMBER email list, and I'll send you the full, angsty version of "Erin's Humiliation at Senior Prom," the titillating details of "The Squire's 'Reward' for His playmate," the yummy play-by-play of "Master Ronan's First Taste of priss," and Erin's erotic punishment in "The Rest of the History between priss and The Saint." It's really juicy stuff that will whet your appetite for the next instalments.

You'll also get lots of fun stuff like contests and free gifts, and details about new titles in this series before the general public hears. Dillon is breathing down my neck (oh, yeah, feels sooo good), threatening to punish me (even better) if I don't tell his story of redemption next. The Saint will have me on my knees and at his mercy because Jerry muscled his way into the lineup with a few things to say about his plans for Erin (what does it mean to be "finally his"?) and how he's going to keep her when she runs one more time as his past life as Snapper catches up with them. *Regis Rules the Lion's Den*, DYKKC Book 1.1 (a novella),will be available very soon, if Snapper cracks his whip just right for me. *Grrr!*

< ♂ + ♀ >

Afterword

Please remember that *Velvet Purrs* is a work of fiction. Even though my characters spoke to me, would wake me, begging me to tell their tales of trauma and triumph—and often sending the story in directions I couldn't predict—I had the ultimate control of what ended up on the page and could choose how to make it all work out in the end. Life isn't always that easy to figure out and direct, especially when dealing with the subject matter of this story.

Whenever you are playing in the BDSM realm for real, always remember the prime directive—safe, sane and consensual. Even when what's happening in a scene feels very bad, it should, ultimately, feel very, very good, for *all of the players*. If you have emotional issues and trauma to work through, you may be better served talking to a qualified kink-friendly counselor rather than expecting too much from a Dominant or submissive, no matter how experienced they are or how much you trust them.

That being said, not all who are involved in the BDSM lifestyle have been traumatized. I believe every individual soul who is born to this world comes for its own reasons and has its own To Do List of experiences to explore and lessons to learn. Some may be clearing karma not related to this current lifetime. Others may simply have a different energy profile and darker or more unconventional appetites. Whatever the reason, thank God we're not all the same; otherwise, this game of life would be just like playing with yourself. And that's no fun—well, okay, sometimes it is, just not all the time.

I believe that, whether through following the righteous path of the sacred or the irreverent route of the profane, we are all on a quest to, as the inscription at the ancient Temple of Apollo at Delphi admonished, "Know thy self." With knowledge comes acceptance. By exploring what's lurking in our dark shadows as well as what's revealed by the light of our brilliance, we will find the signposts pointing to our wholeness. For each of us, the path is ours to choose; our life is ours to determine.

Leya Wolfgang
Calgary, 2013

< ♂ + ♀ >

About the Author

Life should be rich and juicy. In my writing, I like to explore the many ways we block ourselves from joy or get stuck in following our dreams, mostly because of how often I find myself having to loosen up or push forward. The sexy characters who reveal themselves to me and about whom I write in the DYKKC BDSM Erotica Romance Series are, in some way, aspects of my own mind, heart and soul. They come to help me resolve my issues, heal my wounds and tear down my barriers to bliss. And they get me wet while they tell me their stories. I truly hope that, while I am entertaining you, you come to understand that you need no one's permission to pursue your passions and to remain faithful to your personal truths. You'll be happier if you just go for it. You deserve bliss. We all do.

An indie writer relies very much on word of mouth to gain positive exposure and buzz. I'd be very grateful if you went to the **Amazon** purchase page or to the **Goodreads.com** website and left your honest thoughts in a review. If you enjoyed the book, please help other readers find it and recommend this novel to your friends who might like a racy and romantic read. Just remember that this is Adult Content and share accordingly. Thank you.

Authors live to hear from the people who read our stories. I would love to hear your reactions, questions, kudos or complaints. Reach me at **www.Facebook.com/DYKKCnovels** and on my website at **www.DYKKC.com**.

Made in the USA
Charleston, SC
31 July 2014